CW00556120

This Realm of Hatred
'Approaching Horror'

Christina Wells

Copyright © 2023 Christina Wells

All rights reserved.

ISBN:9798852734761

"Oh Lord, Thou knowest how verie busy I shall be this day. If I forget thee, do not Thou forget me!"

Sir Jacob Astley – before the battle of Edgehill 1642

ACKNOWLEDGMENTS

Initially, I would like to thank *you* for purchasing a copy of a work begun several years ago now which, due to various issues, has taken a considerable time to complete. However, I now wish to thank the following people, in no particular order, all of whom have encouraged me along the way.

Firstly, to my late mum who always wanted to see my work "in print," but who sadly passed away in early May 2020 during 'lockdown'. I know she will still be really pleased that at last it has finally come to fruition. Thank you so much mum!

To my good friend Diane who assisted with editing the finished manuscript of Book One. Thank you for your honesty, editing skills, and for your ongoing encouragement, it's much appreciated.

Special thanks must go to the late Paul McAvilley, (Kit) who was a member of the Sealed Knot Society and whose knowledge of Prince Rupert and aspects of the Civil War were immeasurable, fascinating and extremely varied. A talented artist, Paul's wife has kindly allowed me to use one of his many paintings as the cover for this book.

To my cousin Andy Fawthrop for his patience in teaching me how to finally get my novel in print.

Finally, thank you to ALL my wonderful friends and family for showing such patience in having this crazy lady boring you to bits with constant tales of the civil war and its participants.

PROLOGUE

Yorkshire - 17th August 1642

A dust cloud almost completely enveloped the group of riders pounding their way along powder dry roads. Eventually, on the brow of a hill, they halted. In the distance, silhouetted against the bright blue sky, dominated by the towers of a Minster, stood an ancient walled city.

At the head of the party, a swarthy skinned, dark haired young man pivoted in the saddle, smiling gregariously.

"See gentlemen, there is York and our journey's end, though alas I must crave your forbearance a little longer and insist we make a brief detour that my plans might be fulfilled."

His heavily breathing horse scraped the ground impatiently with one foreleg, instantly receiving a gentle pat on the neck before being urged onward. The small party steadily made their way down the hillside weaving through pockets of woodland and gorse until reining in once more in an area of open land. Before them lay a sleepy looking hamlet and nestling someway off to the right, a large Tudor manor house surrounded by high walls.

The lead rider again turned to address the others.

"Has to be it, wouldn't you say, Crane?"

A man rode forward rifling inside his doublet, drawing out a paper.

"Assuming Lord Bynghame's instructions are accurate Sir, it certainly appears so."

"Note the family arms emblazoned on that flag above the gatehouse, much as drawn by Bynghame, wouldn't you say?" An ephemeral smile briefly crossed his lips, quickly turning into a frown when a large white dog rushed back and forth barking excitedly. "I would say my dog may well be hungry gentlemen."

"I think we'd all appreciate a little food, brother," a dark-haired younger man of similar appearance in the midst of the others remarked.

"And a flagon of ale," another yelled.

"Come then gentlemen, let's test the measure of greeting to be had at this…Haveringham Manor," the lead rider announced, kicking the sides of his mount.

The majority peeled off to dismount in the extensive outer grounds whilst the dark-haired pair slowed their mounts to a steady walk. In turn, each took an admiring glance at the imposing gatehouse with its four domed topped, angle turrets and, welcomingly open, pair of centrally sited huge wooden doors. The horses' hooves clattered loudly on the stone pathway beneath, until ultimately, they rode out into a courtyard of considerable size, finally dropping from the saddle outside the impressive front façade of the large dwelling itself.

In the stables, Miles Ashford, the 2nd Earl of Benningford and his head groom, Matthew Redworth, tended to a grey mare laid out on the straw. Clad in shirt sleeves, Miles raised his greying head at the unexpected entrance of Lambert, his Steward.

"By God man, I haven't time for any interruptions today. With this mare about to foal any time and all the nonsense going on tomorrow…." The mare gave a pitiful whinny. "Easy now girl…" Miles patted the animal's sweat smeared neck. Then turning back to his steward said, "Go back and tell my wife that I can't be found."

"My Lord, the matter is imperative…. two gentlemen of consequence have arrived wishing to see you urgently…"

The look hurled the steward's way was not to be envied.

"What, to be involved in more debate about the King and this wretched Parliament; not today, Lambert, not today."

"My Lord, you misunderstand…these men are not from York."

"Then, whoever they are and wherever they are from, you deal with them, I've neither time nor inclination."

"But Sir, I may not……they are far above my station in life..."

Miles threw a scowl at his faithful retainer.

"You talk in riddles man, out with it, who the devil are they?"

"The Palatine Princes' Master Robin used to speak of so often…though as to their exact purpose…."

Miles' eyes grew wide, a vein pulsating in his neck.

"What…Rupert and Maurice…here?"

Lambert nodded fervently.

"Why the hell didn't you say so at once? Dear God, where are they now?" Miles snarled, grabbing his doublet from the top of a straw bale, and thrusting an arm into one sleeve.

"I left them in the Great Hall with the Countess and Mistress Gilbert."

"And my daughter?"

"I believe Martha has been dispatched to locate her my Lord, somewhere in the grounds."

Miles failed miserably attempting to push his arm into the second sleeve.

"Hell's teeth," he snarled.

"The mare, my Lord?" Redworth interjected.

"You'll have to tend to her yourself, lad."

"Walter'll give me a hand my Lord, we'll see her right."

"You'd better, she's one of my best," Miles said hurrying out into the sunlit courtyard.

CHAPTER ONE

Haveringham Manor - 17th August 1642

Frances Ashford, only daughter of the Earl of Benningford had fled what had fast become absolute uproar in the house to enjoy a portion of relative tranquillity in the gardens. One day away from becoming a bride, Frances' thoughts were mixed as she walked steadily onward, one hand absently trailing across the open roses, oblivious to the number of pink and red petals tumbling in bright showers onto the soil. Having seen a mere nineteen summers, Frances seemed to be experiencing waves of excitement and trepidation in equal measure. Off to one side, a number of full leafed trees instantly evoked a long-overlooked memory. Now, as then, the intertwined branches almost blotted out the sunlight, forming an avenue of lush deep green. Years ago, at the age of only seven, she had strolled hand in hand with a childhood companion of roughly the same age, even sharing an innocent kiss beneath that same tunnel of greenery, hidden from observation from the house.

"When I'm a man, I shall wed thee, Frannie..." Thus, had been the young lad's forceful and adamant declaration.

"You know that can never be," she had responded. Even at such a tender age Frances had been mindful of the dictates of rank and privilege, systems instilled by ancient lineage and persistent schooling.

"Then we'll run away from Yorkshire......to somewhere neither of us are known...they'll not be able to find us ya know...."

A naïve resolve, almost dreamlike, but to children of such tender years, achievable. Maturity would bring irrevocable change of course, compelling acknowledgment of the differences in station and of the guidelines associated with those differing situations. Frances had been born into one of the noblest families in England, whereas her childhood playmate, Matthew Redworth, was merely the son of lower-class folk whose family had been employed on the

Haveringham estate for several generations.

The plaintive cry of a blackbird broke her reflections and strolling further on, Frances' thoughts moved on to a more recent kiss, far more adult in nature and of much deeper intimacy. In the grounds of London's royal palace of Whitehall, and newly betrothed Frances' lips had been briefly captured by those of the man she had come to adore. His had parted hers so gently and sweetly in a manner that almost denied her breath, making her desirous of something far more. Her face then must have portrayed shock.

"T'was but a kiss, my love." Thus, he had said, leaning closer to whisper, *"tis naught compared to the delights of the marriage bed."*

Biting her lip, Frances looked up at the green canopy and the manner in which the leaves rustled softly in the gentle summer breeze.

'Not long to wait until I find out….'

John Fitzherbert, a handsome dark-haired, blue-eyed gallant just happened to be the elder son of a Kentish Earl and therefore considered an ideal match for her. A gifted soldier, John had willingly served the Protestant cause in the troubled Low Countries, as had her brother Robin, the pair only returning to England little over a year ago when her sibling had been wounded in a battle. Now England seemed beset by similar woes to Europe, disagreements between King Charles and his Parliament increasing in severity as the months advanced, so much so that accounts of all out violence seemed to be reported almost weekly even in the north. Frances knew how serious matters were becoming having witnessed a measure of it first-hand herself last November in London, yet she didn't care to think of such things, not today.

'Tis not right to ponder such gloomy matters,' she thought to herself, pushing a tendril of hair back from her face. Having purposely left it loose with only two sections tied back at the nape of her neck with a bright blue ribbon to match the shade of her simple gown, she could almost hear her father's rebuke.

'You should at the very least wear a coif, my girl.'

A plain-spoken Yorkshireman, her father never was one to mince his words, much as her mother, whose voice suddenly drifted out through an open window.

"The Melton's must see Haveringham looking its best Moll, therefore I want all the arrangements checked and re-checked. I'll not tolerate oversights, none whatsoever, is that understood?"

"Yes, Countess," the housekeeper responded. Moll Gilbert sounded courteous, but Frances knew enough of her mother's exacting ways to realise that she would be feeling increasingly vexed.

"Now, the wedding gown, is it completely finished?"

"I believe so, Countess, tis hanging in the sewing room."

"Then go and examine it yourself Moll, it must be flawless."

"I can assure you Milady that the seamstresses have adhered to all your instructions faithfully, ever since you remarked upon…several flaws."

Outside, Frances stifled a giggle with one hand to her mouth.

"Where is Frances, do you know?"

"In the gardens somewhere or so I believe, Milady."

"Where she has no business being…send Martha to find her."

"At once, Milady."

Having little desire to be seen, Frances crouched and hurried round the side of the house, heading toward the formal garden. Once certain of being unobserved, she paused to consider the southern side of the magnificent Tudor house that had been her home since birth. Bathed in bright sunlight, Haveringham Manor looked superb. It had been the contrivance of her late Grandsire,

William Ashford, the 1st Earl of Benningford whose desire had been to have a grand dwelling erected on the site of the previous Norman building. Fortunately, William had been fortunate to secure the services of the late Queen Elizabeth's master mason, Robert Smithson, whose finished design, and build was impeccable in both taste and appearance. The impressive frontage benefitted a number of resplendent half circular bow windows, contrived to flood the inside area with the greatest amount of daylight. The upper floors boasted a long gallery, the playground of Frances' youth and latterly, a place to exercise during inclement weather.

The sudden clatter of horses and constant barking of a dog broke through her reflections, producing an instant scowl.

"I hope that's naught relating to the King…. not today of all days," she said aloud.

She was at the wrong side of the house to see the arrivals, but from the excessive noise, it sounded as if there could be several visitors. Unexpected guests often arrived to visit her father, ever since King Charles had fled to the north from London in the early part of the year, taking up residence in York. If today it were more of the same, her mother would not be best pleased.

She still had no desire to return to the house and be given a task to do, so she hurried on toward the pretty little Norman church in the grounds where the very next day, she would be married. Picking her way down the grassy slope, ignoring several gravestones, the resting place of many kinsmen, she finally stopped in front of a relatively new one and sank to her knees on the grass. Absently tracing round each letter carved upon it with a finger, she said, "I still can't believe you won't be with us on the morrow," she said wistfully as further noise from outside the house reached her. "Even today it seems we must receive unwanted visitors. I'd best go and find out who it is. Sleep well, dearest Robin."

A kiss of her fingertips was lightly transferred to the gravestone before she headed back the way she had come, only to be confronted by two serving girls.

"There you are Mistress Frances, we've been lookin' for ya," a slightly flustered Martha, Frances' personal maid said. Petite and dark haired, Martha was a good-natured girl who had served the daughter of the house for several years. The other, Rachel, seemed to be struggling to hold an armful of freshly cut flowers.

"Here, give me some of those Rachel, I'll wager they're for the Great Hall," Frances remarked with a grin.

"Aye Milady, the Countess said we should cut plenty," Rachel admitted.

"But Mistress Frances, we were sent to find ya cos there's visitors come that are…."

"Yes, I know, I heard," Frances interrupted. "No doubt mother said something similar to, *'These men have ridden here from York and my daughter should be present to greet them.'*

Well used to her young mistress's tendency to mimicry, Martha laughed, "Oh Mistress Frances…. but they're not….." she began, but Frances had already turned away to run back across the lawn.

"Tiresome as they probably are, I'd best go and face them," she shouted over her shoulder.

Vaguely aware of a deep male voice as she hurried into the Great Hall under one of the archways, Frances caught only a segment of what was being said.

"And whilst we appreciate the celebration taking place here on the morrow my Lord, our purpose for calling is most pressing, we would scarce be here else…"

Conscious of eyes following her, Frances carefully placed the flowers on a table beside one of the large windows, startled by the unexpected appearance of a large white dog, sniffing the hem of her gown.

"Oh, who do we have here?" she asked. The animal's appearance was nothing like the sleek beasts the family had owned in her youth. This one had tightly curled white fur, large ears and a long snout that sniffed the air continually. Reaching forward, she stroked its broad head.

"Daughter, you forget yourself," her father stated more firmly than she was used to. Realising she had been ill mannered she stood upright and dipped the merest hint of a curtsey, though her focus was still on the dog, lifting one paw in the air.

"I trust your ride from York was a pleasant one, gentlemen?" she said, distracted by the dog pawing her skirts and having to disguise a sudden desire to giggle.

"Daughter, heed me at once. These gentlemen are not come from York but much further afield. Tis my honour to present Prince Rupert of the Rhine and his brother Prince Maurice."

Apart from the gentle tick of an ornate clock further down the room, silence seemed to dominate the ambiance for some time.

'Prince Rupert of the Rhine....'

One hand almost welded to the dog's head; memories assailed her. That was a name she had heard her late brother speak of so often and now he stood beside her father in her own home. After what seemed an age, she finally dared to lift her eyes toward the silently watching royal pair. Both were young that much was obvious, very well dressed, despite the dust on their clothing, and exceptionally tall, towering above her father who could never be described as slight of stature. Blushing intensely, Frances sank into the deepest deferential curtsey.

"Your Royal Highnesses may have already concluded that this is my daughter, Frances.... the Viscountess Haveringham," the Earl explained.

CHAPTER TWO

Haveringham Manor - 17th August 1642

Motionless in a deep curtsey, Frances only dared to raise her head on hearing Prince Maurice voice, "Rise, Viscountess, if you please."

Neglecting one of the most basic of elementary protocols had proved mortifying as very slowly, Frances stood, heat infusing her face. Such a blatant error would, without doubt, afford her a deal of chastisement from her mother later, but for now, all Frances could do was apologise. Bizarrely, she noticed a flash of amusement cross the face of the elder Palatine before he turned to examine a tapestry on the wall.

"If I might be allowed to give account for such lack of propriety?" she asserted soundly.

"If you wish," Maurice responded. What she had to say might prove interesting to hear and he was in no mood to prevent her.

She began very slowly.

"You see we often receive visitors from York, seeking my father. Hearing you arriving, I wrongly assumed you to be more of the same…."

A curious Rupert turned at a decidedly feminine voice, tinged with the merest hint of a northern accent.

"Justification is wholly unnecessary, Viscountess," he declared. "You were not to know of our visit this day." The dog impatiently nudged Frances' hand. "My dog seems unoffended by it; therefore, how could we be so?" With an unpretentious smile he quickly added, "His name is Boye and usually I find him an excellent judge of character."

Frances again considered the curly white head, when with a whine, Boye lifted a paw for her to grasp.

"Then Boye you are most benevolent, though I do believe tis your master who should be offered the greater measure of gratitude," Frances said, lifting her eyes to look straight into Rupert's. Curiosity drew the prince nearer, keenness to take a better look at an unusual female who had so easily enthralled his dog. For a woman of her rank, she certainly appeared less than she should. The colour of ripened corn, her hair certainly wasn't arranged formally. It fell loosely across her shoulders, saving one small section tied at the nape of her neck with a pale blue ribbon. Her gown, though cut well and of good material, could only be described as plain as was her lace edged collar. Unusually, the nearer he drew, the more disinclined she seemed to be to look away, deepest blue eyes, almost violet, holding his keenly. Why was that? Defiance, dislike, or something else entirely? Unwilling to consider that thought for long, his brows lifted dismissively as he headed for the ornate fireplace. A plethora of carved biblical figures, depicting good triumphing over evil, covered its surface and Rupert reached out to touch one angelic being wielding a sword. Eventually, his gaze traversed upward to the centrally sited Benningford coat of arms. Its motto *'Honneur et Valiance'* almost set the young soldier's teeth on edge.

'Time will certainly show if that is true,' he thought.

With a sigh, he strolled off again down the Great Hall, considering the remarkable room in detail. A minstrel's gallery was obvious above the three ornately carved oak archways framing the main egress to the outer corridor, where he also witnessed a broad oak staircase leading to the upper floors. Suitably impressed, he turned to walk back, casually trailing a hand along the huge, centrally sited, oak table with several red velvet upholstered chairs positioned beneath.

Nervously, Moll Gilbert approached bearing a tray of goblets.

"Wine, Your Highness?" she asked, bobbing a brief curtsey, waiting for a response.

Rupert took a goblet with a nod of the head as Miles came to join him.

"I can only apologise for not being here to greet you in person, Your Highness, urgent business had me in my stables but……"

Rupert's hand shot straight up.

"Be at peace my Lord, we were not expected to come here," he said, noting the Earl wincing and rubbing his thigh. "But you are pained my Lord, pray be seated if it would help?"

"Unnecessary Highness," Miles said shaking his head. "Tis but an old injury gained three years back at Newburn in the northeast. From time to time, it pains me, but not so much as to make it intolerable."

"So, you drew swords against the Scots I assume?"

"I did indeed," Miles responded catching a wide-eyed glare from Elizabeth. The mention of the clash still brought painful memories of the day he had told her of his intent to ride north with the King to address the Scottish unrest. After all, their only son Robin had not long since left Yorkshire to fight for the Protestant cause in the Low Countries and Elizabeth could not bear to think of either event nowadays and looked for the means to change the subject. Maurice stood alone, so she sidled up to him, forcing a smile to her lips.

"Your Highness, might I make a request of you?" she asked slightly reservedly.

Maurice flashed a questioning glance at his brother, a mere nod assent to proceed.

"You may ask what you will Lady Benningford, though any response may depend upon the nature of the request," Maurice said quietly. More reserved than his elder sibling, Elizabeth felt she could speak freely.

"I wondered if you and your brother might care for quarters here this night and in addition……attend the wedding celebrations on the morrow?"

Here she paused, watching his expression steadily for any sign of reluctance or annoyance. Thankfully, Maurice simply smiled.

"A tempting thought Countess but alas one that must be declined. Our intent is to set out again shortly, for York," he said, another glance at his brother confirming the response, though Miles had heard.

"My wife speaks on impulse, Your Highness," he said to Rupert. "Though I must say I believe it to be a rational suggestion?"

"In what way?" Rupert asked.

"In that I should deem it a great honour to offer you the comfort of my humble home for as long as you wish."

"Lord Benningford, this magnificent house should never be described as humble, not when compared to the formidable edifice in which I was so recently held captive," Rupert answered, removing his hat, and raking back his mop of raven hued hair.

At the table, Boye's head resting contentedly on her lap, Frances narrowed her eyes. Even now, Rupert could be little more than two and twenty at most, having been captured in a battle and incarcerated at the age of only eighteen, so her late brother had told her.

"May I be permitted to express delight in learning of your release from captivity, Sir?" Miles said. Rupert appeared contented enough, so the Earl quickly added, "Might you be persuaded to reconsider the whole invitation?"

The concept of a comfortable bed for two nights, along with hearty meals certainly was tempting, aching limbs from being in the saddle so long certainly making a positive response all the more alluring. Maurice, it seemed needed no more convincing.

"A day's delay won't really make much difference surely brother?" he enquired.

Rupert pursed his lips, taking time to mull over the notion, much as he did with any propositions.

"Well, it's a thought.... given my requirement of speaking with Bynghame and Fitzherbert..."

"My own thought exactly brother?" Maurice smiled warmly at the countess and given her close proximity; a gentle blush crept up her face.

Frances however felt nothing but a sense of foreboding. Why did Rupert need to speak with John, on the eve of their marriage? It didn't make any sense and yet deep within she already suspected the reason.

Chivalrously, Rupert approached the countess, lifting her hand to kiss it.

"It appears your wishes are granted," he said simply.

"Then we are truly honoured Your Highness," she simpered. "And as for Lord Fitzherbert, why he is due to arrive here this evening with Lord Bynghame. Doubtless there will be opportunity for your discussion then. Now if you would excuse me, I intend to ensure that everything is made ready to receive you both."

Rupert tilted his head in answer as Elizabeth engineered a faultless curtsey and swept regally from the room.

"Might I ask where you made landfall, Highness?" Miles enquired, at the table pouring more wine.

"We hoped to make Scarborough, the ship carrying a cargo of arms, but it was not to be so, alas. Close to the headland at Flamborough, we were hailed by a vessel bearing Parliamentarian colours, demanding to look us over," Rupert explained.

"I'll warrant you didn't oblige?" Miles ventured cautiously.

"Nor would I," Rupert retorted with Maurice adding, "My brother went up on deck wearing a sailor's cap, my Lord, ordering the captain to raise the Dunkirk colours and run out the guns."

"The scoundrels didn't fire on you?" Miles asked.

"Oh, they did, but the incompetent fools shot to leeward, missing us by considerable distance. Eventually we were able to outrun 'em and finally made landfall at Tynemouth. We've ridden hard to get this far," Rupert said almost casually.

"Tynemouth is considerable distance north?" Miles suggested but Rupert merely shrugged.

"We were left with little choice, my Lord," he said as Maurice chortled.

"Wherever it was, my brother was mighty relieved to stand on firm soil once more my Lord. Seafaring does not agree with his stomach."

Frances did not miss the irritated glare Rupert hurled at his brother.

'So, you do have a weakness then?' she thought smugly.

"My late son suffered bouts of sea sickness," Miles admitted, and Rupert's expression softened at once.

"Yes, I recall him once telling me," he admitted with a reflective smile.

The brothers had left the cargo of arms aboard the vessel, the captain giving assurance of making Scarborough to offload under the cover of darkness. Attesting to his belief in the captain's reliability, nevertheless Rupert had ensured a number of his own men remained aboard the ship to ensure delivery of the much-needed cargo to the Yorkshire port. Miles decided the younger man had displayed great wisdom in that one decision alone, something that would doubtless be tested and stretched to its limit, should it come to all-out war.

Rupert fingered the goblet on the table before asking, "Might I now make a request of you, my Lord?"

Wondering just what he might want, Miles said, "I am at your disposal, Highness."

"A number of my companions currently wait in your excellent grounds. They too will need quarters this night. Should they have your permission to camp here, it might save considerable time and effort to locate an alternative?"

Miles readily agreed of course, considering it best to ensure tents were pitched as far from the main driveway as possible. There were enough trees and bushes in the grounds to guarantee it would not be viewed as a military encampment by arriving guests, even though effectively that's just what it was. After all, it could be considered to be related to the nuptials, nothing more sinister than that.

"Excellent," Rupert said, pacing up and down. "Now whilst we are happy to stay for the wedding, we must rise early the following day to head for York and the King."

The Earl frowned.

"Then…perhaps you have not heard?" he said causing Rupert to look back with a deep scowl.

"Heard what exactly, my Lord?" he demanded.

"Why that His Majesty is no longer in York. Tis my belief that he and several others have headed south toward the area around Nottingham."

Rupert's scowl deepened and picking up his goblet, he drained it completely.

"It appears our plans may well have to be adjusted," he voiced as Maurice came to stand beside him questioningly.

"We shall still remain here tonight though?" he asked.

The elder's expression darkened, like a storm threatening to break, a look Maurice knew well from experience. "I'm not certain we should now, Maurice," he said.

"But surely, if we are no longer required to go to York, then we can set out the day after tomorrow and head straight for Nottingham. One more day won't make that much difference, and I'll wager the men would welcome chance to relax a little after that perilous journey?"

Again, Rupert removed his hat to rake back his hair. Silent and thoughtful, he made his way across to the window, looking out at the sun-drenched courtyard giving himself space to contemplate all the implications.

"Well brother?" Maurice urged.

At length Rupert threw a glance over one shoulder.

"I dare say it will be in order, though I insist we leave for Nottingham before sunrise the following day," he said.

With a grin at the Earl, Maurice dropped onto a chair by the fireplace.

"Excellent," he said, interlocking his fingers.

At the table, gripped by increasing unease that made her nauseous, Frances absently fondled one of Boye's long ears, watching her father continuously with a determination to speak privately with him as soon as possible.

From then on, Miles regaled the royal pair with details of the King's movements whilst in York, most of which came as a surprise to them. The King, he told them had been forbidden entry to Hull in April by the governor, Sir John Hotham, Charles intent on securing the port with its store of weaponry left over from the Bishop's Wars, but also a place for his wife to return from Holland.

A second attempt was made to lay siege to the town, again thwarted by Hotham when the sluices were opened, completely flooding the area making any form of attack virtually impossible. Hotham had been declared a traitor by the King of course, yet Parliament had praised him for his actions.

Frances distinctly heard Rupert mutter what sounded like some form of derogatory remark, though it was in a language she didn't recognise, so couldn't be sure. Illuminated by light streaming in through the large window, she could now scrutinise his features with ease. By anyone's standards Prince Rupert of the Rhine was a remarkably handsome man, having a determined brow, aristocratic nose, lips topped by a youthful moustache and a strong jawline. His hair was very dark, almost black, cascading in soft waves onto his shoulder across a dusty looking scarlet cloak slung casually over one shoulder. Despite his looks, his stance and demeanour, for some reason he seemed to annoy her intensely.

Sensing her staring, Rupert suddenly swung round, his cloak narrowly missing an ornate vase on the tabletop littered with the flowers she had previously left there. Briefly their eyes connected but this time, she seemed unable to hold his for long and looked down at the dog's head resting on her lap.

"Surely there is still hope for a peaceful solution to all this?" Miles enquired as Rupert strode toward him.

"I think not. The King has been pushed beyond endurance making his position untenable, my Lord," he said. "Before long the royal standard must be raised, mark me on that and irrespective of the location, Maurice and I must be there to offer support to our uncle."

The stark reminder of the high-born status of these two young men, nephews to the King of England, royal blood flowing through their veins as direct descendants of both James I and his mother, the executed Mary, Queen of Scots made Frances look up once more.

"So, England is to face a conflict……where there's no real enemy," Miles said, almost to himself.

"Any rebellion against God's anointed must always be addressed, my Lord. Tis my intent to raise an army, to put a swift end to this nonsense." Again, the elder Prince began pacing. "I am already created General of Horse, answerable to His Majesty alone."

Rupert's fingers playfully teased the pommel of the sword slung at his hip from an elaborately embellished baldric, words tumbling from his lips with as much ease as if merely describing the cut, colour or style of a new doublet.

"Such roles are already decided, Highness?" Miles enquired wondering if matters were much worse than already feared.

Rupert's lips formed an almost indolent, confident smirk.

"The Queen bestowed the commission upon me in Holland before I left, my Lord. Tis in this respect, I need to speak with Bynghame and Fitzherbert."

Frances quickly supressed a gasp, unable to prevent tears stinging her eyes. Boye, sensing her distress, gave a whine and licked her hand repeatedly. It felt as if something terrible were brewing, something she would be unable to stop, no matter how much she would wish to. Thankfully, Lambert, loitering beside one of the archways, indicated his need to interrupt.

"Yes Lambert…. what is it?" Miles asked.

"Your pardon my Lord, but rooms are ready for their Royal Highnesses. Once your discussions are at an end, I should be honoured to show them upstairs myself." Lambert gave a low bow.

"Then do so now, Master Steward. We have spoken enough I think for the present…would you not agree, my Lord?" Rupert's dark eyes flicked toward an ashen faced Frances staring sightlessly down at his dog.

"I comprehend your meaning, Your Highness and fully agree," Miles said.

"Perhaps word can be sent to our servants out in the grounds that we require them to attend us?" Rupert asked.

"As Your Royal Highness wishes. If you would care to follow me?" Lambert said.

Only when Rupert drew level with Frances did she finally stand up and dip a curtsey, lifting tear filled eyes to his. Outwardly unmoved, Rupert strode straight past, shouting for Boye to follow.

CHAPTER THREE

Haveringham Manor - 17th August 1642

Miles dropped onto his favourite chair beside the fireplace, extending his legs and crossing his ankles, sipping contentedly on his wine.

Frances watched, drumming her fingernails lightly on the table. She needed to speak openly and taking a deep breath, she said, "Is it to be war then, father? Are matters really so dire?"

Miles blew out his lips and shook his head.

"It would certainly seem to be moving that way," he answered distractedly. He had a great deal to think about and wasn't going to tell her too much about his deepest fears, not when his darling girl was to be married the next day. But he had to say something, her enquiring look almost demanded it. "Just think of the unrest we witnessed ourselves in London last November and there's been outbreaks here in Yorkshire too, not to mention what's going on in the south according to John's letters. It doesn't bode well, that much I can say."

Of course, Frances knew all about the spasmodic events erupting all over England, even in her home county, but it seemed things were intensifying and that was alarming. For the last few months, it had been relatively easy to push such worries to the back of her mind, after all the area around Haveringham remained peaceful enough. But the sudden and unexpected arrival of these two royal men with all this talk of war, had made all her anxieties resurface, frighteningly so.

Tracing her fingers up and down the grain on the oak table, she suddenly thought of something and stiffened.

"He's come here to take John away with him," she gasped.

"Who?"

"Prince Rupert. Didn't he say he needed to speak with John and Ralph urgently. If he's already General of Horse, what other reason could he have?"

Miles tutted.

"Be at peace my girl, there can be any number of reasons."

His daughter was no fool and Miles hoped his attempt at sounding positive wouldn't be received as a feeble excuse. It hadn't worked, she was growing distressed that much was clear from her trembling hands.

"But I can see John being torn from my side the very moment we are declared wed, and swiftly on his way to Nottingham before I can even think. Oh, I wish Prince Rupert had never come here… I really hate him!"

She spun away, hands covering her face.

With an elongated sigh, Miles set down his goblet and went straight to her, enfolding her in his embrace, kissing her head.

"Come, come now, what foolishness you speak. John won't be torn from your side by Rupert or anyone else for that matter."

"But he's a Prince after all… and General of Horse with the King's blessing, so can demand whatever he wishes, surely?"

Her tears were falling now, running down her cheeks in little rivulets, staining the blue material of her gown with salty droplets.

"Yes, he could, but Robin spoke of him in the most glowing terms as being honourable, so I doubt very much that he'll demand such a thing. And just think, all this unrest may yet come to naught. For all his faults, and Lord knows he has many, this King of ours won't easily choose to wage war on his own subjects."

Trying to be a good father and holding her close to his shoulder, Miles felt a wave of relief that in this moment, she couldn't see the tangible concern on his face. Privately he feared that England was spinning out of control, afflicted by a disorder that no physician would be able to cure. Setting a smile to his lips, he took her shoulders looking down into her tear-stained face.

"This is no way to be, not on the day before you wed. Go and change your gown into something more befitting the daughter of an Earl and have Martha dress these fair tresses more appropriately."

"You don't care for it worn this way?" Frances asked with a sniff.

"Of course, I do, but without sounding too Puritanical, even though scripture does speak of it as your 'crown of beauty,' it should be covered unless it is formally styled. Now obey your father in this, daughter."

"No longer from the morrow though?" she asked a tad impudently. Cupping her face, Miles searched her features.

'Just where have the last nineteen years gone?' he thought to himself. For one brief moment, he was back in one of Haveringham's bedchambers where in 1623, having endured hours of childbed agony, Elizabeth had reclined limply against a pillow in an oak four poster, looking at him with tear-filled eyes. With significant effort, she had pointed to the cradle in the corner in which the new arrival lay contentedly. Peering down at the small bundle, Miles remembered vowing that this, their tenth child, would be the last time Elizabeth would endure the ordeal. Over the years they had lost precious infant after infant, some still born, others dying before the age of five years, their son Robin their only surviving child until that day. Miles had reached for the new arrival's hand, the babe gripping his finger tightly, eyes opening to stare up at him. That one action alone had melted his heart.

'Dear Lord, let this child live….' he had prayed silently and from the bed, Elizabeth had added in a whisper, *'Francesca…. her name should be Francesca…. after your Grandmother.'*

Leaving the child, Miles returned to his wife, sitting on the coverlet, kissing her cheek.

'We shall my love…. but Elizabeth also, for this new little mite is destined to be as precious to me as is her mother.'

Young Robin had interrupted then, running into the room with his nurse in tow and Miles, lifting him in his arms, had taken him across to see his baby sister.

'She's very little, can I show her my new pony?' Robin had spluttered.

'Not yet a while, she's too small, maybe when she's grown a little….' Miles had said, ruffling his son's hair.

Now that small boy was no more and the bundle in the cradle a fully grown woman, was about to be given in marriage.

"Father, are you alright?" Frances asked.

"Simply memories dear daughter, simple memories," he said.

CHAPTER FOUR

Haveringham Manor – 17th August 1642

"You've been down in the graveyard again, haven't ya?" Martha scowled as deftly; she curled a section of Frances' hair before it was pinned in place. The girl had served as Frances' personal maid for several years and during that time, the pair had developed an easy rapport, at least when alone, though each observed formality at all other times.

"What of it?" Frances almost snapped.

"Well, it tends to make ya so cheerless," Martha remarked, conscious of being careful when speaking on a subject she knew still pained her mistress so greatly. Expertly, she pinned a fair ringlet in place, stepping back to admire her own handiwork, checking it meticulously. Glancing up in the mirror, she could not escape Frances' scowl.

"Am I not permitted to be cheerless sometimes then?" Frances asked.

"Not when you're getting wed on the morrow. It ain't right if you ask me, ya brother wouldn't want ya allus going to sit by 'is grave. I remember 'im once sayin……"

Martha's voice faded as memories of bygone days and the brother she had held so dear, came to the fore.

Haveringham Manor – Early Spring 1637

He was always known as Robin, though his baptismal names were William, Robert, James Ashford. Fair haired and amiable, Robin had been fascinated by Frances from the moment he had first seen her. Before long, it was noted how many times the babe turned her head to watch her brother playing in the nursery and as the pair grew, so did their relationship until they became as close as siblings could possibly be. Youthful capers often resulted in bed with no supper in addition to a harsh rebuke from their father. All too soon Robin was forced to face the demands of a formal education and though the propensity of the age was for males alone to receive teaching, forward thinking Miles ensured that Frances too had her own tutor in order that she might be educated in more than just the usual feminine subjects.

When it came to the gentlemanly art of swordplay, Miles took charge of his son's schooling himself, Frances often watching with more than a touch of jealousy. One such day, Miles took her completely by surprise when he proffered a sword to her, the ornate work on the hilt glinting tauntingly in the sunshine.

"Would you care to take a turn, daughter?" he asked.

After only a slight pause, a sceptical Frances shook her head.

"Don't tease me so, father," she said, making as if to walk away, though Miles reached for her arm.

"I'm in earnest daughter," he said with a broad smile, but added, "Not a word to your mother though eh?"

The lightness and balance of the weapon as her fingers coiled around the hilt amazed Frances, as did the highly fashioned guard circling her hand perfectly. Strangely she felt at ease having such a killing weapon in her hand and though her first attempts were slow, painstakingly so, gradually under Miles' patient tutorage, inaccuracy and clumsiness made way for a good measure of competency. And then Elizabeth found out about the secret lessons.

"What were you thinking Miles, allowing her to use a sword and a pistol? For heaven's sake, it's most unseemly and must stop at once," she declared.

Miles listened with raised brows, winking at Robin as he said, "Very well Bess, I promise that I shall no longer teach our daughter."

And so, he didn't. Robin took over instead, steadily instructing his sister how to hone her skills in thrusting, parrying, countering, and deflecting, always explaining to expect the unexpected by dodging, ducking or even how to use the pommel itself should the need arise. Frances treasured these occasions, despite Robin being on occasion less patient than her father had been. Miles sat observing of course, making suggestions here and there for Frances' betterment, thus ensuring that his promise to Elizabeth was kept, albeit tenuously. As with most young men of noble birth, despite being crestfallen, Frances had ultimately had to face the time when Robin left Yorkshire to further his education in Oxford at St John's College, the very same Miles had attended in his own youth.

A number of years elapsed before Robin returned, greatly changed. The gangly youth she had seen ride away was gone, replaced by a confident young man who seemed fixated on certain subjects that Frances knew little about. Endlessly he spoke of the protracted war in Europe, a conflict that had commenced long before Frances had even been born.

"I really don't understand your obsession with this……this Bohemian King," Frances remarked one day, when despite the cold, she and her brother had ventured out into the grounds, swathed in fur lined cloaks.

"Frederick…. his name was Frederick," Robin declared irritably. "To be declared King, only to have his crown stripped from him less than a year later, forcing him to flee into exile in Holland with his entire family……. sad indeed."

"His wife being King Charles' sister, Elizabeth?"

Robin grinned.

"So, you do remember some things then?" His remark sounded a tad sarcastic.

"But why does the fighting continue if King Frederick is dead?" she asked.

"Dear little sister, the reasons are many and far too complex for one of your tender years to fully comprehend."

A candid, straightforward remark, nevertheless it stung and lifting her chin, Frances pressed her lips firmly together, feeling anger rising.

"I'm thirteen now and if you won't explain it to me, then I shall ask Master Johnson to tell me more about this Bohemian family you seem so obsessed with."

Robin dropped an arm round her shoulder, familiarly.

"I'm sure he'll be extremely happy to oblige. He and I have spoken for hours on this very subject."

Despite her youth, Frances felt nothing but unease when Robin spoke of a fixation for something that seemed so far removed from their peaceful life in Yorkshire. In slightly pained tones, he told her of the demise of Frederick from an illness contracted in Germany, though he keenly added that many believed the true reason to be a broken heart. Horrified, Frances had listened to the tale of Frederick having to witness a terrible event that no parent ever should. He and his elder son, Prince Henry had apparently been aboard a ship that foundered and though the King himself was rescued, Frederick had to witness the ship disappearing beneath the waves, taking his precious first born with it. That, Robin insisted, must have had a truly adverse effect upon the Bohemian monarch's health and for once, Frances had to agree. Picking his words carefully, Robin went on to explain that since that time, three of Fredericks remaining sons, Charles-Louis, Rupert, and Maurice had joined the fighting in Europe themselves, along with many an Englishman. Here he paused, unable or unwilling to look at her. In that moment, Frances had felt an inner disquiet that refused to leave. Europe seemed so far from Haveringham's sun-drenched gardens as she watched Robin pushing a stone about with the toe of his boot before kicking it with force into a pile of dead leaves, scattering them in all directions. Picking up another stone, he bounced it on his palm several times before it too followed the first.

"I may be young yet Robin, but I'm neither witless nor blind…."

With an almost silent chuckle, Robin shrugged his shoulders.

"Mother won't approve," he said evasively.

"Approve…. of what?" Was it right to ask for an answer to what she suspected already? He took off his hat, shaking out the ostrich plumes set in one side.

'I have to do this, I have to.'

A sudden gust blew his hair about, almost mirroring an inner turmoil that neither he, nor she, could escape in that moment.

"I intend to go to Europe myself, Fran," he said, clamping the hat back on his head.

"But why Robin, all this unrest in Europe has naught to do with us here in England, surely?"

"As I said, you're too young to understand," he snapped, angry with himself for saying far too much. With a grimace, Frances stamped her foot.

"I'm old enough to be wed should father insist upon it you know!"

Like a thunderous cloud, Robin glowered.

"Don't you be shrewish with me, little sister. Just be thankful father isn't the type to thrust someone upon you merely for our family's advancement."

Frances' head drooped almost in unison with her spirits. She would never get used to him speaking so harshly to her and despite her best attempts to prevent it, tears sprang to her eyes.

"I don't want you to go, brother," she murmured, and Robin clenched his fists.

"Your tears will not affect my decision, so you can cease this attempt to manipulate me. There are things a man must do, and this is one of them."

Unused to him berating her so harshly, Frances wandered over to a leafless bush, noting that it held the tiniest of buds on each branch, a promise of spring growth. Turning to face him she said, "In but a few weeks everything here will look so very different, don't you want to be here to see it, Robin?"

With a shake of the head and pursing his lips, he walked up to her, taking her hands in his. "I know what you're trying to do but it won't have any effect upon me. If you could but comprehend the wickedness in men's hearts when they seek power that's not rightly theirs. Tis an evil that must be stopped by force, if necessary, Fran and that's the point in question."

Whipping her coat aside, it suddenly felt like nature itself portended some sinister warning or counsel. Swiftly, she tugged it closer.

"Mother won't like what you wish to do," she said.

"Ah, but she won't be able to protest, once I have father's blessing, which I am certain to receive once I speak with him about it." He touched her face and smiled in that genuine way she loved. "Just think of the gifts I'll be able bring back when I return, some sparkling little trinket or mayhap a bolt of the finest fabric. Will that lift that sour little countenance, eh?"

Laughing along, Frances wondered if she even knew her brother anymore at all.

Miles slapped Robin stoutly on the shoulder.

"What nobler pursuit for a restless young man in these days?" he said. "I'm elated."

Elizabeth however, pacing back and forth wringing her hands, was anything but.

"He won't be furthering his education, Miles; he's going to join the fighting there…."

"Yes, but he's sure to discover himself in pertinent ways Bess, remember he is one day to inherit all this," Miles said with a sweeping wave of one hand.

Gripping the edge of the table-top, Elizabeth stared.

'If he survives long enough' she thought, shaking off an imagination she couldn't bear to consider for long.

"I really cannot comprehend the reasons for encouraging our only surviving son to undertake such a foolhardy endeavour Miles," she said, one hand over her eyes.

Robin went to join her, lightly touching her arm.

"Tis not something I do on a mere whim, mother. I have considered it long and hard for some time as do many other Englishmen who will be doing the same. Tis a matter of honour."

Slowly, Elizabeth's head turned to look at the son she adored.

"Honour? Where will the honour be if you are wounded…. or worse? Tell me that, my dear son."

Shoulders back, Robin stood firm, head defiantly erect.

"I defend the faith I was raised in Mother against those intent on crushing it completely."

"You can't fault the boy for that, Bess," Miles interjected.

Elizabeth knew she was beaten and turning toward him, she cupped her son's face with both hands.

"You are determined upon this course?" she asked.

"I am but would rather go with your blessing," he retorted.

"Then my son, you go with my blessing and prayers," she said, defeated and then he did the very thing that melted her heart. He bowed deferentially.

"Thank you, mother," he said.

With a loud sigh, Frances flopped onto a chair covering her face with her hands until she felt a hand ruffling her hair.

"Sulking won't alter anything, but cheer up, my good friend Ralph Bynghame is due here within the week. You'll like him." Robin laughed.

'No, I won't,' she thought.

Standing demurely beside her mother, Frances considered Ralph Bynghame, the good friend Robin had made whilst in Oxford. To Frances, this young Lord was nothing but an interloper, one she had not looked forward to meeting, after all she suspected that he just might have been the one to persuade her brother to go to Europe and for that alone, she was determined to dislike him. He was handsome enough, no one could deny that, youthfully lean with curling brown hair worn fashionably long and with a soft moustache that took on a silky sheen whenever he smiled, which she had to admit, was quite often.

"Little point in returning to Cumberland if you're to leave for Europe so soon though," Miles said cheerily. "No, I insist you stay here, my boy."

"Aye, just send word for the things you'll need to be brought here Ralph," Robin agreed, passing him a glass of Rhenish.

"Please don't assume it would put us out to have a bedchamber prepared for you, Lord Bynghame, it certainly wouldn't," Elizabeth remarked, though Frances didn't think much of that idea.

Finally, Ralph smiled.

"It appears I find myself outflanked Countess, thank you," he said.

A nod from Elizabeth was sufficient to send Moll Gilbert scuttling off with a serving girl in tow, to undertake necessary arrangements above stairs.

"Forgive me Countess, but I should deem it a great honour if you would use my given name whilst I am here? Rob…. your pardon, the Viscount Haveringham that is, has spoken of his family so readily that I feel you would not be offended by such forwardness?"

Pursing her lips, Frances rolled her eyes but said, "If that is true, perhaps he has also told you that I am Lady Frances Ashford." She lifted her chin pertly. Only then did the young Lord's attention turn upon her.

"I had already deduced as much, young lady," he said with a grin. "As you might expect, your brother has told me a great deal about you."

Everyone seemed to find the comment amusing except Frances who with a grimace, looked down at her hands.

'Why did you have to come here, spoiling everything.'

Despite all this, as the days went by, Frances could not help but like Ralph Bynghame. His wit and relaxed manner made him difficult to dislike and the easy interaction between him and her brother was infectious to the point where she began to consider Ralph almost akin to another brother. In turn, Ralph found Frances' antics hilarious, especially the manner in which she mimicked Robin's manly gait or the way he dropped onto a chair, elbows on knees. One particular day, after making a disparaging remark, sticking out her tongue at Ralph and running off down the Great Hall, he followed, chasing her round and round the oak table until he caught her with ease and tickled her until she begged him to stop.

But time rushed by far too quickly and very soon it was the final night before their departure for Europe. With Elizabeth at her sewing frame and Frances at the table busy sketching what she hoped would be a fitting portrait of her brother to keep in her room, the two young men excitedly discussed their arrangements for the following day. At one point, Frances looked up from her sketching, pulling a face.

"You know sister, you really should show more respect. I am a Viscount remember, and Ralph not only a Lord but heir to his father's estate, whereas you…."

"Am merely Frances Ashford, yes, I know……. there's really no reason to rebuke me in that manner in front of your…. 'friend'!"

Ralph instantly guffawed, throwing back his head.

"Oh, such wit from a mere child," he said sarcastically, laughing with Robin. Hands on hips, Frances scowled petulantly. "Child, I said because child you are, my little poppet; you'll be sorely missed," Ralph added.

"Little poppet?" Frances demanded acerbically. "Why, I'll have you know that…."

"Enough Frances," Robin snapped. "Anymore and you can go to your bedchamber to cool your temper. We've far too much to discuss to have these constant childish interruptions."

Spoiling his last evening was never what Frances wished to achieve and with tears pricking her eyes she looked down at her sketch of him. She thought she had captured his features well, but setting down her pencil she murmured, "I wish I were a man, so I too could leave for Europe."

Elizabeth gave a tinkling little laugh.

"What a ridiculous thing to say, Frances," she said. "You my dearest daughter are more than fortunate to be born female and therefore kept well away from ought to do with warfare."

"But think how glorious it would be to travel overseas and take up one's sword to fight alongside the likes of Charles Louis, Rupert and….and…. oh, yes, Maurice," she said with satisfaction, glad to have remembered. Looking to Robin, she hoped to see approval and was rewarded with a grin.

"You'll survive without him, little one," Ralph stated casually.

"Not so little that I don't have a heart, just you remember that Lord Bynghame," she said, biting her lower lip.

CHAPTER FIVE

Haveringham Manor – Autumn 1641

Robin had been gone for little more than eighteen months when he wrote of taking part in a decisive battle at Vlotho in October 1638, where the late King Frederick's son, the Elector Palatine Charles Louis, had attempted to regain control of the Palatinate. Sadly, the outcome had been a crushing defeat and in addition, the Elector's younger brother, Prince Rupert had been captured and taken to Austria to face indefinite imprisonment. Thereafter, from time to time, Robin's letters arrived, each assuring his family, Elizabeth in particular, that both he and Ralph remained perfectly safe and unharmed.

Then after four and a half years had elapsed, a messenger arrived unexpectedly one afternoon bearing a letter from Ralph Bynghame. Elizabeth had been in near hysterics when Miles, reading from the letter, explained that Robin had received injuries in a skirmish and though his wounds were not life threatening, his commanding officer had nevertheless ordered him home and that Ralph would be accompanying him. Only then when Miles noticed the date on the letter did he blanch significantly, pointing out that it had been written almost a month previously and therefore the two men could potentially appear on Haveringham's doorstep at any moment. Elizabeth went swiftly into organising mode, demanding various servants attend her immediately. Within a matter of hours, Robin's bedchamber had been aired, the room cleaned and polished till it gleamed, fresh linen put on the bed and his clothing removed from the press to be dealt with. The cook was told to start preparing his favourite dishes the very moment the young Viscount was safely established in his room and Elizabeth ensured that two other chambers were prepared, just in case more than Ralph arrived. Yet of the men themselves, there remained no sign for the next few days. Then one morning when Frances and her father had been out on an inspection tour of the estate dwellings, she had returned home alone, leaving Miles dealing with an issue raised by the gamekeeper. When she walked into the Great Hall, aside from a distant hum of laughter and conversation drifting out from the kitchen, the house seemed distinctly quiet. Untying her cloak, Frances noticed Martha coming down the staircase smiling broadly, a pile of men's clothing in her arms.

"Such joyous news, Milady," she said. "Ya brother's finally home."

"What?"

The cloak dropped to the floor as Frances sped off, taking the stairs two at a time, totally disregarding the coif falling from her head and the hair tumbling freely across both shoulders. Dashing along the corridor, she reached Robin's chamber and flung open the door. There he was, propped against a pillow in the bed, looking pale but a little older, his face now adorned with blonde facial hair.

"Robin," she gasped, launching herself at him.

"Arghh, have a care, little sister," he cried out vociferously.

"Oh Robin, I'm so deeply sorry…. please say I didn't hurt you?" Absently, Frances raked back her long tresses revealing more of her face. At last, after an open-mouthed gape and rising brows, Robin gave a low whistle.

"My God, look at you….," he declared. "What have you done with the girl I left behind over four years back, for in truth I recognise not this fair young beauty before me now!"

A blush infused Frances' face as she smiled, lifting her head defiantly.

"What do you expect brother, I'm almost eighteen now," she replied, startled by an unexpected movement at the opposite side of the bed.

"I have to agree Rob…. why I scarcely recognised her, she's so altered," a bedraggled Ralph Bynghame declared. She bore no resemblance to the young girl they had left here several years ago, and the remarkable change astonished him. Her features were much softer, the chubbiness of childhood replaced by a smooth porcelain complexion, a long, elegant neck and the inescapable mounds of womanhood protruding from the top of her bodice, something he found difficult to look away from as they repeatedly rose and fell. She was staring straight at him, forcing him to look down at his boots.

"You may be having trouble recognising me Lord Bynghame, but I well remember you with your constant teasing. Perhaps now I'm grown you'll be less inclined to call me 'little poppet' as once you did?" she said.

"I…. I imagine not," Ralph almost spluttered, glancing nervously to his left where now another man could be seen, clearly having before been obscured by the bed curtains. Aghast, she heard Ralph say, "John my friend, you'll probably already have surmised that this is Frances, Rob's sister."

"As you now see, Ralph isn't the only one to return with me," Robin said. "This fellow goes by the name of John Fitzherbert, heir to the Earldom of Melton, in Kent," Robin explained. Frances scarcely heard, finding it difficult not to stare at the stranger with long dark wavy hair and the most striking pale blue eyes she had ever seen. Slowly she stood and dipped a curtsey.

"Welcome to Haveringham Manor, Lord Fitzherbert," she said a tad huskily, heat infusing her face.

"Your most humble servant, Lady Frances," he responded in a voice that seemed to almost bathe her in warmth. Finally, she turned back to her brother in time to see him grimacing when he hauled himself further up the pillow. Instantly, she was back at his side, straightening the coverlets.

"Do you need anything brother…. wine, food… a potion from Old Aggie in the village perhaps… or maybe I could fetch you something from the stillroom…."

"Good heavens, take a breath sister, do," he snapped. Frances closed her eyes, embarrassed to feel that he could speak so harshly to her in front of Lord Fitzherbert, but then she wondered why that mattered so much? With a scowl, she looked down at her hands, hearing Robin laughing. "Do you really think I need the ministrations of that old hag from the village? All I need is a rest from fussing females such as you and mother," he said, but then his face contorted, and Frances reached for his hand. Despite every assertion and his attempt at humour, he was in pain, that much was obvious from his pallor.

"Is the wound deep?" she finally asked.

"Wounds sister," he admitted. "One to the arm and another to the thigh, the rogue caught me off guard you see." He smiled, looking into her eyes. "Now, what news of my horse?"

"Hermes? Oh, he tends to be restless I'm afraid. I've had him out often, but I don't think I ride quite as adeptly as you...."

Robin's eyes widened.

"You've ridden my stallion? What was father thinking, allowing you to do that?"

"Because I ride so well now, Robin. Oh, I grant you Hermes can be difficult to control at times, but I manage him well enough, and I love to feel the wind whipping my hair when I allow him his head."

"It sounds as if you've become quite the proficient horsewoman?" Ralph remarked.

"Of course," she answered sweetly, taking the opportunity to have another swift glance toward the dark-haired stranger.

CHAPTER SIX

Haveringham Manor – Autumn 1641

Ralph Bynghame soon returned to Haveringham on the pretext of enquiring after Robin's health, though it soon became evident that there was an alternative reason.

On returning home to Cumberland, Ralph had been informed that whilst he had been away fighting in the Low Countries, a marriage contract had been arranged, his bride would be Anne Winthrop, elder daughter of a respectable family from Westmorland. Two years Ralph's junior, Anne came with a substantial dowry that had proved significant in sealing the deal. The news had come as a complete shock to Ralph and eager to escape and clear his head, he voiced the necessity of checking on Robin, thence fleeing to what he hoped would be the relative peace of Yorkshire.

The day after his arrival, Frances sat beside Ralph in the small dining room with her parents, Robin still taking all his meals in his bedchamber.

"Do you think you might grow to love her though Ralph?" she asked, in between mouthfuls.

"And just how would you have me answer that?" Ralph responded a little sharply, sparkling blue eyes a tad too perturbing as they looked questioningly into his. Surprisingly, Ralph had begun to question the logic of coming here at all, the grown-up Frances proving an undeniable distraction, adding to his already beleaguered thoughts.

"I merely wish to learn more about this bride of yours, you say so little about her. For instance, is she pretty?" Frances asked, taken aback when Ralph's brows rose, and his top lip warped with what appeared to be disdain.

"I suppose she is…. but then I already knew what she looked like, our families have known one another for many years. She and I even played together as children, along with our siblings."

44

"So, the match was planned some time ago?"

"Apparently, though neither Anne nor I were aware of it until recently."

"Upon your return from Europe?"

"Exactly."

For some reason, Frances did not feel as if Ralph were being totally open, probably choosing his words with particular wisdom, none of which was sufficient to satisfy Frances' inquisitive nature.

"Is that why you seem so unwilling to speak about her?" she asked, and he scowled.

"I answered, didn't I?"

Twirling the stem of her spoon between thumb and forefinger, Frances pursed her lips into a smirk, lifting her brows.

"Yes, but you gave no indication of what she looks like. For example, what is the colour of her hair, fair like mine?"

'She's naught like you,' he thought but said, "Her hair is dark brown."

"Her eyes then, are they blue like mine?"

'Yours aren't merely blue….' Ralph reached for his glass, draining it completely before lifting it for Lambert to refill. "They're brown, I think."

"You think? Goodness Ralph, you seem to know more about me than the lady you're destined to wed. Perhaps you have little inclination to know her better, is that it?"

The knife in Ralph's hand fell onto his plate with a clatter and pivoting his whole body, he grimaced.

"Let me explain something to you, Frances. You are correct in assuming that I'm not particularly happy with this arrangement, but it is what it is and there's nothing to be done about it. To go against my father's wishes would be to face disinheritance. Do you really imagine I seek that?" he asked.

"Heavens, you make it sound more like a business transaction rather than a possible prospect for marital harmony."

Ralph rolled his eyes heavenward, shaking his head slowly.

"How naïve you still are," he said snidely. "Marriage is for one purpose only and that is to beget heirs to prolong the family dynasty. This harmony you speak so freely of is purely fictional for most, don't you understand that yet?"

"In a way, but you cannot know how Anne feels. Why don't you ask her, who knows, her answer may well give you greater insight into her character and feelings on the subject."

For some reason, he didn't answer at first. Instead, he reached for his glass and drained it yet again.

"I have no mind to be alone with her at present," he said at length.

"Why ever not Ralph, for all you know Anne may feel exactly the same as you."

"It's not about how one feels, Frances. I could tell she'd been well trained at the betrothal ceremony, standing beside me demure and silent as the arrangements were read out, her eyes dutifully downcast, as expected."

"Nonetheless, whatever you say, Anne may well have her own misgivings and yet dare not express them."

"Perhaps," he admitted, raising his glass for Lambert to replenish once more. "I would have liked her to show a little spirit, even a morsel of reluctance, but she didn't." He looked directly in Frances' eyes. "I doubt you would endure such an arrangement meekly without making some form of comment?"

Nor would she, but then glancing at her father down the table,

Frances doubted he would ever enter into a similar contract without informing her beforehand. As her father, he was free to do so of course but when at that very moment, he looked her way and smiled, she knew she was worrying needlessly.

"Perhaps not," she admitted.

"Then there seems little point in discussing it anymore, Frances," he said. "The die is cast and soon Anne Winthrop will be my wife, whatever her character flaws."

Frances pursed her lips and said, "Or yours."

At first Ralph did not reply, searching her face from brow to chin.

'You really have no idea, have you?'

Eventually he said, "Your wit hasn't improved either I see?"

"Nor has yours," she countered, blaming herself for responding in a manner that sounded lame and a little childish. There were times when she knew she had been outspoken, this being one of them. The pair sat in silence for some time, each concentrating on the excellent repast, until Ralph suddenly spoke.

"I will say this, on the day you are informed of the one you are to marry, I shall be questioning just how you feel, particularly if your father plans it all without your knowledge."

They glared at one another until Frances reached for her fan, fluttering it in front of her heated face.

"Father would never force me…." she said evenly.

"He might you know, if it were to be of great benefit to him."

"I intend to wed for love," she declared firmly, and Ralph let out a loud guffaw.

"Your innocence is perfectly charming you know, Frances," he said almost mockingly.

No more was spoken on that particular subject that night and the very next morning Ralph Bynghame left Haveringham Manor for Cumberland and a marriage to Anne Winthrop two weeks later.

October 1641

"Shall we go across?" Robin suggested. Having made a swift recovery, he and Frances had ridden out together across the flat land near York, pausing only when they reached the river Ouse.

"You shouldn't tire yourself, Robin," Frances said patting her chestnut mare, Phoenix, on the neck.

"I'm perfectly able to go a little further on… Hessay Moor perhaps?"

Robin knew his sister would not be able to resist, the expanse of moorland between the villages of Long Marston and Tockwith, one of her favourite places to ride.

"Do you really need to ask?" she grinned.

At the river's edge, they dismounted leading the horses onto a small ferry that afforded the easiest means of crossing at the point. The small craft was manned by a ferryman who removed his hat, greeting the pair with a bow.

"God give you good day Milord, Milady. I 'eard you was back from them foreign parts. Wounded so I were told?"

"I was simply caught off guard, Master Drew. Thankfully, the rogue hadn't the proficiency to finish the job."

With a gasp Frances touched her brother's arm.

"Don't speak that way Robin, I can't bear the thought…."

Casually, her sibling dropped an arm round her shoulder as the ferryman untied the ropes and the little craft began the short journey to the opposite bank.

"Beggin ya pardon Milord, but I'm told there could well be fighting 'ere in England afore long," Drew remarked, Robin silencing him at once with a resounding glare.

"Take no notice sister, tis all rumour." Then to the ferryman, "I'll thank you not to speak about matters you don't fully understand, Drew. Just do your job and get us safely across."

"Yes, milord," Drew said wisely remaining silent for the remainder of the short trip.

On the far bank, Robin pressed a coin into Drew's palm before helping his sister into the saddle.

"To Hessay Moor then," he said, mounting up.

"Yes, but let's head over the marshes toward Long Marston first, eh?" Her eyes twinkled with excitement.

"Very well, but stay close to me, the ground can oft be treacherous there."

They hadn't gone far before curiosity got the better of Frances.

"What Drew was just saying, is trouble brewing here in England?"

"I won't lie to you, Fran, the King seems to be having more than a few issues with the Parliament these days. They seem to dislike the King's advisers. Remember what happened to Lord Strafford?"

She did. No one could forget the execution of the King's foremost counsellor. Lord Deputy of Ireland, Strafford had imposed a rule in that land many considered far too authoritative. When the King had been left with no alternative but to recall the very Parliament, he had previously dissolved. Strafford returned from Ireland to be turned on by members of the House of Commons almost at once. Accused of treason, Strafford endured a long and protracted trial during which it was said, he defended himself admirably with both bravery and honour. Despite a not guilty verdict, Parliament continued to accuse Strafford with one member, John Pym, issuing a Bill of Attainder against him, leaving the King with little option but to sign a warrant for Strafford's execution. With Strafford gone, Parliament felt increasingly that they now had the upper hand, constantly battling with the King over the smallest of issues, especially a tax levied against grand estates 'ship money' it was called, whether those estates were near a port or not. Miles had certainly been unhappy about paying for something he thought he shouldn't, but had faced it boldly, gritted his teeth and paid it in full, as required.

"Let's see what that chestnut mare of yours is capable of, shall we dear sister?" Robin said.

"If you wish, but don't forget that Hermes is her sire and therefore she has inherited some of his attributes."

With a flick of her whip, Frances urged Phoenix to the gallop, leaving Robin some way behind, though eventually Hermes' prowess showed through, and he soon drew alongside.

"You've certainly grown into a fine horsewoman," Robin said, the freshening breeze catching his voice as he patted the stallion's neck.

"I did tell you she is capable of good speed," Frances said looking around the vast area of moorland with marshes here and there. Ancient hedges formed barriers, one in particular leading to an area locals referred to as 'Four Lanes Meet' a simple dirt track providing access from one village to the other. The only blemish on an otherwise serene landscape was a deep, wide ditch scarring part of it for some considerable distance. To their left lay the gentle undulating slopes leading up to the pretty little ancient church at Bilton and to their right, a thickly wooded area.

"Wilstrop Wood is decked out in such wonderful autumnal shades. How I would love a gown in that copper colour…."

"Only a woman could think of such fripperies when looking at a bunch of trees," Robin guffawed.

"I don't care what you say, all I know is that the county of York is the best in all England. I should hate to ever leave it."

Robin manoeuvred Hermes closer to Phoenix.

"Really, now that is a surprise sister for, I thought the county of Kent might hold some attraction for you?"

Frances' mouth dropped open.

"Whatever do you mean?" she asked almost willing him to respond in the way she hoped. Nervously slipping the reins through her fingers, she waited until Robin reached for her hand.

"You know, I'd wager fifty crowns that John Fitzherbert thinks often of the county of York and......Haveringham Manor in particular," he said.

"Of course, he doesn't, that's just foolishness on your part." She was delighted inwardly but wasn't about to admit how frequently she did think of Kentish Lord, not even to her brother. Nothing would come of it anyway, he was now in the south on his father's estate, whilst she was here in the north. Quickly, she changed the subject.

"Have you not left any ladies in the Low Countries with broken hearts, pining for the Viscount Haveringham, dearest brother?

"What makes you ask that?"

"I'm just curious that's all."

"We weren't actually speaking of me, but of my valiant comrade from Kent," he countered.

"No Robin, *we* weren't, only *you* were."

"Ah, I see that's the way the wind blows, is it? Then I don't suppose it will matter to you should our paths cross next week in

London," Robin said examining his gloved hand.

Miles had declared his intent to visit England's capital in order to conclude a portion of urgent business and despite rumours of increasing unrest there, he had decided that the whole family should accompany him, even to visit Whitehall, should the opportunity arise.

Robin noticed the flash of excitement cross through Frances' eyes.

"You believe he might be there… at Court?" she asked at length and reaching for her hand, Robin said, "For certain."

John Fitzherbert had returned to Melton Abbey in Kent with unsettled emotions and troubled thoughts. He couldn't quite comprehend why he found the blonde-haired, blue-eyed sister of his Yorkshire comrade so appealing nor why his thoughts continually seemed to turn toward her. Having noticed how pre-occupied his son had become, the Earl of Melton questioned him one day.

"What darkens your mood these days my son, the things you witnessed overseas or something else entirely?" he asked.

"I'm just concerned for Robin I suppose…."

"Really, and is that all?"

"Well, I do still recall that your desire is for me to consider marriage in the near future…."

"Have you then discounted all the previous matches I suggested?"

John appeared uncertain how to answer. For a moment he thought better of what was in his mind, but his father seemed in more positive frame of mind and therefore he took his chance.

"I believe so…… Father, when I was lately in Yorkshire at Haveringham Manor, I was introduced to Robin's sister." There, it was said and somehow John felt more than relieved, a weight somehow slightly lifted, though his father's response remained unspoken and of the utmost importance.

"Ah, I see, so that's what occupies your thoughts. Benningford's daughter isn't she.... well now, there's a match to possibly ponder more, she is after all the daughter of an Earl."

John gave a hopeful smile.

"I have only met her once though, father?"

"Oh, that's naught to afford issue; why your mother and I never met till our betrothal day. I'll write to Benningford to test the water."

"Little point father, they are all to be in London next month you know."

"As shall we, my son. Find out where they are to stay and I'll pay Benningford a visit," Melton said with a satisfied smile.

John Fitzherbert strolled about the crowded room at the palace of Whitehall, searching each and every female face until he saw her entering the room on the arm of her brother. His breath almost caught. In a gown of royal blue silk with her hair formally styled, she moved sedately from person to person tipping her head when Robin made introductions. Occasionally, she looked about as if searching for someone and John hoped it would be him. Briefly their eyes met, and colour rose to her cheeks, confirming John's suspicions. Purposefully, he strode over.

"Well met Haveringham," he declared, sweeping off his hat and offering a bow, protocol dictating he greet Robin first, though he longed to speak directly to his sister.

"Ah, Fitzherbert. Do you recall my sister, I hope? I dare say she looks a little different now from when last you laid eyes upon her?"

"Indeed, she does. Lady Frances, I am charmed," John said, reaching for her hand and lifting it to his lips, retaining it a little longer than was required. He could sense the way she trembled and that again made him hope he was the reason.

"Oh, there is father, I must go and speak to him," Robin said. "Fitzherbert, would you mind looking after Frances for a while?"

"My pleasure, Haveringham," John responded and to Frances, "shall we go to yonder window, that we might hear one another speak with more ease? It is impossibly crowded and quite noisy in this spot."

"As you wish, my Lord," Frances said, resting her hand on the manly arm swathed in deep brown velvet braided with gold, glad of the chance to be alone with him. By the window, he looked down at her.

"I truly believe your brother left us alone on purpose," he said lightly.

"We're hardly alone my Lord," she said looking around at the number of flamboyantly dressed courtiers in the room. Her attention strangely fell on her brother with Miles and another elegantly attired gentleman.

"That's my father, the Earl of Melton," John explained.

CHAPTER SEVEN

London - autumn 1641

Only the bravest souls had ventured out into the grounds of the royal palace the following day, a cold snap ensuring the majority stayed indoors in the warm. John, Frances, and Robin, swathed in thick cloaks walked along together until Robin was forestalled by someone he knew. Glancing about, John ushered Frances into a secluded arbour.

"Don't look so startled, I merely wish to speak privately that's all," he said.

"So privately that we need to hide in here?" Frances asked, feeling her heart beating faster. Reaching for her gloved hands, John suddenly appeared awkward, like a bashful boy about to admit to some folly.

"I wished to…. no that's not right, I need to…. Frances, you must be aware that our fathers have been discussing an arrangement between us?"

He felt uneasy, not knowing how she might respond and yet hoping that she would be as pleased and agreeable to the notion as himself.

"I did notice them conversing last night. Are you suggesting they are planning to have us wed?"

"Yes. I shall be honest Frances. For some time, I have been urged to contemplate marriage and yet only when I returned from Yorkshire did I finally consider having found someone I favoured. It's strange and we may have only met once before, albeit briefly, but I couldn't stop thinking about you, even when I was back in Kent. I shared my thoughts with my father who wrote to yours, speculatively. For the son of an Earl to be matched with the daughter of an Earl, there could hardly be any objection…. that is unless you do?"

Her breathing grew erratic, and with a pounding heart, she swallowed deeply.

"I…. I agree, we don't really know one another," she admitted and yet she could hardly deny her feelings. After all, there were hardly any moments when she hadn't thought about him.

"I know, irrational, isn't it?" he laughed nervously. She hadn't shown any reluctance, so he pressed on. "Your brother wrote to me and reading between the lines, he suggested that you mentioned me often in discussions. Therefore, I began to hope that possibly you felt as I did…."

"I didn't know Robin had done that," she said, turning aside with a scowl.

"Is there something wrong, have you no wish to be a bride perhaps?" he asked.

Frances swung back, held by eyes full of apprehension.

"I'm not sure. I've been raised to expect that I shall be required to wed one day."

Believing her reluctant, John again grasped her hands.

"Don't trifle with me Frances, I need to know if you are willing to take this rogue for a husband?" When a dark tendril of hair blew across his mouth, impatiently he brushed it aside, watching her steadily. In that moment, Frances considered him insecure and yet so very handsome, the pale blue eyes boring into hers. She smiled.

"You are no rogue in my eyes, my Lord," she admitted, though this was still not quite enough to convince him, the hardened soldier feeling she may well be prevaricating. With a faint tremor in his voice, he answered. "Are you suggesting that you might be persuaded to consider being my bride?"

Tracing a finger up and down the braid decorating his slashed sleeve, she slowly raised her head.

"I need no persuasion, none whatsoever," she whispered.

Joy washed over him and without warning, he hoisted her in his arms, whirling her round and round.

"Do set me down John, I'm going dizzy," she gasped.

"You have just made me the happiest of men, darling heart." His eyes brimmed with tenderness but then with a roguish grin he added, "This may sound very presumptuous, but mayhap our proposed union might be sealed… with a kiss?"

Feeling as if her thumping heart might burst through the tight constraints of her bodice, she sensed his hands cupping her face and bending his head, he gently brushed his lips against hers, slowly and effortlessly deepening the pressure until she sighed and closed her eyes. They remained closed even when he released her and she heard him laugh and say, "What's amiss sweetheart?"

Only then did she look at him. "T'was but a kiss my love….naught compared to the pleasures awaiting us in the marriage bed…" he said quickly adding, "I think perhaps we should locate Robin, for if we tarry much longer in this hidden manner, I may forget that I am a gentleman."

Trying to look suitably affronted, despite the desire to laugh, Frances replaced her fallen hood, dipping beneath the branch he held high above. On the pathway Robin appeared to be looking for them.

"Ah, so there you are, now what have you two been up to?" he said not missing his sister's flushed cheeks and John's almost triumphant expression.

"We are both content, Rob," John admitted, turning to look down at Frances, one arm encircling her waist.

"Excellent, then it's back to the Inn for a celebratory tankard or two," Robin suggested.

"Let go I say!" The postilion's raised voice rang out as the carriage came to a jolting halt. Robin peered out.

"This looks a tad worrying," he admitted to John inside.

Several civilians armed with sticks, cudgels and other basic weaponry had blocked the narrow street, encircled the carriage, hindering further progress.

"Try 'owt with that whip an' we'll drag ya from that beast, ya bastard."

"I'm not having this," Robin snarled, leaning out through the window. "What's the issue, Moresby?" he barked.

"Unable to proceed for the moment, Milord," the postilion shouted, and the crowd jeered, pounding fists repeatedly against the carriage sides, the Benningford arms emblazoned on the doors, adding to their hostility.

Robin made a hasty retreat inside.

"God damn 'em," he snarled.

Filthy faces began peering in through the window.

"Got ya whore with ya milord?" one shouted.

"Wanna share 'er?" another yelled.

Frances cowered against John's side, drawing her hood forward trying to hide her face but the noise increased.

"They think they's better than us….."

"Devil take 'em, an' the King."

"King Pym, God bless 'im."

Again, and again threats bombarded the occupants and Frances cowered against John, wondering just how they might escape this riotous mob. John drew her into the hollow of his shoulder, free arm hovering over his sword, but it was noticed.

"Draw that and ya'll regret it!"

Verbal onslaught continued unabated, increasing in volume as the minutes ticked by.

"Trust us, my love, we'll get out of this soon," John whispered unconvincingly into Frances' hair. Slowly she noticed Robin's hand moving down his leg to the top of one boot from which dagger was drawn. Keeping it below the door line, he held it ready, beaming at their would-be attackers.

"Good citizens, I assure you we pose no threat to your good selves." His tone remained light; his words as false as the crowd's regard for their safety. "We are but transitory in London and know little of your grievances against the King. We merely wish to return to our lodgings. Pray be good enough to stand aside and allow us to proceed."

Frances had never heard her brother sound so much like a skilled diplomat, his face bearing the facade of peace, though she could tell from his eyes that he intended quite the opposite. His words had insignificant effect.

"An' why should we believe ya?" The jeering intensified. "These 'ere arms on this door proves you's gentry and we 'ates all gentry."

Frances shuddered, John's grip tightening around her. Even through her cloak she could sense how taught his body was and how alert his senses.

A girl, not much more than Frances' own age stared directly at her until her face unexpectedly contorted and she spat out a great globule of spittle. Frances looked with horror at the stain creeping down her velvet skirts, suddenly feeling nauseous.

"I like them clothes she 'as on…..maybe we should 'ave 'em….

imagine me wearing that in Spitalfields...."

Great guffaws greeted that, and someone shouted, "It's yours Lucy.....if ya wan' to 'ave it...."

A sturdily built, balding, chubby faced man with rotting teeth gripped the door frame, making as if to haul himself inside. Robin's grip tightened on the dagger, ready to thrust it hard and deep. Frances turned her head into John's hair, closing her eyes. *'Dear Lord, please help us.'*

Then a voice rang out.

"Hey, see yonder, that's one of them bastards from two days' back and, e's alone this time.... leave them, let's go after 'im."

Little by little, the hammering on the carriage subsided as one by one the crowd dispersed, eagerly pursuing less complicated prey.

Robin leaned back on his seat puffing out his lips.

"That was a close call," he said slipping the dagger back inside his boot.

"Are you alright, my love?" John enquired, tilting her chin to see her face.

"I am, though I can't seem to stop shaking," Frances admitted.

"Hardly surprising, sister," Robin declared, then leaning out of the window, addressed the postilion. "Is all clear, Moresby?"

"Aye Sir, they're off down the next street."

"Then get us back to the Inn and make haste about it."

In less than ten minutes the carriage drew up outside their accommodation. Robin alighted first, drawing his sword, glancing back and forth, up, and down the street. "Take Frances in," he counselled, John who helped her from the carriage. "Moresby, see the carriage is housed round the back and out of plain sight!"

Robin instructed.

"Yes Milord."

Once in the warmth of the upstairs parlour, Frances went to the window, taking off her cloak and gloves. The grotesque stain on her skirts remained, a stark reminder of the ordeal they had just endured. She shuddered and joining her, John said, "Come away sweetheart, tis unwise to stand by the casement, if they come back this way, they may see you." He led her to a chair by the fireside.

"Why do they hate us so much, John?" she asked as she sat down.

"I don't think it's us as such my dear, their main grievance seems to be against the King and his policies, but they're simpletons if they believe he won't retaliate at some point. This rise in violence is just wilful and unmerited."

A sharp rap at the door preceded the entrance of a somewhat rotund host, carrying a tray of goblets, tankards, and bottles. Setting it carefully on the table, he tipped his head.

"Thought they'd put me windows through they were that fired up. Tis that John Lilburne causes all this, with 'is ideas of freedom from the King's rule, inciting rioting, and damage to property, harassing 'onest folk just going about their business... beggin ya Lordship's pardon for talking that way.... will that be all, Milord?"

"For now, Master Gregory," Robin said, tossing him a coin, then removing his baldric and sword added, "We'll need you again, once the Earl returns."

"Certainly, Milord, it's my honour to serve you..... Might I just add that I've no inclinations myself such as them rioters, none whatsoever, may it please you....."

A harassed John went over to the tapster and grasping his elbow, escorted him to the door.

"We'll let you know when you're needed again," John said, closing the door when he had gone, joining Robin at the table filling two tankards with ale.

"The man must be addled if he thinks we believe such protestations. Like as not he'd knife us in our beds, given the opportunity."

Robin glanced at his sister by the fireside, warming her hands.

"Lower your voice, my friend. Here take her this aqua vitae, it'll quell the shock."

"Who is this John Lilburne he spoke about?" Frances asked as she sipped the warming liquid.

"A rebellious cur who thinks more of himself than he should. 'Freeborn John' so he calls himself," John explained.

Robin dropped onto the chair opposite, unbuttoning his doublet, leaning forward, and gazing into his tankard.

"His aim is to indoctrinate the innocent with rebellious philosophies Fran, by handing out seditious pamphlets to anyone willing to heed what's printed on 'em. He even brought in subversive material and books from overseas, all unlicensed of course."

"And for it, was publicly whipped at the cart-tail from the Fleet prison to the pillory at Westminster and yet still his ravings continue unabated. I wonder why no one puts an end to him," John said taking a long draft of ale. Then touching Frances on the shoulder, he asked, "Where shall we dine this night my love, here or elsewhere in the city?"

"We'll all have to dine here." Framed in the doorway, Miles Benningford's expression appeared like thunder. Slamming the door behind him, he strode up to the table, quickly filled a goblet with aqua vitae and downed it all. Robin immediately stood to his feet.

"Has something happened, father?" he asked.

"Go to your mother, Frances," Miles demanded, refilling the goblet. With a squeeze of her hand from John, she obeyed at once.

"If it's aught similar to the encounter we endured earlier father, then it's hardly surprising you're so troubled," Robin said.

"What encounter?" Miles demanded.

"Oh, simply a mob of hot heads haranguing us when they noticed the arms on the carriage door. Thankfully, they soon turned their sights on someone else," John explained. Miles poured more Aqua Vitae, drained it in one and slammed the goblet onto the tray.

"That settles it; we shall return home on the morrow. I'll not have my wife and daughter subject to these mischief makers. You and your father should do the same if you've any sense, John my boy."

"Father and I are obliged to await His Majesty's pleasure, for the present," John explained.

"Mayhap not for long though eh? I learned today that if things do not change for the better, the King may be forced to quit London," Miles said.

"But that's unthinkable, father," Robin stated.

"Unthinkable or not it's what's being implied. The King won't accede to Pym's demands that much we all know, and therefore his position grows more tenuous by the day. They're constantly at loggerheads, neither willing to back down and reach any form of agreement. The unrest in the populace grows at an alarming rate and then all these trained bands drilling on the common every day…..for what purpose I ask, there can only be one to my mind. If I am right, I daren't contemplate what might ensue."

"Military intervention, you mean?" John enquired catching a nod from Miles.

"It certainly seems to me as if London is preparing for conflict. You can almost taste the tension out there…. like some great carbuncle getting ready to burst. And if it does, I want my family back in Yorkshire, far away from it."

Miles trudged across to a chair by the fire, sitting down with a huge sigh.

"Go down and arrange for the carriage to be made ready, Robin. I want to leave at first light. Then you'd best fetch your mother and sister. John, could you locate that whinging tapster of ours and arrange for food to be brought up? Now there's another I wouldn't trust with as little as two farthings."

The journey out of the city proved relatively easy with little sign of disturbance as they traversed the narrow streets and everyone expressed relief to finally reach the road north, except Frances, who kept looking back toward the ever-diminishing city knowing her betrothed remained there.

It took just over a week for the travel weary party to reach Haveringham Manor and once there, the formal arrangements for the marriage were finalised. In only a brief time, documents arrived setting out the agreed dowry and jointure terms to be signed and sealed by all parties, the date of the ceremony set for the 18th August in the year 1642.

CHAPTER EIGHT

Haveringham Manor - Early 1642

Robin strode into the Great Hall, spurs jingling lightly with each step.

"This has just arrived, father," he said, wafting a letter in the air.

"Oh, from whom?" Miles asked.

"John Fitzherbert," he replied.

Leaping to her feet, Frances caught her graphite box, catapulting it to the floor, scattering pieces of black lead all over as she hurried toward her sibling, holding out a hand.

"He writes to me, sister," Robin said breaking the seal, touched by her crestfallen appearance. "Somehow though I suspect this might be of interest to you…."

Another folded paper was held forth and making a grab for it, she stared with fondness at her name written on the front before consigning it inside her bodice.

"I shall read it later brother," she explained, stooping to retrieve all the bits of black lead.

Robin dropped onto a chair by the fireplace, scanning the open letter.

"Dear God," he suddenly declared.

"Frances, go to your mother," Miles stated firmly.

"Nay father, allow her to stay," Robin said. "What's written here will be common enough knowledge before long, it's best she hears it first-hand, if you would permit me to read it aloud?"

Glancing from one progeny to the other, Miles rubbed his chin thoughtfully, eventually tapping the chair beside him.

"Very well, sit here daughter."

Robin began by assuring them that the missive had come directly from Melton Abbey in Kent and therefore both John and his father were safe, then he read aloud.

'I am bound to write of dire issues facing us in these sad times, my friend.

At the beginning of last month, accompanied by many supporters, including father and myself, the King went to the House of Commons, demanding entry, bearing a warrant for the arrest of five members and another from the House of Peers, each accused of treason. Making use of the Speaker's chair, His Majesty addressed the house declaring the 'treason hath no privilege.' It was noted none of the impeached were present and therefore stating that 'the birds having flown, he would take his leave,' the King quit the chamber to chants of 'privilege, privilege, privilege' from its members. Father remarked that this show of open defiance must have affected His Majesty dreadfully, though he displayed little sign of it. Ultimately, it became known that John Pym and the others knew of the King's intent that day and had fled by river, a boat having been moored at the steps in readiness.'

"They must have been forewarned," Frances suggested.

"Weren't they just," Robin scoffed. "It's thought that a member of the Queen's own household was to blame, Lucy Hay, no less."

"Countess of Carlisle? Now that is interesting, she was Strafford's mistress, so they say," Miles announced.

"Some form of twisted revenge on her part. Perhaps she blames the King for her lover's untimely demise?" Robin suggested.

"Well, if that's true, she should be tried for treason," Frances said, though Robin guffawed.

"That won't happen sister, she'll be hidden away somewhere either by Pym or her cousin, Lord Essex," Robin stated, contemplating the letter once more.

London had, for the most part, openly declared for Parliament, access through the city being even more perilous for any supporter of the King. The King and his entire household had fled Whitehall for the relative safety of Hampton Court, as had been feared. Parliament had seized control of the Tower of London, securing the vast array of weaponry stored within its walls.

"But here's a bit of good news," Robin said with a wide grin. "Rupert's been released from captivity in Austria."

Rupert had sailed for Dover, intent on supporting the King, though he had scarcely set foot ashore before being ordered to escort Henrietta Maria back to Holland, her hope being to sell her own jewels to buy arms for her husband's cause.

"Rupert won't have been happy, father," Robin laughed. "Mark me on it, he'll be back here before long, with his brother, Maurice."

The most pitiful sight proved to be the King and Queen bidding one another farewell, the depth of their affection obvious to every onlooker. The King had remained on the quayside, calmly watching the vessel bearing his lady continually until it was no longer possible to make out anyone on the deck.

"That's just awful," Frances remarked sadly.

"Where is the King now, does John say?" Miles asked.

"Coming north to York with a profusion of followers," Robin said, tossing the letter onto the table. "We should go and offer our support father."

"Of course. I'll send word to Glemham, he'll know exactly where the King is to reside."

"King's Manor?"

"Probably, or Ingram's house," Miles said, rubbing his chin pensively.

"So, these rebellious curs think they can drive our King from his own capital, do they? Well now, I just might have to sharpen my sword again," Robin stated, and Frances suddenly felt chilled.

Haveringham Manor – May 1642

The northern gentry soon flocked to York to show loyalty to their threatened monarch. Miles and Robin went most days, riding out each morning only to return after sundown. One unusually cool afternoon, surprisingly Robin returned early, feeling unwell. Listlessly trudging toward the oak table in the Great Hall, he removed his hat, steadying himself on the back of a chair. Sensing something was wrong, Elizabeth went across and laid a hand on his brow.

"You're burning up, my son," she declared, then to Moll Gilbert, "Fetch cool water and cloths, then go to the still room and get a tincture of Feverfew."

Robin tried to smile, but suddenly his eyes rolled as he plummeted to the floor, Elizabeth's piercing scream resounding through the room.

The Steward was at the young Viscount's side in a flash, signalling to two male servants to assist him in lifting Robin from the floor.

"Send to York for the surgeon Lambert, at once, do you hear me?" Elizabeth ordered following the prostrate body of her son being carried upstairs.

"At once Countess," Lambert replied, scurrying away.

Frances went to the foot of the stairs but further up, Elizabeth rounded on her. "Stay back daughter, don't you dare go anywhere near him till we know what this is."

Unable to concentrate on anything for long, Frances paced the Great Hall endlessly, unaware of what was happening above stairs, in Robin's bedchamber. The surgeon arrived, ultimately diagnosing a fever of the type many fell victim to during the winter and early spring and whilst every remedy was tried, nothing seemed to work and gradually, Robin's condition deteriorated. Walking down to the little church, Frances endeavoured to pray, but found it difficult to vocalise much other than the word 'help.' Back in the Great Hall, sightlessly thumbing the pages of a book, she heard a series of anguished screams coming from upstairs. Dropping the book, she ran to the foot of the stairs and looked up. Moll appeared escorting Elizabeth towards her own bedchamber and Frances experienced a rush of fear.

"Mother?" she gasped, making as if to ascend but Moll stated. "Nay Mistress Frances, stay where you are. There's naught to be done now....your brother is with God. I really must put your mother to bed, she's scarce slept these two nights past."

'Robin gone.... how could he be, it was unthinkable......'

Robin's unexpected demise plunged the entire household into the deepest grief. For hours on end, Frances stared at his portrait in the Great Hall, dejected and withdrawn. She ate little and slept even less, little caring that by virtue of the nature of her father's Earldom, she was now the Viscountess Haveringham.

When she had watched her brother's coffin lowered into the cold earth, she had collapsed in a dead faint and had to be carried back to the house to be put to bed. Frantic that her daughter had somehow contracted the same illness as Robin, Elizabeth had beseeched Miles to send again for the surgeon, though this time the diagnosis was nothing more serious than exhaustion brought on by grief. She was put to bed and Martha never left her side, even sleeping in her mistress's room on a small truckle bed. Yet Frances' melancholia continued. In the end, Miles wrote a hasty note to the Meltons, requesting John to come north as soon as possible, believing that his presence might just make a difference to Frances' health. In little more than a week, a mud splattered John Fitzherbert rode into the courtyard, leaping from the saddle.

Pausing only briefly to greet the Earl and Countess, he bolted up the stairs two at a time. A startled Martha, seeing the figure framed in the doorway, dipped a curtsey.

"Leave us," he ordered, striding across to the bed and sitting on the coverlet, grasping Frances' hand. "Dear heart, look at me."

Her eyes flickered open. The face looked familiar, dark hair and pale blue eyes filled with concern. Was she dreaming?

"John, is that you?"

"Yes, my love, I'm here," he said, stroking back her hair. Sitting up, she fell against him, sobbing.

"Hush now. Rob wouldn't wish you to grieve so much for him, now, would he?" he said rocking her back and forth. Tilting her chin, he kissed her very gently before standing up.

"I'll leave you now...."

"But you've only just arrived?" she said frantically reaching for him. Shaking his head, he sat down again, taking her by the shoulders.

"True enough, but as you can see from my grubby attire, you foolish wench, I need to go and bathe, then change into something more appropriate for spending time with my betrothed," he said, firmly, stroking her cheek. "Now heed me, Frances, I intend to tell Martha to come to you, see you up from that bed and dressed in something better than a mere shift. Then when I return, we shall take a turn about the gardens together, after which, we shall go to the small dining room and you will eat something that the cook will have made to tempt you into eating once more, is that clear?" he said.

"Perfectly John," she said.

He stood once more and strode purposely to one of the windows draped with black fabric. Grasping a piece firmly in both hands, he ripped it down, moving on to the others that soon suffered the same fate.

"Robin hated this kind of outward show of sorrow and so do I!" he said.

Two weeks later saw Frances greatly recovered, so much so that John made the decision to head back to Kent. Having already taken his leave of the Earl and Countess, he and Frances made their personal farewells in the Courtyard before he mounted up.

In only a few weeks' time he would return for their wedding and that day could not come fast enough for Frances, the memory of his lips planting feather-light kisses on her neck far too alluring. Her fingertips strayed to that area of her throat as she watched him finally disappear from view.

'Dear God, if you are willing, allow me to bear this man several sons and I vow that my first born, shall be named Robin, after my beloved brother…...'

CHAPTER NINE

Haveringham Manor - August 1642

"Mistress Frances....."

Dazed, Frances shook herself back to reality and the confines of her bedchamber, Martha's voice resonating in her head.

"Sorry Martha, what were you saying?" she asked.

"I was saying that going down to that graveyard does you no good at all. You allus end up melancholy." Adeptly, she worked on an unruly curl, holding it carefully in place before securing it with a pearl tipped pin. "That's not all I said though, I was making you aware that I thought I'd 'eard a carriage...."

Frances' eyes grew wide.

"Oh Martha, do take a look, it may be John," she gasped.

Setting down the comb she had been using, Martha went to the window.

"Aye tis him indeed, and that must be his father and mother. Oh, and Lord Bynghame's carriage has just pulled in too."

Pressing a hand to her chest to steady her beating heart, Frances looked at herself in the mirror, turning her head from side to side, admiring Martha's handiwork. Her hair certainly shone now with soft ringlets cascading in profusion, framing both sides of her face, whilst high up at the back, a coil of plaited hair, threaded with tiny pearls had been pinned in place.

"Make haste and help me into my gown, I must go down at once," Frances ordered.

Slowly she stepped down each tread, one hand trailing casually over the intricately carved banister. Candles burned brightly in sconces set at various intervals, casting strange shadows across portraits of long departed ancestors, painted eyes almost following her with approval. Hearing voices and laughter drifting out from the Great Hall, she paused to primp her full sleeves, lovingly caressing the sapphires at her throat, a wedding gift from her mother, much as they had been from her own.

'In time, I hope they will be passed to your own daughter.'

Thus, her mother had spoken that very morning when handing them over and smiling at the memory, Frances stepped down the remaining stairs, pausing at one of the archways. The Princes,' now clad in black velvet, braided with silver, stood beside her parents and Haveringham's resident minister, Reverend Bankes. By the fireplace Ralph Bynghame conversed with the Earl and Countess of Melton, an attentive dark haired young woman beaming up at him whenever he spoke, devotion etched on her face.

'That must be Anne,' Frances thought. *'She's really pretty, trust Ralph not to describe her accurately.'*

Her search for John continued, without success.

'Where is he?'

"Ah, here's the bride…..better late than never, eh John?" Miles' light-hearted quip finally brought the bridegroom into view, having been hidden by his father and mother. Oblivious to anything, Frances darted forward, flinging herself at him and though he caught her, he drew back holding her by the shoulders.

"Now whilst I am truly touched by such a fervent greeting Madam, I must remind you of something overlooked….."

The pale blue eyes flicked towards the royal brothers.

'Oh no, not again….'

Slowly Frances turned, heat infusing her cheeks. Both bore strangely mystified expressions, thankfully not of annoyance. By their side, her father's furrowed brow proved him to be less than pleased. She moved forward until she stood directly before the Princes where she sank into a deep curtsey.

"Your Royal Highnesses, I beg your pardon. I meant no offence……"

Rupert put one hand to his mouth to keep from laughing and looking down at the large rosettes on the front of his chisel toed shoes, thought *'Twice in one day.'*

Repeatedly Prince Rupert's attention turned toward the laughing bridal pair and curious for information, he asked, "A love match, I take it, Lord Benningford?"

"Indeed Highness, much as was my own," Miles answered taking the opportunity to smile at the demure lady by his side, but then Rupert had already detected the marital harmony shared by his hosts and gave a nod of perception. When Lady Elizabeth blushed, he noted how greatly alike mother and daughter were at times, complete to the fair hair and vivid blue eyes.

"I once had a sister, of whom I was very fond, who died due to what she described as the miseries of an enforced marriage," Miles explained. "I vowed that were I to ever be blessed with offspring then I would try my best not to see them affected in that manner."

"You believe an arranged marriage was the cause of your sister's death?" Rupert asked.

"I know so Highness. Her affections lay elsewhere and though he came from a good family, my father did not consider him appropriate enough. She was simply informed of the arrangement with a more fitting family, told to obey without complaint…..and sadly died in less than a year of the match."

"May she rest in eternal peace," the sycophantic Reverend Bankes said, crossing himself and looking heavenward.

Miles scowled.

"When it came to my daughter, Sir, I allowed her a measure of choice even though the final decision would always be my own. In the event, Melton's elder son satisfies both our requirements perfectly," he said.

"They do display a positive regard for one another," Bankes bleated through thin lips.

Rupert turned in time to see John Fitzherbert fondly tracing a finger down Frances' cheek and his brows rose.

"The marriage terms are excellent, Your Highness. Frances will be well provided for, should aught happen to John......God forbid, of course," Elizabeth said, and Miles patted her hand.

"I'm sure His Highness doesn't need to know the exact details, Bess," he said.

The affinity displayed by this Yorkshire Earl to his spouse was once more tangible, Lady Elizabeth evidently unperturbed by the mild correction offered by her husband, her sweet smile so reminiscent of that of her daughter.

"My daughter can be headstrong.....as you have witnessed yourself on more than one occasion this day, but I confess to being mighty proud of her, Sir," Miles said.

"To my honour, Your Royal Highness, I have personally instructed her as to the nature of her wifely duties, such as submission and obedience." Bankes clasped his hands together as if communing directly with the Almighty.

Rupert almost expected him to burst into the kind of 'fire and brimstone' form of rhetoric he disliked so greatly, but pragmatic as always, the minister was ignored, and he addressed Miles instead.

"Tis rare for a woman to show such spirit, though my Lord," he stated. "Most females of my acquaintance display little more than passivity and compliance, leaving little opportunity for healthy debate." Once more, the languid, Stuart gaze returned to the animated woman in blue conversing with the Earl of Melton. *'Yes, most unusual,'* he thought.

"You must concede that some aspects of your bride's behaviour must change once you're wed, John," Edward, Earl of Melton said, twinkling mischief filling his eyes.

"Should she not already be aware…." his Countess began, forestalling her words on noticing her husband's expression.

Edward decided that comment would be addressed a little later when they were alone. Now was certainly not the occasion to reprimand her in public, however tempted he felt. A distinguished man in his forties, Edward Fitzherbert's greying locks fell in abundance over his broad, lace edged, collar. Slim faced, nevertheless he remained a handsome man with an unrestricted air of elegance and pale blue eyes, similar to those of his elder son.

"Better to discipline her early John, lest she shame us all in the future with even graver misconduct in public," Edward said, encompassing his wife with a harsh glance when speaking.

Frances reached forward, tapping the Earl on the arm with her closed fan.

"My Lord, would you have me so reduced that I become like a newly broken colt with no spirit left at all?" she demanded with an exquisitely charming tilt of the head.

"Better than ending up a constant torment to your husband with shrew-like tendencies, Madam," Melton said coolly, again glancing at his wife.

"I can assure you father, that this lady will be left in no doubt who is master, once we're wed," John proclaimed. For a brief moment Frances was unsure whether to laugh or cry, until Melton reached for her hand.

"Rest easy my dear, we jest with you," he assured.

Secretly, Edward heartily approved of his son's choice of bride and not merely for the ample dowry she brought with her. The fact that due to her brother's premature death she was now a Viscountess, destined one day to be Countess of Benningford in her own right, added to a character that he already considered her wholly endearing.

Pondering his own marriage, the difference appeared starkly obvious. His had been arranged purely for the benefit of the Melton purse, though as time had passed, he had developed a measure of affection for his bride, Catherine. As any good wife, she had done her duty of course with solemn dignity, presenting Edward with several children over the years, the first two being sons. Increasingly, their relationship underwent a change, surprisingly Catherine finding a voice hitherto governed by self-control and the desire to please. Sadly nowadays, she often expressed unsolicited opinions on all manner of issues to the extent where her tone irritated Edward so greatly that he increasingly sought solace in the arms of his much less antagonistic mistress. Now as he again looked at Catherine beside Ralph Bynghame, she appeared bright eyed and unquestionably keen to include the younger Prince in their conversation, an appealing strategy, providing she did not ask too much.

"I understand that you are to attend the wedding on the morrow, Highness," she asked.

Similar facially to his elder brother, swarthy and dark eyed with almost raven black hair, Maurice smiled politely.

"Indeed, Lady Melton," he replied simply.

"Are you to remain long in England?"

Edward felt he may soon have to intervene should she press much further on a subject that was none of her business. Thankfully,

Maurice remained entirely composed and in control.

"We are not here for pleasure, Countess," he explained. "My brother and I are here to assist the King against these rebellious men in the Parliament."

"Ah of course, the King's troubles, yes my husband and sons speak of little else these days," Catherine remarked, casually examining her fingernails.

Frances scowled, wondering the reason for the number of meaningful glances passing between Melton, Maurice, Ralph and her betrothed.

"In that regard Highness, I hear this rebellious Parliament have recently ruled that anyone aiding His Majesty is a traitor," Ralph announced.

"Merely a response to the King calling them traitors to the Crown, Ralph my friend," John observed, taking a sip of wine.

"It becomes a tad sobering though when one considers how many in this very room would be hailed as such by this so called…. Parliament," Edward replied.

"Then all I say to that is *'God save the King'* father," John declared, lifting his goblet in the air.

Frances fell silent, finding it difficult to understand why they could jest about 'troubles' that could potentially prove so serious.

"Fret not my love, all shall be well," John whispered, leaning toward her. He seemed to have the knack of realising when she fretted, the distinctive dark lashed eyes exuding love and reassurance, calming her fears at once.

"High time these upstarts in London were taught a swift lesson though, would you not agree, Highness?" Ralph asked.

'Trust you to say something to worry me again, Ralph Bynghame,' Frances thought, disturbed even more by the princes' cool

response.

"Rupert certainly thinks so…. why should we venture here else?" he said almost nonchalantly.

CHAPTER TEN

Haveringham Manor - August 1642

Keen eyed as a kingfisher poised to dart into the water for a meal, from a low hanging branch, Lambert's steely eyes surveyed every item being positioned on the damask covered table, moving this or that to aid perfection. In his forty-eighth year, Joseph Lambert had served the Benningfords for almost two decades and despite the unusual circumstances of this particular night, he was determined that nothing should go wrong. Retrieving one of the newly fashionable, dual pronged forks, he gave it a quick polish before it was set back beside a matching knife and round bowled spoon.

Another glance to ensure exactness and Lambert gave a predetermined signal to Miles who cautiously drew Rupert to one side.

"Your Highness, might you…. that is, may I suggest….."

The younger man interrupted almost at once saying, "Ask whatever you wish my Lord, this is, after all, your home."

"Then by your favour, I was about to ask if you might be agreeable to less reliance on precedence at table this night?"

Miles steadily watched the dark features for any sign of reluctance, but the moustache edged lips simply formed an indolent smile and a Princely hand dropped familiarly onto Miles' shoulder.

"This is of concern to you, my Lord?" Rupert asked. "Seat us wherever you wish, tis more our honour to be included in what is, a family event."

In that moment, Miles felt he had been given another glimpse of the diverse and complex character this young royal possessed and to some extent began seeing a little of the person Robin had spoken of so often with pride and enthusiasm.

"Then with your permission?"

"Go to it," Rupert assented.

No one seemed in the least put out by the relaxed manner of dining, especially once innumerable platters of tempting deliciousness were set before them. Woodcock and other game birds were positioned alongside dishes of oysters, spinach tart, dutch pudding, citron pudding, 'grand salats' made from oranges, radishes, hard boiled eggs, figs, violets, capers, and herbs. Steaming plates of chicken frykesy, forcemeat balls, roasted beef and mutton followed, each dish inspected by Lambert before being set before the diners. Baskets of manchet bread rolls were proffered, the 'upper crusts' only suitable for such grand diners of course, the lower blackened portions, being retained in the kitchen for the servants.

Standing beside a group of musicians in the minstrel's gallery, the sweet falsetto tones of a young man permeated the room, adding to the relaxed, jovial atmosphere. Beside John, Frances, could not help but glance occasionally at the princes seated opposite. Whispering together, their close relationship was obvious to any onlooker. At one point, indicating the dutch pudding, a singular dish made from minced beef totally encased in cabbage leaves, they seemed to share a jest, both saying *'eten, eten, eten'* in unison and the name *'Louise,'* prior to laughing. Frances assumed this particular dish held some form of amusing memory perhaps. She might never know of course and would never dare to ask outright. Without warning, Rupert looked up ensnaring Frances with questioning eyes. Blushing deeply, she hastily considered the food on her plate. It still rattled that the brothers were here and yet annoyingly, she couldn't help but feel a little intrigued by them. When eventually it was safe to do so, she looked about at the other guests happily enjoying the repast, though when she reached Ralph Bynghame, he was staring. With a lift of his brows, he offered the strangest of smiles, raising his goblet in silent toast before turning away abruptly to speak to his wife.

'What was that all about?' Frances thought.

One by one, the diners eventually drifted from the table, though when Frances made to rise herself, Elizabeth waylaid her.

"Wait a moment, Frances I need to speak with you," she said.

"But mother, I want to be with John."

"It is of importance, daughter."

Sitting down once more, Frances suspected that her mother might just be formulating some kind of proposal but just what, she could not tell. She didn't have long to wait.

"We have been presented with such an opportunity here, dearest daughter," Elizabeth said, flicking her eyes toward the royal brothers. "They are both unwed, you know."

"And this is notable because….?" Frances enquired hesitantly with a scowl.

"Well, just think how impressed our guests would be if you had…. royal Brides-men?"

'So that's your plan, is it?'

"We could never be so impertinent as to ask that of them and anyway Matt and Ned have already agreed to be my Brides-men."

"Oh, they must be made to understand," Elizabeth stated firmly, smiling at the younger Prince when he glanced their way. "Just think how amiable they have been thus far. But see, Rupert is alone, come with me."

Before she could object, Frances' hand was grasped firmly, and she was virtually dragged across to the fireplace where the elder Palatine stood in deep thought.

"Your Highness, might we interrupt your reflections and speak with you momentarily?" Elizabeth said, setting what she hoped was a dazzling smile to her lips as the royal head turned. The expression facing them seemed almost indifferent.

"As you wish," he answered simply, his brows flickering upward.

"My daughter seeks a favour of you." Elizabeth turned to Frances as she spoke, widening her eyes purposefully.

'Oh, well done mother you're leaving it to me....'

Frances smiled nervously at the man she would prefer not to speak to at all. If he were as intelligent as Robin had alluded to, then surely, he would realise the true source of the request, once it was ultimately voiced; she could only hope.

"You must have a great deal to think about Your Highness, I would not wish to burden you further," Frances began cautiously. Rupert examined her face, sensing annoyance but at whom? Her mother for placing her in this awkward position, or at him? Deciding to be playful and not relieve the embarrassment of her plight, he fixed her with a direct stare.

"Not at all, what would you ask of me, Viscountess?" he asked.

'How insufferable,' she thought, shifting from one foot to the other, unwilling to look the Prince in the eye. She could tell that he wasn't about to make things easy for her and that rattled her even more than his unrelenting gaze.

"Well Madam? If you do not speak it, I cannot give an answer," he finally said.

Only then dare she raise her head to observe the royal expression.

"Your Highness, my lady mother would……" Elizabeth cleared her throat and after a pause, Frances began again. "Sir, I would ask if you and your brother might be willing to…" Again, she faltered. Why would she even want to have this man escorting her on the most important day of her life.

"Willing to what?" he asked.

It was no use, she would have to ask the question, despite being more than just reluctant.

"I wondered if you might consent to being my escorts on the morrow." There, it was said and all that was required now was for him to respond, but Rupert wasn't quite done tormenting her.

"Escorts, what does that mean?"

This was horrendous, Frances couldn't believe that a man alleged to be so highly intelligent showed such a lack of basic understanding of something that was an elemental part of the marriage tradition in England.

"'Tis a country custom for a bride to be escorted to the church by two unmarried men known as 'brides-men.' I am reliably informed that you and your brother are both unwed, Your Highness?"

All the time she spoke, her hands made little gestures and only occasionally did the violet eyes dare to look into his.

'I unnerve her a little, it seems.' He smiled indolently before asking, "And this is the favour you seek from Maurice and I?"

"It is."

'She doesn't appear convinced.'

"Would the role entail anything further?" he asked, vaguely amused by her palpable reluctance to even speak with him.

"They escort the bridesmaids back to the house for the wedding breakfast," Frances said, waves of annoyance coursing through her. What was it Robin had found so fascinating about this man, she felt anything but interested in him.

"Very well Viscountess, it seems your Brides-men are now in place."

'They already were.'

Frances dipped a hasty curtsey.

"I'm obliged…. Your Royal Highness," she said, trying not to sound too sarcastic.

"I feel certain that Frances will forever be indebted to you," Elizabeth simpered, scarcely able to hide her delight.

'What a delightful concept,' Rupert thought, but voiced, "Perhaps this service might be considered as recompense for the hospitality we have been afforded here, Countess."

He glanced across the room to where his brother laughed with both John and Ralph.

"Now, if you would excuse me, I must address a matter of some importance."

Both ladies sank into curtsies as he strode away.

"There, did I not say he would agree?" Elizabeth asked, but Frances was watching the prince urging the three others to accompany him outside. Why, for a private conference?

She dashed to the window, peering out into the mounting gloom, though it was still light enough to make out the four men. Rupert was speaking, John and Ralph nodding from time to time. Her breathing became ragged, and her hands felt unexpectedly clammy.

Rupert grinned, placing his hands on John and Ralph's shoulders. It was unbearable, something had definitely been arranged and all Frances' greatest fears resurfaced. Anxiously, she turned back into the room, seeing Anne Bynghame watching her with what appeared to be empathy. Of course, Anne would be affected too in whatever had been arranged outside in the courtyard. No words were uttered between the two women and yet in that moment, Frances felt they were united emotionally. There had been little opportunity to get to know Anne Bynghame, but Frances instinctively knew how deeply Ralph was loved by his wife.

CHAPTER ELEVEN

Haveringham Manor - August 1642

The strains of fiddle, hurdy gurdy, laughter and loud singing filtered from the barn as the little party approached. The estate workers had been given permission to enjoy their own revelries in one of the barns and it had been decided that the bridal party should make a fleeting visit.

Some distance behind the main group, the Countess of Melton tugged at her husband's sleeve.

"You cannot deny this is all a little reprehensible husband?"

Edward Fitzherbert stopped walking and with a contemptuous grimace, grasped his wife's elbow, thrusting her a little roughly, to one side.

"What of it?" he snapped abrasively, swiftly adding, "I urge you to cease these relentless criticisms of others, Madam. If this gesture of goodwill pleases our son and his bride, then it should be of no concern to you."

Devoid of much affection these days, nevertheless, Edward still appeared so much like Catherine's elder son John, the same boyishly handsome features even though he now carried a little more weight than once he had, his hair and beard flecked with grey.

"Is it fitting for a future Countess to mix so freely with.....servants and the like? Did you not see the way she dragged our son out of the house by the hand?"

Edward pursed his lips, shaking his head.

"I grant you Frances can be singular at times Catherine, but if I'm being totally honest, I admire that trait in her and if the Palatines have no issue with this, then why should you?"

"But some of the behaviour you admire so much in her, does need addressing, if only for the sake of John's reputation."

"Are you sure it's not your own you think more of?"

"Of course not. I'm certain John will appreciate more... restrained behaviour in her, she is a Viscountess after all."

"And Benningford's heir Catherine, don't forget that."

"Then as such she should conduct herself. You would not have appreciated me behaving as she does before we wed?"

'You wouldn't have known how to.'

The veins in Edward's neck pulsated visibly and for one heart-stopping moment, Catherine thought he might actually strike her, but the raised hand fell to his side, though his hot breath brushed her face when he snarled, "You try my patience woman with your constant whinging. Leave Frances be, I like her just the way she is, but more importantly your son adores her. Now let's join the others before our absence is noted."

Walking beside her solemn husband with her shoes crunching on the gravel, Catherine pondered that as always Edward had misconstrued her meaning. Perhaps she had worded her concerns wrongly, as she invariably did these days. She wanted to explain, wanted to draw him to a halt and beg him to listen to what was really on her mind. Whilst John and Frances would be starting out on marriage come the morrow, Catherine felt increasingly as if her own were just about finished. Edward couldn't really expect her not to know where he was headed every time he went out riding by himself. Was she really so entertaining this mistress of his? Had Catherine not been willing to allow him to do whatever he wished in the bedchamber, was that not enough now? Catherine truly wished for the best for her first-born son, but truth be told, once Frances had come along, she felt almost supplanted in John's affections and that was difficult to bear on top of Edward's lack of care. A glance at her husband's profile surfaced age old emotions and reaching for his hand, she urged him to a standstill once more.

"But a moment Edward," she begged. "I am truly sorry……forgive me?"

The look on her face and tears glistening in her eyes assuaged Edward's wrath, touching his emotions as he looked at her hand resting on his sleeve. On her finger, the gold and emerald ring screamed memories of bygone days when his feelings had been so vastly different, and he had gifted it to her. He sighed deeply.

"Very well. See that there is no repetition of your disapproval whilst we are here. We are the Earl and Countess of Melton, and no one should suspect there is aught amiss between us. Do I make myself clear?"

"John knows," she murmured.

"I realise that."

Catherine reached up, briefly touching his cheek.

"Edward, I miss you….."

Time almost stood still as Edward took in the dark lashed hazel eyes and pink quivering lips allowing his eyes to drift down over the soft brown curls topping her shoulders to the almost translucent quality of the mounds protruding from her bodice, bathed as they were in the playful light of the full moon. He drew her into his arms, hungrily seeking lips that responded at once, in a way he had almost given up on.

"Cate," he whispered into her hair. "Why can't you always be this way?"

The music and laughter stopped the moment the grand party entered the barn and cheering broke out. Leading Frances forwards a little, John acknowledged the estate worker's good wishes, waving one hand. Eventually, Miles joined the bridal pair, eagerly reminding everyone of the work awaiting them the following day that would be better undertaken with clear heads. Hoots of merriment and cheering broke out as the Earl shook his head, encouraging the musicians to strike up once more.

Frances stood beside John, glad of his arm around her waist as she looked around the barn. Off to one side, several men lounged lazily on straw bales, drinking ale, and laughing together. John informed her that they were companions of the Princes from Holland and that some, he knew. One in particular nodded at John as he picked his way around the edge of the barn until he reached Rupert. This was Richard Crane, John informed her, someone who had known Rupert for several years, even visiting him whilst in confinement in Austria.

"He's an excellent soldier, my Lord, and in that respect, he is to be Lieutenant Colonel of my Lifeguard," Rupert explained, once Crane had bowed and wandered back to his colleagues on the straw bales. "I trust you have no objection to my comrades being here. After a momentous sea voyage, I suggest they may well be eager for a little recreation?"

"Think naught of it Highness, they are most welcome here," Miles said as Frances once again considered the one John had named Crane as he relaxed on a hay bale, drinking occasionally from a tankard in one hand. Astonishingly, another man had a girl draped across his knees, kissing her energetically.

"O'Neill never could resist a pretty wench, Highness, could he?" John laughed over one shoulder but other than a slight flicker of one eyebrow, Rupert made no other response, though Elizabeth made a mental note to address the inappropriate behaviour with the girl, once the celebrations were over and done.

The simple country tunes proved inviting and very soon Frances began to sway along, tapping her foot to the beat. Then from her right, a little worse for drink, the shadowy figure of a Matthew Redworth appeared, an inane smile playing across his lips.

"Mistress Frances will ya not dance wi' me…..afore ya leave

Yorkshire?" he slurred.

"I don't……" Frances got no further once her hand was grabbed, and she was hauled down the barn.

"Matt, no… I can't, do you hear me? We have important guests….." she endeavoured to say.

"Ya'd deny me one final dance with ya?" he asked, looking like a whipped dog.

Frances glanced back at John beside the others, most looking astonished if she were being honest. Prince Rupert even appeared as if he were trying not to laugh, though she could not be certain. Perhaps, being from such a privileged background, the Prince did not quite apprehend the easy-going relationship both she and her father had with their estate workers. Robin had always declared Rupert to be perfectly relaxed in any form of company, but as yet, Frances had to witness it herself.

Thankfully, Lady Melton seemed content enough, controlling herself admirably as with a fixed smile, she held onto the arm of her husband, though John's expression appeared a little thunderous.

"We are no longer children Matt. I am now a Viscountess about to be married to a future Earl, now pray release my hand," Frances said, and Matt's smile disappeared as a tanned muscular arm rose, one hand raking back his long hair.

"I know me place….." he muttered.

This was true. What Matt had done was clearly a breach of the social gulf that separated them, but she could tell he was vexed, and she wouldn't wish for that. "Very well, one dance but then you must return me to my Lord," she said lifting her head.

Matt laughed out loud, leaning close enough for her to smell the ale on his breath.

"That I will……Frannie."

"You must not address me in that manner now, you must henceforth address me formally."

"An' I will, from the morrow, but not tonight…..Frannie."

CHAPTER TWELVE

Haveringham Manor - August 1642

Making their way back to the house, it troubled Frances that John had not mentioned anything about the dance with Matt. It had only been one short, simple country dance before she had been restored to a stony-faced John. The atmosphere between the two men had been a little tense as Matt offered a slightly inebriated bow, expressing his thanks to John for allowing the privilege of partnering his betrothed. John had simply tipped his head and said, "Redworth."

Sauntering across the courtyard side by side, the silence felt tangible. Ultimately John slackened his pace and drawing Frances to a standstill he finally spoke.

"Now then, what should I make of that unseemly display just now eh?"

Frances scowled, her head falling forward. Strangely, she noticed just how dusty her shoes appeared.

"Don't scold John; t'was only a dance," she murmured.

"But something never to be repeated."

"John, you don't understand. Matt and I are of an age, we even played together as children. He's now father's head groom and Lambert is schooling him to be assistant steward, why he can even read and write, such are his capabilities. He only wished to bid me farewell, that's all."

Her eyes appealed for compassion in a way that made it impossible for John to remain indignant any longer.

"I could see that, my love," he admitted. "The joy of the other dancers when you joined them was a delight to behold. They have a fondness for you I think, even Rupert said as much."

"Did he?"

"Yes, he speaks as he finds Frances. If he is not displeased, then I can scarcely be so, can I?" he said planting a quick kiss on her lips.

"If I might interrupt?" Elizabeth said, having wandered back to them.

"Of course, Countess," John said.

"I wish to steal Frances for a moment, if I may?" Then to her daughter. "This is the ideal opportunity to address that we discussed earlier?"

"Is something wrong?" John enquired.

"Nothing, though Frances does need to speak to two of the servants urgently," Elizabeth said.

"Then I should come with you," John remarked.

"There's no need," Frances said, "Mother and I won't be long. Everything will become clear tomorrow, I promise." Frances turned on her heels and hurried back toward the barn, beckoning to Matt and Ned as soon as she entered.

"Milady?" Ned enquired cautiously. Frances was not inclined to beat about the bush, nor did she wish to sweeten the blow she had been forced to deliver. Matt wouldn't be any happier with what she had to say than he had been by the earlier reprimand.

"There's no uncomplicated way to say this, so I shall be direct. You are both to be released from the role of Brides-men…"

"What?" both declared in unison, anger flashing through Matt's eyes.

"Because I dared to dance with ya?" he snarled.

"No, not because of that Matt…it's more that…"

"The Palatine's are to be my daughter's Brides-men," Elizabeth said forcefully giving no chance for them to speak as she joined them. "Tis an honour indeed for the Benningford's, I'm certain you will comprehend."

Neither man uttered a word, though their body language spoke volumes to Frances.

"Come daughter, we mustn't keep our royal guests waiting," Elizabeth said walking off once more.

"No best not….." Matt sneered, and then directly to Frances, "You asked us months ago when you got back from London. Are we not good enough now since those two fops have come 'ere?"

This was the very reaction Frances had hoped to avoid and yet she realised just how disappointed both men must be. She had to make them understand that this was not of her doing, her mother was behind the whole plan, after all, she disapproved the idea almost as much as they did/

"I cannot go against my mother's wishes, surely you must realise that?" Her chin lifted defiantly. She didn't need this, not on the day before her wedding, having far more prominent issues to worry about. "Don't you dare show anger toward me; remember who I am!"

Matt's eyes narrowed, willing himself not to respond. Never before had she spoken to him with such harshness and his disappointment was undeniable. What he desired to say would without doubt land him in deep trouble, but despite the effects of drink, he still had the sense not to jeopardise his situation on the estate for the sake of a 'tradition.'

"Frances do make haste, our guests await," Elizabeth announced from the doorway.

The rejection etched on Matt's face was all too much for Frances.

"I wish it were different, but I too have to go along with it…..now I must return to the house." She turned to go but Matt wasn't done.

"I'll still be outside the church watchin, Frannie…..Beg pardon, my Lady Viscountess," he said performing an almost mocking bow before walking off, kicking at a hay bale with such ferocity that it tumbled over, spilling the contents of an abandoned tankard across the ground.

CHAPTER THIRTEEN

18th August 1642

Frances woke early and deciding to venture out of doors for a
while, she hastily retrieved a dressing robe from the back of a chair
and slipped it on, fastening each of the ribbons down the front.
Picking up a pair of mules, she carried them to her bedchamber
door, opening it slowly to pause and listen. Everything appeared
peaceful so she made her way along the corridor and down the
staircase, pausing momentarily by one of the archways. The Great
Hall was devoid of servants, though already looked stunning,
decorated with flowers and the oak table partially set. Voices
echoed toward her from the far corridor leading from the kitchens
and not wishing to be seen, Frances rushed to the front door only
opening it far enough to squeeze through, grimacing when it
creaked loudly on its large hinges. On the top step, the heady
scents of early morning invaded her senses and glancing around
she noted how stunning the gardens appeared, gossamer-like
tendrils festooning many of the bushes and trees, like pearls at a
woman's throat, as if nature itself had been decked out for her
special day. She stifled a giggle, slipped the mules onto her feet,
and ran round the side of the house, crossing the lawn close to the
fountain, only stopping on reaching the pathway that led down
toward the walled garden. The flat countryside spread out as far as
the eye could see beyond the walls appeared tranquil, golden, and
lush with an abundant harvest, almost ready for gathering. The
church bell chimed, and she strolled on a little further, singing a
country ballad to herself as the breeze toyed impishly with her
undressed, loose hanging hair. Nature's perfumes were certainly
intoxicating and inhaling deeply, Frances closed her eyes,
spreading her arms wide as the sun bathed her face in early
warmth.

"You are abroad early, Viscountess?"

Frances spun round so fast that she would have tumbled over, had
not Prince Rupert reached out to grasp her arm. For a second or
two the pair stared at one another until Frances sank into a curtsey.

97

"No, there is no need for formality, I just heard you singing and…...." he began.

'How long have you been there?'

"I didn't think anyone else would be about at this hour…...," she interrupted, quickly adding, "I trust you slept well, Your Highness?"

Dressed casually, almost palpably so, Rupert's doublet and shirt hung open, the latter affording a tantalising glimpse of dark wispy hair in the hollow just beneath his neck.

"I slept remarkably well, for once," he replied.

"For once?"

"I do not always seem to require extensive sleep," he explained offering an indolent smile that did not quite reach his eyes. "I noticed you from my window, running across the lawns and wondered if you might appreciate a little company, though please say if you would prefer to be alone."

'Never be alone with a man you do not know; you must always be chaperoned.'

Her mother's rigorous schooling and propriety of the age, resounded in her head.

"Well, I…..."

"You have my word, you will be perfectly safe," he declared.

Her head shot up. *'Are you able to read minds too?'*

"I'm sure I shall," she said, her own smile wavering.

Prince Rupert was the last person Frances wished to be with, especially on such a special day but to blatantly admit she wanted nothing to do with him would show a form of disrespect she dare not allow. Instead, she heard herself saying, "I should be honoured to have your company for a while, Your Highness, though you must forgive my appearance, I had no wish to dress fully…. until later."

Brown eyes unashamedly surveyed the pale pink and silver silk robe, though he had no opportunity to speak, for Boye suddenly darted forward and excitedly leapt up at Frances,

causing her to almost stumble had not a Princely hand once again stayed her arm.

"Boye, away," he snapped. "He did not hurt you?"

"No, I'm quite well, thank you," she answered honestly, brushing pieces of grass from the front of her robe. Rupert scowled at his canine companion who, hung his head in shame, making Frances giggle at the almost comedic behaviour. Boye took this as his chance, and slowly crept forward to lick her hand, an eye constantly on his master.

Rupert shook his head and said, "I have never known him to take so readily to anyone." "Then he must be a dog of great perception," Frances said, drawing back her hair when the breeze blew it across her face. "Would you perhaps care to see our maze, Your Highness?"

"Possibly, though I don't think you should venture inside, lest you be unable to find a way out….and miss your own wedding," he said.

'Goodness don't say you actually have a sense of humour?' she thought, instantly remorseful for even considering such a thing about a man she knew so little about. Rupert certainly was proving a bit of an enigma now. Currently, he was all consideration and apparent kindness, whereas the previous day he had seemed more arrogant, self-confident, and determined. Despite the quality of his clothing, made from only the finest materials, one might never guess at his high status, such was his pleasant demeanour now.

"Then I shall show you the walled garden instead, where my

brother and I often spent time talking together."

"Lead on," he responded.

Walking beside him, Frances felt dwarfed, such was his height. John was considered tall at a little under six feet, but Rupert surpassed that by more than four or five inches at least. Boye trotted on happily behind, pausing now and then to sniff at interesting things. They had to enter under the archway to the walled garden and it came as no surprise that the Prince was forced to stoop a little. For some time, side by side, they admired the well set out gardens, neat little boxed hedges bordering areas containing vibrant hued flowers. Intoxicating scents filled the air, insects buzzing about continually, sipping from first one bloom then another.

"My sister, Louise would capture this splendour so well," Rupert voiced ardently. "She is a gifted artist thanks to the tutorage of Honthorst."

Frances gave no response, though her eyes widened at the stark reminder of Rupert's high rank. For his sister to have received instruction from Gerrit Van Honthorst, the Dutch Court painter was something unimaginable and yet Rupert hadn't boasted about it, the information had been spoken so calmly, without a hint of superiority.

"I too often like to make sketches, though I cannot boast such a grand tutor myself," she finally admitted.

"But it's not about the calibre of one's tutor, Viscountess," he answered. "Tis more the time one spends studying any given subject. In my experience, there is little hope for proficiency else."

Unexpectedly, Frances had the strangest impression that Rupert's direct approach sounded so similar to her father's straightforward manner and for the first time, she felt her curiosity growing.

"Shall we perhaps sit?" Rupert said, indicating a recessed seat in the wall. "There is something in particular I wish to say."

Curiosity plummeted, resentment and mistrust straight back in her thoughts as grudgingly she complied, the Prince removing his hat before sitting beside her.

"I will be direct, Viscountess. I dare say, you saw me speaking with Lord Fitzherbert last evening?"

"I confess I did."

"Then it will hardly surprise you to learn that both he, and Lord Bynghame, have accepted a commission in my cavalry."

How coolly and without obvious emotion, this Palatine imparted this piece of information that could very well change Frances' life irrevocably. Despite the warm sunshine, she shivered and turned away to look at a large oak tree beyond the walls in the distance. She imagined herself in her bridal gown beside John, the imposing figure of Prince Rupert hovering close by, poised to pounce upon her new husband to spirit him away.

"I see," she murmured, her mind in turmoil as she bit her lip.

The profile Rupert considered displayed a definite lack of pleasure, as with most females the Viscountess being unable to disguise her emotions. Bizarrely, he felt the need to explain further.

"You must attach no blame to Fitzherbert I think. If you must bear a degree of malice, then let it be to me alone for my need of him is great...."

Slowly her head turned and for once she stared unashamedly.

'My need of him is great. How dare you say such a thing so calmly!'

Openly declaring his intent to separate a newly married couple was both sobering and distressing in equal measure and yet from somewhere deep inside, common sense began permeating. John could never be described as anything but his own man, strong willed and determined no matter what, something that had endeared him to her in the first place. The final choice would always be his, no matter how difficult it would be for either party. Surprisingly, she felt Rupert's hand covering hers.

"Will you not say anything, Viscountess?" he asked.

"John is hardly likely to be influenced by anyone, even myself, so there is little for me to say… except to ask…." How could she ask something of this man that even to her sounded irrational, but Rupert merely folded his arms and said, "You have leave to speak freely."

Surprised by tears pricking her eyes Frances decided to be honest and pivoting her whole body toward him she said, "I should be most grateful if… in the heat of any battle, you might watch out for my Lord?"

Rupert's expression darkened in a way that reminded her of clouds suddenly obscuring the summer sun.

"You ask too much, Madam," he said.

'Oh no, I've angered him,' she thought, closing her eyes. How could she have asked him such a thing; it would be impossible. When he inhaled deeply she opened her eyes to see him frowning and stroking his chin.

"You have little concept of warfare, I think," he declared at last. "In battle there is scarce chance to look to oneself, let alone anyone else." A golden curtain formed a barrier between them when her head fell forward. "Lady Frances, I will say only that, if possible, I shall endeavour to honour your request, but I….."

Instantly she sat upright, sweeping back her hair.

"Please Your Highness, you must think me immature and witless to ask…."

'You're anything but…' He scowled at the unexpected thought, quickly shaking it off by saying, "You express a desire for Fitzherbert's safety, naught more."

She noticed the way the sunlight played on his notably, freshly shaven face, the raven locks occasionally blowing back in the breeze revealing a small gold earring. Those dark eyes benefitted from long lashes but only when her gaze fell to the moustached edged lips did she blush.

'Ah, so she's curious about me?'

Rupert smiled but said nothing.

"Forgive me, I didn't mean to stare," Frances finally admitted.

"No matter, tis most flattering to be examined by a pretty woman. You consider me handsome?"

"No…..I…." Her eyes closed. When would she learn to choose her responses carefully before replying? What she had meant to express was that, though handsome, Rupert was naught compared to John, at least in her eyes. Believing he would indeed think her witless, she wondered why that seemed to matter so much.

"What I mean is…. of course, you are very handsome, Your Highness, but … " She stopped mid-sentence and chuckled. "Oh dear, I seem unable to speak coherently in your company… perhaps you are at fault by making me so nervous…."

"What, when all I endeavour to do is put you at ease?" he said, then narrowed his eyes. "You seem to wrongly assume a great deal about me, Viscountess."

"If I do then I beg your pardon," she said, drawing back her hair again.

"Then let me allay your fears regarding Lord Fitzherbert," he said, and Frances held her breath. He noticed, a smirk at his lips. "You will be relieved to learn that he is ordered to remain in Yorkshire for the next three weeks," he said.

CHAPTER FOURTEEN

18th August 1642

"Did you hear me, Madam?" Prince Rupert asked, and though Frances nodded, she remained in shock. "I dare say such an arrangement will dispel any concern regarding Lord Fitzherbert's departure?" he remarked as her stare continued, unswervingly.

"He is not to go with you, when you leave on the morrow?" she finally asked.

"Would I not then be accused of cold-heartedness to a bride?" He smiled briefly though it dissipated rapidly, when he added, "There will, however, be certain duties I require him to accomplish in the meantime."

"Oh, I see," she responded.

"You do not care overmuch for my being here, I think?" he said unexpectedly. As if physically struck, Frances wondered just how to respond with any sense of politeness. She could hardly admit to saying more or less the same thing to her father earlier in the day, but she knew a response had to be made; he was after all, of royal blood and under the direct stare, she felt decidedly guilty.

"I confess to questioning the reason for your unexpected arrival, especially when you mentioned John by name. Forgive me Sir, I may have misjudged you, for in truth, I know so little about you…."

Rupert shrugged his shoulders.

"Then let me rectify that now, in the hope that perhaps thereafter, you might look upon me a little differently?"

Frances considered her hands, unsure of whether he was being totally candid or just pacifying her. There could be little harm from learning more of his character, in fact it might prove fascinating; she had no desire to return to the house just yet, so what better way to pass the time?

"If Your Highness is not required elsewhere, there is still time before I must return," she said, glancing quickly at the position of the sun in a now vivid blue sky.

"Very well," he said, folding his arms. "I would say you miss your brother incalculably, am I right?"

"Very much," she admitted, not expecting him to begin in that manner.

"What you may not be aware of, is that I too lost a brother."

"My brother once spoke of the accident Sir; it must have been dreadful for your family," she admitted.

'So, she does know something,' he thought.

Informally, Rupert interlinked his hands behind his head, extending his legs and crossing his ankles. He was feeling indulgent and for once quite willing to speak about himself. After all, it was more than pleasant in these sunlit gardens, especially since it meant time spent with a woman possessing such an unusual reputation.

He began by saying that he very nearly did not enter this world at all, his mother's carriage being struck by a landslide when she was close to her confinement. One large rock in particular penetrated the carriage and struck her on the belly. For a time, it was feared she might miscarry, but mercifully Rupert was born safely on the 19th December in the year 1619 in Prague. In less than a year, the whole family were forced to flee the city, but even then, the babe was in peril. A nurse left Rupert lying on the floor whilst retrieving an item from another room, then forgot all about him. Fortunately, the mistake was discovered in time and the young Prince was unceremoniously thrust into the last carriage to leave. Forced into exile in Holland, his parents at The Hague, Rupert, and his siblings at Leiden, under the care of governors and governesses, their number increasing almost every year as more were born. During that time, one of his sisters decided to play a prank on her governess and dressed in some of Rupert's clothing. She looked so similar to her brother that for a while she was believed to be the Prince, until Rupert sauntered in through the door and the ruse exposed. Needless to say, the Princess received harsh castigation for unseemly behaviour.

Rupert suddenly stopped, narrowing his eyes suspiciously.

"You doubt what I tell you?" he demanded on seeing her frown.

"Not in the least Highness……though something about you does puzzle me greatly," she finally admitted, hoping he would not be offended.

"And what might that be, or should I not ask?" he enquired.

"Well, when you speak English…..why tis almost perfect," she said and throwing back his head, Rupert laughed out loud.

"Ah, you perhaps believe I should speak with an accent of some kind?"

"My brother is to blame, Your Highness, for he would often mimic the way Dutchmen spoke English……"

"And upon your brother's notion of wit and because I lived in Holland, you assume I should speak the same way? Or could it be because you consider me……a foreigner?"

Frances could not tell whether he was angry or just testing her and not wishing to find out which, she simply said, "Not at all, Highness."

Once again he folded his arms across his chest, chuckling to himself.

'That's gratifying to hear.' He bent his head to examine his hands, a satisfied smirk hidden from her by his long hair. "I am reliably informed though, that if ever I am overtaken by excessive zeal, there can be the slightest trace…."

Suitably chastened, Frances smiled.

"I stand corrected Sir," she admitted.

From the way he went on to describe it, Rupert's upbringing sounded formal and rigid, his sisters required to curtsey to their brother's whenever they entered or left a room. A keen student, Rupert had quickly mastered mathematics, law, music, art, and languages, being fluent in English, French, German and Latin. His accomplishments seemed endless, though only when he mentioned his profound interest in warfare did he grow sincerely animated. The siege of Rhynberg afforded the fourteen-year-old Prince a first-hand taste of war, though that experience had been short-lived when his mother, fearing for the morals of her young son being so often in the company of older men, recalled him to The Hague. Nevertheless, his unrelenting interest in all aspects of warfare continued unabated, particularly the finite tactics used by the Swedish King, Gustavus Adolphus in relation to cavalry charges and sieges.

Frances wondered if those tactics might soon be required in England, brushing the though away as quickly as it had come.

"I was concerned to learn of your brother's wounds and even though by then I was imprisoned, nonetheless, I still used my influence to have him sent home," Rupert said. Very slowly Frances' head turned, her expression this time incredulous.

'I still used my influence….' Did he really just say that he was in part responsible for Robin being sent back to England?

"In truth Highness, you did that for my brother?" she finally voiced.

"Naturally. Encampments are unforgiving when it comes to recovery from any injury gained in battle, he stood better chance at home."

Frances fought the desire to stare, fiddling with her hands instead.

"We knew Robin's commander had ordered him home, but he never mentioned you having had influence over it," she admitted.

"Ah, but then he may not have been aware of it," Rupert said, rubbing his palms repeatedly on his thighs. "It is regrettable he was to fall ill so soon after his return…."

He stared out across the gardens, giving Frances an opportunity to study the handsome profile once again. "He would have been of great use to me now, had he lived." He sounded distant, almost ethereal as if not only addressing himself but some spectre on the far side of the village.

Frances felt she should say something, if only to lighten the mood. An idea struck her.

"Robin told us of your capture at Vlotho and of your imprisonment, but might I enquire how you came to gain release?" she said.

Very slowly the dark eyes turned to scrutinize her, almost indolently.

'You taught her well Robin, my friend.'

He seemed delighted to relate the complex terms, part involving a pledge never again to take up arms against the Holy Roman Empire, affirmation of which would be complete, by the Prince kissing the Emperor's hand. Rupert paused, absently brushing a leaf from where it had landed on his leg, relishing a look of puzzlement flashing through her eyes.

"But I don't understand, if you were imprisoned, how could you…..?"

"Ah, but my confinement was not restrictive. I was allowed outside from time to time, provided I was accompanied. On one such occasion, a hunting party rode up, beset by a wild boar. I grabbed a spear and killed the beast outright in front of them. One of the party, the Emperor himself, offered his hand in gratitude….."

Wide eyed, Frances pivoted round, raking back her hair.

"Oh of course, a kiss upon it and your freedom was assured," she gasped, and Rupert nodded in satisfaction.

His three-year incarceration, he explained, did hold some lighter moments, one being a relationship developed with the Governor's daughter, Suzanne. Frances wondered if this Suzanne had become his mistress, though would never dare ask. Rupert's love of animals became self-evident when he mentioned catching a wild hare, teaching it to perform simple tricks but being mindful of its wild state, eventually he set it free.

Visitors had been few, though amongst them were Richard Crane and the Earl of Arundel, the latter having given the Prince Boye as a pup. Sprawled out under the Princes' long legs, Boye raised his head on hearing his name, receiving a much-appreciated fondle of one ear, from a princely hand as the church bell chimed the hour.

"Though this has been a vastly informative time, Your Highness, I think I should return to the house," she said rising to her feet. Rupert followed, retrieving his hat as she paused by the entrance and looked back, grinning. "I'd hate to think my mother finds my empty bedchamber and assumes I have run away, rather than be wed."

"Better yet if my room is discovered vacant…. what might be made of that?" Rupert said with a smile that reached his eyes.

Unexpectedly, Frances finally felt as if her initial perception of this Palatine Prince had been so wrong. Having spent time in his company, she finally comprehended a little of what Robin had admired so much about the man's unique but complex character. For Rupert to have been open enough to tell her about his life was something that in her view, no other royal would be likely to do. Without being told, she realised that his deepest thoughts would always be kept to himself, this man would never want anyone to know anything about him that could be considered weakness.

"I believe your sense of wit and mine may be quite similar, Sir," Frances quipped as they left the walled garden and as the swallows dipped and swooped about them, Boye trotted along behind, stopping to sniff at various points of canine interest.

"My humour is oft considered sardonic and habitually misunderstood," he said with a guileless smile.

CHAPTER FIFTEEN

18th August 1642

Murmurs rippled through the guests in the Great Hall when, at the foot of the staircase, the Earl of Benningford greeted two well-dressed young men with excessive deference.

"Honoured guests, I crave your forbearance?" Miles' then announced and a precipitous hush descended. "I am honoured to present their Royal Highnesses, Prince Rupert and Prince Maurice of the Palatinate."

Eventually, the distinct rustle of silk accompanied curtsies, men's hats being swept to one side as they bowed. Both Princes' looked on with equanimity, faintly bemused by the incredulous expressions facing them.

Beside the fireplace, James Pettigrew, husband to one of John Fitzherbert's sisters, watched the royal pair with great suspicion. A slim built, shrewd man with hooded eyes and a serious countenance, Pettigrew's short hair barely reached the almost plain collar falling across his bony shoulders. His attire was also decidedly dour in comparison to the brightly clad peacocks around him and one hand gripped tightly to a black steeple style hat, devoid of decoration or plume, that had eventually been removed when the requirement had been to offer deference. It rankled to show excessive courtesy to the pair of dark-haired men in conversation with his brother-in-law, John Fitzherbert and as to what was being discussed could only be speculated upon. Pettigrew's top lip curled contemptuously, witnessed at once by his wife.

"Husband?" Pettigrew's head partially turned. "These men cause you some unease, I think?"

"Aye, don't they just," he responded a little acerbically. The Captain-General of the Parliamentary forces, Lord Essex, would without doubt be interested in learning of this development. It had long been surmised that assistance might well come to the King from his extended family in Europe and now here was the proof of it.

'Once this sickening display of wealth and pomposity is done with, I'll write to Essex,' he thought to himself. Pettigrew hadn't wanted to attend this celebration at all, saving the fact that his wife was sister to the bridegroom necessitating their presence. *'Should Essex be pleased to learn this portion of intelligence, a reward might well be in the offing.'* Suddenly Pettigrew recalled the row of tents in the grounds. At first, he had assumed it to be connected to the wedding, but now as he thought more on it, he speculated that it might well have something to do with these two foreign mercenaries. *'Yes, Essex would be glad to learn of their arrival and the fact that Benningford freely affords them the hospitality of his home can only add more weight.'*

With the greatest solemnity, Lambert indicated the staircase down which Frances carefully progressed, the train of her pale blue gown trickling across each step like a silken waterfall. At the foot, Miles held out his hand.

"You've never appeared more striking than you do today, my dear," he said leading her toward the Princes where she sank into a deep curtsey. Rupert leaned down to lift her by the hand.

"Far more appropriate than a simple dressing robe," he said with a flick of his brows. A deep blush stained her cheeks as Miles then led her toward the bridegroom. Dressed in deep red velvet, braided with gold, John's dark glossy mane cascaded in rippling waves over a lace edged white collar, his handsome looks almost taking Frances' breath away.

"Well met, my Lady, I trust you are willing?" he said voicing the words of a country tradition.

"I am willing, my Lord," she responded almost shyly, looking up at John as he took her by the shoulders and kissed her soundly.

"I shall await you with eagerness, in the church," he whispered. Barely had the words left his lips before he was dragged away by Ralph Bynghame and the giggling bridesmaids carrying branches of Rosemary, a symbol of love and constancy, the guests following, until only the Princes' remained.

"Shall we?" Rupert enquired simply. Frances took the Princes' proffered arms, each bound by ribbons in her chosen colours and making their way out from the house, they progressed down the driveway until reaching the little Norman church in the grounds. A small crowd of estate workers waited outside, Matthew Redworth among them, leaning against the wall stripping bark from a twig. On seeing her with the Princes,' the stick was thrown to the floor, and he stood upright, tipping his head politely. Frances smiled though she was hastily given over to her father's care and the final walk down the short aisle to the waiting John Fitzherbert.

CHAPTER SIXTEEN

18th August 1642 – Haveringham Manor

Emerging from the church, John and Frances were met by the ear-splitting sound of a musket volley. Rupert's European comrades had decided to greet the bridal pair with a guard of honour, using the age-old tradition of loading their muskets with feathers that now cascaded down over them. A number of flower festooned hoops were then raised above them, forming a floral tunnel, under which the newly-weds progressed as Martha flung handfuls of pink and red rose petals high above them. Several settled onto their clothing and much to Frances' amusement, into John's hat brim. One floral hoop was then laid out on the ground.

"Leap, leap, leap." The shouts were repeated until the happy couple sprang over it, though Frances lost her footing, stumbling into her new husband.

"Brazen woman, can you not wait till we're alone?" he whispered with a look of such affection that drew a deep blush to Frances' cheeks.

A small band of musicians with fiddle, fife, and hurdy gurdy, led the whole party on the short walk back to the house. Frances glanced at the distinctive ring now on her right hand. In addition to the formal wedding band, this was a special love gift from John, chosen in London and slipped on her finger the moment they had been proclaimed husband and wife. Made from the finest gold, it had two intertwined lovers knots framing a deep red ruby in the centre and Frances adored it.

'I shall wear it always, to remind me of this day,' she thought, smiling up at her handsome husband walking alongside.

An exultant Lambert hurried down the steps of the house, clasping his hands together.

"Hearty felicitations, Lord and Lady Fitzherbert," he said with a bow, stepping back to allow them inside. In only a fleeting time, the great hall rang with animated conversation, laughter, and gentle music from the minstrel's gallery. Beribboned flower garlands adorned the large oak table that boasted the best silver and glass that Haveringham had to offer. A steady stream of servants carried in platters filled with the finest fare, the most impressive being an 'endored' peacock. The previous day, Frances had been in the kitchen watching the cook stuff smaller birds inside, each one slightly larger than the previous, until finally the peacock's flesh was put back in place, brushed with a mixture of saffron and melted butter and the tail feathers were repositioned giving it the appearance of being alive.

Platters were brought in with game, fish, various cheeses, pies, pasties, salats and sweet delicacies, enough to tempt even the most fastidious of appetite. Copious amounts of wine, beer, sack, aqua vitae, and several cordials were offered throughout the meal, glasses being refilled repeatedly. Finally, the cook's infamous sack posset was set before them. Made from eggs, sack and spices scalded with sweetened cream, it was Frances' particular favourite, and she not only consumed her own but eyed up John's half-finished dish. Pulling it aside, he shielded it with one hand.

"Would you steal from your husband?" he asked pointedly.

"Can you really deny your wife a dish she esteems so greatly, my Lord?" she said with what she hoped was an endearing pout.

Shaking his head, John offer the remainder to her.

"Today, I can deny you naught my dear wife, but trust me, it will not always be thus, I assure you," he said, planting a kiss on her nose.

Maurice noticed what appeared to be his brother's unremitting interest in the group of people down the room.

"Why are you so absorbed by the dancing?" he asked pointedly.

"What if I am?" Rupert answered.

"I only remark upon it."

"Well don't, there's no need……I'm just curious."

"As to what?"

"The way she looks at him."

"Who?"

"The Viscountess, who else?"

"What do you expect, she's clearly in love with Fitzherbert, brother."

Rupert threw a less than amused scowl at his sibling.

"*Merde*….. You can be so annoying." Rupert gave no further explanation but when he looked, Maurice noticed Frances briefly touching a lock of her husband's hair, her eyes sultry. "One day….."

Maurice almost choked on his wine.

"One day? Is your memory so short Rupert, have you forgotten all the flirtatious drabs in The Hague? You only had to walk into a room to have them fluttering their eyes your way."

Rupert scowled.

"*Ach du, Maurice*, this is different…..look now," Rupert said.

No one could doubt the devotion in Frances' expression, the bridegroom almost teased relentlessly with feather light touches of his hair, sleeve or lace cuff, the result, John appeared totally engrossed. Manoeuvring slowly around her husband, the bride occasionally lifted her skirts slightly, giving an alluring glimpse of slender ankles and even once or twice, a tantalising peek of ribbon garters encircling her knees. Those same skirts were hastily dropped with appealing giggles, whenever John tried to make a grab for her.

Maurice turned back.

"You need more wine brother," he said with a grin. "I grant you she's comely enough, but no more than many another. What a privilege to select one's own bride though? I doubt we'll have such a freedom; brides will be chosen for us and may well look like the back end of a horse."

"No woman will ever be thrust upon me, even if the union would aid our status in Europe," Rupert snarled, with a derisory curl of the top lip.

"Is that why you are indifferent to Mademoiselle de Rohan, tis said she pines for you in France you know?"

This was a match set before Rupert, though one he was reluctant to consider and had declared as much often. As soon as the words were uttered, Maurice knew he had overstepped the mark from his brother's darkening expression.

"We have far more important things to consider in England than frivolous women, Maurice," he said and strode off to join Ralph Bynghame by the fireplace.

CHAPTER SEVENTEEN

18th August 1642

"To bed, to bed!"

Frances made a grab for John as the mantra broke out throughout the room, but he was quickly manhandled away by a group of male guests and escorted up the staircase to the accompaniment of bawdy jests.

Meanwhile, Frances became surrounded by a group of giggling females and once the men were gone from sight, she too was bundled up the stairs and into the bridal bedchamber. The walls had been draped with floral garlands, the same encircling each of the four bed posts whilst the coverlet had fragrant pink and red rose petals strewn across it.

Ultimately stripped of her beautiful bridal gown, Frances stood nervously in just her shift as someone removed each of the pins holding her hair, shaking it loose and setting an elaborately embroidered coif on her head. Frances kept her gaze lowered, unwilling to make eye contact with women who surprisingly saw no wrong in voicing the occasional innuendo. Abruptly, her shift was tugged lower, and Frances finally looked into the eyes of a lady with a slightly perturbing smile, holding a small phial of liquid.

With a pronounced smirk, she tipped the bottle back and forth using the stopper to lightly touch Frances' neck, shoulders and shockingly between both breasts.

"Don't be alarmed my dear," the lady said. "This fragrance is said to greatly enhance the experience of love making. Trust me.....Lord Fitzherbert will not complain...."

Lady Benningford pushed through the group of giggling females surrounding her daughter, bearing a pale blue and silver embroidered bedchamber robe across both arms.

"Show a little decorum ladies, please," Elizabeth said, slipping the robe around France's shoulders and tying the ribbons down the front.

"I'll wager they won't stay fastened for long."

"Imagine if he slices through each one with the point of his sword?"

Frances hurled a beseeching look at her mother.

"He'd be an absolute rogue to despoil such a fine garment," Elizabeth said, primping the lace round the neckline. "I doubt Lord Fitzherbert would do such a thing, tis not in his character."

In a room down the corridor the bridegroom was enduring much the same as his bride. John's rowdy male companions had seen him stripped of all finery and encased in a bedchamber robe of red and black silk. Most being worse for drink, the bombardment of advice seemed increasingly crude in nature.

"I'm well aware of what I must do, gentlemen," John said to further bellows of joviality. Ralph drew a little closer, proffering a goblet.

"What, you too Bynghame?" John enquired.

"I merely offer a little sack to…..enhance your performance?" he said.

John shook his head, folding his arms protectively across his chest.

"I need no strong drink my friend, no one would…..just think of her, all that sweet innocence waiting to be plucked…..wouldn't anyone want to keep their wits about them?"

'Definitely,' Ralph thought , draining the goblet himself.

Banging on the door became increasingly insistent, manly shouts demanding to be let in.

"Not yet, have patience," one woman shouted back, ushering Frances into a position directly in front of the door. "Now, open it."

A crescendo of voices accompanied the door swinging wide but Frances kept her gaze on the floor, until a pair of red and black mules came into view, and John's fingers lifted her chin.

"To bed…..to bed….to bed." The cries grew ever insistent as John's smile, intended for his wife alone, held up one hand to achieve quiet.

"I am sorry to disappoint everyone, but I care not for the rest of this bedding custom," he declared.

"But we must see you abed, t'would bring ill tidings, if not," a woman's shrill voice rang out to the agreement of most except the bridegroom.

"Superstitious nonsense," he scoffed. "I intend to dispense with such unnecessary ritual, whatever you say. I wish to be alone with my bride, before entering the marriage bed."

Frances tried to ignore ribald comments about the floor not being soft enough or John having to be shown what he must do.

"Out, all of you…." John said ushering most from the room until only the royal brothers remained by the door.

"We are certain to have left long before you see daylight, I think," Rupert said, raising his brows expressively.

"True enough, Highness," John said, turning to smile briefly at his blushing bride.

"I'll expect to see you again before too long. We'll soon see this rebellion crushed," Rupert said, then to his brother, "Come

Maurice, let's leave these love birds to their nesting."

CHAPTER EIGHTEEN

18th August 1642

The lock emitted a definite click when John rotated the key and offering a smile, he joined Frances and grasped her hands.

"We don't want any interruptions," he said.

'Oh goodness,' Frances thought, swallowing deeply as she endeavoured not to look at the vacant marriage bed.

"I must thank you for the gloves John, they are truly beautiful.....I do believe they will compliment my finest cloak, exceedingly well," she said far too quickly.

Sensing she might be trying to forestall matters, John determined to address that issue before much longer. Common sense told him she would be nervous of course, all brides must be but soon she would realise that there was no reason to be fearful.

"Are gloves not the accepted love token from a bridegroom to his bride?" he asked lightly. "Now, my darling heart, there is something I must speak about before....."

Her head slowly lifted, and eyes widened.

"If you intend telling me of the commission you have accepted with Rupert, I already know," she said softly.

'What.....?' His brows almost knitted together; such was the intensity of his scowl. "How?" he finally asked.

"From the Prince himself. He joined me in the gardens this morning and told me of the arrangement." She paused, unsolicited tears filling her eyes. "You are a soldier John, could I really expect you to reach any other decision?"

He smiled with relief, glad that she already knew and yet partly wondering why she had not shown the slightest indication of it during the day, her behaviour as sweet and agreeable as usual.

"I am to be a Staff Officer to the Prince himself, with men under my direct command. Tis such a privileged position," John declared proudly.

'Privileged? Must you really be so blasé about this?'

She withdrew her hands and wandered over to the window, staring out at nothing in particular and all the time John watched her, waiting for her to say something, anything that would reveal what was on her mind.

"Sweetheart," he said wandering across to join her, touching her shoulder. "I have to do this, you know that."

Other than gently breathing in and out, she made no move. Was this really to be the one blight on what had been an otherwise perfect day? He certainly hoped not, but he had to make her understand the importance of a decision to join the Prince and more importantly explain what had been arranged for her.

"Can you really blame me for wishing to show loyalty to my King?" he ventured and very slowly, she turned about.

He looked so very handsome in the red and black silk robe, dark hair spilling across both shoulders. From his expression, Frances could tell how much he wanted her to realise the agonies he had gone through in making such a choice, though in the end there could only be one. If the King were beset by trials, naturally men like John would always offer their swords in his service, but then had she not always suspected as much?

"I know you will have considered your decision carefully," she admitted.

John lightly touched her cheek with his fingertips. "Do you really think I didn't ponder long and hard the effect my resolve would have upon you?"

"You had no need to, after all, I am merely your chattel now…."
She would have turned away again had he not gripped her

shoulders.

"Chattel? How foolish you can be, Frances, I don't see you as that."

"I just thought….."

"Then stop thinking," he said lifting her chin to plant a quick kiss on her lips.

Though she didn't like the thought of him going to war, she realised she had a choice to behave like a petulant child or to support her husband completely. They were hardly likely to be the only couple separated in the weeks to come, countless others would no doubt be bidding farewell to one another, no matter which side they supported. Reaching for John's hand, she kissed it tenderly and held it to her cheek.

"Rupert said I should blame him, but I can't do that," she said and then sighed deeply, searching his face. "Dearest John, you go with my blessing."

"My most courageous, adorable little wife," he said looking down into her upturned face.

"There will be a civil war then?" she asked.

"It's almost unavoidable now," he answered taking her in his arms. Frances frowned, her fears coming home to roost on this of all nights. "There is something else I need to say to you," he added, feeling her abruptly stiffen. "Don't worry, my love I dare say you will like what I have to say. Your father and I have spoken and agree tis best for you to remain in Yorkshire, at least for now."

"Really, I can stay at Haveringham?"

"Well in my view Kent is too close to London for comfort. I don't want you in any danger and the north remains predominantly loyal to the King, thus far."

"Your father, does he approve of this plan?"

"He considers it wise. Then, once everything goes the way Rupert hopes, it won't be long before the King returns to Whitehall and you and I can start our new life at Melton Abbey. Oh yes, and Ralph has suggested that Anne remain here too, so you won't be short of company."

Throwing herself at him, Frances kissed his face over and over till he gently pushed her away.

"Steady now," he laughed.

"But John, that's so good to hear on top of the Prince allowing you to delay your departure….?"

In no mood for more talking, John kicked off his mules, stripped off his robe and flung it across a chair.

"Forget all that now, I want you in that bed, Madam," he said, kissing her hungrily. She did not resist, even returning it with equal enthusiasm, aware of mysterious urges within her as his fingers skilfully untied the ribbons of her robe. With each capitulation, Frances' heart seemed to beat a little faster. Finally, the robe surrendered and eased gently from her shoulders till it slithered down onto the floor, leaving her in only her chemise, the translucent fabric hiding little from John's attention.

"Away with this too," John whispered, dragging the coif from her head, freeing her fair tresses.

His breathing grew laboured as tenderly he began caressing her, each touch sending ripples of fire through her. Frances felt unusually alive, as if some hidden joy were about to be set free. Emboldened by desire, she assisted with the removal of his nightshirt, allowing it to simply fall to the floor. John stood completely naked before her, smiling at the way she seemed unwilling to allow her gaze to drop below his shoulders. Frances' chemise became the next garment joining the pool of clothing on the floor and eventually, tilting her chin, John said, "Your mother spoke with you…?"

Frances nodded, suddenly conscious of a subtle change to the lower part of his body, pressing against her thigh.

"She…..told me it may hurt a little…."

"Only the first time, my love," he said allowing his fingers to caress her shoulder. "Once your maidenhead is breached, thereafter it will not be thus, I promise." His lips followed his fingers, tracing lightly down her neck, along her collarbone and down to her right breast, where his tongue did things she never thought to experience and when she moaned, he smiled. "Trust me Fran, I shall teach you everything."

Hoisted in his arms, he carried her to the bed, placing her upon the petal strewn coverlet. Her fair hair lay fanned out across the pillow as he manoeuvred himself above her, taking long admiring looks at her whole body.

"You're beautiful Fran, I love you," he whispered into her hair and as his lips moved down her body, she experienced a longing for something far more. She wanted, no needed, him doing whatever he wished and was not about to stop him. He kissed her with a passion that almost took her breath away, deftly parting her lips with his tongue, using it in ways that felt strange but tantalising. Eager for fulfilment himself, nevertheless, John knew to hold back and wait for her, unable to prevent a groan in his throat when her fingers moved on from his hair to rake teasingly up and down his sides and back. He could sense her spiralling toward the moment of total surrender when at last they would be one flesh and she would truly be his.

CHAPTER NINETEEN

18th August 1642

"Despite the King's policies being exacting at times, he is nonetheless our Sovereign and as such no-one should oppose him," Melton said.

Smoke hung above the heads of several male guests enjoying a pipe of tobacco, after the days' hectic festivities. Wine had been flowing copiously all day and, despite the presence of the young royals, tongues were becoming a little loose.

"Even if the number of taxes he imposed were unacceptable?" One enquired, erupting into a fit of coughing.

"Aye, none of us were happy being forced to pay 'ship money,' not when our estates are nowhere near a port," Miles ventured, puffing thoughtfully on his pipe.

"But to oppose the King with the vehemence of this Parliament?"

"Beyond mere opposition when our King is left with no alternative but to quit London," another said, to murmurs of agreement.

The Earl of Melton's attention alighted on the ostensibly disinterested elder Palatine beside the hearth instinctively knowing that not one word would have evaded him.

"I would say the die is now cast; would you not agree Highness?" Edward ventured, interested to see how Rupert would respond. The dark head turned, a languid gaze falling upon the older man.

"Without doubt, Lord Melton. One only hopes those professing loyalty will be willing to provide everything required to put a swift end to this foolishness."

With an all-encompassing sweep of every face present, Rupert was hardly surprised when no one spoke. He suspected that requiring even these men to part with anything to aid the royalist cause might prove problematical and yet he was determined to try.

Eventually, one hardy soul asked, "What manner of requirements do you mean, Highness?"

Rupert wrestled the need to grimace, fixing a calm expression on his face, one his brother could read at once. Could these men really be so simpleminded in not knowing what a war would need? Almost reading his thoughts, Miles stepped in.

"If you will permit me, Highness?" he asked.

A royal nod was all the affirmation required.

"I think we must all understand that His Majesty may seek provision for his cause in any number of ways. Equipment and of course men…. I intend to raise a regiment from here under the Benningford name."

"No matter the name, all regiments will ultimately form part of the King's army," Maurice explained. One look at his brother had shown the younger sibling how annoyed he was, though Rupert always managed to cover it well.

"The most difficult part will be convincing my Steward to dip into my already overstretched purse," Miles chuckled, refilling his pipe with tobacco. Maurice watched him with a smile. Two days at Haveringham Manor had heightened the younger Princes' penchant for the guileless Yorkshire Earl whose frank manner of speech was refreshing to say the least.

"I'll warrant there'll be much for us to provide," Edward mused.

"Armour won't come cheap," one ventured dourly.

"Then buff coats are the answer; they afford some protection from sword strikes," another remarked.

"But they are remarkably heavy when wet and if it should rain….."

"Then all we can do is pray for fine weather or make agreement with the enemy to delay encounters until it is."

Maurice noticed Rupert's eyes briefly close, his expression tense.

'Oh dear, he's not liking this at all,' he thought, the men in the room conversing freely.

"We'll see these upstarts off as soon as they take to the field. Most of 'em will be low born anyway, no backbone or intelligence you know……and they think to take on gentlemen?"

"I hear the theatres in London have been closed, doubtless the actors will need some form of gainful employment?"

"I wouldn't jest about such matters if I were you gentlemen. Noble blood opposes our King as much as common, Lord Essex for one," Melton remarked, having noticed Rupert's jaw tightening.

"As I said Melton, naught but rogues and cuckolds…. a bad lot if you ask me."

Miles set down his pipe and turned toward the speaker.

"Tis imprudent to speak jovially about such serious matters for England. We prepare to fight, no matter our status."

Rupert pondered the brace of Earls with gratitude.

'I'm glad you two speak with such sense. Others here tonight might as well throw in their lot with the rebels from the start, such will be their usefulness to me,' he thought. *'I believe my role in England may prove more challenging than I first envisaged.'*

"There will be other choices for us all gentlemen," Ralph Bynghame interjected, every head turning his way. "All must decide either for King or for Parliament, no easy task; families may soon face divisions."

A reflective Edward Melton studied his burgundy sombrely. His own son-in-law James Pettigrew would unquestionably side with the Parliament, insisting his wife do the same. Edward's cherished daughter Mary, schooled to be submissively obedient to her husband, would be left with little choice. Conforming to

Pettigrew's decision would set her on path of direct opposition to that of her family and Edward determined to speak to her before leaving Yorkshire, in an effort to make her see sense.

"Makes one think, doesn't it?" Miles said studiously.

Well aware of his brother's multi-layered character, Maurice wasn't fooled in the slightest by Rupert's solemn bearing, knowing full well that whatever bothered him would be vocalised once they were alone. Curious to know, Maurice gave an exaggerated yawn, stretching out his arms.

"Your pardon gentlemen but this day, though joyous, has been long and as my brother and I are to have an early start on the morrow, I believe it only right to retire," he said.

Rupert comprehended at once, glad to have the chance to escape a conversation that troubled him deeply. Standing to his full height, he heard chairs being vacated.

"Might I say how greatly your presence has enhanced the day," Miles said with a bow of the head, a flickering smile briefly touching Rupert's mouth in response.

"T'was our pleasure, my Lord," he said.

"I shall ensure food is provided for you in the morning, ahead of your long journey. I dare say my steward and some of the servants will be on hand should there be anything you require," Miles said.

"Thank you, my Lord," Rupert replied.

Moments later traversing the oak staircase, Maurice asked, "And just what preoccupied you this night, brother?"

Rupert stopped in his tracks.

"What would you have me say to that?"

"The truth. I noted how reluctant you were to join in the conversation and even less by their…. notion of wit."

"Wit, you call it. They seem to consider warfare purely as a means to pass the time, a sporting event or the like…..suggesting no conflict should it rain? God in heaven, can they be serious?"

"I think so."

Rupert shook his head.

"Well, I tell you this Maurice, if actors need employment or the Welsh or Irish, then I'll take 'em all, along with any other who will vouchsafe to serve me well."

"I'm sure they'll come to their senses once they realise the seriousness?"

"They'd better or I'll be forced to take them on as well as this damned Parliament."

Maurice burst into laughter.

"You laugh at that?" Rupert snapped.

"No of course not, I agree with you. Tis more I wondered if you were not wholly concentrating just on warfare tonight?"

"What do you mean by that?"

"Only that perhaps your contemplations related more to the couple down yonder corridor in the chamber next to your own?"

"What?"

"Don't be so defensive, Rupert."

"Believe it or not, I had far more on my mind than the coupling of newly-weds." Rupert ascended two or three more stairs then turned back. "It was wrong to break our journey here, we should have made straight for Nottingham. The King may well be displeased should he learn that our tardiness was the result of attending a social gathering."

Maurice joined him on the higher stair.

"We're not tardy brother; our Uncle may not even be aware of our arrival in England."

"Nevertheless, we ride at first light with no more distractions, whatever the circumstances. Now to your bed brother, I bid you goodnight."

Maurice watched his brother stride up the remaining stairs and down the corridor, slamming the door behind him when he entered his bedchamber.

For some time, Rupert leaned against the closed door, a scowl scarring his face. Eventually, he went over to the dresser, laying his hat and sword belt on the top. Unbuttoning his doublet, he raked back his hair and dropped onto the bed, staring up at the tester. Confined to the room for much of the day, Boye leapt up beside his master, licking his face repeatedly until the Prince urged him to lay down at his side. The young soldier pondered the hour or so spent in the company of men who didn't seem willing to acknowledge the severity of the situation in England. Such flippant attitudes would have to change or be changed by force if necessary. Only the Earls of Benningford and Melton seemed to display any form of good sense, a tad alarming especially if the royalist cause were to have any shred of superiority. With a sigh Rupert determined upon the only possible solution and that was to oversee as much of the recruitment and training process as possible to ensure the Royalist Army performed in a manner that would gain the upper hand.

Nonchalantly slipping one arm beneath his head, Rupert paused at the distinct sound of a woman's laughter filtering from the next room.

CHAPTER TWENTY

19th August 1642

It was still dark, and yet the weakest shafts of light filtered through a small gap in the curtains. The sound of a dog barking and horses hooves crunching on the gravel, finally eradicated all remains of sleep and Frances raised herself up on her elbows to listen. Muffled voices could be heard, though not what was being said. Throwing back the covers, she tip-toed to the window and peered out. Though the light was dim, she could clearly make out the undeniably tall figure of Prince Rupert speaking with his brother, beside their waiting horses. For one moment, he looked up at the house and Frances darted back behind the curtain, after all she was still naked. Eventually when she ventured a look, the princes were mounted up with others alongside, including she noted, Ralph Bynghame. The little party moved off, riding toward the gatehouse, Boye's distinctive white fur making him easily visible.

'That's them gone then.'

Frances padded back toward the bed where John was still asleep, his lashes forming dark crescents on his cheeks and wavy hair spread over one shoulder. Slipping under the covers, she rested her head on her pillow, examining her husband with fondness.

"What's wrong, why did you leave me?" he asked drowsily.

"I went to watch the princes' leaving," she said.

"I heard 'em, but wasn't of a mind to leave this comfort," he whispered huskily, eyes still firmly shut

Her fingers trailed from his shoulder, across his chest and further downward until her wrist was grabbed, and she was pushed onto her back where he rolled on top.

"Brazen hussy," he said searching her face. "Don't you know it's for a man to instigate such things?"

"I'm not sorry…. I merely blame my husband," she answered.

"Oh, for what?"

"Well, t'was he who enlightened me to such…. pleasures. I hope I've been an able student?"

She could feel his body changing.

"An excellent one," he said, licking his lips but when she thought he would continue, he rolled away, pulling her down against his shoulder. "I hurt you," he said simply.

"Only a little," she whispered, playing with the sparse, curling dark hair on his upper chest. "It was…. wonderful."

"It gladdens my heart to know I gave you pleasure," he laughed, trailing his fingers up and down the arm laid casually across his stomach. "Your gratification will ensure the getting of children, everyone knows that."

Propping herself up on one elbow, Frances looked down at his face.

"When did you first lie with a woman, John?"

The pale blue eyes widened in horror.

"What?"

"Well, I cannot be the first?"

"Of course not."

The brutality of the response left her feeling a little crestfallen. Could she possibly have dared to believe that he too had been as pure as she had been?

"My dear Frances, a man's needs are far different to those of women," he remarked as she drew away and sat up on her haunches.

"But why should that be?" He made no response, so she added. "I take it then that you've lain with many…."

She sounded almost petulant and yet she felt the need to ask. Like some wild innocuous dream, she had really hoped that what he had done to her, he had never done to another and yet how foolish that had been. He was after all two years her senior and a man.

"Very well, Mistress Curious, if you really wish to know, I shall tell you," he said lifting her chin. He wouldn't mention the number of youthful fumblings with estate wenches of course, no he would begin with what was a more memorable encounter.

"When I was at University, I met the prettiest girl and arranged to call on her."

"You mean she allowed you to…"

Frances could not accept that a woman would give herself so freely and yet he was almost saying that this woman had. Casually, John slipped an arm behind his head, watching her carefully when he said, "No, she was not at home…but her mother was."

Gradually, Frances' eyes grew wide.

"You cannot mean…?"

As she was still kneeling before him, he blatantly took in every inch of her nakedness before answering.

"Oh yes, I can…. she entertained me for most of the afternoon, her coaching highly enlightening and far more pleasurable than my usual studies. She taught me a great deal, especially how a man should pleasure a woman, not just himself."

Frances couldn't help feeling jealous, even though she realised this had happened long before she had even met John.

"You took her as your mistress then…?" she asked, and John almost choked with laughter.

"Good heavens, no. I came to realise just how close to my mother's age she was and that curtailed my ardour, somewhat." Casually, he reached out to fondle one of her exposed breasts, the rebellious article responding almost immediately. Wanting to know more, Frances brushed his hand away.

"What about when you were in Europe, with Robin?" she asked.

'Oh no more woman, I've no desire to talk, just to possess you again!' He dragged her down against his shoulder once more and caressed her back.

"There were women in the Low Countries willing to offer any weary soldier a measure of light relief," he said and felt her shudder.

"Whores you mean?"

"No, camp followers," he answered honestly.

"Did you…. did you love any of them?"

He broke into spontaneous laughter, planting kisses on the side of her head.

"My dearest wife, they weren't the type of women to grow fond of. They provided a service that's all."

He paused to lift her chin and look into her eyes.

"Wait now, I can see what this is all about. You think that when I leave here, I may well succumb to that same kind of 'entertainment' on army encampments?"

Frances scowled deeply.

"Your father has a mistress…."

He drew away from her.

"Tis no business of mine…. but definitely none of yours," he announced firmly. "Within marriage a man may do just as he wishes."

She rolled onto her side, tears pricking her eyes. This was true and yet having daily witnessed the relationship between her mother and father, Frances had hoped that her own would prove similar. Was John almost suggesting that in the future, he may well stray to another….?

Almost sensing her thoughts, John pulled her back to his shoulder, enfolding her in his arms, caressing her skin.

"I am not my father Frances, I would never betray what we have together," he said resolutely with an almost sad tone to his voice.

"No, you aren't, are you?" she smiled drawing back to look down at him.

Slowly, he cupped her face, kissing her until she returned it with equal measure, both soon lost in mounting desire, all previous conversation forgotten.

CHAPTER TWENTY-ONE

August 1642 – Haveringham Manor

Wisps of smoke rose heavenward from the recently vacated encampment in the grounds as Frances and John rode past.

'I wonder where they are now,' Frances thought to herself.

The day being so bright and warm, John had suggested taking a ride into the countryside, something to which Frances readily agreed, relieved to be able to escape the somewhat subdued atmosphere in the house. The morning had been surprisingly eventful ever since the newlyweds had ventured downstairs. Anne Bynghame seemed unusually reserved as she greeted them, hardly surprising given Ralph's sudden departure. Though she had only known her a brief time, Frances comprehended the depth of love Anne seemed to hold for Ralph, though whether it was reciprocated was debatable to say the least.

Frances started when John suddenly sped past. Not to be outdone, she urged Phoenix onward, catching up with John relatively easily. Side by side they rode on through the open countryside, eventually slowing their pace on reaching the village of Skelton with its pretty little church in the centre.

"You're clearly known?" John remarked as several villagers paused from their daily business to show deference.

"Of course, I often come here with father when he tours the surrounding villages," she answered.

"Are they loyal?"

"Why shouldn't they be?"

"No reason, I'm just pondering something I heard Rupert say."

Frances wondered what was alluded to, but she had no mind to find out, the day being far too fine and sunny to worry about such trivialities. Before long, Skelton was left behind and once again, they were able to canter out across the open land, the magnif towers of York Minister visible in the distance.

"You know, I'd quite like to see the Minster at close quarters if we have the opportunity," John remarked.

"I could ask father if we could use our house in York?" Frances said pivoting in the saddle when John didn't make a response. She hadn't noticed, but John had reined in and dismounted beside a rippling stream. Frances rode back.

"Had enough already, my Lord?" she asked. Hat removed, John crouched down on his haunches and turned to gaze up at her.

"I merely thought it might be pleasant to tarry here a while," he remarked.

"You like my home county then husband?" Frances asked, slipping from the saddle to join him. Phoenix sauntered off to join John's mount enjoying some lush grass beneath a tree.

"I'd like it even more if you weren't blocking the view." John removed his cloak, spreading it out on the ground beside a large boulder. "For you my love," he said.

It wasn't long before the sun proved soporific and resting back on the soft fabric, Frances slipped an arm beneath her head, the babbling of the stream and the sweet song of a skylark high above, the only sounds.

Unbuttoning his doublet, John watched her, resting on one elbow.

"Contented sweetheart?" he asked, fiddling with the ribbons on the front of her gown.

"Perfectly…. I wish these days would never end," she murmured.

John leaned down, kissing her until she began to return it and allowing a hand to move inside her bodice, he was taken aback when she pushed him aside and sat bolt upright.

"We can't John, not out here." Hoping her objection sounded genuine, Frances couldn't deny how rebellious her body was being.

"Don't you turn prudish on me, wife. Do you honestly think the only place to enjoy one another is in the bedchamber?" Pulling Frances back down onto the cloak, he straddled her, staring down into her alarmed face. "I assure you, tis most enjoyable out of doors, after all we only wed yesterday."

When he began kissing her neck, Frances' perfidious body responded, almost willing his hand to creep ever deeper inside the top of her gown.

August drew rapidly to a close, neither John nor Frances willing to consider that fast approaching day when he would take to his horse and finally leave for an unknown length of time. They did end up spending several days and nights in York, dining more than once at the Olde Starre Inn, returning to the York house where, in the privacy of their bedchamber, their joint passions played out freely. One particularly warm evening, they rode past the Minster and out of the city under Monkgate Bar. In an isolated spot on the banks of the river Ouse, they lay contentedly in one another's arms, feet trailing in the cool water as the sun set in spectacular fusions of orange, gold, and crimson.

"It's as if the sky is ablaze," Frances remarked casually, but John didn't answer. He had noticed of course, feeling as if nature itself were offering some form of sinister portent. *'That's nonsensical, it's just the sun setting,'* he thought and standing to his feet, hoisted her from the ground. "Let's go back to the house, before it grows dark."

That night, though they had given and taken from one another more than once, for some reason sleep eluded Frances. Unendingly, England's impending future ran through her mind with alarming clarity as if some new kind of pestilence stalked the land, waiting to pounce on the unsuspecting populace. Her knowledge of warfare was limited of course but Robin had taught her enough about military encounters to bring that nagging fear to her. She rolled over, hugging her pillow. Somewhere in a distant street a dog barked repeatedly, a voice bellowing for it to be silent as a church clock chimed the hour. Three of the clock and still sleep evaded her. Looking at John next to her, Frances envied his steady breathing proving he was in deep slumber.

'It's as if the sky is ablaze…..' Her own words suddenly made Frances shudder and a wave of overwhelming panic assailed her. Reaching for John, she gently shook his arm attempting to wake him.

"Be at peace my love…..all shall be well," he whispered drowsily, drawing her down to his shoulder. The warmth of his body and regular rise and fall of his chest eventually lulled Frances into a shallow sleep, though almost at once a vivid dream woke her again. Distorted faces floated along in crimson tinged river water. Wailing women ran along the banks, as mutilated bodies of men and horses floated by. Smoke pervaded the whole area, shielding what in the dream looked exactly like York Minster, though it was in ruins and all the while women wrung their hands and howled with grief.

Gasping for breath, Frances sat upright, one hand to a chest in which her heart beat so rapidly and loudly that she felt John must hear it. All the while, he slept on.

CHAPTER TWENTY-TWO

Late August 1642

The pane of glass helped to cool her fiery cheek. Frances had been weeping for some time that morning, ever since making a shocking discovery. This particular window seat always had proved a sanctuary whenever some issue or other bothered her, this day no exception. John and Lambert were outside with her father, her mother and Anne Bynghame in the still room, so Frances felt no one would interrupt her. There was no way of telling how John would react once she told him what had happened, and this troubled her more than the problem itself. Always a deep thinker, Frances liked to examine issues from all angles before deciding on the best solution. Another wave of weeping overtook her and burying her head in her hands, Frances was unaware of a footfall drawing ever closer.

From the moment he had pushed open the large oak front door, John had become aware of a sound emanating from somewhere in the Great Hall and went to look.

"Hey now, what's all this?" he asked, recognising his wife's skirts cascading down the side of the window seat. He sat beside her taking her hand in his and gradually a tearful expression turned toward him.

"I…. I have failed you.…" she whispered, through faltering lips.

"How so?" he asked, stroking the back of her hand with his thumb.

"My…my…'flowers' have come.…" she managed to say, but John scowled little comprehending her meaning, then realised.

"Ah…. you speak of your monthly sickness?" he asked. With a grimace, Frances answered with a simple nod. "And this is the cause for all this anguish?"

Her head shot up. What could he possibly mean by that and why did she perceive him to be faintly amused?

"You don't seem to realise what it means though, I had hoped to find myself with child before….."

Frances turned back to the window, closing her eyes, tears escaping in little rivulets down her cheeks.

"Before I leave," he finished for her. Reaching for her chin, he gently turned her head from side to side. From the number of dark stains spotting her skirts and the undeniably swollen eyes, he observed she had been weeping for some considerable time. John never could bear to see a woman cry without compelling cause, especially Frances.

"Why didn't you come and find me?" he asked.

"You were busy with father," she answered quietly.

"But to become so distraught over such a trivial matter? I thought it to be something far worse."

'Trivial?' Again, Frances scowled. "How could it possibly be worse? Did we not wed so that I might provide you with an heir?" she said.

John shook his head laughing.

"That wasn't the only reason we wed, Frances," he said, laughter in his eyes.

"Oh no, we must not forget the generous dowry I brought….."

Frances noticed him stiffen; all previous humour gone from his eyes.

"I'll not tolerate such talk, Frances," he said firmly. Though he adored the unusual side to her character, nevertheless, John felt the need to occasionally address anything he felt had overstepped the mark and this particular comment required it. No man wished for a fractious wife, John no exception. Letting her hand fall from his, John heaved a sigh and stared across the Great Hall a frown scarring his brow.

'Oh no, what have I done now…..'

Frances realised she had spoken rashly with little thought to the consequences. He was annoyed, of course he was, wouldn't any man be on hearing such an intimation?

"John…..forgive me?" she pleaded and only when he looked round did he notice just how distressed, small, and undeniably remorseful she seemed.

"You my dearest wife will never again imply that I only wed you for your dowry. Tis not so and you know it. As for children, we must have patience, trusting God to favour our union before long."

Even if time is now against us….'

This time Frances knew better than to voice her thought and merely offered a flickering smile. John traced a finger down her cheek, settling his forehead against hers, pursing his lips in a contactless kiss.

"Don't you want to know why I came inside to look for you?" he eventually asked.

"Of course," she said sitting upright and dabbing her eyes with a kerchief.

"I've received word from Rupert," he said, casually rifling inside his doublet, drawing out a folded paper that made her recoil suspiciously.

"Please don't say he requires you at once?" she gasped.

With a steady stare, John's brows rose heavenward.

"You are quite determined to see the worst in everything today aren't you?" he remarked.

"But why should he write else?"

"Perhaps you'll will understand if I read it to you," he said unfolding the paper, scarred on one side by the Prince's personal seal.

The journey south had been eventful to say the least, Rupert's horse having taken a tumble, falling on him, dislocating his shoulder. Thankfully they had been fortunate to locate a bonesetter in a nearby village and after only three hours, the Prince was back in the saddle. Frances found her thoughts straying to the enigmatic young royal who had conversed with such ease in the walled garden on the morning of their wedding. After spending time alone with him, it came as little surprise to Frances to think that despite excruciating pain, Rupert had continued his purpose with a determination few could deny.

"Now here's a portion you're sure to like," John said. "I am given a direct order to remain in Yorkshire until the middle of September."

John watched Frances' eyes grow wider.

"Truly?" she gasped.

"Tis written here, in Rupert's own hand."

"Will he make a good commander, John?"

"If he's given the freedom to do what he considers fitting, then yes he will. He's not one to take criticism easily though, especially when he already knows some are sure to resent him being here in England at all."

In Nottingham, the Princes' soon discovered that the King had left for Coventry, forcing the little party, after taking food and having a brief rest, to head out again. In the end they had located the King close to Leicester, the whole party returning to Nottingham together where a few days later on the 22nd August, the Royal Standard was raised.

Frances noticed the way John's grip tightened on the parchment, his knuckles blanching considerably as he stared at nothing in particular. She was under no illusion that he must have desired to be present on what had been a momentous and pivotal day when the monarch openly declared war on his own subjects. Would he blame her for not being there? He certainly gave the impression of being deeply disturbed, confirmed when he whispered, "Englishman against Englishman…. who would have thought such violence would ever happen and yet tis confirmed here, in Rupert's own hand."

The letter quivered under John's grip and for some time, neither spoke, each pondering just what this would mean for England and more importantly to individuals. John had witnessed many atrocities in Europe, done against the populace in the name of righteousness and unbeknownst to Frances, the vast amount of his concern related to his wife and the effect war would have upon her.

John looked down at the letter, pointing to a portion in which the Prince spoke of renewing acquaintance with the son of the Earl of Bristol, one George Digby and he laughed.

"Hmm, Digby is a jumped-up popinjay who thinks too highly of himself," John explained. "Listen what Rupert writes about him."

'The King sent Digby to my lodgings in order to request a petard from me. From the manner of his speech, it was obvious Bristol's son had not the faintest notion of what a petard was. My opinion of Digby remains much as it was in Holland, that the man knows more of politics than soldiering.'

"The Prince sounds very direct," Frances commented, and John smiled.

"Tis his way. Rupert won't have forgotten Digby's part in persuading the King to go to the House of Commons last January to arrest Kimbolton and the five members. Remember, I wrote to Robin about that fiasco?"

"Yes, I do recall him reading it to father and myself," she said.

Rupert's mistrust of George Digby had begun in Holland when

both men had been attending the Queen. Disturbingly, Digby was overheard saying that in his opinion, the Prince was found far too regularly keeping company with those of lesser standing. Once Henrietta Maria had been informed of this, she insisted that Digby make a full public apology to Rupert. This incident alone had soured the relationship before it had almost started. From an early age, Rupert mistrusted anyone showing disloyalty or unreliability and following this episode in Holland, Digby had fallen foul pf that view.

Eventually, John folded the letter, slipping it back inside his doublet, but not before Frances had seen the signature 'Rupert' at the foot, in addition to what appeared to be even more words underneath. She would have questioned it, had not John encircled her in his arms and begun planting kisses on the side of her head.

"Now, what do you say to a ride to York? We could dine at the Olde Starre again?" he suggested with a grin.

"Only if we use a carriage John… I really cannot ride Phoenix today."

CHAPTER TWENTY-THREE

The Olde Starre Inn, York - Late August 1642

The hum of conversation gradually tailed off when the well-dressed couple entered the Inn. The Tapster noticed and depositing a fistful of empty tankards on a table, he went to greet them, wiping his hands on the apron round his waist.

"Welcome Milord, Milady," he said tipping his head. "You require a private room again perhaps?"

"The same as before, if you please, Master Foster," John replied.

"Of course, Milord, if you'd both care to follow me?"

Foster led the way up the narrow staircase turning right at the top where he opened a door, standing back to allow John and Frances to enter. The room was basic but comfortable enough with wood panelled walls, a number of padded chairs, a dresser, and a large table. Whilst John spoke to the Tapster about food and wine, Frances went over to the window, removing her cloak and gloves.

"There's such a fine view of the Minster from here," she said opening the casement to peer out, as John joined her once Foster had gone.

"No strolling by it this day, though. This rain grows heavier by the hour," he remarked.

"The Ouse may well flood again if it continues like this," Frances said, suddenly grimacing when a painful spasm shot through her lower abdomen. Even though he was removing his hat and sword, John noticed.

"You're unwell, my love," he said.

"No, I shall be back to normal in a day or two," she said.

"Well, you know best; I know naught of such womanly matters."

"Tis the curse of Eve for all women to suffer thus. Martha will attend me once we are back at the house, she's done so for a number of years now….."

Frances turned away, closing her eyes as another wave of pain assailed her.

"Fortunate then that we came in the carriage," John began as a sharp knock sounded at the door. "Enter," he shouted.

Foster carried in a tray with a bulbous bottle and two goblets upon it.

"Place that on the table Master Foster and bring the food in about half an hour?"

John opened a small leather pouch and dropped several coins into the Tapster's outstretched palm.

"Right you are, my Lord." Touching his forelock, Foster left again.

"A good host that, very obliging," John said pouring wine into two goblets. "Come and have a little of this wine my love, it might help?"

Frances wandered across to the chair by the fireside and sat down, contentedly sipping on the wine handed to her. John drew up a chair beside her.

"Now we're here…. there is something I need to speak to you about," he said.

Frances recalled the portion of writing below Rupert's signature on the letter and her heart ran cold. John suddenly seemed nervous, edgy even and she waited, dreading what he might have to tell her.

"There was something else Rupert had to say?" she asked.

"Yes, but I wasn't about to speak of it when you were so distressed earlier."

"Though you don't mind doing so now?" Frances said watching yellow tinged flames licking across several logs in the grate. "Very well husband, speak what you must."

John reached for her hand and when she turned to look, his lips spread into a smile.

"There is a good reason for me being ordered to stay in Yorkshire," he began. "My orders are to recruit troops and procure supplies in this area, to assist your father in his compliance with an official document he received from His Majesty."

Frances scowled into the pale blue eyes.

"Father said nothing to me about receiving an official document?" she said and with a smile, John stroked her cheek.

"He had no desire to spoil our nuptials, though I assure you the document does exist, I've seen it myself and Lambert knows of it. I am to source horses, after all there are many breeders in this county, and I want to get my hands on them before the enemy does."

Frances' eyes widened and pivoting round, she grabbed his hand.

"Well now, in that, I can truly be of assistance," she declared, colour flooding her face for the first time that day. John, noticing how sparkling her eyes had become, narrowed his own, speculatively.

"What do you mean?"

"Only that I know the area better than you and therefore, if we were to...."

John released her hand and stood upright.

"Oh no, no, no Frances, this is no task for a woman."

Undeterred, she placed her goblet on the hearth.

"Don't chide, John. It would make perfect sense since I'm known on most of the estates where horses are bred. I've been often with father to several of them."

"Nevertheless, I say no. You may suggest names and places, but actual visits will be done by your father and myself, not you."

Frances' expression fell and wandering back to the window, she peered out at the relentless rain.

"You are to leave so soon and yet you intend to spend time away from me, with my father?" Her head fell forward until a surge of anger rose from within. "Now I see it…..you cannot love me as I love you…."

Her hands flew to her face, and she sobbed. Watching her, John heaved a sigh and depositing his goblet on the table, he slowly rose and went to her.

"You grow hysterical Frances; you need to rest…. you're clearly unwell," he said.

"Not unwell my Lord…..just unable to bear you a child!"

She watched the hurt spread into his eyes, realising that yet again, she had acted like a petulant child toward the man she purported to love. She wanted, no needed to make him understand just how desperate she was in desiring to spend as much of the time they had left, together. How would she cope with the knowledge that he and her father were only a few miles away, whilst she was forced to remain at Haveringham. It was not fair and yet she couldn't have him leave to tour the locality with the knowledge that he was angry with her playing on her mind. Frantically, she made a grab for him.

"John, oh John, I'm sorry…I didn't mean…. t'was wicked to speak thus…"

Eventually, he gently placed both hands on her shoulders.

"I believe such wildness is due to your present condition, naught more," he said.

"But to speak so to my husband….?"

"Tis certainly not to be envied and not what any man desires to hear from his bride," he admitted.

"I only wished to suggest that I could be of great use were I to help with sourcing of horses," she said so tearfully that he could sense her dejection. Enfolding her in his embrace, he was immediately assailed by her perfume. Despite his annoyance and though loathe to admit it, some of what she had implied did make sense.

"How am I to refuse such a heartfelt plea to help?" he said, pressing his fingers to her lips when she would have spoken. "Tis a fact, you do know this county better than I but before you crow too loudly wife, remember that your father may insist on accompanying me himself."

Surprisingly, Frances gave a small giggle.

"Ah but such a venture would be best undertaken on horseback and father is unable to be in the saddle for long these days, remember. He would need the carriage which in turn would limit the speed and distance you would be able to cover in a day…."

John drew back, narrowing his eyes.

"Why you cunning little….."

"Not at all…. I just state facts," she admitted with a smile. "I only wish to be with you, is that so terribly wrong?"

"Not wrong, but know this, should your father and I deem it unsafe, then you will remain at Haveringham, do I make myself clear?" he said.

"Why would it be unsafe?" she enquired innocently.

"Don't you consider Parliament's supporters in this county will be about the same task as your father?"

"Oh, I hadn't thought of that."

"But I had," John insisted. "Now, no more till I speak with the Earl and Frances?" She stared questioningly. "Never again doubt the depth of love I have for you!"

CHAPTER TWENTY-FOUR

Late August 1642

The large document, with an enormous seal dangling from a crimson ribbon at its foot, quivered slightly under Miles' ever tightening grip.

"Are you are obliged to comply with all the terms, father?" Frances enquired, peering over his shoulder as Miles grimaced at one particular portion.

"Explain it to her, John my boy," he almost snapped.

"Remember me speaking of a certain document being sent to your father some weeks ago?" John asked and Frances nodded. "This is the very one, the Commission of Array. It requires your father to muster local inhabitants and ensure they're kitted out in readiness for war, that's why he is to raise his own regiment."

"You didn't mention receiving this though, father?" Frances enquired.

Miles didn't even look up, muttered something incoherently and absently tossed the whole document onto the table.

"With your usual succinctness, you've hit the nail on the head, daughter," he eventually said. "The damned thing did arrive a while back but with the wedding and so forth, I had no mind to give it consideration. Alas, now I have to and the men attending today's meeting must be told of its implications and thereafter choose which side to take in this…. unpleasantness."

Miles spoke with his normal transparency with no hint of guile and Frances smiled. This trait was something she admired, trying to emulate it herself by stating, "And if they decide for the King, pockets must be delved deeply."

She noticed John shaking his head.

"They must though husband, the King would scarce have issued such a formal plea for help else," she said.

"Perhaps the manner in which assistance is sought should be tempered a little though?" John said and squeezing his hand, Frances started to walk away.

"Fortunate then that the task falls to you and father, husband. For now, I shall be in the sewing room with Anne.....where no doubt I belong."

"You'll go nowhere, daughter," Miles announced. "You and John will both attend the meeting."

Frances turned back and concluding she was being teased said, "Father, I do wish you wouldn't jest so......"

"Tis no jest, Francesca." The inexplicable use of her formal name confused Frances, all the more when Miles added, "I care little for proprieties when England faces such events as now it does. You are my heir and as such I require your presence. John will be beside you to advise, should it be necessary."

Frances threw a beseeching look at her husband.

"You must do as your father wishes," John advised.

To be attending something predominantly male dominated was unusual to say the least, and yet extraordinary times called for unexpected measures. Thankfully, Frances had been taught a great deal about estate matters, ever since Robin's death, but suddenly she wondered how these men would react, not only to her presence, but more alarming still, if she might actually be required to say anything. Sensing her misgivings, John took her hand and gave it an affectionate squeeze.

"All shall be well, my sweet," he whispered.

"What concerns me most is the thought that some of these men, I've known for so long might actually decide to support the rebels," Miles admitted a little gloomily.

"You believe they will be foolish enough to side with Parliament father?" Frances asked.

"Don't be naïve daughter. James Hughes has a son who is a Member of the Commons, his daughter wed to yet another, now he will be one to watch. Of late I've had little contact from Hughes and that doesn't bode well. I dare say we'll know where his allegiance lies before the end of this day."

"Conscience clashing with family allegiances, eh?" John suggested.

Absently pulling on his beard, Miles heaved a huge sigh. Times certainly had changed in England, factions clamouring for power against a King who, in Miles' view, had made some glaring errors during his reign thus far. Nevertheless, Miles's loyalty to his monarch remained without question.

"To think that before long, father will be against son, brother against brother and even father against daughter."

"How so daughters?" Frances questioned with a frown.

"If they be from Royalist families but wed to rebels," John answered and only then did the poignancy of that one remark alone strike Frances. She reached for him.

"John, your sister?" she ventured and with a fleeting smile, he patted her hand. His wife had just voiced the very thing that had scarred his thoughts for some time, ever since noting Pettigrew's expression on seeing Rupert and Maurice standing in Haveringham's Great Hall.

"Mary will be loyal to Pettigrew of that I'm certain," John admitted. "I hate to consider it Frances, but before long my sister and I will be on opposing sides…. divided by the sword, so to speak." He tried to laugh but couldn't.

'Divided by the….sword.'

Such a simple phrase with so many connotations attached to it and

Frances could not escape the palpable distress within his eyes.

"How will you bear it?" she asked tentatively.

"Bear it I must," he answered simply. "To rebel against one's King is to commit treason. My sister is wed to someone who sees naught wrong in rebellion and as such will be… my enemy."

John meandered across to the window, Mary and their close relationship since childhood embedded in his mind. The siblings had always been relatively close as they had been born within a year of one another, their days when growing filled with adventures, joy, and laughter, until the day when Mary had been informed that a marriage had been negotiated for her to James Pettigrew. A member of Parliament from an excellent Sussex family, Pettigrew was four years Mary's senior and from that day she and John were parted. Mary faced schooling in wifely attributes and duties whilst John was eventually packed off to finish his education in Oxford and thence heading for the war in Europe. John still cared deeply for his sister, only questioning the divisions a civil war might have upon them both. Aware of Frances' arms encircling his waist and her head resting softly against his back, John slowly turned round.

"We mustn't ponder such cheerless thoughts," he admitted.

"Might your father not make Mary see sense?" she enquired.

"He'll certainly try, but my sister will not wish to offend God by denying her marriage vows, nor will she wish to bring disgrace or shame to Pettigrew by siding with the Fitzherbert's. I'm sorry to say it, but Mary will show loyalty to her husband."

Despite the warmth of John's embrace, Frances shuddered, and John held her closer, only drawing back when Lambert appeared under one archway with two men in his wake.

"Sir Clifford Ainsty and Mr James Hughes," Lambert announced.

"Welcome gentlemen," Miles greeted. "You know my son in law,

Lord Fitzherbert and of course my daughter, Frances, his wife."

"Lady Frances, hearty felicitations on your recent marriage; you seem most joyous for the situation," Ainsty said.

"I am, indeed, Sir Clifford," Frances responded holding out her hand. "I trust your wife is in good health?"

"She is Madam and bids me pass on her compliments to you both."

Frances barely heard, instead she became fixated on Hughes removing his hat and gloves at the table. It had been noted that Hughes had given the newlyweds nothing but a cursory glance and tip of the head, no good wishes or respectful felicitations and recalling her father's previous concerns, Frances braced herself for what might ensue.

In only a brief time, the Great Hall held more than twenty men and one lone female.

"Lift your head, my love," John said grasping her hand as he led her to the table. "You are a Viscountess remember, something they must all acknowledge."

The enormity of what she was about to undertake suddenly felt overwhelming and taking a deep breath, Frances concentrated on keeping her head erect and face serene.

John drew out a chair for Frances, making sure she was sited beside her father before taking to his own to her left.

"My thanks for attending this day gentlemen," Miles began. "You will all be fully aware of the troubles besetting England and in my capacity as Magistrate for the area, I am instructed by His Majesty to make the contents of this document known to you all."

Every head was turned toward Miles, with the exception of James Hughes seated directly opposite Frances who seemed more disposed to stare continually at her.

"Your pardon my Lord, but your daughter remains present, hardly fitting surely?" Hughes said and calmly, Miles set down the document.

"What of it?" he asked.

Smirking, Hughes glanced repeatedly up and down the table, hoping to see others feeling the same way.

"Only that if our discussions are to be of a serious nature, then surely she should withdraw?"

"No, my daughter will remain where she is," Miles answered succinctly, reaching for the document again. "Now gentlemen, if I might…." Scarcely had he begun before Hughes interjected again.

"I must protest, my Lord. Serious matters relating to the state of events in England are scarcely suitable for women's ears."

Frances concentrated on the hands, clenched in her lap, her insides almost replicating their rigidity. She could sense her heart beating rapidly and felt slightly nauseous until she felt the comfort of John's hand cover hers.

Again, Miles allowed the document to fall from his grip.

"Your pardon gentlemen, but it seems I must deviate from our business this day to give account for my daughter's presence." Miles leaned back on his chair folding his arms, his gaze alighting briefly on each man in turn. Inwardly he was somewhat annoyed but was not about to let anyone see just how much. "The title I bear was first bestowed upon my late father by Queen Bess, of blessed memory. Tis unusual in that it is hereditary and had he lived, my son would have inherited, though God saw fit to take him earlier this year. Consequently, my daughter has become my sole heir and when my days on this earth are done, she will be Countess in her own right. You will however observe that Lord Fitzherbert sits beside her and will, I assure you, advise his wife, should it be necessary."

Sir Arthur Redbourne, a long-time associate and friend of the family, greying at the temples though still nonetheless of considerable stature and presence, felt the need to intervene.

"I certainly have no objection, Miles. As you rightly say, she is your heir who I know to have been schooled in estate matters by yourself and your steward, since Robin's death. Tis of little consequence to have her remain."

"Thank you for showing sense, Arthur," Miles said.

"It seems I must concur, my Lord Earl," Hughes said evenly with a tip of the head, a disingenuous smile at his lips as Miles retrieved the parchment for a third time.

"Right, if there are no more objections, perhaps we might proceed?" he said. "This document is the Commission of Array issued by His Majesty, furnishing me with a commission, requiring me to seek compliance to its terms locally."

"What manner of compliance, my Lord?"

Miles fixed the enquirer with a charitable smile.

"I have a mind to allow my daughter answer that William, she is after all fully conversant with the particulars of it."

Frances' head shot up; her hand given a gentle squeeze by John before being released. Her mouth suddenly went dry at the sight of every head turned her way.

"Gentlemen……" She faltered, swallowing hard. "Gentlemen, the document requires that all those loyal to the crown should come at once to the King's aid. My father is to raise a regiment from here and will be pursuing the provision of coin, arms, and men from the various estates hereabouts, hence we lay this before you all."

Fumbling with the fabric of her skirts, Frances could not look up, not wishing to witness anger on the faces still watching her. Where Hughes was concerned, she could already sense his reticence.

"Nobly spoken, dear lady," Sir Arthur Redbourne said leaning across John to speak.

"And what if we do not wish to consider making such provision, Viscountess?"

Frances looked down the table, supressing a desire to laugh at the questioner who strangely reminded her of an old bull they once had on the Haveringham estate. It took some effort, but she made sure to set a composed expression on her face before answering.

"I am persuaded that individual consciences must be searched as to whether it is appropriate to provide aid for one's troubled monarch, or not, Sir," she said and directly opposite, Hughes gave a loud snort.

"This is intolerable. No matter her rank, for any woman to address men so unashamedly about such weighty issues as these? It cannot and must not be tolerated," he sneered.

Frances shot a glance at her father whose jaw suddenly seemed to tighten and lips pale as they pressed together.

"I would have you know my daughter speaks naught more than I intended this day," he finally managed.

"That's as may be my Lord, though I can only reiterate that her time might be better spent at her sewing frame or other similar harmless activities rather than advising men to search their consciences… whatever next," Hughes said.

Only then did Frances dare to look directly at the man seated across the table from her. Her stomach churned and her breathing shortened, though above it all came a wave of disdain and definite irritation. Never having received such outward disapproval before, Frances felt adamant that Hughes was not about to be victorious where she was concerned.

"I may be a member of what you might term as the 'weaker sex' Mister Hughes, but nevertheless, I have far more to offer my sovereign than mere skills with needle and thread," she declared, lifting her chin, conscious of John quietly chortling with pride beside her.

"And thus, by her own admission, we are to be influenced by the misguided concepts of this....mere chit of a girl," Hughes declared.

John's whole demeanour changed. In that moment he stiffened, sword arm itching to be used, but deciding prudence should be the order of the moment, a sharp glare through narrowed eyes sufficient.

"Have a care Sir, you are mighty close to insulting my wife," John said very slowly and deliberately, staring Hughes out.

"Then mayhap you should bring her more to heel, Lord Fitzherbert," Hughes voiced, glancing at his fellow attendees. John leapt to his feet, the sword from its scabbard with alarming rapidity, his chair toppling over and clattering to the floor. A little slower, but nonetheless with the same purpose, Arthur Redbourne mirrored the response, a brace of blades soon poised perilously close to Hughes' face.

"Tis perhaps most unwise to speak thus to me, Sir," John snarled, the sword blade glinting in the sunlight streaming through the windows. "If you continue in similar style, Haveringham Manor may well experience bloodshed."

Frances reached for John's arm.

"Put up your swords, both," she said. "I am sure Mr Hughes is merely a tad.... Misguided in his view."

"Aye indeed, such raised passions gain naught," Miles declared, scowling at the pair of men on their feet. Slowly, weapons were consigned to their scabbards and Arthur retook his seat as John stooped to pick up his own, moodily sitting upon it, arms folded across his chest as with a continuous stare he glared at the impervious looking man opposite.

"Before we continue, I should dearly like to know the reason you seem to display such marked aggression toward my family," Miles enquired.

"If I might be given leave to answer without receiving harassment?" Hughes asked.

With a look, Miles silently urged his son-in-law and old friend to conform and say no more. Despite feeling much the same, Miles wasn't prepared to accept acts of open hostility toward a guest within the confines of his home.

"Truth be told, I felt loath to come here at all this day," Hughes admitted with interlinked fingers. "After all, I am already conscious of just where the Benningford allegiance lies."

Miles exhaled loudly and shaking his head said, "I have never tried to disguise my loyalty. I am, and always shall be, a true Kings' man. What of it?"

Hughes again encompassed everyone at the table with a swift glance before answering. "Well, my Lord, according to my son, you are already identified as delinquent by the Parliament in that only recently, you harboured two members of the King's own family under this very roof."

Miles felt a sudden urge to replicate John and Arthur's reaction at the man's audacity, though with a concerted effort, he mastered it quickly. Pronounced delinquent by these rebellious men in London was he, well he certainly wouldn't recognise that insult.

"Do you expect me to deny it?" Miles finally said.

"By no means, my Lord, though Parliament would be interested to know why you considered it necessary," Hughes replied, casually examining his fingernails as if he felt bored.

John and Arthur exchanged a look of outright dismay.

"Would they now?" Miles sneered. "I freely admit to offering the Palatines the hospitality of my home of late, but would dispute strongly, the term 'harboured,' they were invited guests, much as you are this day."

Frances loved this determined side to her father. As always he appeared in full control of his attitude and temper, even though she knew he would be as angry as John had been at the blatant impudence shown by Hughes.

"I hardly think so, given the reason for them being in England in the first place," Hughes chortled. "The elder Palatine for example is said to secretly support the Irish Catholics, perhaps even sharing in that... misguided faith."

John's anger quickly resurfaced and leaning across the table, he snarled, "That insult is beneath even you, Sir. You seem unaware that Prince Rupert is known to follow the Calvinist faith."

"I merely speak as I have been informed," Hughes said almost casually.

"Unbelievable," John said so quietly that only Frances heard.

"As to your plea, Viscountess," Hughes said looking directly at Frances. "According to good conscience, I am resolved to comply with Parliament's Militia Ordinance and not this so called..... Commission of Array."

Pursing his lips, John gave an insincere laugh.

"Pah, the Militia Ordinance?" he commented. "Naught but a bill passed by the Parliament without assent from the King."

Hughes impassively eyeballed the young Lord across the table.

"Nonetheless, whatever you say Lord Fitzherbert, it is now law being passed on its first reading by one hundred and fifty-eight votes to one hundred and twenty-five."

"Is that so?" John sneered and indicating the formal parchment on the table, added, "I think you will find that this particular document negates that highly questionable of laws."

"I do not recognise that document," Hughes responded coolly, pointing to the parchment.

"Then I take it that you will be rallying troops against His Majesty?" Frances asked finding her voice again. "If so, that would put you in direct opposition to everything I hold true and honourable."

"And I would consider you a traitor, Sir," John declared soundly. "One day you are sure to face judgment for such an erroneous choice…. unless I first encounter you on the field of battle."

Frances perceived the narrowed blue eyes to suddenly display what could only be described as, loathing. The sentiments could not be denied of course but the intensity of her husband's anger was something she had not witnessed before. Was this a sign of what would be happening throughout England, men displaying the kind of behaviour normally alien to their normal character? Hoping she could be wrong, somehow deep within remained a nagging doubt that it might well be true.

"Lord Fitzherbert, I am no traitor, I speak from the heart," Hughes said with a disingenuous smile. "The King alone must be held responsible for the impasse we now face. He placed excessive demands upon the populace, taxing them till they could take no more. Parliament merely speaks with the voice of England's people."

John shook his head.

"You really are moulded into Parliament's will, aren't you?" he said, a pulsating vein visible at the side of his neck. Frances placed a hand on his arm and when his head turned, the hard expression softened at once. She needed reassurance, that much was obvious from her eyes, but from the manner of this one man alone who had proved arrogantly inflexible, proved what was to come, and it wasn't peace.

"There seems little point in debating this matter further with you or any other sharing your stance," Miles said to Hughes. "I am saddened that even within my comrades here, we are to face division, but I beg all of you, think well upon it before finally deciding."

"I never thought to see you so irate," Frances whispered, leaning closer to John.

"Such events force an end to all politeness," he answered simply.

"Can't we make them understand though?" she asked and with a smile, he tenderly touched her cheek.

"The chance for such niceties has gone, Fran. There's naught to be done now but direct action."

As he rose and retrieved his hat, Hughes glanced briefly at Frances, though she did not meet his gaze. Beside Miles, he nervously fed the brim of his hat through his fingers.

"My Lord Earl, I feel the need to ask your pardon for what must have appeared a harsh posture. This sorry business seems to increase all our passions one way or t'other."

Miles was not about to let that pass without a direct and honest response.

"I care not for these so called 'passions' being expounded quite so vehemently within the confines of my home," he stated firmly.

Hughes nodded silently again looking toward Frances beside her husband.

"Your daughter is much grown, why it seems only yesterday that she and her brother were running about the grounds here. To look upon her as a Viscountess and a married woman….." Hughes frowned. "Her husband is…interesting to say the least, and spoiling for a fight I would say."

"Blood is up on whatever the side," Miles said and looking Hughes directly in the eye added, "It seems we are destined to pursue conflicting paths."

"Alas so.... God be with you, Miles," Hughes said holding out a hand which Miles shook firmly.

"And with you, James," he answered and as Hughes and four others left Haveringham Manor's Great Hall, Miles shuddered to think they might never meet again.

CHAPTER TWENTY-FIVE

Arthur Redbourne contemplated the Earl pouring wine into goblets with an expression that seemed to exude both hostility and disappointment at the same time.

"By God Miles, your daughter would make a fine diplomat," he said, accepting a proffered goblet.

"Aye, she does well enough," Miles admitted, glancing to where she still remained seated beside John at the table.

"Managed Hughes' notable bias remarkably well in my opinion," Arthur remarked.

Other than a slight sound in his throat, Miles merely drained his goblet. "Well, let's get back to it. My heart's not really in this, but it has to be done," he said.

Scanning those remaining, Miles asked, "Am I given to understand that by your continued presence here, you will be pledging support to the King, gentlemen?"

"I speak for us all when I say that to a man, we are, Miles," Sir Marcus Harrington declared.

Frances smiled at her Godfather. *'Trust you to show sense.'*

On arrival, Sir Marcus had greeted the newlyweds warmly giving opportunity for them to thank him for the generous gift of silver tableware that had arrived some days previously in a large straw filled crate.

Miles heaved a sigh, retrieving the Commission document once more.

"We must now reflect upon the implications written here, the main consideration being that all men from fifteen to sixty should come forward for military training."

Looks of bewilderment and whispering spread around the table.

The effect of surrendering their strongest workers would mean there would be no one left to undertake the heaviest of tasks and that alone did not sit well with some.

"What, all of them?" one finally enquired.

"It appears so," Miles said, inwardly pondering the implications to the Haveringham estate.

"If most of our menfolk are gone, then who is to man our estates?" another asked.

"It will be left to the women and the men over sixty," Frances said when her father hesitated. Miles had already considered the effects on the Haveringham estate and wondered how they might survive.

"May I ask where this 'training' is to be done?" another enquired.

"The Earl is to raise a full regiment and having a large amount of land hereabouts, there will be ample space on which training may be accomplished," John explained, noting the number of blank expressions, and shaking of heads. "It will be the same throughout the land," he added.

"And the financial implications to us?"

"We shall all need to dip into our already overburdened purses," Miles answered. "I am told that a troop of cavalry will cost in the region of two shillings and sixpence per man…per day."

Audible gasps ensued causing Frances to respond.

"Ah but then most 'gentlemen' will already possess their own horses and weapons, so the ultimate cost will more relate to equipment for foot troops," she said. Despondent expressions met her gaze and she quickly added, "It is to aid our King, gentlemen."

Again whispering, nodding of heads and bemused expressions spread around the table until Clifford Ainsty turned to Miles.

"I take it you will be Colonel of this regiment then, Miles?"

The Earl pursed his lips and shook his head.

'God damn it, if ever I were needed more....'

"In name only alas," he replied. "This damned leg injury excludes me from actual service; therefore, I shall have to content myself being Colonel Proprietor only. The various companies within the regiment will be led by experienced officers chosen mainly by the higher command here in the north."

"Sounds as if a lot has been decided already?" Ainsty countered.

"I believe so. I lately conversed with His Highness, Prince Rupert on this very subject, it was most enlightening." Miles could have said far more and yet he felt wise council was the better option. "The Prince agreed to my design that, at my own personal cost, I would also raise a small company of cavalry under the direct captaincy of my son in law, with Lord Bynghame as his second in command. This company will go by the name of the Haveringham Troop of Horse."

"Why, the need for that, my Lord?" one enquired.

"Because this smaller troop will be under the direct control of Prince Rupert himself in his capacity as General of Horse and as Lord Fitzherbert's commission is with the Prince, the Haveringham Troop will leave here when he does."

"I dare say the Earl of Cumberland will have a great deal to say on that subject," John laughed, a proud Frances giving his hand an affectionate squeeze.

"Pah, Cumberland will have the Benningford Horse and foot troop. He can hardly complain when the notion has the direct approval of Prince Rupert."

"Then what of weaponry, how is that to be sourced?" another thankfully asked changing the subject.

"Glemham has assured me he will be involved in that as he knows of my contacts in Europe. As for swords, there are suppliers enough in Sheffield, who for the right price…." Miles broke off when at the back of the room, Lambert cleared his throat.

"Hell's teeth man, be at peace, it will all be done as cheaply as possible," Miles said throwing him a look of frustration.

A modicum of laughter cut through the tension, even Miles, ultimately, smiling broadly.

"Seriously, over the next few days, Lord Fitzherbert accompanied by my daughter will tour the area on the pretext of presenting themselves as newlyweds. Their true purpose, however, will be to ascertain allegiance and where appropriate request aid for His Majesty."

Frances turned wide eyes to both father and husband in turn. This was the first she had heard of a plan clearly concocted between them and she felt elated to be included.

"Truly father, we are to do this?"

"Well, I can hardly go myself," Miles answered honestly. "John and I have spoken at length and feel there is no better means of innocently gleaning intelligence."

"So, we are to be spies?" Frances whispered with a twinkle in her eyes.

"Hardly daughter," Miles tapped her hand gently. "We'll speak more of this later my girl."

"Then we had best start with those locally known to breed horses," she said barely able to conceal her excitement.

"Well, I can enquire in the areas around Boroughbridge," Sir Marcus admitted.

"I'm willing to do the same round Malton, Pickering and Helmsley," another said, then addressed the man to his left. "Could you not do the same around Bridlington, Henry?"

"I could…..though I'll avoid Burton Agnes Hall. Matthew Boynton might prove a tad unresponsive."

"He may not come out for the King, you mean?" Miles enquired.

"Who knows, he may initially, though I feel any loyalty may be short-lived. Mark me, Boynton may run first with the hare and then with the hounds, just as the fancy takes him. Best to see how the land lies in that direction before paying him a visit, I think."

"Then leave him for now Henry, there's others you could visit instead out toward Scarborough," Miles said and then to John, "I suggest you begin to the east of York taking a couple of men with you for protection, Redworth for one, he's trustworthy and he knows the roads well. I'll take the carriage out towards Bolton Abbey; I'll be damned if I let the rebels get there before me."

CHAPTER TWENTY-SIX

Late August 1642

"Suffering, dear heart?" John asked, helping Frances from the saddle.

"I ache everywhere," she admitted, arching her shoulders upwards.

"Your face is filthy," John said planting a swift kiss on her forehead.

"You're not exactly clean, yourself, you know," she responded.

"Well worth all our efforts though with plenty of horses for Cumberland and enough to take with me to Rupert," John remarked.

Frances turned away, fiddling with the stirrup dangling from beneath her saddle. She needed no reminder of a day she dreaded, the last few days enabling her to push it to the back of her mind in an effort to block it out. Now they were back at Haveringham, it returned alarmingly quickly, and she struggled to dispel her concern. Almost discerning the reason for her uncharacteristic quietness, John draped an arm round her shoulder and pointed to an area to the left of the house where a variety of horses grazed contentedly in a makeshift enclosure, surrounded by haphazard fencing.

"It would appear your father has had similar success," he said as a voice rang out.

"Welcome back," Miles said, hobbling toward them with Lambert close behind. "Well, my boy, how did it go?"

"Very well. Your daughter has a strangely persuasive manner, my Lord," John laughed, indicating two packhorses with paniers slung at their sides alongside a mangy looking donkey harnessed to a small cart all in the charge of Matthew Redworth. "I believe you may well be interested in what's in these." Delving inside his saddlebags, John drew out two leather bags, handing them straight to the Earl. "They contain a goodly amount of coin my Lord."

"And what is in those?" Miles enquired, looking from the cart to the paniers.

"Clothing, shoes, boots, weapons and old, but serviceable pieces of armour," Frances explained.

Limping across to the cart, Miles lifted the cover and drew out a slightly rust laden sword. Turning it over and over, he nodded and pursed his lips.

"I dare say once it's been honed by the smithy, it'll suffice well enough," he said.

"Old weaponry is better than none at all, is it not father?" Frances enquired.

"Of course," Miles smiled, though it quickly faded. "Just look at the state of you both."

"Inns don't always offer the best opportunities to stay clean father," Frances admitted noting the way John kept scratching at his thigh.

"Damn fleas bite like the very devil," he stated with a scowl.

"I think we will both need to bathe, father," Frances giggled.

"See to it Lambert and arrange for food to be set out in the small dining room for them. But first, take these bags of coins to my study and lock them away, then bring me the keys."

"My Lord," Lambert said scurrying back into the house.

"Redworth, ensure the horses are tended by the grooms, take that lot round to the storehouses, then get yourself to the kitchen, there'll be a jug of ale and some food waiting you, well done."

"Thank you, my Lord," Matthew said, the thought of food and ale filling spurring him into action once more as he dragged the donkey and horses round the side of the main house. He had enjoyed the task they had accomplished, making a change from his normal duties.

"Any problems?" Miles asked following John and Frances into the house.

"Oh, they're about alright, sporting what looked like orange scarves, though we didn't get too close, if you comprehend my meaning," John explained. "I'd say they're mobilising, much as we are, but Redworth proved himself more than capable when it came to taking less direct routes."

"Aye, he'll make an able soldier," Miles said.

"Or mayhap even a Cornet……with your approval of course, my Lord?" John suggested.

Miles puffed out his lips.

"He'd need to be a junior officer for that… but then these are unusual times, I dare say there'll be a way round it. Leave it with me, I'll give it some consideration."

For John to recommend Matt, though unexpected, pleased Frances no end. Previously, she had assumed that John disliked Matt and yet now he seemed to have concluded that Miles' head groom could be of beneficial use. He had, after all proved himself stout hearted and loyal over the last few days, offering John sound advice as to which were the best and safest routes to take. Nevertheless, there had been moments that had proved a little testing.

"You must tell father about the less than hospitable reception we received, John," she remarked.

"Oh, where was this?" Miles enquired.

"Ellington Hall, near Selby," John explained.

"Ah, so Edwin Maddox reveals his true colours eh? I thought he might. He offered you no threats?"

John faltered, saying cagily, "Not directly."

"Indirectly?"

"Well, we approached as newlyweds, as planned, but from the moment we entered the house, something felt wrong. Oh, we were shown the usual civilities of course, though it seemed to me as if Maddox might well have been evaluating the water from some of the comments he made."

"Such as?"

'The King should be taught a harsh lesson, lest he forget the power of his people.' That kind of thing my Lord," John explained.

"He dare speak thus to you, the son of an Earl, knowing full well who Frances is, not to mention myself?"

"That didn't seem to bother him overtly. I explained that we had no interest in politics, but our visit was merely as part of an informal tour of the area," John said, and Frances added, "We left as soon as it was tactful to do so, father."

"Thankfully, I had ordered Redworth and the others to wait a safe way from the house, concealed in a copse. I have the feeling that if Maddox had seen them, our ploy would not have worked."

CHAPTER TWENTY-SEVEN

Early September 1642

Unmistakable manly laughter, and plenty of it from the sound of it, resonated upstairs as Frances left her bedchamber. It felt puzzling, for though she had heard horses arriving, she had grown so used to that occurrence almost daily, she had ignored it. Now, as she made her way down the stairs, it was clear this was different. Quickly, she checked her hair and gown, pausing only briefly to scan the Great Hall. Several men were gathered in groups, one in particular standing beside John catching her interest.

"Well now, Lord Bynghame, I thought you were somewhere in the midlands with Prince Rupert?" she said, and Ralph turned, doffing his hat to bow before lifting her hand to his lips.

"Obviously not," he said coolly.

'Goodness, you're radiant,' he thought.

"No alteration in your attitude I see; still prone to stating the obvious," Frances said cynically. "Does Anne know you're here?"

"I suspect so, though I've not seen her yet," he replied casually, scowling at an impatient companion kept on nudging him. "Fran, lest he burst for the want of it, allow me to introduce Sir Anthony Portman. Portie, this is John's wife, the Viscountess Haveringham."

"Your most humble and obedient servant, my Lady," Portman said planting a kiss on her hand, hazel hued eyes lingering far too long on her décolletage. Hastily, Frances withdrew her hand and with a smile, slipped her arm through John's.

You didn't hear us arriving then, Fran?" Ralph enquired lightly.

"Horses often arrive here these days Ralph, did you not see the enclosure at the side of the house?"

"Ouch, prickly as ever," Ralph retorted, lifting his brows as the sound of her father's voice made her look round.

"Except for isolated pockets around Bradford, Hull and Selby of course….."

Aghast, beside the Earl strolled the unmistakable figure of Prince Rupert. She sank into a deep curtsey, almost knocked over when Boye bolted over attempting to lick her face.

"I see my dog remembers you, Viscountess," Rupert declared finding the occurrence slightly amusing.

Frances rose, straightening her skirts and giving the dog a hasty stroke on the head.

"It appears so, Your Highness." She could feel the blush deepening on her cheeks, so quickly added, "Have you been offered refreshments?"

The Princely head tipped, his expression faintly nonplussed as he said, "I believe the housekeeper attends to such practicalities, Madam." With a whine, Boye pawed Frances' skirts. "Boye, away!" Obedient to his master's order, the dog trotted over to a spot by the window and dropped to the floor, eyeing the Prince unswervingly.

"I confess I am surprised to see you here, Your Highness, is this visit to be of duration?" Frances enquired.

Rupert smiled in an indolent way she had witnessed before.

"I like to dispense surprises," he said with a satisfied smirk. "But in answer, our visit to the north will be of short duration. I am merely here to oversee the training, in particular the cavalry. Ability to ride is not the only attribute required, some riders may be green and need almost as much schooling as their mounts."

Polite laughter greeted the Princes' notion of wit.

"Schooling, Your Highness?" Frances asked tentatively, feeling John's arm slip around her waist.

"The Prince means that horses will need controlling by other means than with reins," John explained.

"Oh," she said and comprehending her lack of understanding, Rupert said, "With both hands bearing weapons, the horse must be turned by movement of thigh or body weight alone, Viscountess." Widening his eyes, he continued, covering any questions yet to be voiced. "Horses must be taught not to shy, no matter what they face."

"Such as weapons discharging?" she asked.

"Anything relating to battle conditions, from the smell of gunpowder, smoke, drum beats, trumpets blaring and so forth. Most horses will be unused to such elements."

"So even though my mare is used to the clamour of the hunt?"

"In the situations we must introduce, your mare would doubtless throw you, Madam. Warfare is seldom quiet."

"I am considered an excellent horsewoman…. perhaps I could assist….?"

Another squeeze of her waist proved she had once more overstepped the mark and leaning down to her, John threw his young commander an almost apologetic look.

"Leave it now, my dear," he whispered.

"Ah now this is more than welcome," Ralph Bynghame said taking a tankard of ale from a tray proffered by Rachel, one of the female servants. Portman mirrored the action, thoroughly sweeping the serving girl with immodest interest and a broad smile that made the girl blush. Quickly, Rachel moved on to serve others in the room, though couldn't help but keep glancing back at the handsome soldier beside Lord Bynghame.

"Pleasant little thing, ain't she?" Portman said as she retraced her steps towards the kitchen, a coy smile playing across her lips.

"Retreat, Portie, t'would be an insult to our host were you to touch her," Ralph warned.

"Shame…..worth a try though, don't you think, on the quiet?"

"No, I do not," Ralph retaliated. "Don't you dare make her one of your conquests Portie. Rupert would have your hide. If you need a woman so badly, take a ride into York and visit a whorehouse, they're not difficult to find."

"Know that from experience do you?" Portman's eyes lightened even more when Martha, carrying an armful of fresh linen, walked through the Hall in Moll Gilbert's "Nor her, lest you offend Fitzherbert's wife; that's her personal maid."

Portman contemplated the remainder of his ale, narrowing his eyes speculatively, swirling it round and round.

"Ah, the fair Viscountess… hard to keep one's eyes from, eh Bynghame?"

"For God's sake, don't think to look upon her….."

"Wouldn't dream of it personally old chap… though if he realised you might well face the wrath of Fitzherbert."

"What?"

"Well, I do have eyes you know Bynghame. I saw the way you looked at her."

"Utter nonsense, Portie. The lady and I have known one another for years, ever since she was a child."

Portman almost choked on his ale, throwing a scathing look at Ralph.

"Well, as any fool can see, she ain't a child now. You hung on her every word just now.

Tell me, my friend, is she the reason you are so tardy in going to find your wife?"

Ralph scowled, pressing his lips firmly together.

"Such lack of intellect is not worthy even of you. False accusations can lead to trouble you know," Ralph snarled, narrowing his eyes.

"Threats Bynghame, whatever next," Portman said with a broad grin.

"Mere warnings, my friend, mere warnings."

"Then I must be mistook, and withdraw the remark," Portman said. "Come then, let me meet this glorious creature you are wed to."

"I'm not sure I should let you anywhere near her either," Ralph admitted, relieved to find the conversation had moved away from Frances. Inwardly he couldn't seem to get over just how wonderful she looked and hoped for an opportunity to speak to her privately before they were required to leave.

"Pretty is she, this wife of yours?"

"Would I have wed her else?" Ralph quipped.

"Then here's toast to all pretty women…..whoever they may be and whatever their rank," Portman said, draining the remainder of his ale.

CHAPTER TWENTY-EIGHT

Early September 1642

Frances waited patiently as John and a man in green engaged in a hearty manly embrace. Bizarrely, Frances felt as if she recognized this stranger, yet couldn't quite fathom where from.

"You certainly appear hale and hearty, Fitzherbert…. little requirement to ask the reason, I suppose?" the stranger said, encompassing Frances with a sociable smile.

"Allow me to introduce my wife, Frances. This is Richard Crane, alongside whom I fought in the Low Countries, my love," John explained.

Finally, Frances recalled Prince Rupert mentioning Crane as being of assistance to him during his captivity in Austria. Thereafter he had been given the honour of commanding the Princes' personal Lifeguard.

"God give you good-day, Colonel Crane," she said, admiring the benevolent features as he bent over her hand to kiss it.

"Lady Fitzherbert," he replied, impressed by her knowledge of his rank in Rupert's regiment.

"You were in the barn on the eve of our marriage were you not?" she asked.

"I was indeed and a most enjoyable evening it was, as many a sore head proved the next day."

"Are you to join the prince in yonder field, Dick?" John enquired.

After a moment's hesitation and raising his brows, Crane responded.

"Aye, not so much for cavalry today, more the correct use of pistols is my lot."

John picked up on the hint of reticence.

"Problems?"

"Naught that can't be managed, though from what I've seen already, some of 'em will need all the help they can get. A few are clueless weaponry wise…. begging your pardon for my direct manner," Crane said to Frances.

"No matter Colonel. My husband has already intimated as much," she confessed.

"Show him what you've made for the Haveringham Troop though, "John encouraged and unfurling a piece of red taffeta, Frances spread it out.

"Ah, a Cornet," Crane exclaimed. "All your own work?"

"Alas I can only take credit for painting the interlinked Benningford and Melton arms in this corner. Most of the stitching was done by our housekeeper, though the fringing and ribbons in Prince Rupert's colours were my idea."

"His Highness is sure to be honoured by that," Crane replied admiring the small flag. "And who is to have the privilege of being Cornet and carrying it?"

"Undecided at the moment Dick, though I've made one proposal in that regard to the Earl. Trouble is the fellow isn't a gentleman," John explained.

"Oh, I doubt Rupert will care about that," Crane scoffed.

"What I don't understand is why both the flag, and the one carrying it, have the name Cornet'?" Frances said and John and the Colonel shared a momentary look of amusement.

"It's of no matter, my love. Do as the French do and call the flag a Guidon if that helps, but the one carrying it will be the Cornet of the Haveringham Troop," John elucidated.

"And must guard this with his life, for they are a much-prized trophy in battle," Crane explained.

'Guard it with his life....'

Frances shuddered, such being the reality of what they were about to face. It was not about a piece of decorated cloth, it was more that Englishmen would be fighting Englishmen, each seeking to purloin such trophies from one another.

Prince Rupert and the Earl of Benningford, having dispensed with their doublets, stood together hands on hips, watching a group of horsemen circling the field. For some time, Frances was content to admire the tasks being undertaken until finally asking, "John, might it be acceptable to have Phoenix saddled?"

"I'm not sure that's a good idea, we have a lot to do here, and I don't have time to join you," John responded, trying not to stare too long into the beseeching expression facing him.

"But if I keep out of the way?" she asked, tilting her head in a way that made something catch in John's chest. Momentarily stroking her cheek, he felt unable to deny her something that would give her pleasure and as he would be required by Rupert for some time, he saw no harm in it.

"Go on then, off with you, before I change my mind," he said.

Barely ten minutes later, Frances returned riding Phoenix, walking the mare slowly to the place where John, Miles, the Prince, and Sir Arthur Redbourne were in deep conversation, the prince insistently pointing to various areas of the field. The paleness of his shirt broken only by long, raven hued locks, almost accentuated his great height, adding a superiority to his entire appearance.

"Fitzherbert, join Bynghame and take these fellows through their paces with strong leadership at their head," Rupert commanded.

With a nod, John rushed across to where a mounted-up Ralph held his horse in readiness, leaping effortlessly into the saddle.

"From the walk to the trot and thence to the canter, my Lords," Rupert bellowed after them, then turned to Arthur, "If you take the smaller group out beyond the walls and put them through the charge with drawn swords?"

"Highness," Arthur said as Miles, using his walking cane, joined the prince.

"If it weren't for this damned leg, Your Highness, I'd be able to put 'em through their paces myself," he admitted, and Rupert offered a magnanimous smile.

"I appreciate how difficult it is for you, my Lord, but I require you here with me. Two heads are much better than one for the finer details, wouldn't you agree?"

Miles wondered momentarily if the prince might simply be humouring him and yet somehow, he doubted it, the younger man's direct manner and insistence setting the Earl at ease. Miles knew enough of Rupert's character to realise this straight-talking young man would never say anything merely to flatter.

"T'would be my honour, Your Highness," Miles said.

Frances had heard enough and walked Phoenix slowly round the edge of the field toward the church, briefly waving at her husband. Then unexpectedly a series of sharp explosions caused the startled mare to rear, tumbling Frances backward onto the ground.

"My God, Frances!" John yelled, galloping across to where his wife lay prostrate and motionless. Leaping from the saddle, he dropped to his knees, cradling her head in his lap, fearing the worst but with a soft moan she slowly opened her eyes, grimacing as she hauled herself upright, nestling against him.

"What happened?" she said, arching her back with a frown. "Oh John, I've never been more grateful to be wearing so many petticoats."

A manly guffaw drew her attention and looking up, she saw Ralph Bynghame on his horse, staring down at her.

"You weren't meant to hear that," she murmured.

"Then sweet lady, I humbly beg your pardon for knowing you wear a number of petticoats......I see you are as unharmed as is your wit."

"I am only winded, Lord Bynghame. I think you may safely return to your duties," she said, as John helped her to her feet.

Mockingly, Ralph flourished his plumed hat and bowed his head.

"Then I thank thee for precipitously dismissing me so benevolently …Lady Fitzherbert."

Turning his mount to ride away, Ralph closed his eyes and uttered a silent prayer of gratitude to the Almighty. She could so easily have badly hurt…or worse, many dying from injuries sustained when tumbling from horseback. Heading toward the anxious looking Earl and the prince, Ralph quickly reassured them that Frances was perfectly unharmed, saving a little embarrassment.

Back across the field, Frances looked John full in the face.

"Oh John, to think how I boasted of my prowess as a horsewoman to Prince Rupert, only to show such woeful inadequacy…. I'm so ashamed of myself," she bewailed.

"You were just unaware of Crane conducting pistol practice," John said as right on cue, another volley resounded in the air.

"Phoenix?"

"Over yonder." John said pointing to a group of trees some distance away where the chestnut mare grazed almost contentedly, though her ears flicked back and forth. Frances gave a low whistle and instantly the mare's head lifted.

"I'd best get her," Frances said walking across to where the mare had gone back to munching on the lush grass, and grasping the reins, gave her a sound pat on the back, just as another series of sharp cracks rang out. Phoenix reacted immediately, whickering in alarm, and tossing her head, but this time Frances remained in full control, holding her steady and whispering soothing sounds.

"Take her back to the stables," John said on joining her.

"Don't chide, John. I'll go out of the grounds to watch Sir Arthur with the others, we should be safe enough there," she said, gathering up the reins and allowing John to hoist her into the saddle.

"I haven't time to argue Frances, the prince is waiting," John said.

"Then you'd best lead me down toward yonder gate," Frances responded adroitly.

"You have the capability for great cunning and that is not pleasing in one's wife…" John said.

CHAPTER TWENTY-NINE

Early September 1642

Frances slowed Phoenix to a plodding walk. Having been watching Sir Arthur taking the small group of troopers through the charge with drawn swords, as instructed by Rupert, she had grown increasingly bored. No one seemed concerned about her, so she decided to take Phoenix for a gallop, after all her mare had not been out for a number of days. The feeling of the wind whipping at her hair and sitting low in the saddle always exhilarated Frances, though she realised she shouldn't go too far from the estate and soon turned back, heading through Haveringham village. A small crowd were gathered on the village green, laughing and jeering as a young man seemed to be reading from a paper in his hand. As Frances drew closer, a tangible edginess spread through the gathering as the crowd slowly parted to allow her access.

"What have you there Maynard? It must be something worth sharing to cause such hilarity in these sad times?" Frances enquired lightly.

Strangely, the paper had been consigned to the young man's rear.

"Tis naught, Milady," he said.

As she looked around the worried expressions in the gathering, Frances thrust out a hand.

"Give it to me, I wish to see it," she demanded.

"Best not, Milady…."

The woman daring to speak received a harsh dig in the ribs, not unnoticed by Frances. Something was very wrong here and Frances was determined to find out what. Pulling on the left rein, she turned Phoenix about, eyeing the crowd cautiously, on her guard. She felt glad to have the whip in her hand and knowing that Phoenix could be urged to rear on command, and flourish her hooves, proved comforting.

"I shall be the judge of whether to see it or not, now hand it over," Frances demanded, staring Maynard out until reluctantly complied.

The more Frances read, the more her eyes widened, and she felt the colour draining from her face. There, in stark black ink, above the crudest of caricatures, England's populace was warned to mistrust Prince Rupert of the Rhine, listing the foulest allegations against him, branding him a sexual deviant, not averse to having intercourse with his own dog. Feeling physically bilious, Frances finally looked up. Every eye seemed focused on her, though Maynard's expression appeared contemptuous.

"Where did you come by this nauseating filth?" she murmured but no one spoke. "Answer me, I demand to know how you came by this."

The crowd shuffled about, no one wishing to be the first to admit what they knew, until the woman, brave enough to speak beforehand said, "A man rode by a while back handin' 'em out Milady."

Instantly, the recipient of glares and scowls, proved the estate workers to have a code of conduct none should break, but Frances was not yet finished.

"What man?" she demanded.

"Gave no name Milady, just said Parliament wants everyone to know that for all his 'andsome looks and fine clothes, that prince can't be trusted…..."

More felt inclined to join in after that, and the floodgates of explanation opened with full force.

"Told us we should know the truth, Milady."

"Aye, that's right. 'e did."

"And due to the lies this man uttered, you consider it acceptable to read this... this depravity to these good people, Joseph Maynard?" Frances stared the young man out and though momentarily shaken nevertheless, he lifted his chin, staring back, scorn in his eyes.

"Tis right for everyone to know what's really going on…. Milady," he said with an arrogance that wasn't missed.

"But this is not the truth," Frances answered shaking the paper angrily. "This is intended to discredit the prince, naught more. Can any of you really believe that Prince Rupert could behave in such…. such repulsive ways? The evil ones are those perpetuating falsehoods such as this." Her gloved fist closed around the document, crushing it completely before it was slipped into a pocket in the side of her skirt. "My father will certainly be interested in seeing this and hearing what has occurred here today, though what he will decide to do thereafter, I cannot say."

"What do you mean by that?" Maynard sneered to gasps from the crowd.

"How dare you speak to me in this manner," Frances snapped. "What you must all bear in mind is just who gives you employment on this estate, and the dwellings in which you all live. Can I speak plainer?"

Mutters of *'Nay Milady'* spread throughout the group, though Maynard remained proudly defiant, shaking his head, and silently mouthing *'threats now….'*

A woman forced her way to the front, making a grab for Maynard's arm.

"Hush now my son…. this is foolishness," she begged, then to Frances, "Ya pardon Milady, I'll take 'im 'ome. He's had these strange notions ever since them Puritan folk passed by here a while back, fillin' 'is 'ead with nonsense."

Roughly the same age as the countess, nevertheless Sarah Maynard's life had proved so vastly different to that of Elizabeth. Time had not been kind to Sarah, repeated childbirth, and the rigours of day-to-day labouring on the estate, taking its toll. Her hair was tinged with grey, and her face deeply pitted with lines. Slight of build, her plain clothing had quite clearly been repaired in several places, the woollen skirts pinned up front and back to keep from trailing on the ground.

"Grown 'e may be, but I'll box 'is ears if'n 'e thinks on such things much longer, you see if I don't."

Maynard jerked his arm free, grimacing at his own mother.

"I'm a grown man with a mind of me own mother, and I've been using it, that's all," he snarled. "I say there's truth in what's written on that paper. Haven't we all seen that white dog of 'is wherever 'e is? I've even 'erd it sleeps on 'is bed." Maynard scanned the crowd, pleased by the number of amused expressions and sniggers of agreement.

Frances urged Phoenix closer, glaring down into Maynard's face.

"If you repeat such defamations, I'll have you thrown off the Haveringham estate," she declared, and Sarah reached out for Frances' skirts.

"Milady, please don't…. 'e don't know what 'e's talking about."

"No, you're so wrong mother, I know exactly what I'm saying and stand by it all, 'er threats don't scare me. Times are changing in England, mark me on it. Before long, the likes of 'er family won't be 'lordin' it over the common folk anymore and it can't come soon enough if you ask me."

Sarah Maynard stared open mouthed at the son she scarcely recognised.

"Joseph?" she managed.

"No mother, I'm done with being paid a pittance for long hours of toil and being punished for the slightest thing. Just think how they flogged Jacob last year for taking a rabbit to feed his little 'uns bellies, that's all. Rabbits to my mind is God's creatures, free for us all to take and eat; they don't belong to the Benningford's."

"They do if they are caught on my father's land!" Frances snarled.

Hands on hips, Maynard stared her out.

"Typical. It's just like we was told, why should they have so much when the rest of us have so little? Wanna know why I didn't come forward for military training, Milady? Because I don't hold with fighting for this dishonest villain calling himself King, that's why."

Audible gasps resonated throughout the gathering and once again Sarah made a grab for her son.

"Tis treason you now speak, my son. Lord Benningford could have you hanged for less..." she gasped.

"He'd have to catch me first mother and I ain't afeared of 'im no more. I've got freewill by the grace of God, and I intend to make use of it. Benningford don't own me."

Sarah now had tears coursing down her face as she looked with a mixture of pity and unbelief at her first born.

"Joseph, we've served the Benningfords for nigh on twenty years and have allus been treated well. We've a roof over our 'eds and food in our bellies thanks to the Earl's generosity. He's a fine master and we serve both him and the King with loyalty....as should you."

"Should? I'll do as my conscious dictates and it's no longer in this God-forsaken place."

Frances raised her whip, paused as if to strike but thought better of it. Any act of violence could well cause an adverse reaction from the rest. Instead, she lowered it once more and snarled, "Devil take you, rebellious cur. You have just declared yourself an enemy of my family and henceforth will no longer receive any form of succour here. Leave now or I dare say my father and my husband will come and see you off with the points of their swords."

Maynard's top lip curled contemptuously, and he stepped closer staring up at her, venom spreading across his expression. Frances' felt her heart racing but determined not to allow this traitor to see the fear that tried to overwhelm her.

"Tis for ya father to order such things, but as I was leavin' anyway I'll say no more about it. I just hope to persuade a few more to come with me." He peered round the little crowd, though most seemed unwilling to even look at him anymore. With a disconcerting laugh, Maynard strode off. Sarah fell into the arms of her youngest daughter, weeping openly as from some way off Maynard yelled back, "Know this, I'll have my revenge 'pon you and yours one day... Milady... I swear it before God!"

CHAPTER THIRTY

Early September 1642

Tears stung her eyes as ,with an infuriated shriek, Frances hurled her gloves to the floor and John rushed straight across to her.

"Whatever's wrong, my love? Arthur presumed you'd come back to the house when he could no longer see you; has someone hurt you?"

"Not exactly," she managed.

"How not exactly, what's happened Frances?" John asked, anger flashing through his eyes. Slowly she removed the crushed pamphlet from her pocket.

"This was being read to a group of our villagers," she said slowly.

John straightened out the paper and after reading it, tossed it toward the remaining men at the table.

"A decidedly low form of attack," he snarled.

Ralph, Arthur, and others gathered round to examine the document.

"Who do they find to compose such offensive drivel?" Arthur declared.

"Offensive drivel such as this?" Prince Rupert's voice boomed out as he entered the Great Hall beside the Earl, brandishing what appeared to be another paper in one hand.

Chairs scraped against the floor as each man stood to bow and Frances dipped a shallow curtsey, still tormented by emotion.

"We would have kept it from you, Highness," Ralph Bynghame began but the prince dismissed the remark with a wave of one hand.

"No need Bynghame," he said. "This particular copy was nailed to a tree in the grounds, but as to how it got there, now that's some mischief to be solved." Frances looked down, chewing her lip, one hand to her throat. "You know of this, Madam?"

Heat infusing her face, slowly Frances raised tear filled eyes. It had to be Maynard, who else could it have been, everything in his behaviour pointed to guilt.

"I.... I believe I do know something, Your Highness. Seemingly, a man has been in the area handing these out and I am sorry to admit that the culprit may well be one of our own estate workers."

"Who?" Miles asked, though Rupert marched up to Ralph, snatched the paper from his hand and ripping into several pieces, hurled it into the fire, watching it curl into black ash with an impenetrable expression. The blatant content must have affected the young royal, though Rupert gave no indication of it. One hand resting on the mantel, one foot on the hearth, the prince appeared studious and little inclined to speak, though eventually when his head turned, it was Frances the brown eyes sought.

"Fire is a fitting way to dispose of such rebellious hogwash, Viscountess. By such means the enemy will endeavour to convince those of naïve nature to believe exactly what they desire." He stood upright, rifling inside his doublet. "Here is another pamphlet doubtless left by the same culprit. Read it aloud Fitzherbert, for I dare say it will amuse us all."

John began, *'England's gentry are naught but 'Cavaliers'.... scarcely better than peasants on horseback, fit only for drinking, swearing, wenching, and festooning themselves with gaily coloured ribbons, sporting outlandish feathers in their hats.'*

"Outrageous Highness, where did you find it?" John asked, guffawing along with the others.

"In the hedgerow, close to the main gate. I'm surprised you did not see it yourself, Viscountess?"

A deepening blush made Frances lower her head and scowl. She would scarcely have noticed anything having ridden as speed through the main gates, intent only on reaching the house where her anger might be assuaged.

"This term 'cavalier' implies we have naught more to offer our King than debauchery and other dissolute habits," John sneered, greeted by more laughter.

"That could well be true of some of us," Portman grinned, digging Ralph in the ribs.

"Posterity may well speak of us as 'cavaliers' be it our choice or no," declared the prince with a half-smile that appeared more like a smirk, reaching even to his eyes.

"With your good self as the epitome of one, Highness, eh?" Portman put in.

"Possibly," Rupert replied casually, then with a forced smile added, "Given the distances I've traversed of late; I'm surprised there aren't more declaring my 'supernatural powers.' I am after all said to be in the south in the forenoon and then in the north but a few hours later…"

Frances frowned. Such a feat would be nigh on impossible to achieve, the length of time required to cover even the smallest of journeys prohibitive to say the least.

"Do we not have anything similar to scatter about for the enemy to find?" she eventually asked.

"Naught that could be repeated before a lady of your delicacy, Viscountess," Portman quipped, again grinning at Ralph.

"We often describe them as 'puck-eared' Puritans, possibly due to them deciding for some unknown reason, to crop their hair so short," added Ralph.

"I once recall Her Majesty in Holland referring to them as……

'roundheads,' which I dare say is remarkably apt," Rupert said almost nonchalantly.

One by one they drifted through to the small dining room, though Miles, held back saying to John, "You go with Rupert my boy, I'll join you presently. I want to speak to Frances first."

John had seen her wandering off to one of the windows realising something was not quite right. He would have joined her himself had the Earl not prevented him. Presently, Frances felt a hand on her back and her father's voice saying, "Come on then my girl, out with it."

She turned and with trembling lips said, "I think…. that is, I believe…..I may have spoken over harshly to one of our tenant."

Miles encouraged her to sit beside him on the window seat.

"Best tell me all about it then," he said.

"I am your heir, am I not?" Pulling a kerchief from her pocket, she dabbed her eyes.

"You know you are."

"Then in that capacity… I ordered the elder Maynard son to leave Haveringham."

Miles' forehead creased.

"So, he was the one reading the pamphlet to the villagers was he; and doubtless responsible for the others we found."

"He has never spoken to me as he did today, father."

"What exactly did he say?"

"He was inciting rebellion if you ask me. I heard him openly declaring his intent to join Parliament's army. Had I not arrived when I did, doubtless others might have followed his example. He spoke vociferously against the King….and Prince Rupert, father."

Sighing deeply, Miles grasped her hand.

"And thus, you ordered him to leave Haveringham?"

"I did."

"He did you no physical harm?"

"No, but what he suggested was somehow far worse. He swore that he would no longer take orders from the Benningford's and certainly not…. not from the likes of me…."

Her voice trailed off and the kerchief was pressed to her mouth.

A wave of anger rose within Miles, spilling out when he snarled, "Joseph Maynard dared to address you, a Viscountess, in that manner?" She could only nod. "Then be at peace daughter, for you have done no more than I would. By God, I'll not have such bare-faced revolt on my estate."

"His mother as greatly distressed, weeping openly when I left…."

"Aye, Sarah, and Tom Maynard don't deserve such a faithless son. Tom wasn't present then?"

"No."

"Thought as much, he'd have had a lot to say to the lad, had he been." Miles could see how distressed Frances was and yet he was proud of her. "Know this my girl, you spoke with nothing but authority, as I would have done. I'll not tolerate rebellion like this. I take it you saw him leave?"

"No, though he said he'd go once he'd packed his belongings."

"Then I'll go and check after we've eaten," Miles said.

"He spoke against me personally, father." Finally, she felt free to admit what had caused her the most distress and what filled most of her thoughts thereafter. Whilst she didn't easily fall into the trap of believing in superstition, nevertheless such venom had been disconcerting.

"In what way?"

"He swore to have revenge one day……upon me and mine."

The colour rose in Miles' face, his lips pressed so firmly together, they almost disappeared.

'By God, I'll see him hanged for this,' he thought but voiced, "That good for nothing dared to curse my daughter, did he? Well, I'll take John, Ralph, and others with me once we've dined and if he's not gone by the time we arrive, he'll be seen off at pistol point." Miles stood, hoisting his daughter to her feet.

"You did well, daughter," he said softly, kissing her cheek.

CHAPTER THIRTY-ONE

Early September 1642

Secured together with nails and placed upright, side by side, roughly hewn planks of wood had a crudely chalked outline of the human form upon them, ready to use for target practice. A serious looking Richard Crane strolled up and down in front of the recruits, eyeing each one cautiously.

"Courtesy of the Earl of Benningford, you will each receive a brace of these pistol to be sited in the holsters on your saddles. Now, to function perfectly, they must be kept clean and dry. Watch whilst I prepare this one for firing."

A measure of powder was tipped into the barrel followed by a ball and then wadding. A small scouring stick then rammed the charge home and finally, using a special key, he spanned the mechanism.

"Did you hear the sharp click?" he enquired, eyeing the would-be troopers. "That will tell you that the correct position has been reached in order to generate the spark that will discharge the weapon." Placing a little powder in the pan, he closed the cover, and the pistol was primed and ready to fire. Turning to the targets, Crane extended his arm and gently squeezed the trigger. With a flash and a plume of smoke, the weapon discharged its deadly load splintering a section of the wooden target in the area around the head.

Smugly satisfied, he turned back to the men.

"Regrettably, they can be prone to misfiring, therefore the best way to counter that is to keep 'em clean gentlemen. Remember, doing so might very well save your life. Now, come to the table, pick up a piece, load it and fire when ready."

For the best part of an hour, the practice continued each man taking several shots at the targets until a contented Rupert sent them off in pairs to the far side of the house, to continue with sword drill.

Frances wandered up to the table, trailing her long fingers across the butt of one of the pistols laid out upon it.

"Would you care to take a turn, Viscountess?" Rupert asked.

'You're in for a surprise if I do.'

With an engaging smile she said, "May I?"

"I see no reason why not, Crane prepare one for her," the Prince ordered.

The loaded weapon was soon sitting in her palm.

"Oh, my word, it's so heavy," she commented, hoping her father wouldn't say anything. He didn't. Crane reached forward, settling the weapon more firmly in her hand.

"Don't grip it too tightly, Lady Fitzherbert," he instructed. "When you're ready, raise your arm, extend it fully and give fire."

Lifting her arm, she closed one eye to view a particular area of the target, then firmly squeezed the trigger. The weapon discharged and when the smoke cleared, the ball had obviously struck the area around the heart. Giving an enthusiastic guffaw and clapping his hands, Rupert walked toward her shaking his head.

"You have done that before Madam, and I'll wager on far more than one occasion," he said speculatively.

With a shy grin, Frances replaced the weapon on the table.

"I confess I have Your Highness. My father taught me when instructing my brother. I trust the deception did not displease you?"

'Not a bit of it, you're proving to be quite remarkable in many respects.' The Prince tipped his head and, with one of his all too rare smiles that both gratified and disquieted at the same time, said, "It merely proves that you are not only an able shot, but a talented actress also?"

"I can also use a sword?" Frances hurried in, though John interrupted.

"Something that will not be proven to the Prince this day," he said firmly, then to Rupert, "Pray forgive her tendency to excessive exuberance, Your Highness."

"Might prove interesting to witness though, eh?" Rupert chuckled, arcing one dark brow upward whilst scrutinizing Frances for some considerable time with expressive eyes that gave little away.

At the table, Miles picked up a pistol turning it back and forth in his hand for some time.

"I'm contented to have acquired these, but I am concerned that they're said not to be too accurate," he remarked. Joining him, Rupert picked up another, loading and spanning it swiftly.

"Do you see yonder weathervane on the church, my Lord?" he asked, and Miles found it difficult not to laugh.

'You'll never hit that….'

"Tis some distance Highness, I'd say nigh on sixty yards or more," Miles voiced.

Without another word, Rupert raised the weapon, straightened his arm, and pulled the trigger. All eyes focused on the church tower and through the smoke, the vane could clearly be seen spinning round and round. With a look verging on arrogance, the young royal set the weapon back on the table.

"Well, I never…." Miles began but the Prince asked, "Mere coincidence you think, my Lord?"

Quickly another pistol received the ministrations of the Prince and once primed, Rupert pointed it toward the same target. Once again, when the smoke cleared, the weathervane could be seen spinning on its pole, two definite holes visible in the cockerel's tail feathers.

Miles shook his greying head in wonderment.

"My apologies for such scepticism Highness. I never thought to see such precision or range from these," he said painstakingly examining yet another of the pistols.

Rupert gave a chuckle.

"I confess to being grateful that neither failed me," he said, then added almost wistfully, "One day I shall give greater thought to improving the accuracy and firepower of such weapons."

CHAPTER THIRTY-TWO

13th September 1642

The day Frances had dreaded for so long dawned dank and chilly, mist pervading the whole area, almost mirroring the depth of her inner emotions. Fine drizzle fell relentlessly, almost as if nature itself were weeping as much as she was inwardly.

The courtyard was a hive of activity, the now stylishly attired Haveringham Troop of horse only awaiting final orders to set out for the midlands, from their newly appointed Captain, Lord John Fitzherbert.

Pulling her cloak closer, Frances almost wished time would stand still and yet despite that yearning, everything seemed to be progressing all too quickly. At her side, a noticeably quiet Anne Bynghame also waited, the two women watching their husbands constantly.

Just what kind of emotions Anne was going through, Frances could only speculate, though she knew her friend tried her best not to show the depth of her suffering, much as she did herself.

Frances took in everything about her husband, the tilt of his dark head, the long hair she loved, the gestures of his hands and the depth of his voice as he issued order after order. Like some macabre overture, the dark cloak at his shoulder swayed almost rhythmically as he strode about purposely from place to place in the courtyard. Finally, he turned, and eyes fixed on hers, he came to join her, drawing her to one side, for more privacy. As he looked down into her eyes and she into his, both tried to memorise every facet.

"You're cold darling," he eventually said. "You should go indoors."

'Go indoors, no I won't, I can't……'

"I'm not cold John…..I'm just…"

Closing her eyes, she fell against his chest.

"Now, now, my love, don't be like this…. all shall be well, remember that."

Cupping her face, he tilted her head slightly to gently kiss her lips.

"Come back to me, John," she whispered.

"Of course, I will, and before too long if Rupert gets his way. These rebels will soon be put in their place, mark me on that!"

'Are you trying to convince me or yourself?'

Trying to smile Frances actually said, "God keep you safe till that blessed day then husband."

He would never admit it to Frances, but he too was finding this moment exceedingly difficult.

'If only I wasn't so torn' he thought.

They had been together for such a brief period of time, and this pulled at every emotion he possessed. The look of her, the smell of her perfume and those deep blue eyes would be so hard to let go of and yet he knew he must. He was a hardened soldier whose skills and talents were needed by the King of England, how could any man possessing loyalty ignore such a plea from his monarch and yet to leave the woman he adored was proving much harder than he had expected.

"Dearest wife, remember everything we said last night as you lay in my arms. My passion for you defies all comprehension, you are dearer to me than aught else in this world. That alone will spur me on to the time when the rebels are defeated and I come here to take you to Kent where we shall live contentedly until we die of old age, surrounded by all our children and in time…. theirs too."

He grinned infectiously, forcing her to do the same.

"If God is willing, yes we shall," she said, adding, "I truly love thee, John."

The epitome of a dashing Cavalier John wore a doublet and breeches of blue, braided with silver, a bright scarlet sash across his body, tied at the hip with loose ends that swayed with every movement. His arms encircled Frances and he drew her closer.

"I love you, dear heart and promise to write as oft as I can."

His lips crushed against hers with a ferocity that had become the very nature of their joint passions, each trying to draw every inch of love from the other. Eventually, with great resolve, John broke away, holding her at arm's length. He had tormented himself enough and knew that if he didn't leave now, he might very well be unable.

"I must go," he said with determination, releasing her hands and striding toward his horse.

The moment had finally arrived, and Frances almost gave in to a mounting desire to scream his name and beg him to stay, despite realising she could not, must not do so. She was a Viscountess after all, the daughter of a peer of the realm and as such should behave. Watching him climb into the saddle made it all too real and with a pounding heart, she went to stand beside him. She had to convince him that though she would miss him, she supported him fully and that she was proud of him. Setting a smile to her lips hoping they would not tremble and give away the truth of it, she said, "Go to it, my Lord and may God keep you safe until His Majesty gains a swift and resounding victory over his enemies."

John reached down, grasping her hand.

"My brave and courageous lady. All shall truly be well, remember that, Frances."

"I shall," she nodded, her smile now slightly tremulous. "Think of me often?"

"You'll never be far from my thoughts or prayers, my love," he said and with a slightly tortured expression, turned to address his men. "Come then gentlemen, let's away before this day grows much older."

Ralph Bynghame rode a little closer.

"God be with you Fran, look after Anne for me?" he said.

"I shall," Frances said, smiling when Anne joined her and the two women linked arms, each watching their husband progressing across the courtyard. The clatter of hooves made every nerve in Frances' body rattle and her head pound as Matthew Redworth, now the Cornet of the troop as suggested by John and appointed by her father, rode past. The significance and poignancy of that promotion alone, as well as the image of the interlocked Melton and Benningford arms on the little flag he carried, finally hitting home. This was the reason John had chosen to serve his sovereign in this way, this was why he had to leave. Frances looked once more toward the front of the little procession and its lead rider, heading under the gatehouse now. He turned once, waved, and was gone.

CHAPTER THIRTY-THREE

Early October 1642

Life at Haveringham Manor took on a whole new perspective once the men had gone. Having gathered his residual staff in the courtyard, Miles addressed them all making it clear that due to the unusual events besetting England, everyone must be called upon to undertake anything of benefit to the Benningford estate. Thereafter, the remaining older men and the womenfolk began undertaking more strenuous duties, even the children being given menial tasks to ensure the estate functioned as normally as possible.

Frances seemed to suffer bouts of melancholia, following John's departure and despite encouragement from her father, felt little inclination to leave her bedchamber. One particular day, Frances looked down from her window to see a girl of roughly her own age, forcibly dragging a heavy sack along the stony ground. Every now and then, the girl stopped drawing her sleeve across her forehead until at last another female came out from the barn and together, they bore the sack with greater ease, the first obviously grateful for the second's help.

'How can I sit here with such gloomy thoughts when they are working so hard…..' she thought, watching the pair of women disappear round the back of the house. Perhaps it was merely that her mother and father were humouring her, given the separation she faced from her new husband and yet was it right for her to do nothing at all? With determination, Frances rose and went to the clothes press, rifling through its contents until she found an old woollen gown that, being front laced, made it easy to slip into without need for Martha. After the addition of a plain collar and coif, she hurried out of her room and down the stairs, slipping out of the house and down to the kitchen garden where Old Jake, the Gamekeeper was digging.

"You come to help then, Milady?" he asked, lifting his head on seeing her approach.

"I have Jake, though you may have to instruct me what to do."

"Course I will. Grab that hoe over there and give me a hand with some of this, it's not too difficult."

In a matter of days, Frances had been taught how to grow and tend simple crops, what each might be used for, and her previous limited knowledge of the medicinal properties offered by certain plants, increased considerably. She assisted others in the orchards, harvesting apples, ensuring the bumper crop was eventually safely stored in the roof space of two of the barns. Apples would be used for pies, pasties, preserves and cider in order to ensure they would have a goodly supply during the long winter months. When it came to the estate beasts, Frances learned how to milk cows, slaughter and skin rabbits, hares and even wring the necks of chickens as well as butcher sheep and cattle for meat. A goodly amount of her time was spent in the kitchens watching the way the cook peeled and chopped vegetables, made pies, pasties and prepare all manner of dishes, adding fresh herbs for greater flavour. Once back in her bedchamber, she made sure to make copious entries in her journal, believing the information contained within its pages might very well prove useful one day when she was mistress of her own household. The greater part of her days though were spent in the company of her father and Lambert in the Steward's room, going through estate matters in finite detail being shown how written records had to be kept and updated regularly. Despite the amount of work to be done, she was allowed some free time and one particular afternoon, Frances lounged in the window seat with a favourite book when Lambert interrupted.

"Beg pardon Lady Frances, but this arrived for you," he said. In his hand was a folded paper.

Sitting bolt upright, Frances said, "A letter, but I didn't hear a messenger arriving?"

"Alas, it came whilst you were in the kitchen and being busy myself, it slipped my mind. I've only just recalled it being in my pocket......I am deeply sorry, Milady."

She couldn't be angry with a man whose expression looked like that of a whipped pup, though she dropped from the seat and took the letter.

"Oh, it's from John," she said excitedly, recognising the hand at once and with a precipitous flick of her fingers and a smile, Frances resumed her place on the window seat and broke the seal, reading the letter through twice before resting her head against the glass. It was still raining heavily, much as it had been for most of the day. In her mind's eye, she imagined John riding in under the gatehouse, leaping from the saddle to pick her up and whirl her round in his arms.

'If only,' she thought.

"Heard from John I take it?" Miles said, limping across to the table to fill a goblet with wine. "Do you wish for some?"

"No thank you, father and yes, tis a letter from John," Frances answered joining him at the table.

"And does it contain anything you might be inclined to share with me, or is it full of sentimental nonsense only?"

"There are portions I can share father, yes. He speaks of rendezvousing with His Majesty, Rupert and Maurice at Stafford, along with two Lords….." She looked down considering the letter. "Ah yes, Wilmot and Digby. Do you know them?"

Frances well recalled one of the names herself and of John's derogatory comments.

"Digby eh…. Earl of Bristol's son. Handsome enough to captivate ladies I dare say, but a little too shifty eyed for my liking, mind you, his father's not much better." Frances smiled at her father's turn of phrase and direct manner. "Bristol wanted the King to wed the Spanish Infanta all those years ago, but a Spanish bride would not have gone down well in England. Remember what happened last time England had dealings with Spain in the time of Queen Bess?" Frances nodded. No one could ever forget the Armada

210

levelled against England and of the magnificent victory that had
ensued.

"Does he say aught of the Haveringham troop?" Miles eventually
asked.

"He does. They've seen some action already," she answered. "I'll
read you what John says.

*'Intelligence revealed that Lord Essex was heading in our direction from
the south, attempting to reach Worcester. Rupert had ordered us to wait
in a field close to the bridge at Powick to be in advantageous position
should the enemy approach. We had discarded our armour, relaxing with
open doublets when without warning, the enemy horse began crossing the
bridge. Rupert ordered warning shots to be fired, yelling for us to follow
him, straight to horse. I was immediately behind the Prince, charging the
enemy at full gallop, leaving them no chance to deploy. We cut them to
pieces, many falling into the river with their mounts, the water
soon......tainted with blood......'*

She paused from her reading, staring at the fireplace as the
nightmare she had endured in York came rushing back. A river
running red with blood and the bodies of men and horses floating
in its depths.

"What's wrong daughter?" Miles asked putting down his goblet.

Swallowing deeply, Frances gave a hesitant smile.

"Nothing father… tis but women's foolishness…."

"When was this?"

"Two weeks ago, the 23rd September," she read.

"Does he say whether we had any losses?" Miles asked, refilling
his goblet.

John went on to explain that the battle lasted little more than fifteen
minutes but was a great victory for the royalists. Over one hundred
and fifty enemy troops were lost, and Prince Maurice and Lord

Wilmot received minor wounds, though both were recovering quickly. Unfortunately, Walter Hawkins, one of the best estate workers, suffered a severe injury to his arm which was almost severed, leaving the surgeon little choice but to remove the lower part of it. Thereafter he was dispatched back to Yorkshire, though no indication was given as to when Walter would actually arrive.

"Oh, my word, not Hawkins, he was one of our best workers, solid and trustworthy," Miles commented. "I'll tell you this much, once he's fully recovered, he'll be found some type of role here, that's for certain.

"Then we must see him taken good care of once he gets here father, but listen, here's a bit of the letter I don't fully understand…."

'Being elated by such a swift and resounding victory, Rupert sent Richard Crane to the King, thus ensuring he received a knighthood.'

"Ah, now it's often the case that the bearer of good news of that kind, is rewarded with a knighthood. I'll warrant Rupert sent Crane intentionally."

"You think so?"

"I do indeed."

CHAPTER THIRTY-FOUR

Late October 1642

"Cawood Castle, but that's less than twenty miles from here," Elizabeth gasped, one hand held dramatically to her chest.

"It's far enough away to be of little concern to us here, Bess," Miles answered casually, far more disturbed by recent events than he was willing to admit in front of his wife and daughter.

Alarming news had reached Haveringham of Parliamentary forces inexplicably attacking Cawood Castle. Standing in a village close to Selby, Cawood was always known as a royalist stronghold and believed safe from any form of assault.

"What possible excuse could they have for doing this, father?" Frances asked.

"Well, it stands in a prime location between Selby and York for one and being garrisoned, perhaps their suspicions were aroused a little too greatly." Miles tugged on his beard. "In attacking it, Hotham has blatantly violated the treaty of neutrality drawn up months ago by Lord Fairfax and local royalists, including me."

Miles could scarcely disguise his anger, that much was clear, not from only his lips pressed firmly together but in the manner in which he filled a goblet with wine and downed it in one, slamming the empty goblet onto the table. Keeping his eyes on his daughter, he rifled inside his doublet and drew out a paper.

"This proves Hotham's open hostility to the treaty…. here, read it my girl. In Glemham's opinion, such as this will have been distributed throughout the north and if he's right then it doesn't bode well for the Royalist cause if you ask me."

After reading the pamphlet, Frances looked up.

"But if Lord Ferdinando Fairfax put his hand to the treaty of neutrality father, surely he did so on behalf of the Parliament and like as not, with their full knowledge. How then could any of their supporters go against it?"

Miles' brows rose with derision.

"There's the nub of it, my girl," he answered. "Hotham seems to make decisions without the need to confer with Lord Fairfax. If you ask me, those two just might be vying for control of Parliament's northern forces."

"So, it was Hotham's design all along, to attack Cawood?" Frances asked.

"Stands to reason. What other purpose could he have for sending his son out from Hull with five hundred horse and foot?"

"Whatever the reason Miles, tis all most disturbing…. I doubt I shall sleep easy in my bed henceforth," Elizabeth voiced ominously.

"That's why the gatehouse doors are to be kept closed from now on," Miles said with determination and Elizabeth's mouth dropped open.

"In all the years we've lived here, they have never been closed. They stand open to declare hospitality, Miles," she said.

"You'd be perfectly content to see an enemy raiding party ride directly up to the house then, Bess?" Miles asked and when her hand covered her mouth, added, "No I thought not."

"You believe they would dare to venture here?" Elizabeth eventually asked, a slight tremor in her voice.

"Bess, we are in the midst of a civil war, and this is a known royalist house. They just might be curious to know what we're doing here."

"We're not doing anything of interest to them, Miles. This is a family home after all, not a garrisoned castle like Cawood," Elizabeth said.

"Ah but they'll know who owns Haveringham and that I chose to raise a royalist regiment." Once more he delved within his doublet. "This nonsensical pamphlet of theirs states that all supporters of the King stand in peril of having revenue sequestered from their estates, unless.....they contribute to Parliament's war effort."

"Can they be serious?" Frances asked, snatching the paper from her father to scan it thoroughly.

"I dare say so, hence my decision regarding the gatehouse doors," Miles said pouring more wine. "I intend to have much of our wealth buried in the grounds. Lambert will prepare a coded map showing the location of assorted items, the said document then being hidden in a place known only to us."

Listening closely, Elizabeth's anxiety slowly began to be replaced by pride in a husband who had been compelled to take unusual precautions to ensure that both the family and the most precious of their possessions remain as safe as possible. The thought of a group of rebels paying an unsolicited visit to Haveringham Manor filled her with trepidation, but nevertheless she had a sudden desire to stand firmly alongside her husband in aught he thought best.

"You are content to have us pronounced 'malignant' then Miles?" Elizabeth asked tentatively. His head turned to look at his wife with a mixture of love and resignation.

"Malignant indeed.....I'll show 'em what loyalty to our King means, Bess. From this day the Benningford flag will be flown not only above the gatehouse, but moreover the house itself. There'll be no requirement to question my allegiance!" Then addressing Lambert at the back of the room, added, "See to it at once."

"Yes my Lord," the steward responded and left.

Watching his face steadily, Elizabeth gave a gentle smile and laid a hand on her husband's arm.

"You are determined in this, husband?" she asked and as Miles considered the elegant fingers resting lightly on his sleeve, he felt compelled to lift them to his lips with such passion that momentarily, Frances felt like an intruder and looked away.

"Beloved wife, I shall always stand for what is right and proper before God. These upstarts have chosen to rebel against an anointed King and that cannot and must not be tolerated. For all his faults, Charles Stuart is our monarch, and I will defend him to the end."

Tenderly, Elizabeth stroked Miles' face.

"Then even though I am fearful of what might come upon us, I am proud to stand beside you, husband."

Miles took her in his arms and kissed her openly, Frances turning away to saunter down the room toward the archways, just as Lambert reappeared.

"Pardon my Lord, but the flag is even now being raised above the house," he pronounced and as he drew back from Elizabeth, Miles enquired, "And the gatehouse doors?"

"Closed, my Lord, though before they were…..," Lambert faltered.

"Yes?"

"A messenger arrived outside, with a communication…..for the Viscountess," Lambert said holding out a letter, a broad smile at his lips.

Closing her bedchamber door, Frances sat beside the window, staring at John's familiar hand before breaking the seal and opening out the letter.

Shrewsbury – 11ᵗʰ October 1642

Beloved wife,

Tis eventide and the rain falls relentlessly. Tomorrow we are to make for

Bridgenorth and Kenilworth, though our progress may well be hindered by the state of the roads should this rain continue as it is. I determined to write to you of an amusing incident, knowing how it will make you smile. Prince Rupert and myself rode out recently searching for any sign of the enemy and came upon two farmers intending to sell a cartload of apples to the rebels. Rupert paid them handsomely for the fruit and loan of their clothing, bidding them wait for our return. Thus disguised, we went right into the heart of the enemy camp, selling apples. I dare not look at the Prince for fear of laughing and giving us away, but in the end, we sold the full load before returning to the farmers. Once back in our own clothes, Rupert bid the farmers to go into the camp and explain how they had just bought fruit from the hands of Prince Rupert and Lord Fitzherbert. My love, if I say that the Prince is a born actor, stooping to disguise his great height and speaking so well with a local accent, one should consider him a native. Even now I am smiling at the memory of his performance. Greet your father and Lady mother for me and inform the Earl that the Haveringham Troop continue to equip themselves with much bravery, remaining stout hearted in support of myself, Prince Rupert and of course, the King's great cause. My beloved, I urge you to believe how greatly you are missed and that I despise all those miles that so cruelly separate us. I often imagine being beside you in that most fortunate of beds that currently holds you alone, longing to taste again those sweet intimacies we partook of so often only weeks ago. Be assured, precious lady, that I will write again as soon as I am able, and my desire is to be able to return to Yorkshire 'ere long.

Pray for me sweet wife, as I do for you each and every day. Until I rest in your arms once more, I remain your most devoted husband,

John

Frances held the letter to her chest, tears infusing her eyes. How greatly she hoped that John would indeed soon be able to return to Yorkshire. The winter was fast approaching after all, with little chance to do battle, surely? That alone might afford chance for what she desired, a fleeting visit from the man she adored. Looking about the room everything looked exactly as it always had, the only thing missing being John himself. With a sigh, she refolded the letter and took it across to a dresser, opening a small casket on the top and placing it inside with several other missives from him.

'I must tell father the tale of the farmers with the apples, he'll certainly find it amusing,' she thought, darting from the room, giggling.

CHAPTER THIRTY-FIVE

Mid November 1642

Frances dashed forward holding out both hands.

"Ralph, tis good to see you. Please say John is with you?" she said glancing about the room, but of her husband, there was no sign., Ralph seemed less eager to meet her eye than he normally did, though when he kept glancing across the room toward Anne standing beside the seated Countess, fiddling with a kerchief, Frances wondered if, for once, he were keen to be alone with her.

"I take it your reluctance to answer means that he's still in the south with Rupert and you just dare not tell me?" she enquired. It certainly was disappointing to think of John being so far way, but Frances understood that his orders might differ from those afforded to Ralph. Nevertheless, she couldn't help wishing that it were John who had ventured north and not the grubby attired man before her. Strangely, Ralph still seemed reluctant to say anything and for some reason, Frances felt a surge of apprehension, her heart quickening as she stared into features that appeared decidedly weary.

"Where is he, Ralph?" she asked tentatively. With scowl, he seemed to prefer examining the mud splatters on his breeches and boots rather than answer and taking a step closer, Frances would have spoken again, had her father not grasped her arm.

"Child, heed me now……you must be prepared for what Ralph has to say," he said in soft tones that built Frances' anxiety to a pitch where she spun away, covering her ears with both hands. If she couldn't see Ralph or hear him, she'd be able to ignore what he would say.

"I'll not hear it…. I'll not, no I'll not….." she spluttered until Miles turned her by the shoulders.

"My precious girl, you must be brave," he urged, nodding once at Ralph to do what was necessary.

"Fran….." Ralph faltered, his frown deepening even more. "There's no easy way to say this, but……John…..John was slain in a bloody battle, some days ago."

Frances stared; wide eyed, unsure she had heard correctly. What he had said made no sense at all. Then a thought struck her, Ralph just might very well be up to his old tricks, acting out a part designed to tease. Of course, that was it. Ralph would know all about John's escapade with the Prince and the two farmers and this could be his perverse way of bettering that, despite the callous subject.

"Ah…. now I know what you're about, tis mere play acting and you're all part of it," Frances said encompassing her father, mother and even Anne with a grin. "What a fine jest, Lord Bynghame for them all to look so dour too? Now tell me the truth, where is John hiding….in the corridor perhaps, merely awaiting a signal to jump out and surprise me, eh?"

Ralph didn't even blink, staring her out with a stunned expression and pallor that, despite the grime on his face, seemed to blanch by the second. Could she seriously believe he could be so uncaring and deliberate? What kind of person would use such a sensitive topic only as the means to tease? The truth was that this was the most challenging task Ralph had ever had to undertake in his life.

'She'll hate me once she realises the truth of it…...'

"Fran, I would never be so cruel. Tis the truth I'm afraid, he is gone." He reached for her hand, but she snatched it away, narrowing her eyes.

"Then tis a mistake…..yes that's it, you are mistaken, Ralph Bynghame. Why I had a letter from John only recently…..the apples remember father, it made us all laugh, did it not?"

Miles's expression showed nothing but sorrow, as was that of the Countess, the kerchief now held firmly to her lips and Anne appeared to have tear-filled eyes. Frances' heart plummeted and returning to Ralph, a knot of something indescribable rose from deep within as she looked at him. Then with an anguished shriek, she pounded her fists against his broad chest.

"It's not true….it can't be…. he promised to return, he promised, promised…. promised…."

'Yes punish me if you must…. I'll take it for being the one to break your heart,' he thought, receiving every blow without flinching. Eventually spent, Frances grew still and fell against him. Gently, he enfolded her in his arms.

"Please hear me out, Fran…..please let me tell you…." he begged. His tone, so serious and composed, reached through her distress.

"Tell me then," she whimpered through trembling lips, tears trickling from her eyes. Tenderly, Ralph took her hands in his, tracing his thumbs across her knuckles.

"We took on the enemy in a great battle in Warwickshire some days ago now, Edgehill to be exact, close to a village by the name of Kineton. Under direct orders from Rupert, we charged the enemy, but John was unhorsed, surrounded, and set upon. He fought courageously of course…. you know his proficiency with sword and dagger…..killed several outright, but the odds were too great….." Glancing at the ceiling, Ralph licked across his dry lips in an attempt to dispel images he cared not to revisit. "I was in pursuit of the enemy cavalry but saw what happened, though there was little I could do…. I wheeled my mount as soon as I could, only to be set upon myself. All was confusion, the battle so fierce with deafening noise and choking smoke making one's eyes water. I could scarce make out where I was in relation to my own regiment, let alone……." He stopped mid-sentence, Frances' expression being one of incredulity, her eyes growing narrower by the second.

"You…..you left him……to die, alone?" she snarled.

'No, oh my God Fran no, no….'

The sharp response stung far more than any musket ball and Ralph visibly winced, forcing Miles to step in.

"Such callousness is totally unmerited daughter! In a battle there is scarce opportunity to look to oneself, let alone locate a single person in such chaos. John was well aware of the risks involved in warfare…..no one can be blamed for what has happened to him, least of all this man who has chosen to come north to inform you personally. Now cease accusing him at once!"

Frances lifted tear filled eyes to her father with a mixture of despair, pain, and incredulity. Never had he addressed her so mercilessly and yet somewhere deep within, Frances knew he was only being truthful. To be angry at Ralph really was a fruitless exercise, the blame needed to be laid where it truly belonged, at the enemy's door. Cruelly, if the Parliament had not rebelled against the King, then John would not have gone to war and if he'd not gone to war, then he would still be alive now and they would be living in Kent at Melton Abbey.

By the fireplace, Lady Elizabeth gave Anne's hand a gentle squeeze, then rose and made her way across the room to her daughter.

"Francesca, your father speaks wisely. No one is to blame for what happens in the midst of a battle where naught is ever certain. Do I not know the cruel results of warfare first hand?" This was a clear reference to Miles' injured leg; a legacy Elizabeth had never quite been able to accept.

With her mother thus involved, along with her father, a subjugated Frances turned back to Ralph. Now she looked at him properly, she noticed how dishevelled, drawn, weary and even emotional he appeared, even to the point where his eyes sparkled with undeniable moisture.

"Fran…..it gave me no pleasure to tell you…." Ralph said shaking his head. "I shall miss him too, you know."

A single tear dripped from his lower lashes, leaving a distinct blemish on what was already a very grubby buff coat over his doublet.

"Ralph," Frances voiced, lips quivering. Ralph enfolded her once more until she asked the one question he had feared.

"Did he…..did he suffer?"

Closing his eyes fleetingly, Ralph took a deep breath.

"I doubt he'd have known much at all, the assault on him was far too swift…." Ralph hated speaking untruthfully, but what else could he do, he could hardly be totally honest, could he?

"Then, for his swift end, I imagine I should be grateful," Frances said before doing something that took the young soldier completely by surprise. Reaching up, she planted a gentle kiss on Ralph's cheek. "Be at peace now, my Lord, for your duty is fully discharged…. I have been informed and there's an end to it…."

Feeling suddenly and inexplicably nauseous and battling emotions he dared not consider for long, Ralph watched Frances wander off down the Great Hall. Unwittingly, his fingers strayed briefly to the spot on his cheek so recently touched by her lips.

When she reached the window seat, Frances sat down leaning back against the wall, her face contorting and not only from grief. A spasm shot through her lower belly reminding her of the first heart-breaking discovery that very morning. Her 'courses' had once more arrived and now that Ralph had delivered the second blow of the day, it was obvious that her desire to bear John's child would now never happen.

"I take it Rupert gave you leave to come north, my boy?" Miles enquired.

"Aye, he was most magnanimous and greatly affected by John's death himself. I was present when the list of names was reviewed. The Prince was clearly shocked when the name 'Fitzherbert' was mentioned. Fortunately, Rupert required dispatches to be sent north, so I volunteered for the task. The Prince holds this family in highest regard I would say and bid me confer his personal condolences to you all."

Anne Bynghame sauntered up to Ralph, slipping an arm through his.

"You spoke with great courage and much gentleness, husband," she reassured and with a passing smile, Ralph kissed her head.

"Thank you, my dear," he said, gazing down into adoring green eyes, strangely wishing they were dark blue.

"When are you required to return?" Miles asked.

"Once I have received replies from Glemham and Newcastle....so perhaps in a couple of days' time. There is a great deal to be done following this first major encounter, we cannot afford to lose pace now."

"You think we were victorious in this battle then?" Miles asked and Ralph shrugged, blowing out his lips.

"Difficult to say for certain, my Lord but tis thought the King was marginally successful. Either way, it was the following morning before either side left the area. Lord Essex withdrew toward Warwick, leaving the road to London wide open. Rupert was champing at the bit to press on to take the capital."

"Sounds as if you're inferring that didn't happen?

"It didn't. Some of the King's closest advisers considered it far too risky and Rupert's fervour a tad excessive in the extreme," Ralph explained.

"Waste of a God given opportunity then, I'd have thought," Miles said, shaking his head.

"I think the Prince does himself little favour, my Lord. A number of the older generals consider him arrogant in the councils of war. You've met him, he can be outspoken and little disguises his contempt if he believes them in error. Despite all that, Rupert is a brilliant soldier and invariably his strategies and objectives prove sound."

"Aye well, one must forgive the impetuosity of youth, I suppose…." Miles responded.

Quietly beside Miles, Elizabeth asked, "How is the King…..following such tragic events, Ralph?"

"Said to be greatly shocked and traumatized by the spilling of so much English blood, Countess," Ralph answered, though his attention kept straying down the room to the waterfall of blue silk cascading from the window seat.

CHAPTER THIRTY-SIX

Mid November 1642

Encouraged by Anne Bynghame, a now visibly trembling, Elizabeth was led back to a seat beside the fireplace where she was given a glass of aqua vitae proffered by Lambert. Moving on, the Steward held out the tray to both Miles and Ralph, though when he would have taken a glass to Frances, the Earl forestalled him.

"Set it on the table for now Lambert, I'll take a glass to her myself in a moment," Miles said.

Following the customary bow, Lambert withdrew, taking up position at the back of the room, near enough to be on hand swiftly should he be required, but far enough away to allow privacy. Miles urged Ralph to accompany him further down the room, far away from the ladies.

"Now then, tell me the meat of it, my boy," he said.

"If I say it was worse than anything witnessed in the Low Countries, then you may understand just how appalling it was. It's the absolute carnage I can't seem to forget."

Miles knew exactly what the young Lord meant by that, images of the dead and horrifically wounded in Scotland having haunted him for many months following his return to Yorkshire several years back.

"Many slain?" Miles enquired cautiously.

"Initially, thought to be around the three thousand mark, but with so many grievously wounded, the final number may have increased considerably by now."

"Dear God."

"The names of Officers were still being added to the list when I left. John was already registered, I saw his name myself, along with that of my good friend, Anthony Portman," Ralph said sadly.

"Your outspoken, red-haired comrade who came here?"

Ralph nodded, a deep frown scarring his weary features at the memory of 'Portie' and his oft times, atrocious sense of wit and penchant for women.

"Felled by a cannon ball, along with five others behind on their horses; not pleasant to witness," Ralph explained.

Miles certainly had no need to be told the effects of cannon fire, the sights and sounds of battle all too imprinted upon his own memory. There were times even now when Miles woke sweating and breathless at vivid dreams engendered by the past. Now this younger man might very well suffer in the same manner, especially since he had seen not only his friend blown asunder, but moreover, John's pitiless end. Ralph took a sip of his drink, offering a wistful smile.

"Before the off, Jacob Astley was heard to recite a prayer that I shall never forget, as long as I live," he said. *'Lord, thou knowest how verie busy I shall be this day. If I forget thee.....do not thou forget me.'* "Poignant when one considers what occurred thereafter."

"Was Astley slain?" Miles enquired.

"No, he's safe, unlike many others. As night fell and both sides settled beside the field, neither wishing to be the first to leave, the pitiful screams of the wounded and dying echoed through the darkness. Some even pleaded to be shot, such was their plight. Despite their mournful wailings, few tended them, other than the scavengers stripping bodies of aught worth selling....." Ralph's undisguised revulsion could not be denied.

"You don't think John was amongst those merely wounded?" Miles suggested.

"I know he wasn't." Ralph shifted about and with a deep scowl, added, "I'll not speak of this to Frances, my Lord, but when John was dragged from his horse, despite fighting as desperately as he was able, he......he...." Faltering, Ralph felt the Earl's comforting hand on his shoulder.

"Go on...."

Ralph looked into the Earl's questioning eyes.

"It's the strangest thing my Lord and I've thought on it ever since, but I'd say John recognised the main assailant. He seemed to yell a name even as John lifted his hands to request quarter, but the rebel simply grabbed his hair and fired a pistol straight into his head, cheering when his body slumped to the ground. I just can't tell Frances what I saw, I simply can't."

Miles glanced down the hall.

"Oh, my poor girl.....No, I agree my boy, she must never know of this."

"Nor will she from my lips. It would change naught after all."

Silence fell between the two men, broken only by occasional whimpers from Lady Elizabeth and the ticking of the magnificent clock on a nearby table. After a while, Miles drained his glass.

"What of the Haveringham Troop?"

A smile at last spread across Ralph's haggard features.

"You'd be proud of them, my Lord. They fought with such courage, even after John had fallen. Sadly, four were slain. They were shaken by what happened to their Captain but mayhap they now realise the seriousness of what we're about when even the most hardened soldier succumbs."

"Redworth?"

"Safe and well. He guarded the cornet valiantly, despite every attempt by the rebels to seize it."

"It all seems incredible to think on," Miles mused, going to the table to refill his own and Ralph's glasses.

"Particularly when some of the noblest names in England were slain. George Stewart, Lord d'Aubigny, the Earl of Lindsey and the Earl of Foxborough," Ralph explained and handing over the now refilled glass, Miles' mouth dropped open.

"Tom Carlton, dead?" he asked.

"Aye," Ralph answered.

"Were his sons with him?"

"Aye both. Richard, the elder, gained permission from Prince Maurice to take his father's body back to Lymworth House for burial, it being no great distance from the battlefield." Reading the Earl's unspoken query he added, "John was buried in one of the grave-pits for the Officers, on the edge of the field."

"Ah, well that's something you may tell Frances then, I suppose," Miles conceded.

"Yes," Ralph said sipping on his drink. "A notable event relates to old Sir Edmund Verney, bearing the royal standard. He was set upon by the rebels, attempting to seize the standard and though he tried to fight them off, dispatching some with the pole itself, he was unable to maintain it. He was finally felled and to gain the standard, the rogues hacked off his hand."

"Devils," Miles snarled.

"Eventually, the hand was found, still gripping the fragments of the pole, a ring bearing a portrait of the King on it, proving the discovery to be Verney's."

"And all just to gain the standard?" Miles said shaking his head.

"The rebels didn't crow over it for long, my Lord. One of Rupert's own, Captain Smith, rode after them and took it back. When the King was told, Smith was knighted for daring and loyalty."

"And rightly so," Miles nodded.

"The next day we stumbled upon a piece of intrigue that I think you may find fascinating," Ralph said, taking another swallow of aqua vitae. "Essex chose to leave the area first, so a number of us rode after him to attack his rear guard. We seized the baggage and in one of the boxes was a disturbing dispatch addressed to Essex from none other than Blake….." Ralph paused, watching incredulity spread up Miles' face.

"Blake? What, Rupert's secretary?" he eventually asked.

"Yes indeed. It turns out Blake had been spying for Essex for some considerable time. The document not only disclosed a great deal of information regarding Royalist movements, but actually sought greater financial reward for continued intelligence. God knows how much information Blake had already passed to the rebels."

"The despicable cur. When you think how often he will have been in Rupert's confidence," Miles said. Disloyalty of any kind was abhorrent to him, and this man Blake had obviously crossed a definite line where the Prince was concerned. "I dare say Rupert dealt with him swiftly?"

"Aye, Blake was hanged at Carfax Crossroads once we were back in Oxford. I would say that Rupert was seriously affected by a turn of events no one could have envisaged. He's hardly likely to be in a hurry to confide in anyone henceforth, after such a betrayal of trust," Ralph said.

"Well, perhaps that's for the best," Miles said but when Ralph stifled a yawn, raking back his hair in an attempt to disguise it, he added, "Are you quite well, my boy?"

Anyone could see the strain on Ralph's face, both eyes ringed by dark shadows.

"Oh, there's naught wrong with me that a comfortable bed and a decent night's sleep won't sort, my Lord," Ralph responded taking another glance down the hall.

'What have I done to her?' he thought.

CHAPTER – THIRTY-SEVEN

Mid November 1642

Frances turned her head when her father approached, carrying a glass of tawny liquid.

"Drink this daughter," he urged.

"Father…. I just want John…."

Dropping from the seat, her face crumpled, and she threw herself against him, knocking the glass from his hand where it fell to the ground shattering into several fragments, tawny liquid staining the floorboards. Miles held her tightly, resting his head on hers, helpless to say or do anything to ease her pain. At her most vulnerable, there was absolutely nothing anyone could do to alter it. Time would bring some relief of course, but Miles knew that the suddenness of hearing such unwelcome news was bound to have an adverse effect upon Frances for some considerable time. Her grief when Robin had been taken so unexpectedly had been bad enough and Miles had then been able to gain the consolation of John's presence for her. This time, he despaired as to just who might be able to offer her the depth of comfort she would need. With relief, he heard Ralph trudging slowly toward them.

"Fran is there anything I can do to help you, anything at all…. speak it, no matter how big or small…. it shall be done," he said and when her head lifted, he thought, '*My God she looks so pale….*'

Frances tried her best to focus, conscious of a strange humming sensation reverberating through her head that seemed to grow louder. Then everything swam before her eyes, her legs buckled, and blackness overwhelmed her. Sensing at once, Ralph caught her, hoisting her in his arms.

"Frances!" Elizabeth screamed, leaping to her feet.

"She's fainted Bess that's all; Ralph has her," Miles assured, then to Ralph. "Take her up, my boy."

As he watched his ashen faced daughter being carried toward the staircase, Miles decided the only practical thing he could do now was send to York for the surgeon which he instructed Lambert to arrange at once.

Progress up the staircase proved tortuous to Ralph, a sense of hopelessness almost overwhelming him as his eyes continually dropped to the limp form laid across his arms. Her skin was so pale, almost porcelain in quality and yet her beauty remained constant, reaching to his very soul.

'Dearest heart,' he thought, briefly touching his lips to her forehead. She moaned softly as he continued along the corridor and into the bedchamber she had occupied before her marriage, gently placing her on the bed, stroking back a portion of tear dampened hair stuck to her cheek. Gradually with a sigh, her eyes flickered open, widening when she noticed him so close.

"What are you about, Ralph?" she gasped, trying to sit up with a grimace, one hand to her head.

"No, no…. don't be alarmed," he said. "Lay back on the pillow…. there was a strand of hair, I merely brushed it aside…. you fainted and I was told to bring you to your room."

Slowly Frances took in her surroundings, the curtains, the furniture, the bed and even the curved window.

"I don't belong in here…. this isn't my bedchamber now…." She gasped, breathing so rapidly that Ralph feared she might swoon again.

"Calm yourself, Fran…. where would you prefer to be?" he asked, taken aback when she looked at him with an expression close to loathing.

"Where do you think….in the room he and I shared, there to mourn my husband for as long as I choose."

Her hands covered her face as a fit of sobbing overtook her once more. Without speaking, Ralph lifted her from the bed and as her head fell against his, he felt the sensation of her tears trickling down the side of his neck, onto his collar. In the corridor, they were confronted by a worried looking Countess, Martha alongside her continually stirring the contents of a goblet.

"No Ralph, you were in the right place, take her back," Elizabeth said and only then did Frances raise her head.

"I have no desire to be in my old room as if John never existed mother, I want to be in my marriage bed, nowhere else." Her head dropped back against Ralph's shoulder causing him to swallow deeply. Her close proximity, the warmth of her body and intoxicating perfume, proving a challenge.

"I thought only to save you more sorrow, daughter," Elizabeth answered, eagerly wanting Frances to understand she meant no harm. When Frances' head lifted once more, her expression was one of annoyance.

"Then please stop thinking for me mother. I am no longer a child, but a woman grown, a wife and now…. a widow and will deal with my personal grief in any manner I choose."

Then to Ralph, "Carry me in Ralph, please."

Smiling apologetically at the Countess, the young Lord bore his charge in through the open door, depositing her on the large four poster bed, stepping back to watch her.

Looking up at the tester above, Frances could not escape the memories engendered by its ornate expanse. If only it could speak, what tales it would have to relate of a couple totally in love, rolling about on the coverlet, laughing, caressing, teasing and finally making love to one another. Now the man she adored and married with such hope for a long and happy future together, lay cold and decaying in the ground in Warwickshire, so far from Yorkshire.

"He'll never again share this bed with me…." she murmured, and Ralph heard.

"Don't torment yourself, Fran," he said as Elizabeth took the goblet from Martha.

"Drink this daughter, tis to make you sleep," she said.

"Will you leave me alone if I drink it?" Frances asked.

The Countess glanced at Ralph, who nodded approvingly.

"Very well, but only if you drink it all…. before I leave," Elizabeth urged.

Sitting upright, Frances took the goblet from Martha and swallowed the obnoxious tasting contents, handing back the empty cup.

"There, now you can all leave me to reflect upon my…. dead husband." Her voice caught and Ralph wished he could sit beside her on the bed and take her hand, though instinct prevented him.

"Don't speak so, daughter…." Elizabeth said and Frances laughed unconvincingly.

"How else do I speak of him, mother…. he's dead, as dead as my brother out there in the cold ground…. there's naught more to say."

Elizabeth made to answer, though Ralph beat her to it.

"Fran, if you wish to be alone, that's fine but I intend to place a chair outside in the corridor, where I will sit as long as I must, in case you have need of anything."

"Do as you wish…." Frances said, rolling onto her side, away from him.

"Lady Elizabeth, she'll come to no harm if I sit out there," Ralph said, encouraging the two women to the door, picking up a chair in the process, glancing back once before closing the door.

Alone, Frances sat up, hugging her knees. Then she spotted it, a tiny pinkish hued object, almost hidden behind the dresser. Dropping from the bed, she stooped to retrieve it, settling it on her palm. The edges were curled and tinged with brown, but it was obvious what it was. A rose petal, one of the many that had been strewn across the bed covers on her wedding night. Briefly Frances wondered how it had escaped being cleared up by the servants, as the others must have been. Her hand closed over it and as she sank to the floor, she rocked herself back and forth in a wave of agony.

"John… my love." Tears began again coursing down her face, grief once more swathing her in its inhumane grip, building to such a pitch where it could not be held back. Throwing back her head, she produced an agonised, piercing scream and instantly the door flew open. Seeing her on the floor, Ralph rushed to her side, cradling her in his arms until eventually she grew calmer.

"How am I to survive without him, Ralph…...?" she sobbed, trying to focus on his face, her speech becoming slurred as the herbal remedy began its soporific duty. Hoisting her from the floor, Ralph set Frances back on the bed, this time making sure to draw the coverlet over her. Try as she might to fight the effects of the potion, Frances could not keep her eyes open.

"Hush now, lest your heart break; time will bring healing, my sweet, but for now I am here whenever you need me," Ralph whispered, unsure whether she had heard or not.

'If only you would allow my love to comfort you....' he thought, her eyes finally fluttering closed, her breathing much shallower and far more rhythmical.

CHAPTER THIRTY-EIGHT

Mid November 1642

A few days' later, reclining on the window seat, Frances absently watched her father, Ralph, and Lambert out in the courtyard. Her eyes felt prickly and sore from constant bouts of weeping, triggered by the simplest of things. Gradually she was beginning to realise that her beloved John would never now return and that somehow, she would have to find a way of picking up the pieces of a life without him, but how when she felt so forlorn?

Her interest mounted when one of the gatehouse doors unexpectedly opened and a single horseman rode in, dropping from the saddle beside the three men. Ultimately, rifling in the bag slung across his body, he handed a package to Ralph.

'Probably the messages you've been waiting for,' she thought absently.

Thinking little more of it, she noticed Ralph pass something to Lambert who made his way back into the house and entering the Great Hall.

"Sorry to disturb, Lady Frances, but this has just come, for you," he said walking toward her holding out what appeared to be a letter. Dropping from the window seat, she wandered nearer, black skirts rustling with every step.

"Who…..who is it from?" she asked tentatively. In reality, she really hoped it would not be from John, penned just prior to the cruel battle that was to claim him. Lambert smiled as the letter was turned over to display an impressive scarlet seal.

"Prince Rupert writes to me?" she asked with surprise.

"By his direct order, so the messenger said to Lord Bynghame," Lambert replied.

Hesitantly, she reached for the letter, crossing to the fireplace where she sat down, conscious of Lambert waiting. "See that the messenger is offered food, ale and perhaps a place to rest for the night?" she said.

"Already offered milady, though he is unable to tarry. His desire is to reach York before nightfall with urgent dispatches for the Earl of Newcastle."

"Ah, yes of course, Newcastle regards York as his headquarters now, so it stands to reason he will receive and send out many dispatches, I suppose. Very well Lambert, that will be all, you may resume your duties."

Frances felt staggered to think of Prince Rupert taking time out from his busy schedule to write to her personally and was keen to see if the letter included the reason why. There really was only one way to find out, though for some time she could only marvel at the flamboyant manner in which her name was penned on the front. With a shrug, she turned it over, breaking the seal and unfolding the paper. Reasonably brief and concisely written, the letter bore the Princes' unmistakable flourished signature at its foot.

Brentford - November 1642

Madam
I write to express personal sorrow following Lord Fitzherbert's unexpected demise in Warwickshire. Know you this, your husband entered our endeavours with utmost valour and bravery, his commitment and loyalty to the King's cause and to myself unrelenting to the end. Your grief must be testing to say the least, for which I confess you have my heartfelt condolences. Were it possible, I would choose to convey these sentiments in person, but due to the number of pressing obligations besetting me daily, it cannot be.
The morrow will see me attacking the town of Brentford, providential fog in the area being used to my advantage. By the time this missive reaches you, by God's good graces, I shall be triumphant here.
I send greetings to the Earl and Countess, pray tell them their hospitality is oft recalled with much pleasure and gratitude.
Be assured Madam, I remain your humble servant and friend,
Rupert

Briefly, Frances was back in the walled garden on the morning of her marriage, sitting beside the casually attired young royal, pleading that he might look out for John in battle. How foolish and immature she had been then and yet for Rupert to pen these words to her personally, might he too have recalled that very conversation? Re-folding the letter, she rose and went up to her bedchamber, placing it inside the casket on top of John's final letter.

When Frances returned to the Great Hall, Ralph was sitting at the table, his head bent over an open letter, brow deeply furrowed.

"Do I disturb you?" she asked wandering closer.

He looked up, quickly folded the missive, and tucked it inside his doublet.

"No, not at all. Come here," he said standing up and opening his arms. Nestling against him felt comforting and Frances finally asked, "When are you leaving, Ralph?"

"In the morning, early," he said, retaining her hand.

"So soon?"

"I must. Sounds as if I've already missed out on serious action at Brentford. I too had a letter from Rupert," he explained, tapping the front of his doublet.

"I am astounded that he found time to write to me personally," Frances said, running her fingertips along the table top. "He spoke of John's bravery…."

"Tis true Fran, John was a truly fearless soldier," Ralph said, and Frances gave what sounded like an insincere snort.

"Ah, wasn't he just…. brave, fearless and…..now dead."

Frances realised her words sounded more than a little caustic,

Ralph's stunned expression confirmed it when she looked up, but she wasn't about to deny her own emotions either.

Releasing her hand, Ralph wandered across to the fireplace, resting one foot on the hearth, a hand on the mantle shelf above. He had hoped that the last couple of days might have enabled Frances to start coming to terms with John's death, but the outburst just now proved that she had not. Ralph was no fool, he knew she would be going through the stages of grief, anger being just one of them.

"John would want to be remembered as fighting bravely for a cause close to his heart, Fran," he said quietly.

"So close to his heart that I am now left widowed, whether I wished to be or nay. Oh yes, John was *'a valiant knight…. slain under his shield'……* the words of The Three Ravens, seem so relevant, don't you think?"

Unsmiling, Ralph turned his head to briefly glance at her.

"What foolishness you speak at times. In no way does your situation resemble the tale in that song," he said. Seeing the acerbic glare she offered, he braced himself for yet another reprimand.

"No, you're right, for I was unable to…… *'kiss his wounds…'* Do you realise Ralph, that John was dead for nigh on two weeks…..and I never knew….."

With an elongated sigh, Ralph's head fell forward.

"We are at war Fran, I came as swiftly as I could to tell you," he said steadily, staring up at the ceiling as if pleading for divine intervention. A rush of panic unexpectedly struck her, and Frances rushed up to him, making a grab for his hand.

"Ralph, I'm sorry…. truly I am. I suppose I feel so distraught because I haven't had chance to see him buried. If only he could have been brought here and placed next to Robin in the churchyard…..I would then have had one place to mourn them both."

Ralph turned and dropped his hands onto her shoulders, trying to read her mood from the frantic eyes meeting his. To Frances the notion seemed a simple one and yet the reality was that such an enterprise would be nigh on impossible to achieve.

"Fran if he had been taken anywhere, it would have been Melton Abbey, to lie with his ancestors, not here to Haveringham, that you must accept. In the event, Edgehill was too far from Kent for that to happen."

"Then tell me, do you know exactly where he lies?" she asked.

"In a grave dug for Officers, at the edge of the field. His name was recorded as one of the slain, so never doubt it Fran."

Ralph had been at pains to carefully tell her of John's final resting place, a mass grave in Warwickshire and though it would sadden Frances to think she would never be able to look upon the actual site, at least he was certain the Earl would approve of this information being imparted. She looked so innocent and hurt, so much so that he abruptly dropped his hands from her shoulders and wandered across to the window, his mind in turmoil.

Curiosity took hold of Frances as she watched his anxious profile. It looked as if he was struggling with something and fearing what that might be, she rushed up to him, pulling him round to face her.

"What are you holding back from me?" she demanded, and irritation spread over Ralph's features.

"Don't press me Fran. I was wounded myself you know. Do you want me to show you my arm still bearing the dressing put on by the surgeon? Do you? I can do so if you wish…." He began unbuttoning the front of his doublet, but she stayed his hand.

"No Ralph, don't," she admitted with a frown.

Silence fell between them for some considerable time until at last he spoke, very softly as if he weren't present in the room anymore.

"The carnage has affected me more than I care to admit…. all those bodies….men and horses in pieces….gore and blood everywhere….the unspeakable effects of warfare….."

Frances' hand flew to her mouth, stifling a gasp, a sound that brought Ralph back to his senses.

"What do you mean in pieces?" she eventually asked but he merely shrugged.

"Can you be serious?" he said through narrowed eyes. "For pity's sake woman, don't force me to relate sights that even now plague my dreams each night. Do you really not comprehend the effect swords, pole axes, pike, shot, and cannon balls have upon human flesh? Do you really desire me to describe exactly what I saw that day?"

Accompanied by a deep scowl, he ran one hand through his long hair, drawing it backwards, disturbed to see that she had grown pale, and her eyes sparkled with unshed tears. Gently, he wrapped his arms around her.

"I do not speak of John, you know," he admitted and reaching for her chin, tilted her head upward. "Your grief is significant at the moment, which is perfectly understandable, but time will bring healing. One day you will be able to recall the love you and John shared with fondness. To love, even for such a brief time, is something to be envied, you know."

Scepticism instantly returned to Frances. Could he really be so blasé in that view? Taking several steps backward, she glowered.

"Envied? How can you say such a thing? I am nineteen years old and after but two short months, I am separated forever from the only man I am likely to love," she said, and he winced. "You cannot comprehend how I feel Ralph Bynghame, so don't you dare speak to me of time healing……it won't, it just won't." She turned to leave, but unexpectedly swung back. "Your wife is here Ralph…. go to her and show her this 'love' you speak of so freely.

She is the one to be envied, for you are still living, not dead somewhere on a battlefield in the south!"

In a flurry of rustling black silk, she fled, bolting up the staircase leaving Ralph to return to the fireplace where he dropped onto a chair and cradled his head in his hands, tendrils of brown hair filtering through his fingers.

"Fran, Fran, Fran….." he murmured.

CHAPTER THIRTY-NINE

Late Autumn 1642

Long before reaching the river Ouse, Frances had managed to evade the escort her father had insisted she have with her, on a brief and much longed for, horse-ride.

Walter Hawkins had eventually returned to Haveringham after losing part of an arm in the September encounter with the rebels at Powick Bridge and though still recovering, he was perfectly able to sit a horse, therefore Miles had instructed him to accompany his daughter. The days had dragged for Frances, ever since Ralph's departure for Oxford, a letter having arrived from him after almost four weeks, confirming he remained unscathed and safe, despite the long journey south. Frances felt frustrated and almost entombed, so seeking out her father, she had begged to be allowed to saddle Phoenix and take her for a gallop. Reluctantly, Miles had agreed with the provision of Walter being with her.

Glancing behind, Frances saw that Phoenix' speed had made it possible to leave Walter far behind and urging the mare onward, she eventually reached the river at Poppleton where the ferryman considered her suspiciously. Frances made it clear that she had little desire for conversation of any kind, her only wish to reach the opposite bank, nothing more. In that respect, she took out a small purse paying him not only the fee, but a little extra. On the opposite side, without a word, the ferryman assisted her back into the saddle and soon she was cantering off toward the village of Long Marston. She had intended to visit the little church for a time of quiet reflection, but halfway there, she changed her mind and turned Phoenix right along a narrow dirt track meandering across the vast open moorland toward the village of Tockwith. Everywhere seemed quiet and still and urging her mare to the gallop, Frances easily cleared a fallen tree, riding on until eventually she reined in. Dropping from the saddle, she walked Phoenix over to a large log, obviously part of another fallen tree, where she could sit for a while. The whole expanse of Marston

Moor, known as Hessey Moor by locals, looked magnificent in the various autumnal hues ornamenting its vista. This place had always been close to her heart, and she loved riding across the unspoiled moorland despite the memories it now engendered of both Robin and John. The wide ditch caught her attention, scarring the landscape for some distance, recalling the rebuke she had received from her brother when she had set Phoenix to jump it. To the right in the distance, she could see smoke rising from the chimneys of the buildings in Tockwith, weaving and swirling in strange configurations as it was drawn up into the leaden afternoon sky. She had ridden there only a few weeks back with John at her side, the reminder increasing the acute ache in her heart. John and Robin; two men she had loved in differing ways, both now unbearably gone. She certainly had not intended to become emotional and yet this place seemed to make her so. Her breathing quickened and before she knew it, she was on her feet screaming until the pain in her throat stopped her. Sinking to her knees she wept until something warm and soft nudged against her. Phoenix, her placid mare had wandered closer and with a soft whinny, touched her again with her velvet soft nose. Standing up, Frances draped her arms around the chestnut's neck, looking into long lashed brown eyes that seemed to exude reassurance.

"I'm fine, my girl," Frances said, planting a kiss on Phoenix' nose before looking up at the sky. "I think we'd better head back. It'll be growing dark soon and I dare say father will be furious when he discovers what I've done."

Using the fallen tree to mount up, she turned Phoenix several times, looking across Marston Moor with fondness before heading back toward the ferry at Poppleton.

The light was fading when eventually Frances reached Haveringham Manor. Miles stood beside one of the now open gatehouse doors, a lighted lantern in one hand.

"In God's name girl…..where've you been? Your mother's half demented with worry."

"I'm sorry father, I needed some time alone," Frances said, dropping from the saddle to lead Phoenix forward into the courtyard.

"Walter came back saying you'd ridden off at speed and he'd lost you. He was told severely to get back out there and search for you. Did you not see him?"

"I did not, father."

Miles grunted and scowled.

"Jake's in the stables saddling my horse, not that I felt inclined to venture out in this cold, you know how it adversely affects my leg. He spotted a body of riders earlier at the other side of the village….. good grief girl if they'd intercepted you?"

"I saw no one at all, father." Frances patted Phoenix neck to keep from looking at Miles' angry expression. Thankfully, Jake chose that moment to lead out Miles' horse.

"Take him back Jake and Lady Frances' mare, now this… wanton is returned," Miles instructed, curtly.

Frances could not miss the shake of the head Old Jake gave when he reached for Phoenix' reins.

"She'll need a good rub down, then feeding and watering," Frances said, the instant recipient of what clearly was irritation.

"I knows just 'ow 'ta look after 'er… God knows I've done it long enough," Jake said, then to the Earl. "What of Walter, Milord, should I head out to look for 'im?"

"That won't be necessary Jake. I told him to come back before dark, even if he didn't locate this… this one! When he does, tell him to go straight round to the kitchen for some food and a tankard or two, he's earned it."

Jake led both horses toward the stable, muttering to himself all the while. All he had wanted to do after completing his duties that day was to be seated before a blazing fire in his cottage but now it would be some time before he was free to do so.

"Do you see now just what you've caused?" Miles demanded, firmly gripping Frances' arm as he led her toward the house. "I'd not put it past the rebels to accost anyone out there unaccompanied, particularly a lone woman! For heaven's sake, what were you thinking? I am displeased Frances, most displeased."

"Please don't chide so, father. I needed some time to myself, and I swear I saw no one though I think the ferryman might have….."

Her eyes widened with fear at the depth of fury spreading across her father's face.

"Are you saying you've been across the Ouse?"

Frances tried to force a smile, failing miserably.

"I…..I only thought to visit Long Marston church, father…. I….."

"By God Madam, you're fortunate that I don't take a switch to your backside for this. We have our own church here in the grounds, why the need to visit Long Marston?"

"Because I couldn't bear the memory of where I was married…..besides, the Moor is one of my favourite places to ride…."

"Have you lost your wits, Madam, anything could have happened to you up on that moor; inside with you, at once!"

Sleep proved difficult to achieve that night even though Frances felt exhausted. She'd been admonished even more strongly by her father and her mother expressed her displeasure and dismay at what to her seemed a lack of common sense. Their evening meal had proved awkward, containing prolonged periods of silence and annoyed glances from both parents and Frances had been glad to escape to the relative peace of her chamber.

Turning on her side, she ran one hand over the pillow previously used by John. In a dreamlike state, half-sleeping, half-awake she imagined herself in his arms, responding to his kisses and caresses until reality hit once more and she sobbed. Then it happened, a sudden and inexplicable noise made her look at the foot of the bed. John stood there, smiling in the warming way he always had, sweeping off his hat with a flourish as his lips spread into a broad grin.

'Beloved wife, cease weeping for me. All shall be well, remember now…..all shall be well.'

Sitting bolt upright, breathing heavily, and feeling her heart beating so rapidly, she feared it might burst, Frances stared at the now empty void. What had just happened, a dream perhaps or just wishful thinking on her part? Had sleep claimed her without her realising?

Dropping back against the pillow, she stared continually at the tester above, until her heart ceased to beat quite so fast.

'What had he said that I am no longer to grieve for him? Should I then accept that I no longer have a husband? 'All shall be well'…..how many times had John voiced that when he was alive and now in death she felt strongly as if he were repeating it forcefully this time in an attempt to make her understand.'

For some time, Frances lay awake thinking through what she should do to try to reclaim some form of normality to her life.

'I'll start on the morrow and speak to father about the financial implications of my widowhood,' she thought turning onto her side. Hitherto Frances had refused to even think about such things and Miles had complied with that, believing that time would bring her to that stage when it was right. The jointure agreed at the time of

her betrothal to John Fitzherbert would provide Frances with a considerable annual income that much she already knew, but just how much was yet to be explained to her. In addition, a comforting thought was that she would now be staying in Yorkshire, indefinitely.

CHAPTER FORTY

February 1643

News being sketchy, Sir Thomas Glemham, York's Governor, dropped by occasionally to Haveringham Manor, not only to see his old friend and comrade Miles, but to update him with news of skirmishes in the localities of Leeds, Tadcaster and Selby. Invariably these involved Ferdinando Fairfax and one of his sons, Thomas. Miles scathingly described them as 'like wasps during the late summer,' annoying and difficult to get rid of! In reality though, Miles experienced a measure of regret at the exploits of Tom Fairfax, having served with him in the war against the Scots. That campaign had seen Tom Fairfax ultimately knighted by the very King he now seemed perfectly willing to draw swords against and that rankled.

In early December, a letter arrived from John's younger brother, William, not only to enquire after Frances' welfare, but to relate even more ill tidings besetting the Fitzherbert family. Edward, the Earl of Melton had taken the demise of his elder son very badly and having gone out riding one day, had failed to return. Search parties eventually located the bodies of both Edward and his horse. It appeared that the Earl had set his mount to a particularly large hedge unaware of a huge drop at the far side. The horse must have toppled on landing, falling awkwardly, and breaking its neck, rolling on top of its rider, killing him outright. When found, Edward's body was transported back to Melton Abbey to be interred in the family vault alongside many ancestors, John's brother William then inheriting the title of Earl. His mother, Catherine, had thereafter 'run mad' with grief after losing both her elder son and husband in a matter of months, being forced, ever since, to receive constant care to prevent her from harming herself in some way. The level of grief and devastation presented to both families by the one battle at Edgehill, was unthinkable and Frances felt such empathy.

No one felt much like celebrating Christmas and it proved to be a definite subdued affair. It was decided that the usual extravagant manner in which the season was celebrated at Haveringham Manor would be wholly inappropriate in the circumstances, though the servants were allowed to hold a small gathering in the servant's hall, courtesy of the Earl. Miles somehow managed to procure small gifts for his close family, a gold and sapphire bracelet for Elizabeth, a small brooch studded with pearls for Frances and a beautifully engraved, leather bound book of Shakespeare's sonnets for Anne. During those long winter months, the consensus of opinion seemed to be that hopes would be high for the royalist cause as the old year concluded and the spring campaign season of 1643 began.

One particularly chilly February day when Anne Bynghame and Frances were both seated beside the fire reading, Elizabeth sauntered across to one of the Great Hall's large windows.

"Ah, it looks as if we have more visitors," she remarked casually, and Frances snapped her book closed.

"Oh, not again, do we really have to endure the opinions of these men from York when most aren't even involved in the fighting?" she wailed.

Elizabeth turned about with a scowl.

"Don't be so intolerant, Frances. We cannot turn visitors away simply because......"

"Because your widowed daughter doesn't wish to listen to their ramblings....no, heaven forbid."

"Francesca do not speak to me in that manner," the Countess declared.

Rising, Frances deposited the book on a table, immediately dipping a curtsey.

"Lady mother, I humbly beg your pardon," she voiced quietly.

Elizabeth wandered closer, primping the lace at her elbows.

"We have all made allowances for you Frances, knowing how greatly you have suffered, but nevertheless, your father's business has to continue and if that involves receiving visitors, then we must too, with respect… no matter their opinions."

"I understand mother, but may I not be excused? Some of them do speak….. with little astuteness, you know."

Elizabeth had to stifle a smile.

"Yes dear, that is exactly what I have believed myself for many a long year."

"Then I'll not be missed, surely……" Without waiting for permission, Frances started down the hall, barely reaching the archway nearest to the staircase when the influx of manly voices made escape virtually impossible.

"Ah, daughter, where are you going?" Miles enquired and closing her eyes, Frances fixed a smile to her lips before turning round.

"I feel a little weary, father. I beg leave to be allowed to go to my bedchamber to rest?"

"Nonsense, all you need is a little company. Come and greet our visitors," Miles said with a grin as he wandered into the Great Hall, six men following behind and Frances slowly retraced her steps to stand beside her mother and Anne.

"Now Bess, I dare say it's not necessary, but surely you remember our visit to Derbyshire in '34 and the masque staged for the King?" Miles said and Elizabeth's face lit up as she extended her hand toward the elegantly attired man at his side.

"Who could forget 'Love's Welcome to Bolsover,' such a unique performance. Welcome to Haveringham Manor, my Lord. I trust you will find our residence to your liking?"

"My dear Lady Elizabeth, who would not?" he said glancing

around. "I'd say it bears all the hallmarks of Robert Smithson's handiwork?"

"Correct William," Miles said. "My late father insisted on the services of old Queen Bess's master mason, to design and build it."

"A fine job he made of it too," William remarked whilst removing a pair of ornately embroidered gloves that perfectly complimented the blue doublet and cloak, all braided with silver.

"Allow me to make formal introductions, William. My wife you already know, but this is my daughter Frances Fitzherbert, Viscountess Haveringham and beside her stands Lady Anne Bynghame, wife to Lord Ralph Bynghame of Cumberland. Ladies, I present William Cavendish, the Earl of Newcastle."

Frances remembered her parents visiting the Earl's home years ago and her mother extolling the virtues of someone she described as the most handsome of men. Now as the very man stood before them, Frances recalled her father telling of Cavendish's penchant for training horses in a purpose-built structure on his estate of Bolsover Castle. How greatly she had wished to see them herself at that time.

"Viscountess," Newcastle bowed, "I believe you were lately married…?"

"And widowed in less than three months," Frances interrupted aware of the sharp gasp coming from her mother. Realising the mistake, Frances dropped her gaze.

"As I would have added……given the opportunity," Newcastle declared stalwartly, with no hint of animosity. "Lord Fitzherbert was a man of great courage, Madam."

Frances head shot up and her eyes grew wide.

"You perhaps saw him at Edgehill?" she asked hopefully.

"No, no, you misunderstand me, Viscountess. My remark relates more to what I learned of his daring at Powick Bridge; straight in the saddle behind Prince Rupert, so I was informed." Newcastle noticed Frances constantly twirling a ring on her right hand. "Tell me Viscountess, what age are you?"

"Nineteen," she said so softly that Newcastle barely heard. Reaching for her chin, he tilted her head upward.

"What sorrows are afflicted upon England where women are widowed at such a tender age, eh?" he remarked.

"I never desired to be widowed, my Lord," Frances voiced openly, conscious of her father's displeasure.

'Well, well, we've got a plucky one here…. I quite like that,' Newcastle thought.

"I regret to say, but before this conflict is done, many more may find themselves in your…..unhappy situation," he admitted.

"Frances," Miles said, with a cough of irritation that she comprehended at once.

"My Lord Earl, I beg your pardon if I sounded a little unmannerly…. the death of my husband still distresses me," she said softly.

The Derbyshire Earl simply lifted her hand to plant a kiss upon it.

"Hardly surprising, my dear. Have no concerns, your impassioned speech merely proves the level of affection you felt for Lord Fitzherbert."

Despite every attempt to prevent them, tears sprang instantly to Frances eyes, and her lip quivered. Thankfully, her mother had the sense to deflect an awkward moment.

"Might we offer you and your men refreshments, my Lord?" she asked brightly.

"That would be most acceptable, Lady Benningford, though first allow me to make my companions known to you. From the left Sir Frances Mackworth, Captains Fleetwood, Frost and Hemmings and at the far end, Lieutenant General, George Goring."

The Countess allowed a pleasing smile to encompass each man in turn, accepting their bows with a gracious nod of the head.

"General Goring has only lately returned from Holland," Newcastle explained.

"Oh, were you with Her Majesty, General?" Elizabeth enquired.

"I was Countess, for a time but on my return, I was able to bring a considerable amount of munitions back with me for the cause," Goring responded with an air of confident arrogance that somehow seemed to intrigue and repel Frances in equal measure. His eyes briefly captured hers and surprisingly, she felt a blush creeping up her cheeks but when Moll Gilbert carried in bottles, jugs, tankards, and goblets, setting them on the table, he seemed to find what she was about of greater interest. Frances felt unenthusiastic at joining them at the table and wandered across to the fireplace instead.

"Will you require quarters for the night, my Lord?" she heard Elizabeth enquire.

"Unnecessary Lady Benningford, we are required back in York before nightfall, but you have my thanks for the offer," Newcastle smiled.

"I understand from Glemham, that you'll be replacing Cumberland as Commander in Chief of the King's northern forces, William," Miles said, leaning back on his chair, interlinking his fingers.

"By His Majesty's direct command, I am," Newcastle replied.

"Cumberland taking on that role never did sit easy with me," Miles said. "That's one reason I sent a small body of cavalry straight to Rupert, with my late son-in-law."

At the fleeting mention of her husband, Frances' head turned. It seemed as if her father had chosen to speak almost dispassionately about the man she had adored and yet perhaps she was being oversensitive, after all he hadn't actually said anything derogatory.

"Ah, Cumberland was none too happy with you doing that, Miles. He wrote to me at length of his disapproval, though I was at pains to remind him that Fitzherbert's commission was with the Palatine and therefore it stood to reason."

"All academic now anyhow, William. Lord Bynghame wrote of the Haveringham Troop being broken up and deployed in other regiments," Miles added.

"I think there were a number of major overhauls to various regiments after the losses at Kineton fight," Newcastle said.

Frances frowned, stroking an angelic being carved upon the fireplace.

'Whatever you're naming the battle, I don't want to hear about it...' She thought.

"Frances do come and join us at the table," Elizabeth announced lightly, though her expression indicated that it was more of a command than a request. Reluctantly, Frances sauntered toward the table, Goring on his feet at once, drawing out the chair next to his own, a smile playing through his eyes.

"Would you care for a little wine, Viscountess?" he asked as, once seated, Frances rearranged her black skirts.

"A little, thank you General," she responded politely.

Goring reached for the wine bottle, filling an empty goblet, and setting it before Frances, topping up his own in the process. Now that Frances was closer to the young General, no one could doubt he was a handsome man with light brown hair falling in soft waves to his shoulders, but somehow, a mischievous glint in his eyes filled her with suspicion.

The subject at the table moved on to the 'thorny' problems relating to the town of Bradford, some thirty miles to the west of Haveringham. The town's citizens had proved stalwart in defence of the town, refusing to surrender more than once, despite every attempt by Savile, the Royalist commander, to persuade them otherwise. Many of the inhabitants were puritanical in outlook, hardly surprising then that the town had come out in support of Parliament when the war began, curtailing some of Miles' business dealings with particular merchants there, mostly relating to the woollen trade. Bradford boasted a pretty little parish church, set on a slight incline in the centre of the town, information having been received that the inhabitants had ensured wool sacks had been slung over the sides of its tower, for protection. Troops had been sent from nearby Halifax to reinforce the place with Tom Fairfax taking up occupancy himself. Newcastle explained how astonished he had been when learning that the citizens had welcomed Fairfax almost as if he were a hero.

"Well, should he attempt to come here, he certainly wouldn't receive any form of welcome," Elizabeth stated soundly, fluttering her fan.

"Well said Countess," Goring responded, toasting her with his goblet.

CHAPTER FORTY-ONE

February 1643 – Haveringham Manor

Frances couldn't escape the constant analytical scrutiny of Goring, nor did he seem inclined to stop.

'Must you look at me so shamelessly….?'

"Might I ask why you seem inclined to study me so closely, General?" Frances ventured at last.

"Forgive me, but as far as I'm aware, it's no felony to admire a pretty woman?" Goring said with a throaty chuckle and broad smile. "But now that you mention it, I perceive your eyes to carry a great deal of sorrow…. a legacy of your husband's untimely demise?"

Frances felt unwilling to undertake any form of conversation involving John, especially with someone who, to her, proved a complete stranger. Determined to put an end to that particular subject, she merely responded, "No doubt."

Hazel eyes captured hers, almost provocatively, his smile not only reaching them but proving engaging. Into her mind came something Ralph had once said about this very man. Goring had a past and had not always been what he seemed to be now.

Mischievously, Frances thought of a way to assuage the attentiveness that was beginning to feel a little awkward.

"Forgive me General, I know you have been Governor of Portsmouth, and I may well be in error, but I am reliably informed that your current defence of His Majesty's cause has not always been as…. robust as it now appears? Were you not once involved in betraying a number of your colleagues to the Parliament and offering them information that John Pym then used against the King himself?" she said, setting the sweetest smile to her lips as she stared him out.

Visibly taken aback, astonishment visible on his face, eventually, Goring laughed and nodded complacently.

"Your knowledge astounds me, Viscountess, though it is somewhat limited and therefore I must question the overall reliability of what you have been told," he admitted, reaching for his goblet once more. "Time and circumstances have wrought a definite change of heart in that respect, tis a mistake I would never replicate, I assure you. My allegiance remains steadfast to His Majesty, and always shall be henceforth."

Frances certainly hadn't expected such a detailed response and raised her brows. "Then you have my respect General," she said, then after a momentary pause, decided it might be possible to ask a little more without giving offence. "Did I perceive you to be limping when you entered the house? An old injury perhaps?"

'Damn me, you miss very little,' Goring thought.

Briefly, he wondered if she initially felt inclined to press him more in relation to his loyalty, but then perhaps she just wanted to provoke a certain response. Honesty, he decided, would be the best form of attack and just watch for her reaction.

"You are correct in that it is an old injury, Viscountess. I took a musket ball in the ankle during the siege of Breda, in the Low Countries. It pains me from time to time, particularly if the weather is colder, much as it is today," he said.

Frances would have enquired if he had known Robin or even John from Europe, had not her father chosen that very moment to address Goring himself.

"Are there plans afoot for the Queen to return to England then, General?" he asked.

"Most assuredly, Lord Benningford. In fact, she endeavoured earlier this month, but severe weather forced a return to Holland." Goring reached for the wine bottle, refilling his goblet, and downing most of it in one. "Her ladies were in a sorry state, their clothing ruined by seawater, the contents of their stomachs and…. pardon me other less agreeable substances. Most of their attire was ruined and had to be burned. One lady declared that she would rather live in Holland than ever set foot aboard a vessel again. Her Majesty tried to reassure he lady by declaring, *'no Queen of England hath ever yet been drowned,'* but it was all to no avail, the lady remained adamant."

"In all honesty Miles, the convoy could potentially reach English shores within days," Newcastle put in. "My orders are to see the Queen escorted safely to York, once she does arrive."

"Well, if I am able to assist in any way William, you only have to ask," Miles offered, and Newcastle nodded.

"In truth, I was hoping you would say as much, Miles. I shall be happy to convey your willingness to Her Majesty whenever I meet with her."

"How long do you believe she might be resident in York?" Elizabeth queried.

"Several weeks I should think Countess, until better weather arrives. It would be nigh on impossible to reach Oxford currently, the roads being so impassable," Newcastle explained.

"Of course, Lord Bynghame wrote that the King has made Oxford his headquarters," Frances remarked, leaning forward to address the Derbyshire Earl directly.

"That's correct, Viscountess, he has indeed. The King occupies most of Christ Church College, whilst Prince Rupert and Prince Maurice, who are absent more often than not, lodge with Timothy Carter, the Town Clerk, when they are in Oxford," he explained. "It's said Royalist supporters are flocking in huge numbers to Oxford, the citizens being obliged to take in lodgers, whether they wish to or not." Turning his attention to Anne, Newcastle asked, "Do you hear often from your husband, Lady Bynghame?"

Anne almost choked on her wine, startled at being addressed

directly, her cheeks growing ever pinker by the second.

"Infrequently, my Lord," she responded sheepishly and as if thinking of something to say, added, "His last spoke of being quartered at Abingdon?"

"As are the majority of the royalist cavalry, Lady Bynghame, so we understand," Fleetwood answered with a genial smile that served to calm Anne's edginess.

Information coming north always did prove scant, with varying degrees of credibility, but ever since Frances had overheard a conversation between her father and Glemham some days back, she had pondered something.

"Is it true that many garrisons suffer from want of equipment, Captain Fleetwood?" she enquired, and the Captain turned widened eyes upon her.

"Alas tis often the case, Viscountess. I am told that Prince Rupert is frequently the recipient of requests for assistance from commanders throughout the land, and more often than not is unable to offer much succour."

"Then how are troops to fight effectively if they have neither the means nor basic necessities to do so?" she continued, much to her father's growing pride as he looked on.

"How indeed, my dear," Newcastle answered adding, "We are hopeful that once Her Majesty returns, the lack should be alleviated a little, due to the armaments she has been able to procure."

Miles gave a ponderous nod, tapping his index fingers against his pursed lips.

"There'd be little need for any additional weaponry if Lord Falkland's endeavours at peace-making before Christmas had born fruit though, William," he eventually voiced.

"I know what you mean Miles, but sadly neither side would yield an inch."

"Falkland's a first-rate man, pity he wasn't heeded more," Miles mused.

"Ah but not everyone thinks as you, Miles. Many consider Falkland far too weak, though I dare say he'll join the fighting, if and when required."

Goring reached for the wine bottle once more before Moll Gilbert could prevent it, refilling his own goblet and that of Frances before setting it back on the table directly in front of himself.

"I'm unsure whether you are aware of this, Lord Benningford, but supporters of the King are being asked to surrender silver and plate for the cause?" Goring explained, turning the goblet in his hand.

"Could we not add our support to that, father?" Frances asked. "We have plenty of silver and plate here, and I would willingly part with my wedding gifts to assist His Majesty." She ignored the looks of amusement passing between Mackworth and Fleetwood and added, "Are there not others hereabouts who might be persuaded to part with their treasures?"

Miles threw her a look of a predator corning its prey. His daughter had something in mind, that much was obvious, and he felt the need to temper her eagerness a little, particularly in front of these guests.

"Leave well alone daughter, after all, you are not yet fully recovered...."

"I've not been ill father, merely widowed....."

She stopped at once, her father's features darkening like a threatening storm.

"Forgive me, my Lord, but I believe what the Viscountess suggests may hold some merit," Goring put in. "Like many houses of similar age, I take it this one possesses hidden cellars, secret passages…. even priest holes from the past, perhaps?"

'Impertinent rogue,' Miles thought, staring at the younger man.

"Signifying, General?" he asked at last with what Frances knew was an insincere smile.

"I mean no offence, my Lord. Tis more that, were it possible to collect silver from the locality, then if you had such hiding places here, those items could be readily stored safely, until such time as troops may be deployed to transport it south to Oxford, where it could be of most use."

"Not the Mint in York?" Miles enquired with a scowl.

"Preferably not," Goring admitted. "The King has set up the Royal Mint in Oxford now."

'What a splendid notion….' Frances thought to herself with a rush of excitement she had not felt for a number of months.

"Perhaps it might be worthy of some consideration…." Miles finally responded, rubbing his chin.

"Of course, it is, father," Frances put in, receiving an unreadable look from Miles. Inwardly, he was taken aback by what he read on Frances' face. She seemed radiant somehow, her eyes sparkling with a brightness he had thought never to witness again.

'She definitely has something in mind….' he thought to himself, feeling a tad joyous to see her looking so animated for once.

"Leave it for now daughter," he said, and Goring leaned closer.

"A minor triumph I would say, Viscountess. It remains to be seen just which of you will be the overall victor in the siege of 'silver and plate' eh? My wager would be that it may well be you."

CHAPTER FORTY-TWO

February 1643 – early afternoon

The sky had threatened snow for most of the day, though only the lightest flurries had so far fallen, until now when it seemed to be growing heavier by the minute..

Swathed in thick woollen shawls, Elizabeth and Frances sat by the fireplace in the Great Hall, the blaze in the grate crackling and spitting every now and then as it cast a warming glow and smell of sweet wood smoke, throughout the room.

Elizabeth worked on a piece of embroidery at her sewing frame, though from time to time, she looked across at her daughter seated opposite, focused on a book.

'She still appears so melancholy and the black she wears drains her pallor,' Elizabeth thought. Had it not been for the war, Frances would have been taken to Court in the hope of gaining a new suitor, but all that made no sense since if the nation had not been at war then John Fitzherbert would still be alive and doubtless, she would be in Kent. Tying off a stitch, Elizabeth rubbed her tired eyes, when loud hammering at the front door made her leap up and almost topple the sewing frame.

"Oh, my word, whatever is this? Trust your father not to be here….what if it's roundheads?" she gasped.

"I doubt they'd be polite enough to knock, mother," Frances said, placing the book on a table.

Lambert rushed through, heading for the corridor leading to the main entrance.

"Stay here Countess until I ascertain the need for such urgency," he declared as yet again the hammering on the door continued. Reaching for one another, mother and daughter waited arm in arm for Lambert to return with an explanation. Both women realised it must be something urgent if whoever was knocking had been allowed entry through the gatehouse. They could only make out muffled voices until Lambert returned with a heavily cloaked figure in his wake.

"Countess, this gentleman wishes to speak urgently with the Earl, he has news of the Queen," Lambert said with obvious concern.

Elizabeth could only stare open mouthed, so Frances felt the need to comment.

"My father is not at home, Sir. If you could wait a while, he should not be too long. This is the Countess, my mother."

Throwing back his cloak and removing his hat, the visitor bowed.

"Ladies, I humbly beg pardon for intruding in this unexpected way, but the matter is somewhat pressing and may not wait," he said moving closer to the table where the candlelight illuminated his features. He was relatively young, with a square jaw, determined brown eyes and a mop of light brown hair that fell in damp tendrils across his shoulders. Thankfully, the scarf tied about his waist was red, not orange.

"I have just come from, Her Majesty," he said with a bearing of deference, as if the lady herself were present in the room.

Elizabeth grabbed the back of a chair to steady herself.

"She has returned to England?" she stammered, and the stranger offered a relaxed smile that spread to his eyes.

"Indeed, Countess. Her party made landfall at Bridlington on the coast, two days ago. The Earl of Newcastle bid me come here at once to request lodgings for the Queen and her party this night."

Elizabeth's knuckles paled as her grip on the chair tightened.

'Miles, where are you when you're needed?' She gave a hesitant smile. "Her Majesty wishes to lodge here?"

"She does Countess, tis the reason for such insistent knocking. Did

265

not Lord Benningford previously offer of assistance?" he asked, and Frances nodded. "That is why I am here. Forgive me, but the whole party cannot be too far behind me. I must return swiftly with a definite response."

Elizabeth took a deep breath.

"Then the answer is we should be honoured," she said, then to Lambert, "Bid Moll, the cook and all the servants attend me at once, there is much to be done." Bowing, Lambert hurried away but not before Elizabeth shouted, "Lambert, have one of the stable hands ride toward York for my husband."

"Consider it done, Countess," the steward said.

Elizabeth's focus then returned to the young man, who she noted, seemed to glance more than once at her daughter beside the fireplace.

"Will you take a little wine, before you leave?" Elizabeth asked, pouring a measure, and holding it out.

"Thank you Countess," he said, taking the goblet. "If I might be permitted to introduce myself; Henry, Lord Broughton of His Royal Highness, Prince Rupert's Lifeguard, at your service," he said with a dip of the head before draining the goblet.

"Is the Prince with the Queen?" Frances enquired with wide eyes that met his, forcing Broughton to smile broadly.

"No, no, you misunderstand me. Tis true that my commission is with the Prince, though my last direct order was to ride north with communications for the Earl of Newcastle, mostly relating to the Queen's imminent arrival. I was present when the Earl received word that the flotilla had been sighted in the bay at Bridlington and delighted to be invited to join the advance party sent to greet her. I am commanded by Rupert to attend Her Majesty until such time as she can make the journey south to Oxford."

Water seemed to be pooling on the oak flooring, formed from

droplets continually dripping from both his hair and cloak. Frances went across to a dresser, opened a drawer and took out a napkin, returning to offer it to him.

"For your hair, Lord Broughton," she said. Now she was closer, she could see features that were particularly handsome, from sparkling eyes to moustache edged lips that spread into an easy smile as he took the cloth from her hand. Judging him to be no more than a year or two her senior, the cut and style of his clothing proved he was from a family of considerable rank.

"Thank you, Lady…..?" he enquired.

"Viscountess Haveringham," she answered, lifting her chin marginally. She noticed his brows flicker upward in surprise. "Your orders may involve you being absent from your regiment for some time I think, Lord Broughton, for tis said the Queen may remain in York until the late Spring, at the very least."

"It does appear that way, but such are my orders from Rupert and am not inclined to gain say him. I shall of course re-join the Prince once we reach Oxford," he said.

Holding out the now dampened cloth, Broughton watched carefully as elegant fingers took back the fabric and folded it carefully, setting it aside on the table. Her fair hair almost shimmered in the candlelight and her profile was most pleasing.

'To think I initially balked against the order to come north. I'm strangely glad now to have been chosen for this task,' he thought to himself.

Primarily a soldier, Broughton had been aggrieved by an order that would see him, not only leaving his comrades in the south for an indeterminate period but requiring him to almost function as a mere escort rather than a combatant, and that had rankled.

"How soon before the Queen's party reaches us, Lord Broughton?" Elizabeth enquired.

"By sundown I should think, Countess," Broughton replied. "Such a large party makes progress slow, as you might expect, and this atrocious weather is bound to hinder it even more."

Elizabeth gripped the chair back once again, her knuckles blanching.

"Just how large will the party be?" Suddenly Elizabeth experienced a wave of alarm after all their home was a mere manor house, not a castle .

"Our home is not of huge proportions my Lord… surely we cannot be expected to provide lodgings for…."

Broughton's hand shot up.

"Pray do not concern yourself overly in that respect, Countess. The Queen's immediate party only will required lodgings within the house. With your permission, others may make use of your extensive grounds?"

'Goodness, not for the first time,' Frances thought, nodding enthusiastically at her mother's enquiring look.

"I can speak for my father Lord Broughton, I am almost certain he would have no objection to that," she said.

Broughton went on to calm further concerns, by relating that the majority of the military would make straight for York, dispatches having been sent back and forth constantly between Newcastle and Glemham, in that respect. The small troop presently guarding the Queen's person and baggage, would of course be required to camp within the grounds, along with several others making up the royal entourage. When he stated that he would be one of those occupying a tent himself, Frances felt surprisingly glad to hear it.

Thereafter, the house became a frenzy of activity, servants rushing here and there, directed by Elizabeth, Lambert, or Moll Gilbert. Five or six rooms were to be made ready, the Queen being given Robin's old bedchamber, as it was larger than most. The cook was tasked with preparing as many tasty dishes as possible from the depleted stocks of foodstuffs kept in the storerooms and outbuildings.

"A fresh horse awaits you in the Courtyard, my Lord," Lambert declared on his way through the Great Hall, bearing two large silver jugs in need of polishing.

"Excuse me ladies, I must be off," Broughton said, replacing his hat. "I shall return shortly, with Her Majesty."

"Continue with the arrangements Lambert; I shall see Lord Broughton out," Frances said, leading the young officer toward the large front door, where, one hand on the handle, she paused and watched him pulling on his gloves.

"Perhaps when you return, we may have chance to converse a little?" she asked with a hesitant smile.

"By your apparel, Madam might I assume you to be in mourning?" he asked.

"I am, Lord Broughton….. for my husband. He was slain in the battle in Warwickshire."

"Edgehill?" he voiced, familiar sorrow searing Frances' heart as it always tended to whenever the place was mentioned. The shawl slid from her shoulder, Broughton reaching across to replaced it.

"I am grieved to hear it….. Might I know his name?" he asked.

"John… Lord Fitzherbert."

"Melton's son?"

Frances' head shot up.

"You knew him?" she asked.

"Not in person, no, though I do know that Rupert was affected by his death. He was said to grow quiet and reflective for some time after being informed of it."

'I wonder if that was when he wrote to me?'

Tears pricked Frances' eyes and she looked down but not quick enough, Broughton had noticed.

"Forgive me, I did not wish to distress you, Madam," Broughton said, reaching for her hand.

"Tis but memories….. Lord Broughton," she admitted, opening the large front door.

Not wishing to see her chilled, he dashed outside and down the steps, taking the reins from the young lad, leaping up into the saddle and kicking the horse to a hasty canter. Eventually, Frances closed the door and leaned back against it.

'Of all people to come to Haveringham, someone who was actually at Edgehill with John. I must try to speak with him when he returns. Perhaps then I might finally have the answers I crave,' she thought.

CHAPTER FORTY-THREE

Late February 1642

"Miles do keep still for one minute together, all this pacing makes me nervous," Elizabeth said, straightening the lace edging her bodice.

The Great Hall had undergone a rapid facelift. Floors freshly swept; woodwork polished with beeswax mixed with lavender causing a delightful, light fragrance to permeate the whole room. Items of furniture had been repositioned, allowing for more space and the table now boasted a covering of embroidered, blood red coloured, damask. Candles flickered brightly in silver candlesticks sited in various places throughout the Great Hall making the whole room look inviting, warm, and welcoming. The fire had been fully banked up, adding to the bright glow in the room and two large baskets of additional logs had been placed to one side, ready to replenish the blaze when required.

Attired in his best, Lambert almost stood guard near the front door, appearing every inch a nobleman's steward, awaiting the slightest indication of their grand visitor's arrival.

Miles had been located by the stable hand not far from home, the pair galloping their horses back to set about organising the grounds. Miles indicated where horses might be tethered, carriages parked and tents erected, thereafter dashing upstairs to change his clothing. Now as he stood nervously waiting beside his wife, he appeared the epitome of an English Earl in deep green velvet braided with gold. Elizabeth had chosen to wear a court gown of deep peacock blue that served to accentuate her eyes and mirror the sparkling sapphires entwined through her elaborately styled hair.

"She'll be here at any moment Miles, what's keeping Frances?" Elizabeth said primping the lace at her elbows, just as Frances rushed in to assume a stance beside her. With an audible gasp, the Countess stared wide eyed at the burgundy silk gown Frances had chosen to wear.

'Pray don't reprove me mother, I'm done with black whether it goes against everything considered proper or not…..' Frances thought, unwilling to meet her mother's gaze.

"Daughter, I really don't…."

"Leave the girl be, Bess," Miles interrupted but then Lambert's voice boomed out.

"Her Majesty, the Queen!" he proclaimed, bowing deeply as the small but nevertheless imposing figure of Henrietta Maria strolled straight into the Great Hall, several warmly attired courtiers close behind.

"Most gracious Majesty, welcome to Haveringham Manor," Miles declared with a respectful flourish of his hat when bowing. In unison, Elizabeth and Frances sank into the deepest curtsies.

"Milord Benningford, tis a relief to finally be 'ere." Henrietta's soft voice held a pronounced French accent. "Ah, Lady Benningford and your daughter, Lady Fitzherbert, *n'est pas?*"

"*Mai oui, Votre Majesté,*" Miles said, using her mother tongue. The royal mouth spread into a smile, revealing slightly protruding front teeth as she admired the two women repeatedly. Lightly, she lifted Frances' chin with leather covered fingertips.

"*Ah,* je *me souviens,*" the Queen said almost to herself, adding, "Your 'usband's death is the cause of much sorrow, *n'est pas?*"

Violet eyes lifted to meet the brown ones of England's Queen.

'Who told you?' To enquire would be an unforgiveable lapse of etiquette of course, though Frances couldn't help wondering.

"*Oui Majesté,*" she answered simply.

"Ah, but I 'ave an idea. You are in sore need of gaiety and so, when we proceed to York, you shall accompany us." Then over her shoulder, "What say you to that, Mary?"

A young woman with pale brown hair in a fur trimmed cloak, removing her gloves looked up.

"I can think of no better prospect, Majesty," she responded. Undeniably English, the woman threw a brief, sociable smile Frances' way.

"The Duchess of Richmond," Henrietta explained a sweep of one hand encompassing several others. "Henry Jermyn and various others you may already be familiar with, Milord Benningford."

Miles tipped his head graciously, though when he lifted it again, the Queen had sauntered off down the room, dropping on a chair beside the fire holding out her hands to warm them.

"Charmant," she said aloud, gazing about the room.

"Would Your Majesty care for some refreshment?" Elizabeth asked approaching slowly.

Henrietta barely flinched.

"Non, non…… though I should like to change, having ridden so long in this gown, I may well smell as bad as my horse,"

Elizabeth laughed nervously.

"If you would care to follow me, Your Majesty, I will show you to your bedchamber, where your ladies may attend you?" she said and only then did Henrietta offer her full attention.

"Parfait and once I have changed, I shall require food and good wine, if that could be arranged?"

"Already in hand, Your Majesty."

Elizabeth knew Haveringham's cook would deliver the finest delicacies to please even the most demanding of appetites, the Queen no exception. Leading the way, Elizabeth secretly enjoyed the innumerable bows and curtsies as they strolled past, despite knowing they were not levelled at her. Three ladies peeled off to follow, but as she was not required, the Duchess of Richmond sauntered across to Frances.

"You must forgive our 'little Queen,' she is inclined to make free with anyone's property, wherever we find ourselves," she said in a voice holding melodic tones and green eyes that sparkled with mirth and geniality. Judging her to be roughly about the same age as herself, Frances could not help feeling that the young Duchess possessed an air of confidence she could only envy.

"May I show you to your bedchamber, Your Grace?" Frances asked, admiring the cut and style of the riding gown beneath the damp and grubby looking cloak the Duchess hastily removed. Laughingly, the Duchess wrinkled her nose, impishly.

"I think that would be best, yes. Lud, my maid will have her work cut out if she is to make aught of this damp mop of hair," she laughed.

On her way back down the staircase, Frances deliberated the strange events of the last few hours. Not only had the Queen of England arrived unexpectedly at Haveringham Manor, but also the beautiful, flamboyant Duchess of Richmond, whose gregarious character intrigued Frances significantly.

Entering the Great Hall, it seemed that several more individuals had come inside and spotting her father alongside a small group of well-dressed men, she went to join them.

"Ah, gentlemen, may I present my daughter, Lady Fitzherbert, the Viscountess Haveringham," he explained and as Frances dipped a curtsey, smiling at each in turn, she noticed Lord Broughton at the end.

"We meet again, Viscountess," he said brightly, moving to be beside her.

"Welcome back, Lord Broughton," she answered offering her hand. "I see you have been introduced to my father?"

"Aye indeed, a most genial host," he grinned, lifting his goblet of wine.

Frances felt edgy as conversations between the men continued apace, almost disregarding her presence. Secretly she wanted an opportunity to question the man beside her and yet as time went on, he kept being asked about the fighting in the south, what Prince Rupert engaged in and what his orders were. Eventually, she had her chance when servants approached to refill empty goblets and a lull fell. Lightly, she touched Lord Broughton's arm.

"Might I speak with you…..privately, Lord Broughton?" she whispered with a tilt of her eyes.

'Well now, this is a pleasant surprise.' He thought and holding out his arm said, "Of course, tis most flattering to be asked."

As they walked together down the room to a place by the window where few were standing, the thought struck Frances that Broughton might just have completely misconstrued her motive. Would he think her capricious or flirty? First and foremost, she must make him understand that she merely wished for any information he might be able to yield regarding the battle in Warwickshire.

"Lord Broughton, firstly allow me to say that you are mistaken if you think I…..I am not the kind of woman to…..tis not for flirtation I needed to speak alone with you," she explained fiddling with the ruby ring on her right hand. "When you were here earlier, you spoke of a matter I would know more of?"

The young Lord's eyes grew wide. He certainly hadn't expected her to say that, misreading her motives entirely and briefly, he felt ashamed.

"Pray tell me then, what is it you wish to know?" he said hesitantly.

"You…..you mentioned earlier of hearing of my late husband?" she said, yet again twirling the ruby ring.

"Heard of him yes, but I had no real acquaintance with him, if that's what you're asking?"

Frances' heart plummeted.

"Might you then have seen him at Edgehill? I need to know if he…."

Broughton forestalled her by grasping her forearm, the lace at her elbow inextricably catching on an emerald ring on his finger. For a moment, he paused, taking time to carefully extricate the delicate threads.

"I hope the lace is not damaged?" he asked.

She scowled, both in annoyance and frustration. How could he speak of lace when all she wanted was to speak about was John.

"Tis of no consequence," she snapped, then realising her rudeness added, "forgive me, did you see aught of my husband in the battle?"

'She's certainly persistent, I'll give her that.'

Broughton felt a little perplexed and folding his arms across his chest said, "I don't think I can be of any help in that respect, Viscountess. I rode close to Prince Rupert at the first charge. Your husband would have been with his own troops, way off to the right of our starting position."

Her face clouded. Suddenly Frances felt foolish, almost childishly so. A battle such as the one at Edgehill would involve vast numbers spread out over a huge area. How could one person be seen in the mayhem that ensued. She really must stop seeking to know something that no one was likely to be able to provide her with. After all, Lord Broughton was more or less saying what Ralph had told her about that fateful day.

"I comprehend fully that you would wish to know what happened, but....what will it gain you in the end?" he asked. Tears glistened in her eyes, though she made sure to blink them away so he would not see, but he already had.

"I was foolish to ask it of you, Lord Broughton," she admitted. "John and I wed last August....for love....such a short time ago....."

Finally, Broughton understood the reason for her rash questioning and felt a surge of sympathy for her. Unfolding his arms, he took hold of her hands.

"Many good men fell in that fateful encounter, Viscountess," he said. "I lost a lifelong friend, Lord Aysgarth who was like an elder brother to me."

He turned to gaze out of the window at the snow falling steadily, not saying anything for some time, though his thumbs continually stroked her knuckles. Eventually he looked round and smiled.

"You know, I would say that 'Kineton Fight' has already wrought far too much grief in this land. Personally, I should prefer to see those unusual eyes of yours sparkling more with joy and less with tears, as they are now," he said.

CHAPTER FORTY-FOUR

February 1643 – Haveringham Manor

The longer she spent in Lord Broughton's company, the more Frances began to relax and enjoy herself. Broughton proved an amiable and attentive companion with a congenial sense of humour that felt restorative. At long last, Frances felt able to laugh, finding it both cathartic and infectious. Frances was forced to bite her lip, when Lord Broughton described the difficulties in changing from wet clothing in a ridiculously small tent in the grounds. Now that his hair was dry, Frances admired the rich light brown colour and the fact that it was worn fashionably long.

In turn, Broughton felt relaxed enough in Frances' company to tell her he came from Buckinghamshire. Many of his kinsmen owned properties in that part of England and all were supporters of the King, though one cousin, had chosen to side with the Parliament, much to their chagrin. He was two and twenty, had four younger sisters still at home, along with a ten-year-old brother by the name of Tom who, when informed he was far too young to join the fighting, had thrown a massive tantrum, earning him some harsh punishment. Smiling shyly, he briefly mentioned that he, much as the King, once had an elder brother who had succumbed to a fever several years ago.

"I lost my own brother similarly," she explained. "Hence, I am now my father's heir."

"As am I," he said, though his engaging smile quickly faded. "That is, I *should* be."

"Oh?"

"My father is greatly vexed that as, yet I have no wife and therefore no heir myself. I confess that the onset of war gave me the perfect excuse to reject my father's latest choice of bride. She was almost four years my senior and….not to my taste at all."

Frances couldn't help but giggle.

"Tis naught to laugh at Viscountess, before I left home, my father gave me a stark choice that if I should refuse his next selection, then I would be disinherited in favour of young Tom. Hence my remark that I '*should*' be my father's heir. I feel sorry for Tom, being so young, he is still quite biddable, alas."

"Whereas you choose not to be?" she dared to venture.

Broughton stared at the floor, rubbing his boot along the wood as a scowl scarred his handsome features.

"I envy you being fortunate enough to wed for love. That's all I seek….." He paused, the scowl deepening. "When I was but seventeen, I considered myself in love with a girl of sixteen and ready to wed her, though she was forced to marry another…."

"She wasn't considered suitable?"

"Oh, she was at first, yes. Though negotiations had barely begun for me, when a better opportunity presented itself and her father dispatched her to Wiltshire to wed a man of nine and forty years."

Frances read a measure of sorrow in his eyes, coupled with acceptance of an event that had obviously left its scar. Frances felt grateful not to have been forced into such a union herself. The thought of gnarled hands exploring her body in the most intimate of ways, made her almost shudder. After the joys of John's skilful and tender lovemaking, the thought of what this poor girl must have endured, was unthinkable.

"I am no great believer in arranged matches," he admitted. "Thankfully, my mother convinced my father to leave the matter be, once I declared my intent to serve Prince Rupert and I rarely have opportunity to visit my home now." He grinned and winked.

"Fortuitous, eh? Now enough of this, might you be persuaded to call me Harry, Viscountess?"

The arrival of two men clad entirely in black, cautiously approaching the Queen roused Frances' immediate curiosity. Both bowed low over the royal hand, though Henrietta's expression did not change from aloof disinterest. Though they conversed briefly, the Queen's whole demeanour displayed disinclination to continue for long. Summarily dismissed, the pair went to stand beside one of the archways where no one seemed to consider them at all. Lightly, she tugged on Harry's sleeve.

"Who are those men beside the archway?" she enquired.

A quick glance and Harry's eyes narrowed.

"They're from Scotland," he said simply.

'Well, that doesn't tell me much' she thought but said, "And, Harry?"

Taken aback, he pursed his lips.

"They're here desiring an audience with the Queen, that's all but she's making them wait until she reaches York," he explained.

Frances took another glance. The pair seemed perfectly content, but devoid of any of the grand company gathered in the room.

"If they came all the way from Scotland, then surely the need must be great, mustn't it?" she asked.

"I really couldn't say," Harry responded nonchalantly.

'That's no answer at all. What are you not telling me?' she wondered.

"Would you be kind enough to introduce me to them, Harry?"

Broughton almost choked on his wine and clearing his throat said, "What?"

"Well, no one else seems willing to speak to them, so I should like to," she said, tilting her chin.

Shaking his head, Harry handed his goblet to a man at his side, rolling his eyes.

As Frances walked away on Harry's arm, she felt sure she heard sniggers and whispers from a number of people but made her focus the men in black and in particular the taller of the two with his back toward her.

"Your pardon my Lord, but our host's daughter wishes to be made known to you," Harry declared, a definite touch of acerbity in his tone. "Viscountess Haveringham, I present James Graham, the Earl of Montrose."

CHAPTER FORTY-FIVE

February 1643

Frances could not escape the compelling grey eyes of James Graham, holding hers consistently, even as her hand was politely kissed.

"Your servant, Viscountess." His voice was deep, with a pronounced, but soft Scots accent. Neither excessively tall, nor short in stature, the reality was that James Graham stood more or less the same height as Frances' father. Something about him appeared undeniably intriguing, with a presence that could only be described as commanding. He was clean shaven, aside from a diminutive tuft in the cleft below his lower lip and worn long, brown hair cascaded in soft waves onto his collar edged with only a small strip of lace. They grey eyes, still boring into hers, strangely made her feel as if he might be able to read her thoughts.

"I understand you to have ridden considerable distance of late, my Lord?" she finally enquired, believing this was the most appropriate thing to say, but aware of heat infusing her face.

"Aye Madam…tis some considerable distance from Scotland," he responded bluntly before turning to the man at his side. "Permit me to present, Alexander Colla MacDonald, my second in command."

"Of course. I….I trust you like my home, and that the county of York is to your taste, Lord Graham?" she asked, hoping he would see beyond what, even to her, sounded slightly lame.

Bizarrely, he simply chuckled quietly, though his smile appeared genuine.

"From the little I've seen of your home Viscountess, I would say it is most impressive, but as to my opinion of the actual county…… Well, I dare say I may well be forced to see a great deal more of it before I am able to return to Scotland. Perhaps you should ask me the same question again once I have done so?"

His expression seemed amiable enough and Frances felt confident enough to press on with a more personal enquiry.

"I am told you are hopeful of gaining a private audience with Her Majesty?" she asked.

Marginally, she noticed the grey orbs narrowing.

'Now this is singular; someone actually requesting to know why I'm here when others show little inclination.'

The response came in the form of an indifferent smile.

"That's my fervent hope, aye," he admitted.

"Then I pray she will not keep you waiting too long, Lord Graham," Frances responded.

By now Harry, alongside, had heard quite enough and looking about, he spied an opportunity to remove both himself and his companion.

"Pray excuse us, Lord Graham but I see a person yonder whom I know would wish to be introduced to the Viscountess," he said.

Frances experienced a flash of vexation. In reality, she wanted to continue speaking with the Scot, though just why that was, she could not completely fathom. Perhaps she desired to know why some appeared to show an aversion to speaking with him at all. She had little chance to protest when Harry offered his arm and felt obliged to take it.

"If you might excuse us, my Lord Earl," she said brightly.

"As you wish, Viscountess," Montrose said and after acknowledging her curtsey with a polite bow, he turned to back to MacDonald.

"Well now, what do you make of 'The Graham'," Harry said when they had not progressed too far, and Frances frowned. "Well, tis what he's called…..amongst other things," Harry quickly added.

"In my view he seems very single-minded," she remarked almost casually.

"Single-minded…. aye isn't he just…. whenever the mood takes him, that is," Harry replied and Frances stopped, pulling on his arm, forcing him to do likewise.

"You don't trust him Harry? Why is that, perhaps because he's a Scot?" she asked, briefly glancing toward the two men by the archway.

"What you may not know and more to the point Frances, is that he is considered naught but a turncoat. You may not be aware but fought for the Covenanters in the Bishop's Wars, you know."

She gave a little chuckle.

"I know, father once mentioned that. Perhaps he decided to change his loyalties though… much as General Goring did?" she asked with a pert tilt of the head, widening her eyes.

"Your knowledge amazes me Frances, especially relating to Goring," he said with a cynical laugh. "You're proving quite the enigma."

'I'm in no mood for mockery,' she thought but said, "In what way an enigma?"

"Well, I was beginning to consider you different to other females, but now I see you are much the same…. easily swayed by a handsome face and courageous words."

It was her chance to scoff.

"You could not be more wrong, Harry Broughton. I am neither swayed by a handsome face nor by flattering speeches." *'If that were so, I'd already be besotted with you!'* "Perhaps I see something in him that as yet, I don't fully comprehend… honesty, determination, tenacity, I'm not sure which, though I am resolved to find out."

Harry studied her carefully, then gave an almost adolescent shrug.

'Well now, why doesn't that surprise me,' he thought to himself.

"Come Harry, even you must admit that if Montrose were merely playing a part and still supported the Covenanters, he'd hardly have come all this way to speak with the Queen. I know my Father believes he and Argyll have plans to oppose the Covenanters."

Harry's eyes suddenly widened, and he puffed out his lips.

"Tell me Frances, have you read much philosophy?" he asked to which, she scowled.

"Why ask me that?"

"Because obviously you have a precocity to examine matters rationally, absolving those who may or may not, deserve it. You are somewhat of a sage, dear lady," he admitted.

The description made her snigger.

"It's more one can learn from errors in this life. Some may disagree but till I'm shown otherwise, I intend to give the Earl of Montrose the benefit of the doubt…. as I would with anyone."

She smiled in a way that caused Harry's breath to suddenly catch. He certainly found her unfathomable, especially those remarkable eyes, though he wondered if he were just being foolish, swayed by a decidedly pretty face. Time to turn his thoughts to other matters and bizarrely in that moment, Harry wished he were still in Oxford, with all his comrades.

Much later, relaxing on her bed, one arm behind her head, Frances pondered what had been one of the strangest days of her young life. Everything had begun so normally, almost mundanely one might say, and yet by that evening, some of the most noble personages in the whole kingdom had arrived at her home, plunging everyone into uproar. She had been introduced to many people, one in particular filling her thoughts at that moment. Lady Alys Holcroft, fair haired and blue eyed, had proved herself the most remarkably amiable person and she and Frances had easily fallen into relaxed conversation for some considerable time. Alys had explained that she was married but that her husband was serving in the West Country with Prince Maurice, or so she had been informed when last he had written, letters being scarce. She was glad to have been introduced to Lady Holcroft and felt that she would be perfectly happy to spend more time in her company, whilst she remained in Yorkshire. With an elongated sigh, Frances rolled onto her side, this time thinking of Harry Broughton. He certainly had proved himself most attentive and was undeniably handsome, though only when his image was superseded by that of a certain Scottish Earl with penetrating grey eyes, did her heart unexpectedly quicken. She bit her lip and sat up hugging her knees.

'Dare I go to York with the Queen? Might it not prove beneficial and diverting? By all accounts there will be entertainments, gaiety and even dancing… Would not John give his blessing?"

"Why shouldn't I?" she said aloud. After all, the invitation had not been actively sought nor wished for but had been laid out before her as a tantalising proposal. Her parents would have to be convinced of course, but she doubted they would be against the notion, not when it had been suggested by the Queen of England herself.

Laying back down, Frances wrapped her arms around the pillow where once John's head had lain and closing her eyes, remembered his last directive. *'All shall be well…..'*

CHAPTER FORTY-SIX

February 1643

"You've come to the house with the sole purpose of speaking to me, Harry?" Frances asked lightly. She had the inclination to sport with the young officer a little, deciding to feign the appearance of surprise at seeing him. "I thought you might have duties to deal with?"

"Well, I… No, I haven't…. I felt disposed to take a turn in the grounds and wondered if you might care to accompany me?" he said, a tad bashfully.

Pursing her lips, Frances turned away and began walking off.

'Good Lord, what have I said?' he thought, rushing after her, reaching for her arm.

"You don't wish to do so?" he asked with a flash of confusion. Frances made no response, though her eyes dropped to his hand still attached to her arm. He withdrew it at once.

"Harry, if I am to venture out of doors in this cold weather, do you not think that I will need a warm cloak and gloves?" Her eyes widened and head tilted to stress the point.

"Ah, of course," he admitted.

"Then be patient Harry, I won't be long," she said with a laugh and rushed off. Harry watched her hurrying away, the undeniably feminine gait, the swish of her skirts and the soft trail of fabric in her wake. For some time, he strolled around the room, greeting several others with a simple nod until finally, he paused beneath a large portrait of Frances herself, close to the fireplace. The likeness was uncannily accurate. Slightly side-on, one hand held a single white rose between thumb and forefinger, the other lightly gripping a portion of her voluminous skirt. Harry carefully deliberated every aspect, from the sumptuous blue silk gown, exquisite lace, the faintest hint of a smile on her lips and finally, the vividness of the eyes that seemed to almost follow him.

"It was undertaken by an accomplished young artist from York and was a wedding gift from my father."

Harry swung round. The living subject stood directly before him, now swathed in a fur trimmed cloak, pulling on a pair of gloves with elaborately embroidered cuffs.

"My late husband gave me these; aren't they beautiful?" she asked brightly.

"Very," Harry said, turning back to look up at the portrait. "Fitzherbert certainly was a most fortunate man."

At a muffled sound, he turned back to see Frances staring down at the beadwork on the gloves, her brow deeply furrowed.

"Oh, forgive me Frances, I had not meant to remind you….."

The frozen gravel crunched beneath their feet as slowly they made their way across the Courtyard and round the back of the house, the lawn now totally obscured by a covering of snow that shimmered in the weak sunlight. The ornamental pond had frozen solid, its fountain still and silent, petrified by the rawness of winter. They chose to walk past the kitchen garden and keeping to the pathways, around the perimeter of the walled garden, Frances stopped by an arched entrance.

"See yonder recessed seat Harry?" He peered past her. "That's where I sat with your commander on the morning of my wedding," she explained.

'You are abroad early, Viscountess?'

Rupert had certainly startled Frances that day. Then the gardens had been filled with the most vibrant colours, intoxicating fragrances that filled the air, though now they looked quite different. Winter now held the entire area in a grip of nudity and starkness that nevertheless possessed a beauty of its own.

"You spent time alone, with Rupert?" Harry asked with suspicion. Frances took a quick glance at Martha loitering some way behind, knowing that when alone with a man to whom she was not married, the correct procedure was to have a chaperone.

A memory made her smile. On the morning of her wedding, Frances had caused quite a stir in the household when strolling back into the house with the Prince at her side and no chaperone in sight!

"Shocking as it may seem but yes I did. I had decided to take an early walk in the grounds and unbeknownst to me, the Prince had the same notion. We sat together for over an hour or more conversing……he behaved impeccably," she said.

"Might one enquire the subject of such discourse?" Harry enquired.

"He spoke of his life in Holland, of warfare and of his imprisonment and ultimate freedom. T'was most interesting and ultimately, I was forced to change my opinion of him," she admitted.

"You didn't like him?"

"Not initially, no, not one bit. I wrongly assumed he had merely come to take John away with him at once."

"Whereas he had other plans?"

"Hmm, John was given permission to stay in Yorkshire on the proviso that certain duties were performed on Rupert's behalf. In the end, John didn't leave until September and for that alone, the Prince has my gratitude and respect."

"High praise indeed," Harry admitted, nodding his head.

"The Prince graciously dispatched Lord Bynghame north to inform me of John's death at Edgehill...."

"Ralph Bynghame?" Harry asked.

"Yes, he and my late brother were great friends, in fact Ralph is more like another brother to me. I confess I wasn't exactly kind to him at that time, in fact, I derided him most cruelly, more than once."

"A consequence of untold grief, I dare say?" Harry laughed. "Your mother certainly appears fond of Lady Bynghame.....a tad more than the man himself, eh?"

'What do you know about that?' Frances thought, endeavouring to read Harry's unusually impassive expression, and failing. It was clear that he was not about to say any more on that particular subject though, and prudently, Frances chose not to press him.

"The Bynghame's wed for status and fortune.... not for love, as I did," she merely said.

Harry plucked a lone tawny hued leaf dangling almost hopelessly from a branch, rolling the forlorn and fragile item back and forth between his hands until it crumbled into pieces and fell to the ground.

"Oh, to be allowed freedom to choose one's partner in life?" he said more or less to himself. Unwilling to consider a subject that still proved far too painful, Frances walked on, intent on enjoying the weak sunshine hanging low in the February afternoon sky.

"You approve of our gardens, Harry?" she asked cheerily over one shoulder.

"Very much.... despite appearing a little stark currently," he admitted catching up.

"I believe that every season possesses beauty of its own, Harry," she said adding, "You should see it here in the summer when the trees are in full leaf and all the different flowers are in bloom....."

"I should like to see that myself."

With a gasp, Frances swung round. The Earl of Montrose stood casually leaning against a tree, a look of amusement playing through the grey eyes. The two women hastily curtsied and Harry offered a half-hearted bow.

"Good day to you, Lord Graham," Frances managed.

"Forgive me for startling you but when the beauty of these gardens in the summer was mentioned, I felt I had to say something," Montrose said, suddenly looking back along the pathway and frowning. "What's this then?"

A dishevelled trooper hurried toward them with a determined gait and serious expression.

"Beggin ya pardon Milord, Milady…. might I have a word Captain Broughton, Sir?" the soldier said breathlessly.

"Problems, Hakes?" Harry enquired.

"Aye Sir. Corporal Bowater sends his compliments and requests your presence urgently back in the encampment."

'Bad enough the Scot has forestalled us, but now this?' Harry thought. To him this was beyond the pale since he had hoped to spend a pleasant couple of hours in Frances' company.

"What's the issue?" he asked.

"By your leave… I'm not at liberty to speak of it here, Sir… not in front of a lady…. tis a matter of…. behaviour?"

"Where's Newcastle?" Harry asked.

"Gone to York with his officers to meet with Governor Glemham, Sir."

"What all of them?"

"No Sir, some are in attendance on the Queen, at the house….. but I could hardly go and disturb..."

"No, no, of course not," Harry finally admitted. With a sigh he turned toward Montrose. "My Lord Earl, might I impose upon you to see the Viscountess back to the house? It seems I am required."

"Provided the lady has no objection?" the Scot answered.

Martha wandered a little closer to her mistress, clearing her throat quietly. She could tell Frances was perfectly happy to be out of doors especially since two men seemed to be vying for her company, but she was mindful of all the duties still awaiting her back at the house and of time progressing.

"I have no objection at all, Lord Graham," Frances said and then to Harry, "I shall doubtless see you later, for I did note your name amongst those invited to dine with Her Majesty this night?"

Harry's grin broadened.

"Mayhap I might beg a seat beside you?" he asked, kissing her gloved hand.

"Possibly," Frances answered demurely as Harry bowed his head and hurried off with Hakes, a portion of conversation drifting back toward Frances and the Earl.

"What? By God, Newcastle would have him flogged for that...."

Frances and Montrose exchanged bemused glances. Surprisingly, she found herself acquiring knowledge as to the finer points of military encampments, discipline being just one aspect and though she wondered what the problem was, she knew it would be frowned upon to ask, no matter how great her curiosity.

"Matters military, Viscountess," he said. "Ne'er a day goes by without several issues requiring addressing head on. I'm sure Lord Broughton will deal with whatever it is perfectly well. Shall we proceed a little?"

Discounting Martha's obvious desire not to, Frances agreed at once. Fate had brought an opportunity that was not about to be refused. To have a chance to discover more about this interesting Scot was something she had hoped to achieve, ever since being introduced to him the previous evening.

"You are not required elsewhere yourself, Lord Graham?" she asked.

"Not currently," he answered simply. "Perhaps we could converse a little as we walk? Unlike Lord Broughton, I am not invited to dine with the Queen, so this may well be our only opportunity."

"Perhaps then we should walk down this way," Frances said indicating a pathway off to the right.

Martha's lips tightened with a scowl. She knew exactly where this pathway headed, and it certainly was not back toward the house. Eventually the way opened out into an area where the little church stood, surrounded in places by ancient gravestones. As was her want, Frances paused by a particular headstone.

"Here lies my brother," she explained. Briefly she explained their relationship, gave an account of his support for the Protestant cause in Europe and the manner in which he had been cruelly struck down with a fever not long after his return to England.

"It sounds as if you were close to your brother?" Montrose enquired.

"I was indeed. He and my late husband met in the Low Countries...." Here she paused, looking down at the grave.

'Beloved wife'........ 'precious sister.'

Both men had shown her love in different forms, and both were now gone, cruelly stolen from her. Surprisingly, despite the coldness of winter, she detected miniscule specks of moss on the edges of the headstone, almost tauntingly indicating the passage of time. Finally, Frances again looked back at Martha whose eyes almost pleaded for the sojourn to be curtailed.

"Perhaps we should head back to the house now, my Lord," Frances said indicating the narrow path toward the church itself.

"Your husband was slain in Warwickshire, so I understand?" Montrose surprisingly asked.

'Who told you?'

"Yes, in the battle last October," Frances said. "We had only wed a few weeks beforehand, in this very church."

The delight and joy of that summer's day seemed an age away now, the closed and locked doors almost asserting finality.

'Till death do us part.'

Both had spoken that short phrase aloud to one another, though neither had imagined then how quickly that was to come true.

"My commiserations, Madam," Montrose said, taking her hand with a look of genuine sympathy and surprisingly, Frances felt her pulse quicken.

'What is it about this man?'

For a time, the pair considered one another until Martha yet again cleared her throat, a timely reminder for the need for prudence.

"Such sorrowful topics should perhaps be left here…..among the dead," Frances said turning to walk on by herself with mixed thoughts. Eventually, they reached a small gate where Montrose held it open for both women to go through. As she strolled on, Frances considered what detail she knew of this man, facts imparted by her father the previous evening when most had gone, and they had been left alone.

James Graham, he told her, had been married at the age of seventeen to the daughter of Lord Carnegie, Magdalen who had borne him several children, most of whom still lived with their mother in Scotland. When Miles told her of his many lengthy absences overseas fighting, Frances wondered at the nature of the relationship Montrose shared with his wife, though she daren't ask, even of her father.

"Might I ask the reason for your haste in making for Bridlington to see the Queen?" she asked once he drew alongside once more. Under the broad brim of his black felt hat, she noticed his brows lift.

"In her capacity as my sovereign's wife, I need to speak with her urgently.....I still need to do so," he admitted.

"Ah, I see," she responded simply.

"No, I'm not sure you do," he said stopping abruptly to face her. "Few appreciate my true purpose in venturing south so hurriedly."

'Oh, do tell...' She thought, searching his face. "And just what is that purpose, my Lord?" she asked pointedly.

He paused, looking down at the snow on the tips of his boots. Few women ever addressed him the way this one did and deciding to offer a little more information, he wondered just what her reaction might be.

"Few comprehend just how grave Scotland's position grows by the day, Madam," he said forcefully. "The Covenanters only await the slightest opportunity to join forces with the English rebels and attack the King's forces here in the north of England. Should that happen, the consequences for His Majesty would be dire indeed...."

He scowled at the way she merely stared, wide-eyed. Had she understood anything at all of what he had just said or worse still, much as most others, did she even care? Slowly a little frown creased her brow and looking directly into his eyes, she said, "A significant threat then?"

He laughed nervously.

"Without doubt. If, however, the Queen will heed the proposals I have in mind, the enemy's schemes can be speedily and soundly thwarted."

"Dare I enquire just what those proposals might be?" she asked.

Momentarily stunned, all the Earl could do was examine the face of a young woman whose breath formed little clouds of white steam in the frigid air, her fair hair escaping here and there from under a black velvet hood.

"Tis my fervent desire to raise a royalist force to defend the King's interests in Scotland and take decisive action before it's too late. Should the Queen agree to such a venture, then that illiterate 'bastard' Leslie would not dare cross the border……Ya pardon Viscountess, for the graphic words I use, but I consider him naught but an illegitimate rogue."

"Think naught of it my Lord; you speak with great passion, that's all. If it helps, my own father did perhaps hint that the King may well now regret bestowing such a grand title upon Lord Leven."

The truth was that Miles disliked the Earl of Leven intensely, voicing as much several times after encountering him more than once during the Bishop's Wars.

'She's certainly aware of many things,' Montrose thought to himself. "But now he's the commander of the Covenanters and has to be stopped."

"You are resolute in this?"

"Tis the only way."

Frances glanced at Martha stamping first one foot then the other, rubbing her hands together to warm them. It certainly had turned much colder, bitter in fact and if she were honest, she too was starting to feel chilled.

"I think, Lord Graham that I should return to the house now, it suddenly feels much colder," she admitted.

"Then let me take you straight back," he offered.

During their steady walk back, Frances contemplated if it might be too outrageous to enquire more of him. She decided she had little to lose, after all this might be her only opportunity to understand more.

"I hear the Queen won't see you until she's safely housed in York?" she ventured and at first, he gave no response, though she noticed his hands flexing repeatedly.

"No that's right and it's damned annoying….."

Frances had to bite her lip to keep from laughing. Clearly he was annoyed and yet if all that he had told her were true, she could hardly blame him.

"Why could she not have spoken with you at Bridlington?" she asked.

With a very revealing bark of laughter, he responded, "Och, I tried, but was graciously informed that she was too distressed after being fired upon by the Parliament ships."

"You mean her convoy was fired upon?" she asked, pausing by a tree, open mouthed.

"You've not heard?" he asked.

"No." she confessed.

"Then you're sure to at some point," he said with a deep throated chuckle. "Granted, she was in fear for her life at the time, though now she loves to regale everyone repeatedly with her 'brush with death' at the hands of the enemy."

Unexpectedly, his expression seemed to darken and with a growl of frustration, he slammed his fist against the tree's trunk.

"Hell's teeth, she has to see me soon. I have to make her understand that delay gives the Covenanters chance to build an even larger force."

Frances and Martha exchanged a quick look of bewilderment as the dark mood seemed to lift almost as quickly as it had appeared. He turned to encompass Frances with a smile that bathed her in unexpected warmth.

"I beg your pardon for that outburst, Viscountess…… Mayhap now you will comprehend a little of my frustration at being constantly told to wait."

Unthinking, Frances lightly touched his arm.

"You display only the fervent hope to make Her Majesty comprehend the seriousness of matters. If only there were something I could do to assist you in this?"

Grasping the hand on his sleeve, he seemed to carefully examine the ornately embroidered glove, before raising it to his lips.

"For that one comment alone Viscountess, you have my gratitude, but I believe there is naught anyone can do except myself once she agrees to an audience." Releasing her hand, he folded his arms. "Regardless of what is said of me, I am loyal to my King, my only wish is to protect his interests in Scotland."

Violet eyes held the grey ones steadily.

"Despite once rebelling against him yourself?" she ventured, arching her brows upward.

'My but you're surprisingly erudite,' he thought and with a smile said, "May a man not be brought to his senses, despite disagreeing with some of the King's more disputable policies?"

Of course, he could. Frances' own father had vehemently railed against some of the King's more pressing policies. The endless demands from the Exchequer dropping onto Lambert's desk regularly, all guaranteed to put Miles in a bad humour as the amount required from the estate purse increased with alarming regularity. Miles could easily have shown animosity toward this wayward Scot, if only for the reminder of the leg wound, he had received in the battle at Newburn, when he and Montrose had been on opposing sides. But then that was not her father's way and the Scot had been welcomed with as much cordiality as any other member of the Queen's party.

"Perhaps you are right, my Lord," she murmured.

"You speak very plain for a woman, a most uncommon trait," he surprisingly commented, and Frances felt herself smiling.

"I speak as I find, my Lord. No crime, surely?"

Her expression certainly appeared strange, almost provoking as was the smile playing at her lips, setting him on his guard.

"I think perhaps you jest with me a little….no doubt for your own amusement?" he observed. Disturbingly, he wondered if he had spoken too freely to a female to whom he had only recently been introduced and yet she certainly appeared to show a measure of interest in what he needed to say to the Queen. Had she then drawn her own conclusions?

"Lord Graham, I would never be so shallow," she declared forcefully and smiling softly, he responded, "No, I don't believe you would."

Martha moved a little closer, stamping her feet harder to announce her presence and prevent a turn in the conversation she considered a little forward.

"Yes Martha, in a moment," Frances said and then to Montrose, "I hope the Queen will grant you the audience you desire, once we reach York."

Montrose suddenly frowned.

"Forgive me, did you say 'we'?" he enquired.

"I did. I am considering joining the Queen's party heading to York;

she invited me herself."

"And will you go?"

'I certainly will now.' Frances pulled her fallen hood over her hair.

"Well, I believe there is to be entertainments and dancing, so possibly I shall," she admitted.

Montrose looked heavenward.

"Och, such pastimes hold little pleasure for me… though I dare say I shall attend them, if only to keep the Queen sweet." A gust of wind whipped at Frances' cloak and glancing up at the yellowish grey tinged sky, Montrose added, "We'll have more snow tonight I'd wager, and you grow cold. Allow me to escort you and your maid, back to the house. I think we have spoken long enough…. for now."

'For now….?' The thought was to remain with Frances for some time.

CHAPTER FORTY-SEVEN

February 1643

Seated between Harry Broughton and the Duchess of Richmond, Frances felt increasingly uncomfortable, something about the Earl of Montrose bothering her ever since that morning in the grounds. Earlier in the day, the Duchess had given permission for Frances to use her given name, unless propriety dictated otherwise.

"Do you know why Montrose was not invited tonight, Mary?" Frances asked lightly during a lull in the conversation. Mary's expression steadily turned to one of incredulity, until finally, she burst into a fit of laughter. This, of course, brought unwarranted stares from other diners, though Mary remained oblivious to them.

"Because, dear Frances, the Queen does not wish to hear aught about 'Scotland's piteous state' until she is ready," she whispered but this was not enough for Frances. Ever since returning to the house, she had been fixated on what the grey eyed Scot had imparted to her regarding certain activities by the Covenanters and just how they might potentially affect the King. If Montrose were speaking the truth, then surely it would be politic for the Queen to hear him out swiftly, after which he could return to Scotland to put his proposals into action. Everything he had said sounded common sense to Frances and yet she could be completely wrong, reading more into his view than was the actual truth. She was no soldier after all, nor was she any kind of stateswoman and there could well be far more to this issue than she was aware of, but something within her doubted that Montrose spoke falsely about the situation.

"Why the constant rebuffs toward him when he is an Earl, just as my father is?" she asked and with a smile, Mary's brows lifted.

"Montrose is naught like your father, Frances. The Queen considers him too abrasive and his 'icy eyes' as she describes them, certainly unnerve her." Mary giggled and leaned closer, "If you ask me, she finds him attractive," she whispered with a youthful grin.

Frances glanced down the table to where Henrietta Maria almost reigned, flanked at one side by Miles and at the other by Henry Jermyn. In a state of tranquillity, gesturing occasionally with her hands, the little Frenchwoman conversed and nodded as the mood took her.

"What makes you think such a thing, Mary?" Frances whispered and setting down her glass, the Duchess explained.

"I have known the Queen for a long time Frances and have often witnessed her changes of disposition. Right now, for example, she is perfectly at ease with your father and Jermyn, but if it were someone like Montrose beside her for example, you would see an entirely different Queen. I can tell you that she will not agree to an audience with 'the Graham' until she's safely ensconced in York and even then I would say he will have to have a great deal of patience. If he does not, then he's likely to be kept waiting even longer."

Frances scowled. If that were true, then Montrose wouldn't be happy to hear it. He had spoken of acting swiftly, with determination, but if permission was not forthcoming for any length of time, then any action would be delayed and that could only jeopardise the King's situation in the north, affecting even Yorkshire, worryingly.

"But he explained it's vital to speak with her about the movements of the Covenanters, he needs permission to…."

"Dear me, you must have spent considerable time in his company for him to explain such details?" Mary interrupted.

Despite heat infusing her face Frances offered a hesitant smile.

"There was no impropriety Mary, why we spent less than half an hour together and my maid was present the whole time," she explained.

Mary chuckled.

"A little defensive my dear, but tell me, why do you think Montrose spoke of this to you?" she asked.

That was a good question, one Frances really couldn't answer but nor could she reason why she had felt the need to justify herself to the Duchess. She had indeed done nothing wrong; she had merely spent time with someone intriguing, nothing more sinister or for any type of ulterior motive. She was, however, beginning to realise that Mary Richmond had a mischievous side to her character, one that Frances might be the butt of currently.

"I can only think that for some reason, the Earl found me easy to speak to?" she admitted.

Mary retrieved a small piece of bread from her plate and delicately pushed it through rosebud lips in a manner that seemed to captivate the man seated directly opposite.

"So, you like him, Frances?" she asked, tilting her head.

How was such a question to be answered? Frances couldn't help but ask the same of herself if she were being completely honest. Undeniably, Montrose spoke eloquently and with intent, but what else was it about him?

"And just what are you two lovely ladies speaking of so secretly?" Harry interrupted, having put up with their whispering long enough.

Frances shot a wide-eyed glare at Mary, silently urging her to say nothing, but thankfully, the young Duchess wasn't about to betray her new found friend.

"My dear Harry, you have just spoiled my hope of finding out whether or not Frances considers you handsome," Mary said.

Harry leaned an elbow on the table and peering into Frances' face, asked, "Well, don't be timid Frances, do respond, for in truth I should love to hear what you think of me?"

Reaching for her fan, Frances flicked it open, fluttering it rapidly to cool her increasingly heated face as Mary chuckled softly.

"Does her blush not give you an answer," she asked.

"Oh, I do hope so, Your Grace," Harry answered.

'This is intolerable.'

Frances snapped the fan shut with a sharp click.

"Stop it at once, both of you. Tis unfair to attack me from both sides," she said.

"Greater strength in pairs, you know," Harry suggested.

"Just put him out of his misery, Frances and explain what you truly think of him," Mary suggested.

'This is awkward.'

Frances took a deep breath.

"In answer Lord Broughton, I do consider you a handsome man…but more than that, I shall not be prevailed upon to say…" she said.

Mary, finding the evasive answer hilarious, laughed out loud.

Such a captive audience proved too much of a temptation for the Queen and, much as Montrose had suggested, the conversation soon turned to the horrendous journey from Holland. Dark, almond shaped eyes eagerly searched the table as she related the tale of the first aborted attempt that ended in a hasty if somewhat perilous retreat to the safety of the Dutch port of Scheveningen.

Unexpectedly, Frances sensed Harry leaning closer.

"Be warned, this may go on for some time," he whispered.

"You've heard of it before?" she asked.

"Once or twice and I was present for the latter part remember, which no doubt you will hear about shortly…."

"Mon dieu, Milord Broughton…… If your conversation with the Viscountess is done?"

The Queen's raised voice and direct focus produced instant silence. To be singled out in that manner though made Frances feel like a naughty child, though Harry seemed less so, taking it all in his stride.

"I beg your pardon, Your Majesty," he said tipping his head.

Frances caught her mother's horrified expression, certain of chastisement later for being the subject of the Queen's displeasure. Frances realised she should not have been drawn so easily into listening to Harry, not when their monarch's wife was speaking.

Finally assured of everyone's attention, Henrietta began again. Their convoy had approached the east coast, aware that Parliamentary ships would be patrolling the north sea in the hope of waylaying the Queen's convoy. Despite the risks, the whole party made landfall at Bridlington where they were eventually located by the Earl of Newcastle and his men. Henrietta laughed when describing how word had arrived from Ferdinando Fairfax offering to escort her himself to the safety of York, rather than her trusting those whom the highest authority considered 'enemies of the state.'

'There is no authority in this land above that of my husband,' she thought.

"I believed him not," she voiced firmly, breaking into a sudden smirk. "Though Newcastle was delayed for a day or two, I much preferred his company to that of Fairfax, who no doubt would have seen me incarcerated to aid Parliament's mediation with my husband."

"Bridlington Quay is but a mere fishing village, Your Majesty, surely you were not compelled to stay there, when several grand houses were within easy reach?" Miles suggested.

"The hour was late on our arrival, and we were exhausted from the voyage, some even feeling unwell, Lord Benningford. Thankfully we were able to make use of a small cottage on the quayside where eventually, we took to our beds. But then at about four of the clock, four Parliamentary ships in the bay opened fire. Scarcely had I risen from my bed before the balls whistled about us in such style that you can imagine, I loved not their music. We were forced to leave the house, though thankfully my ladies were able to retrieve my thick cloak and then I suddenly remembered my dear Mitte had been left behind in the cottage."

Frances quite liked the little 'lap' dog that seemed to be constantly in the Queen's presence, often scampering around Haveringham's Great Hall behind its grand mistress. It was an ugly looking beast and Frances didn't take to it the way she had to Boye, Prince Rupert's hunting dog.

"We took refuge in a filthy, mud and water filled ditch, though even before we reached it, the balls were singing around us. Not twenty paces from where we cowered, a sergeant was killed outright, one of my ladies splattered with his blood…."

The royal eyes flicked toward a solemn looking lady in green sitting directly opposite Frances, feeding a kerchief repeatedly though her fingers. She seemed close to tears.

'That must be her, poor woman.'

Frances felt a rush of gratitude when the gentleman at the lady's side whispered pacifying and soothing words that eventually gained a hesitant smile.

"Shocking," Elizabeth said, taking a gulp of the yellow tinged canary wine that she favoured far more than Miles' best burgundy or Rhenish.

Interlinking her fingers, Henrietta Maria went on to explain how they had been in the murky depths of the ditch for over two hours, all the time bombarded by the enemy ships, each explosion enveloping them with showers of debris. Ultimately, it came to light that the Admiral of the Dutch vessel, from which they had disembarked, ordered the rebels to desist or he would be obliged to open fire upon them as 'enemies of Holland.' Thankfully, the turn of the tide brought relief and the rebel ships were forced to withdraw from range, allowing the Queen's whole party to return to the relative comfort of the cottage on the quayside.

"Your Majesty could so easily have been killed," Elizabeth mewed and with a magnanimous nod, Henrietta agreed.

"I had no desire to give the rebels chance of boasting that they forced the Queen of England to quit the village she had chosen to stay in," Henrietta explained with a stoical lift of the royal chin. "God has blessed us thus far and come the spring, I am convinced that He will do so again for the onward journey to Oxford and my husband."

CHAPTER FORTY-EIGHT

February 1643

Despite little being observable outside, nonetheless Mary Richmond remained motionless, staring expressionlessly through the window. It was snowing heavily, bathing the courtyard in paleness that gave the whole area a deceptively light quality. Once the Queen had finished speaking of the ordeal at Bridlington, the young Duchess had silently risen from the table and wandered down the Great Hall to sit on the padded window seat, so often favoured by Frances. Memories of that dreadful night constantly plagued Mary. Several of her companions had actually brought up the contents of their stomachs when the sergeant had been blown asunder by the cannon ball. Thankfully, he would have known little, but those witnessing his end would never forget that sight. Lady Catherine had been the most affected of course, being in closest proximity to him and hence splattered with his blood and other unthinkable substances. She had almost run mad in an attempt to scrape debris from her clothing, ultimately tearing at her gown, insisting it be burned, rather than ever wear it again. Mary had rapidly concluded that if the incident in the ditch were even marginally akin to what the men of England faced in battle, then she was heartily relieved not to have been born male. With a shudder, she closed her eyes momentarily until the sound of rustling silk made her open them again.

"Do you wish to be alone, Mary?" Frances enquired, cautiously drawing closer.

With a hesitant smile, Mary patted the cushion beside her.

"Not at all, come and sit by me. I dare say you will consider me to have grown a little melancholy this night?"

"Perhaps you miss your husband, much as Her Majesty does?" Frances suggested, hoping this might detract from any cheerless recollections. Mary's brows slowly lifted, and she gave a simple shrug.

"Perhaps… James and I have been apart for almost a year now," she freely admitted, but then a smile spread to her lips lighting her eyes. "Conversely, there were plenty of handsome gallants in The Hague of course…." Mary's unexpected burst of merriment drew curiosity from some still at the table and for a fleeting moment, Frances wondered if Mary almost eluded to some form of infidelity with one of them.

"Do you not love the Duke, your husband, Mary?" she enquired, and Mary's expression swiftly changed; gone the smile, replaced by a stern look at a proud lift of the chin.

"That, Viscountess is beyond impertinence," she stated firmly. Mortified to have insulted the Duchess, Frances hung her head.

"I beg your pardon, Your Grace; I meant nothing by the remark…" she murmured.

For some time, silence fell between them until Mary reached for Frances' hand.

"No, no, my dear friend, tis I who should seek your forgiveness. You took me by surprise tis all. I am perhaps unused to such directness?" she admitted.

"I am often cautioned for excessive inquisitiveness, Your Grace," Frances admitted.

The Duchess giggled softly, giving Frances ' hand a gentle squeeze.

"It's Mary….remember?" she remarked with a compassionate smile that instantly melted away any fear of offence. "But, since you mentioned him, I do have a great affection for my husband, but then few would not. James Stuart is a tall, fair haired handsome man and his titles of Duke of Richmond and Lennox make him all the more appealing." Again, a peal of Mary's laughter rang out. "You seemed scandalized at the thought of dalliance? Believe me when I tell you that tis the way at Court. There really is no harm in enjoying the attentions of a handsome man, you know, Frances."

Flirtatiously, Mary slowly twirled a lock of hair round one finger, her eyes flicking to two men standing beside the fireplace, their joint bows affirming awareness of her many attractions.

"See Frances, tis but a game of cat and mouse, though let me assure you that I always intend to be the cat….. and never the rodent." Frances wondered how she was supposed to answer something she considered a little shocking and yet she needn't have worried.

"Tell me of your husband, Frances," Mary asked brightly.

"Well, he…" Frances began but then had a better thought. "If you follow me, I can show you."

She led the Duchess out of the Great Hall, down a corridor and eventually, opened the door to the small dining room. Just inside the door, she paused and indicated a portrait on the wall.

'*John, Lord Fitzherbert….September 1642,*' Mary read. "Is it a good likeness?"

"Exceptional," Frances answered. "The artist captured him so faithfully, especially the eyes……" Fondly she traced a finger across the hair, down the face and over the lips. How greatly she missed them ensnaring her own with such passion. "It was painted only days after our marriage….."

Mary dropped a hand gently on Frances' shoulder.

"I'm so sorry. I'm no stranger to unexpected deaths myself, you know. My first husband Charles Herbert, a relative of the Pembroke family, died from smallpox at the early age of only fifteen. We had been wed less than a year and I being only twelve at that time, cannot tell you that I was devastated, why I scarcely knew him."

Frances considered the handsome woman at her side. Daughter of the late Duke of Buckingham, Mary's father had been a great favourite of King James as well as England's current monarch, Charles. Both Mary's marriages had been arranged for her without prior consultation, she given no opportunity to voice any form of objection. The norm for children of the highest-ranking families in the land was this form of arrangement and once again Frances felt a wave of thankfulness that Miles had allowed her the measure of freedom he had.

When overlooked for promotion, a disgruntled officer had assassinated Buckingham, Mary had been raised at the Court with Henrietta Maria actively involved in her upbringing and education.

Frances stared at John's image, until as always, her lips trembled, and tears infused her eyes.

"No, you don't," Mary said, gripping Frances' elbow. "Hear me now before your handsome husband's portrait. You shall indeed come to York with us and there I shall make it my personal mission to rid you of this sorrow." She turned to the portrait and with a tilt of the head added, "What say you my Lord, do you concur with a plan to make your wife smile once more?" In the silence she smiled coquettishly. "There now, I didn't hear him voice any objection," she said with a broad grin.

Frances couldn't help smiling herself. Mary certainly possessed a complex but hugely likeable character, though Frances was mindful of the fact that if crossed, the Duchess just might prove a force to be reckoned with.

"Very well, I shall ask father if I might use our house in the city. I can easily stay there until the Queen leaves for Oxford," Frances admitted.

"Excellent notion," Mary responded.

CHAPTER FORTY-NINE

York - March 1643

In the mirror, Frances watched Martha's expert fingers styling her hair within her bedchamber at the recently re-named Fitzherbert House. For some reason, this second dwelling had always been fondly described as 'The York House' to the family but it had come as a complete surprise to Frances when Miles had suggested renaming it in honour of a son-in-law he had esteemed so highly.

When Frances had broached the subject of attending the Queen's party in York, her father had agreed, on the proviso that Lady Holcroft lodge at Fitzherbert House too. Miles had come to greatly admire Lady Holcroft's calming demeanour, secretly hoping she might prove a steadying influence upon a daughter who could at times be headstrong. In turn, Frances' relationship with Alys, had grown to the point where the pair felt perfectly at ease with one another with the ability to converse openly on a number of subjects, each using the others' given name.

Having been scrubbed and polished till all the surfaces shone and a heady fragrance of lavender and beeswax pervaded every room, Fitzherbert House gleamed. Miles had ordered two staff to be in situ in order that the ladies wanted for nothing, Martha being tasked with attending both Frances and Lady Holcroft to ensure they looked their best when in attendance on the Queen.

Frances turned her head from side to side, admiring Martha's handiwork when the door flew open, and a flustered looking Alys scurried in. Sadly, a curl that Martha had been attempting to secure, fell from her fingers, tumbling down onto Frances' shoulder.

"Alys, whatever is it?" Frances asked, noting the flush on her friend's face as well as her laboured breathing. Unfastening her cloak, Alys tossed it onto the bed, dropping down beside it.

"Well, where do I start," she said breathlessly. "There is such news that I had to come straight here to tell you." One hand pressed to her chest; she took a deep breath. "Sir Hugh Cholmley arrived unexpectedly, wishing to see the Queen."

"What, the governor of Scarborough?" Frances asked, narrowing her eyes suspiciously for Cholmley was known to support the cause of Parliament. "What did he want?"

"You may not believe this, but he's declared for the King," Alys explained, regaining a little more composure. "He was with the Queen for more than an hour...."

The same curl Martha had been trying to fasten in place again fell when Frances swung round to face Alys.

"He's changed sides?" Frances asked.

"Not only that, but he brought a full troop of horse with him."

"But that's astounding.... if Scarborough Castle is now Royalist, the port must be also?" Frances suggested.

"Better yet, there was a ship in the harbour laden with arms that Parliament had previously captured from us." She giggled brightly. "Oh Frances, I would say the wind blows in our favour and we've not even left York yet. Just imagine if the same thing were to happen throughout the land, why the whole country could be back under the King's control before the year is out."

Frances' joy instantly dissolved like frost on a bright spring morning.

'Were that to be true, then John would have died for no reason....' she thought.

Sensing how her young mistress would feel, Martha lightly placed a hand on Frances' shoulder. In the mirror, their eyes met briefly, a simple smile enough to prove to the maid that all was well with her charge.

"I am sure the hostilities won't end so swiftly though Frances;

there's still far too much unrest in places for that to happen." Absently, Alys picked up a phial of perfume inhaling its fragrance. "You know how the Queen confides in me, to her mind the King debates with Parliament far too frequently. Her fear is that he may yet come to terms with them in a way that will make it nigh on impossible for her to remain in England."

Frances spun round so swiftly, that once again Martha's coiffuring attempts were thwarted.

"She can't leave England, she's married to the King," Frances declared.

"Ah, but don't forget that Parliament hate her for interfering so often in matters of state," Alys explained, replacing the perfume stopper, and setting the bottle back on the dresser.

"Can she not express an opinion to her own husband?" Frances asked as Martha threaded a row of tiny pearls in and out of a plait of hair, securing it in a coil at the back of Frances' head.

"That's not how Parliament see it. They consider the Queen to have far too much influence over the King. She feels that Parliament would always insist upon the royalist army being disbanded and should the King agree to that, he would be lost as a monarch." A look of outrage and disbelief flashed through Frances' eyes, but Alys had not quite finished. "Don't forget Frances, the Queen is a papist, a hated and mistrusted faith; Catholicism is seen as a political power remember. Parliament will never allow her to live here in peace, I'm afraid."

"Then what would be her solution?" Frances asked.

"She believes the King should dissolve Parliament once and for all and rule alone, or as she says, *'why take up arms else?'* her exact words, Frances."

'Why indeed,' Frances thought.

The chosen residence for the Queen came as little surprise since the King had lodged in the same dwelling in the early part of '42 when fleeing London. Ingram House, named after its owner, Sir Arthur Ingram, was a medium sized dwelling, described as one of the finest in the ancient city of York. Having extensive grounds crammed with an abundance of flowerbeds, ornate statues, and several fishponds, it proved the perfect temporary residence for the monarch's wife.

Frances and Alys stood side by side, just inside a doorway, the former tapping her foot along to a melody being played by a group of musicians at the far end of the room.

"Are ye not inclined to venture any further in ladies?"

The soft Scot's lilt brought an instant smile to Frances' lips as she turned into smiling grey eyes that held warmth. Both she and Alys curtsied.

"Good evening, Lord Graham," Frances said, strangely fixated on the tinges of burnished, reddish gold in his luxuriant long hair as he bent over her hand.

"Oh, pray excuse me, I believe Lady Catherine is needing to speak with me," Alys said, heading off to join the lady in blue beside a large portrait of Arthur Ingram.

'You did that on purpose, Alys.'

Frances' smile wavered, nerves taking their toll as she wondered what to say. Montrose beat her to it.

"Would ye care to dance with me?" he asked.

"I thought you disliked such frivolous pastimes?" she answered with surprise.

"I do, though to dance with you, would be an honour," he admitted.

"Then I'd be delighted," she answered. "Ah, is this melody not of

Scots origin?"

"It is, indeed, hence we should not neglect the opportunity," he said, offering his arm.

As they walked across the room to join the other dancers, Frances couldn't help noticing the amount of attention they gained. It was really of insignificance; her hand was on the arm of a Scottish Lord whom she had come to admire, and he had requested to dance with her. For what more could she wish? The measure was a slow one, necessitating close movements round one another, intertwined hands, and the ability to look directly into one another's faces from time to time. Frances took in every aspect of his features, from the dark brows, firm jaw and amazing grey eyes that seemed to have the capacity to cause her heart to almost miss a beat. Despite declaring a lack of appeal, Montrose proved a competent dancer and at the final cord, obeisance was jointly offered before he stooped to raise Frances up.

"I must warn you, we seem to be the subject of much scrutiny," he said in hushed tones.

Sure enough, Frances noticed several inquisitive expressions, though most began swiftly speaking again in an attempt to disguise their curiosity. Frances gave a tinkling laugh, innocently touching the Earl's arm.

"I care not, my Lord. Shall we perhaps go across to yonder window and converse with greater privacy?" she suggested.

"What and risk even more gossip?" he answered with a swift glance about the room.

Frances felt strangely lightheaded and not just from the unmerited attention. Being close to this interesting Scotsman made her somehow feel alive again in a way she had not for a long time.

"Let them do their worst," she said, flicking open her fan and hiding her face behind it. "Now they'll no doubt speculate as to just what I'm saying to you...." she whispered.

"And if I were to lean closer, like this…." Briefly his hair brushed across her shoulder when he leaned down, sending a shock wave through her. "May I add how striking you look tonight," he said quietly, his eyes never leaving hers.

'Do I? Please don't…. and yet, yes please do…'

It proved difficult but she forced a smile to her lips.

"Why not be more outrageous still, my Lord and henceforth use my given name of Frances?"

Montrose took a step backwards, standing erect with an expression she could not fathom and brows that briefly flickered upward. For a while, he fiddled with a large emerald ring on one finger.

"I'd be honoured, Frances and in turn, I give you leave to address me as James," he finally said.

"I certainly will not…to me you will be Jamie, for that is the shortened form of your given name, is it not?"

His face unexpectedly clouded, and his smile fell.

"By God Madam, you're undeniably forward," he declared, though Frances felt as if she had almost been physically struck.

'He's offended…. how could I be so irresponsible….'

Blushing deeply, she lowered her eyes, frantically seeking a way to make amends.

"Lord Graham, I beg your pardon. I can indeed be rash and impulsive at times, though in essence I meant no offence to you. I shall, of course, be content to henceforth address you formally…."

Throwing back his head, Montrose guffawed.

"You'll do no such thing. I am merely unused to such spontaneity of speech in a female, but I am becoming aware that this could be part of what is an unusual character? I give you leave to address me as Jamie if you wish, though perhaps you should use discretion as to when? Formality of circumstances must prevail, must it not?"

To be given permission to use an informal style of Montrose's given name was a privilege indeed, he was an Earl after all and therefore should truly be afforded the correct form of civility at all times. As if to seal the matter, Montrose lifted her hand and planted a gentle kiss upon it before standing back and folding his arms.

"Now, Frances… I have news to impart," he said widening his eyes. "I am to have an audience with the Queen, on the morrow."

"But that's wonderful. You must be greatly relieved," she said, unsure why she had experienced a sudden pang of disappointment.

"I certainly am and I'm really hoping that once I have her agreement to my proposals, I'll find myself hastily heading back to Scotland."

'I don't want you to go….'

The thought took her totally by surprise but why she could not exactly say why. Forcing a smile, she quickly said, "I can only pray the Queen listens to all you have to say…."

Inexplicably, Frances had a sudden urge to flee and hastily return to the relative safety and comfort of Fitzherbert House. She need not have worried, right-on cue, Harry Broughton approached offering a broad grin as he bowed.

"Might I be permitted to steal your companion, my Lord, I have a mind to dance, if she would oblige me?" he said. Frances was grateful for any interruption and more than happy to have an opportunity to escape what felt like a strangely emotional situation.

"I'd be delighted, Harry," she said with a gregarious smile as she took his extended arm. "Excuse me, Lord Graham." This was definitely one of the occasions for formality.

They had not progressed far when Harry said, "I must caution you Frances, for I have overheard several remarks about the partiality you seem to show for 'the Graham.' More than one commented 'pon it."

Frances chuckled.

"Tis none of their business Harry… You know their need for scandal is never assuaged, perhaps we simply obliged them with something new to consider for a time."

Seemingly unamused, Harry drew her to a halt and scowled.

"Perhaps not the shrewdest thing to do."

"But tis all unfounded, Harry," she responded seriously. "Do I not converse just as often with you, there is no gossip about us that I know of?"

"That's as may be, but then I am not married," he answered. "I have to say that even I have the thought that you find him, shall we say… engaging?"

"Jealous, dear Harry?" she enquired.

"How could I not be, when I have come to regard you…." He stopped to look down at his boots, suddenly appearing bashful, almost awkward. "Frances, I have given a lot of thought to a matter and am contemplating writing to my father…. regarding you?"

Unexpectedly, Frances felt a pang of uneasiness.

"Whatever for, why would he be interested in me?" she asked innocently, already fearing his response.

'My God, those eyes,' he thought to himself as he lifted her hand and noted how elegantly long her fingers appeared.

"I should really like the opportunity to speak privately with you...." he admitted, and Frances glanced about nervously. Harry was delightful, attentive, and certainly handsome enough and yet considering anything more when she hardly knew him, caused her to feel panicky. It was only a matter of months since she had been widowed, far too soon to contemplate moving on, if that was what he hinted at.

She spotted Montrose standing alone by the window and knew exactly how to respond in a manner that would neither rebuff nor encourage Harry.

"Oh Harry, I dare say there will be plenty of opportunities to converse and even dance quite often, before the Queen leaves York." She knew that wasn't what he wanted to hear, but somehow, she felt the need to distract him. "Lord Graham will be leaving for Scotland before long, he informed me that the Queen has finally agreed to see him on the morrow. The poor man has been kept waiting so long, don't you think?"

"So, he'll be returning to Scotland soon, no doubt?" Harry said, glancing toward the Scot.

"Harry are we not supposed to be dancing?" she asked lightly. "If we tarry here much longer, the gossips will no doubt turn their sights on us too."

CHAPTER FIFTY

York - March 1643

The weather being remarkably temperate for the time of year and keen to escape the stuffiness of Ingram House, a number of courtiers chose to take a walk beside the river Ouse, including Frances and an increasingly agitated Earl of Montrose.

"Why has Hamilton arrived in York, Jamie?" she asked.

"On the pretext of paying his respects to Her Majesty, of course," he almost snarled, annoyance evident in the grey orbs. "It's completely laughable, if you ask me."

Bizarrely, his accent sounded even more pronounced, a consequence of being deeply disgruntled, Frances assumed.

"You doubt his motive?" she asked tentatively.

"That I do…. I know the rogue possesses great cunning. Do you know, the Queen agreed to see him the moment he arrived?"

Silence fell, offering Montrose the chance to mull over the events of the past few weeks, ever since his arrival in Yorkshire. Hadn't he been forced to kick his heels, both in Bridlington and in York, until Henrietta Maria had finally deigned see him and yet Hamilton's unexpected arrival had gained him an immediate audience. Montrose certainly was angry, hardly surprising since this latest arrival revived all those senses of slight and mistrust, all over again. The Queen certainly proved an enigma, at times pleasant to be around, joyful, and almost girlish in attitude, delighted by the merest of hint of a compliment. Yet conversely, she could be petulant and abrasive if the mood dictated. His own ultimate audience had been unfruitful and downright frustrating, Henrietta unwilling to perceive any form of urgency from what he had told her. In answer, he had been firmly ordered to wait until word came directly from the Earl of Hamilton regarding events in Scotland, as if everything he said was mistrusted. Now that Hamilton had come to York, Montrose felt almost pushed aside and surplus to requirements.

Ahead, their faster walking companions soon disappeared round the side of the Minster and though they should have caught them up, he forestalled her.

"Tarry a moment, I need to speak with you. Lord knows you're the only one willing to listen to aught I have to say," he admitted, sadness in the grey eyes.

"I'm not sure…" Frances answered looking toward the open space where the rest of the party had once been.

"We'll join them presently, they're heading for the Old Starre, after all," he said, kicking at the exposed root of a large tree, a forearm resting on its gnarled trunk and cloak fluttering about in the stiff breeze. "Do you know that I'm accused of being over-cautious, rash, imprudent and exaggerating issues that aren't as bad as I make out."

He stooped to pick up a small stone, examining it briefly before it was hurled with some force into the river, scattering a flock of ducks that flew off protesting loudly.

"What does Hamilton suggest?" Frances asked.

Jamie threw back his head, laughing disturbingly.

"Diplomacy my dear, simple diplomacy. He's convinced the Queen there's no need for military action at all and that talks alone will suffice. That damnable silk tongue has convinced her that, far from helping, any act of violence would merely result in the Covenanters choosing to join forces with the English rebels. The oaf hasn't a clue and speaks utter nonsense. Direct action is what's needed and swiftly." Back and forth he paced relentlessly, jaw set, and eyes filled with determination. "He's with her even now, placating her with fine words and untold flattery…. it's just ludicrous, the man's a menace."

A second stone quickly followed its forerunner into the murky depths as patiently, Frances watched him carefully until eventually he turned to face her.

"What am I to do, Frances? How can I compete with such eloquence of speech and manner? I prefer to be more direct as you know, but the Queen obviously dislikes that approach."

Crouching down on his haunches, Jamie picked up a third stone, bouncing it repeatedly in his palm before closing his fist around it. "I'm not wanted here. You've seen the way I'm treated, with naught but suspicion and mistrust."

She moved closer, dropping a leather clad hand on his shoulder.

"Not everyone considers you unwelcome here, Jamie," she said, and he stood to his feet.

"Aye I know that, but the Queen wields the authority here and only seems to respond to appeasement or courtly sycophancy. I'll not pander to such shallowness purely to be heard, Frances."

"Nor should you," she agreed and then with a scowl added, "Has Hamilton given her any definitive assurances?"

His lips seemed to press hard together, a vein pulsating in the side of his neck. When his head shook, he gave a mocking laugh.

"Oh, aye hasn't he just. He guarantees to personally ensure Scotland is kept well out of the war in England…."

Frances grimaced.

"How can he pledge such a thing?" she asked.

"He can't Frances and that's the whole point."

The rushing river became the only sound between them, burbling and gurgling on its meaningless course, every barrier forcing a change of direction as if mirroring England's present twisted directions. Why the Queen couldn't recognise the urgency described by this Scotsman Frances would never understand, after all, it had all sounded so simple to her.

"I am thanked for my endeavours and summarily dismissed, after being informed that Hamilton is appointed as Royal Commissioner for Scotland...." Jamie turned to look directly into her eyes. "In addition, he's been made up to Duke...."

"What?" she said, narrowing her eyes in disbelief.

With a shrug, he consigned the third stone to its watery fate, much as the others, then uttered something that made Frances shudder.

"Mayhap I should throw in my lot with the Covenanters myself."

She made a hurried grab for his arm.

"You cannot mean that, Jamie?"

"Of course not," he admitted, patting the hand still resting on his sleeve. "I'd rather be in league with the devil himself than consider doing that. I only hope that my supporters in Scotland will wait for me to return, before deciding what to do."

A sudden thought struck her, a possible manner of solution. Would he think her foolish if she suggested it? He already knew her to be headstrong, so what point in keeping it to herself?

"Why not write to the King directly?" she asked and when puzzlement flashed through the grey eyes added, "neither the Queen nor Hamilton will be in Oxford to influence his response? Why His Majesty might even send for you."

"I can't honestly see it making much difference, but the suggestion is gratefully received," he admitted with a smile.

Despondently he turned back to the river, his profile causing Frances' heart to suddenly quicken. There was another question that must be voiced and yet she dreaded the answer.

"What will you do now?" she finally asked.

"I'll return to Scotland…. there's naught to keep me here, after all."

'Naught to keep me here…'

Frances felt as if a blade had been thrust into her and twisted cruelly.

"So soon?" she managed to mutter.

He heaved an elongated sigh and again shook his head.

"I think I must, at least there I'll be of some use…."

Thankful for the fur edging her hood she turned her head as tears infused her eyes. Ever since his arrival at Haveringham Manor in February, and their sojourn in York, she had seen Jamie almost every day and his leaving was sure to leave a painful chasm. He joined her, pushing back the hood and lifting her chin with his fingertips.

"Don't you dare be sad for me, Frances Fitzherbert," he declared. "Tis more for me to thank you for having so much faith in everything I said almost from the moment of our first meeting."

Only then did she raise watery eyes to his, forcing a smile to her lips.

"It was a great honour," she whispered sweetly.

His expression changed marginally as he continued to stare into her wide eyes until finally, cupping her face, he stooped and touched her lips with his. Frances felt a surge of elation and closing her eyes, surrendered to a kiss that seemed to grow in intensity and pressure. She felt lightheaded, as if her senses were re-awakening to exquisite sensations, she had thought were gone forever with John's demise. Unconsciously, she pressed herself closer to him, running her fingers through the back of his long mane, a soft moan in her throat. But then abruptly, she felt herself being pushed aside and when her eyes opened, she saw him back beside the water's edge, his expression grim.

'What have I done wrong now?' she thought, stomach in knots.

It was incomprehensible to think that such an intimate moment had ended so unexpectedly, swiftly replaced by what seemed to be annoyance. Was he outraged by an act of female wantonness? Perhaps she should have resisted, shown more decorum, berated him for ungentlemanly behaviour? She had no idea what was wrong, but clearly something was and all she could do was stare at a profile that proved impenetrable. Eventually with a deep scowl, his head turned.

"Forgive me Frances…that should never have occurred," he said but she darted forward, reaching for his hand.

"But Jamie…. you must have sensed…. I did not prevent you….?" she gasped, frantically trying to fathom his present actions.

"Of course, I noticed, but whatever you say… it was very wrong of me to take advantage of you… I have a wife."

"Yes, I know…." She murmured, watching a large section of a tree floating sedately down the river as if that inanimate object might possibly be able to offer some form of explanation as to how quickly such a pleasant outing had taken such a pitiless turn. She felt fragile and strangely cheated somehow, but from what she could only speculate. To her mind, there was but one reason.

"I displeased you," she said, hanging her head.

'Oh, you did nothing of the kind,' he thought, troubled equally in mind but unwilling to voice as much. When he looked round, her eyes were filled with tears, brought about by his foolish and irrational behaviour.

"I shall always remember what occurred with…. great fondness," he said taking both her hands and looking down at them. "Know this Frances, if I were free, I would willingly take you for my wife, such has become my regard for you. I kissed you just now because I wanted to and have done so for some time."

A surge of joy flooded through Frances, but he was not yet done.

"Do not read more into what I just said, for I am not free, and Magdalen does not warrant any form of betrayal. Equally, I would never demean you by taking advantage of circumstances where I should have known better. You are certainly not the kind of woman to… well, let it suffice that I can offer you nothing."

"But Jamie, tis more that I should seek your forgiveness," she hurried in, desperate to make him understand, but he was having none of it.

"No, you're not to blame. You are incredibly young and innocent with the sweetest nature that any man would be proud of," he said and then briefly touched her face. "Tis my belief that it's far too soon after the loss of your husband to seek solace in another's arms."

That much was true. Jamie was the only man Frances had looked upon with any kind of favour, since John. She knew she had been overtly flirtatious at times, enjoying the kind of 'sport' often referred to by Mary Richmond, considering it harmless and yet clearly it had not been. Could she truly ignore her emotions so easily or were they treacherously causing her to experience feelings that were not real. Trying to fathom everything, she wandered down the pathway, wondering if he might follow. He didn't.

"I'd hate to think that…my mistake… could well alter a friendship that I hold dear?" he shouted and slowly Frances turned round, retracing her steps until she stood directly in front of him.

"Lord Graham, I would not have you punishing yourself so. Know this, I pledge here and now that you shall always have the friendship and continued support of the Viscountess Haveringham," she said, dipping a deep curtsey, totally oblivious of the effect that one act had upon him as he looked down at her politely tipped head.

"A pledge I can wholeheartedly return," he said, assisting her to her feet, battling a strong urge to not only kiss her again, but to take her to his bed. Forcing himself to glance toward the Minster, he added, "You know, I suddenly feel quite hungry. Shall we perhaps join the others at the Old Starre?"

'I couldn't eat a thing,' she thought, tugging her glove more firmly on her hand.

"Forgive me, Jamie, but I'm suddenly quite cold. Perhaps it would be best if you escort me back to Fitzherbert House. It's not too far from here, after all."

Disguising disappointment admirably, he tipped his head and smiled warmly.

"As you wish. I agree it has turned much colder."

Neither mentioned the intimacy on their stroll back through the narrow little streets, the conversation purposely kept light-hearted and inconsequential. On the steps of Fitzherbert House, they bid one another a polite farewell and after kissing her gloved hand, Jamie strode away, turning only once to acknowledge her with a wave of one hand, though Frances watched him until he disappeared down a distant alleyway.

By the next morning when Frances finally woke from a slightly disturbed sleep, she felt much better though not surprised when Alys, returning from her duties with the Queen, informed her that the Earl of Montrose and his companions had surprisingly ridden away from York at daybreak.

CHAPTER FIFTY-ONE

April 1643

The days following Jamie's departure dragged for Frances, despondency settling upon her to such a degree that for a time, she even considered returning to Haveringham Manor. Sharing the impression with Mary Richmond brought a response that hardly came as a surprise.

"Nonsense Frances, you'll do no such thing," Mary had said with twinkling eyes. "Time for you to return home once we leave; till then, stay, eh?"

The longer she considered it, the more Frances saw the sense in staying, after all what did her home hold but dismal memories, tedium of day to day living and even more chance of loneliness. York however, held the opportunity to enjoy herself, to meet interesting people and spend time in company with the likes of Harry Broughton. Ultimately, she decided to remain in York, consign any thoughts of Montrose to the back of her mind, and continue with her life, at least until the Queen left, after which was completely unknown.

Seated beside a window in Ingram House, Frances worked diligently on a new collar, stitching portions of 'black work' at the front edges. Never having had much talent with needle and thread, nevertheless she was quite pleased with her efforts. Pausing for a moment, she glanced out at the gardens scattered with signs of the new season, golden daffodils nodding their little trumpet heads in the gentle breeze. Thankfully, the constant rain of the previous few days seemed to have departed, the sky for once displaying portions of brightest blue, dotted here and there with fluffy white clouds.

"Pardon me if I'm intruding Viscountess, for I dare say you have a great deal on your mind?"

The red-haired, green-eyed Lady Sutherland stood beside Frances, her pert little face and rosebud lips, enhanced by some form of rouge, formed into a disingenuous smile. One of the Queen's ladies, Frances had not often been in her company and therefore found it surprising to be singled out now.

"Not at all Lady Sutherland," Frances said, something in the woman's demeanour making her cautious as the sewing was consigned to her lap.

"I simply came to congratulate you," Lady Sutherland said managing somehow to make the remark sound almost scathing. Suspicion aroused, Frances felt it might be unwise to enquire what was meant and yet couldn't help herself.

"Might I enquire what for?" she asked.

"Why your talent for theatricals; even Lord Vevers commented favourably 'pon your performance last evening."

Frances gave a hesitant smile, recalling Mary warning her to be wary of this particular lady, and Lord Vevers too, who in her opinion was not a man to be trusted.

"I merely played the harpsichord and was not the only one to perform. Perhaps Lord Vevers exaggerated a little, for reasons of his own?" Frances said.

"Oh, not at all," came the response with a little disingenuous laugh. For some reason she appeared like a cat having cornered a bird or small rodent.

"Lord Vevers had far more to say about you than just your musical talent. He actually remarked how downhearted you appear of late, doubtless due to you having mislaid something of great personal worth….?"

Frances quickly appraised her gown for any loose thread, missing jewel, or damage of any kind, until realisation dawned. This woman had some other purpose in mind and suddenly Frances recognised that she was about to be the recipient of some form of spiteful cruelty.

"Not your attire, Viscountess; tis more your side that lacks the enhancement of a certain Scottish Lord these days…."

There it was a blow that was meant to knock Frances' confidence. Sadly, it worked and gratified by her obvious victory, Lady Sutherland dipped a contemptuous curtsey before walking off to join the beribboned fop that was Lord Vevers.

Frances was left feeling as if she had been physically struck and glancing at the unashamed pair, little surprised to see them whispering and laughing together, doubtless at her expense. Staring down at the collar in her lap, Frances frowned to see a crimson stain on one corner. Unwittingly, she must have pricked a finger whilst being bullied, shedding her own blood; tears sprung to her eyes.

'Why couldn't I think of a way to respond.'

Frances had heard the rumours herself of course, that Montrose had without doubt bedded her and like a bitch on heat, Frances had openly thrown herself at him. His hasty departure from York was then blamed on her incompetence in the bedchamber, rather than his free choice. Such rumours tormented her and biting her lip, Frances struggled to keep from weeping freely. Turning her head toward the window so her accusers were unable to see the depth of her distress, she stiffened at the sound of a chair being drawn up by her side.

"What did that disagreeable shrew have to say to you?" Harry Broughton asked, sitting down. "I can tell it wasn't anything pleasant, for I can see you are trembling."

"It was naught," she said, turning tear filled eyes upon him before the stain on the collar caught her attention and briefly she wondered if it might be possible to incorporate it into some kind of pattern.

"I don't believe you," Harry said placing a comforting hand on hers. Harry Broughton had never looked upon Lady Sutherland

331

with any kind of favour, having quickly deduced exactly the type of female she was. "She said enough to bring you to tears Frances, much more and you would weep openly, I'd say. Not all women of noble birth are worthy of the title 'Lady' nor is a pretty face indicative of a character worth knowing you know."

Frances felt a wave of relief that Harry had come to her rescue. He must have been watching from the other side of the room and seen what had occurred.

"I thought she was being sociable …." Frances admitted, but Harry blew out his lips, shaking his head as he folded his arms and leaned back on the chair.

"I doubt she'd know how to," he complained. "You're not used to the ways of some of these courtly women, Frances. Outward shows of affability can often hide a disagreeable personality. I dare say you'll learn who to trust and who not, given time."

"But I can't think of any possible reason for her to treat me like that, Harry."

The young Lord glanced across the room when the lady in question, guffawed loudly, meeting her eye as she tipped her head disdainfully.

"Perhaps you've shown interest in someone she favours herself…." Harry suggested at last.

"Such as Lord Vevers? I think not," Frances declared, eventually smiling for the first time since the encounter.

"Now that I can agree with," he sneered. "Vevers is an undoubted rogue. Do you know, t'other night, after too much wine, he remarked that he couldn't see any plausible reason why you seemed so interested in Montrose."

Frances' eyes widened.

"Tis no one's business but mine," she said firmly. "Mark me

though Harry, I shall be on my guard against the likes of that pair henceforth."

"I'm glad to hear it, dear lady," he said. "Now let me tell you a little of her past that hopefully might help you understand more of her.... disreputable character. Lady Sutherland once professed hopes of wedding the elder son of the late Earl of Foxborough, namely Richard Carlton. Seemingly, all her hopes were crushed when Carlton made an unexpected visit and found her in a state of undress in the arms of another man. Carlton was apparently incensed and call the other man out, slaying him in a duel and informing Lady Sutherland that she would never be his bride."

"Perhaps this.... Richard Carlton had a narrow escape?" she said.

"I agree and of course since his father died at Edgehill, Richard is now the Earl of Foxborough.. I would hazard a guess that Sutherland just might regret her actions that day, for if she hadn't, then like as not, she would be Countess of Foxborough by now."

"So, Carlton wed someone else I suppose?" she said.

"No, due to the war, much like me, he remains unwed," Harry explained. "I'll wager Sutherland will be after him once more though, once we reach Oxford, for he attends from time to time when Prince Maurice has need to be there."

"Mayhap then he will rebuff her again and insist on marrying for love," she said almost dreamily with an engaging smile that made Harry lift her hand and plant a kiss on her palm.

"Don't ever change, sweet Frances, for your innocence is perfectly charming, you know," he said and with a deepening blush on her cheeks, Frances stared into adoring brown eyes that she unexpectedly wished were grey!

CHAPTER FIFTY-TWO

April 1643 – Haveringham Manor

"You're an excellent horse-woman Frances," Harry declared as they rode in through Haveringham's main gates.

Persuading Harry to escort her on the short journey to see her parents had not proved difficult, in fact, keen to see her spirits lifted after the encounter with Lady Sutherland, Harry had almost leapt at the chance. In less than an hour, they were riding side by side across the flat land towards Skelton. Everything seemed peaceful and unhurried, though nevertheless it was a relief to know that Harry had arranged to have four mounted troopers accompany them.

"I was taught to ride from a young age," she said, pulling Phoenix to a halt outside the closed gatehouse doors.

"It's best your father insists on these gates being kept closed," Harry remarked.

"They have been for months, though if the enemy were determined enough, I dare say a petard would soon see them breached," Frances said.

Harry smiled, why was he not surprised that this woman knew what a petard was and how it might be used? A face appeared above, peering over the parapet and Frances waved. It took a while but eventually one door slowly swung wide, an older man struggling with the considerable weight.

"One door should suffice, and close it once we're through," she ordered.

"Right you are, Milady," the old man said, touching his forelock.

They rode through, crossing the courtyard to be ultimately confronted by Lambert coming out from the stables, a young lad in his wake.

"Lady Frances, no one said to expect you today?" he declared.

"It was all a bit of an impulse," Harry explained, helping Frances from the saddle.

"Take the horses to Master Jake, lad. He'll tell you what must be done with them," Lambert instructed. Scarcely more than ten years of age, the lad gawped first at Frances, then at Harry only to receive a clip round one ear.

"Don't stare so at the Viscountess and his Lordship. Be off with you," Lambert said and rubbing his ear, the lad dragged both horses across the courtyard toward the stables.

"Is father at home?" Frances enquired, taking off her gloves.

"Yes, my Lady. He and the Countess are in the small dining room."

Harry's face lit up and Frances sniggered.

"If there's enough food, Lord Broughton might be glad of a morsel…. as you can see, he's half-starved," she said.

"A slight exaggeration dear lady," Harry said adding, "I dare say I might be able to manage a little something though?"

Rolling her eyes, Frances made her way up the steps and into the house.

"Frances?"

Elizabeth stood at the sight of her daughter entering the room with the young nobleman behind. Frances dipped a brief curtsey as her father came toward her, holding out his arms.

"Come, embrace me, daughter," he declared warmly.

Though the incident with Lady Sutherland had unsettled Frances, now she was held firmly in her father's embrace, it all felt so trivial and unimportant somehow. Affectionately Miles kissed the side of her head, whispering, "I'm happy to see you child."

'Oh father, how greatly I needed that,' Frances thought. "We decided to take a little air and found ourselves close enough to pay you a visit, father."

"Then you must be hungry, come sit and eat with us," Elizabeth declared and then to Moll waiting quietly at the back of the room, "Tell cook we shall need a little more."

Once Moll had gone, Elizabeth smiled at Harry.

"You must forgive the manner of our table, Lord Broughton. Since the Queen's unexpected visit, much of our provender is gone, though I dare say our cook will find something to tempt you."

"You are most gracious, Countess," Harry said taking a seat himself, after drawing one out for Frances.

Moll returned carrying a tray holding a platter of salted beef, cheese, freshly baked bread, and a dish of creamy butter.

"I noticed a number of cattle and sheep in the fields at the back of the house, father," Frances said, accepting a napkin from Moll and laying it across her arm. Miles' bright expression suddenly seemed to darken.

"No alternative I'm afraid. Thieving rogues rounded up no end t'other side of the village to feed their men...." He mumbled more under his breath though Frances couldn't make out what. It must have been derogatory though from the glance her mother threw at him. Frances stifled a smile glancing briefly at Harry, who did much the same.

"The influx of people to York, hasn't helped, father. The need for flesh is all the greater now the Queen is in residence," she said.

"Not from my estate though and I'm not talking about Royalists either," Miles said tapping the table firmly with one finger.

"Rebels snaffled your beasts, my Lord?" Harry enquired.

"Aye, some sort of raiding party come out from Selby. Jake spotted 'em from the safety of a copse, but couldn't do much about it obviously, not with half the men gone from here and being his age. Thankfully, with the help of women and children from the local villages, we were able to round up a few and drive 'em here to relative safety. There are four milk cows in the barn, so at least for now we have milk to make cheese and butter, but for how long is anyone's guess. They may still yet have to be slaughtered for meat, should matters continue as they are."

"I do wish you wouldn't speak so lightly of these.... raiding parties, Miles," Elizabeth said. "You know how it upsets me to think of them turning up here."

"Facts can't be ignored, Bess, but we are as prepared as we can be," Miles said, patting her hand affectionately.

"Will you both be staying here tonight?" Elizabeth then asked, but with her mouth full, Frances left Harry to answer.

"Alas we cannot Countess, there's a special celebration tonight for the Queen that I doubt Frances would want to miss."

"That's true," Frances agreed. "There's to be music and even dancing."

"You are enjoying yourself a little then?" Elizabeth asked. Delighted that her daughter had eventually chosen to join the Queen's party in York, Elizabeth hoped the diversion might help to facilitate her recovery.

"I am," Frances answered honestly.

"Then why are you here?" Miles asked, covering her hand with his.

'You know me too well.'

Concentrating on her food, Frances pondered that very question herself. Was it because she just craved a taste of normality after the cruel insinuations levelled at her that very morning? The fact remained that the implications, intended entirely for courtly amusement, did hold a measure of truth. Frances could not deny missing Jamie; every day following his departure had proved tortuous, memories of the kiss proving impossible to forget.

"Heavens Miles, must she really have a reason?" Elizabeth exacted, though Miles simply frowned.

"You took a risk coming here at all," he said. "Rebel patrols are often seen around here. Old Jake described a colour some of 'em carried t'other day and to me it sounded like one of the Fairfax's. God forbid that you would've been waylaid by the likes of them."

"I assure you my Lord, that I would never have allowed Frances to leave York had there been any such danger," Harry said. "Truth be told, they appear to have gone to ground ever since the altercation... at Seacroft Moor."

"Seacroft? Do enlighten me, we hear so little, now we are virtually confined here," Miles said, setting his spoon aside to pay greater attention to the young lord.

"It was toward the end of last month. Tadcaster came under attack and Newcastle ordered General Goring to sort the problem. I volunteered to go with him," Harry said proudly. "In all, twenty troops of horse and dragoons left York our intent being to recover the town."

Frances rolled her eyes.

"Harry was so bored in York father, that he willingly accepted any form of distraction...."

She chuckled, but Miles, wishing to hear more, threw her a look of exasperation.

"Nonsense daughter, let the boy finish," he urged.

"Well, my Lord, Tom Fairfax had been dismantling the defences around Tadcaster and we were never going to take that lying down. As we approached, he started marching his troops out across Bramham Moor, trying to head for Leeds, or so we deduced. We'd have been straight at him on the lanes leading to Seacroft Moor, but Goring ordered us to wait and just follow at some distance. It proved a wise move, for once we were out on the open ground of the moor itself, we were able to charge 'em at full gallop. We outnumbered and outflanked 'em, the majority turning tail and running like the cowardly curs they are," Harry said.

"That showed real wisdom by Goring," Miles nodded, wiping greasy fingers on the napkin slung over one shoulder. "Many losses?"

"A few, though the enemy are believed to have lost over two hundred with more than eight hundred taken prisoner," Harry explained with a smirk.

"Goring must be delighted with the outcome," Miles suggested.

"Absolutely, my Lord. The jubilation in York knew no bounds, coming on the back of Scarborough's change of allegiance. Tis for that very reason I concluded it safe enough to bring your daughter here today."

"Then I can only thank you for providing her with protection, my boy," Miles said. "I'd hate to think she would ever be confronted by 'black Tom' himself.

"If I did, I'd not be afeared of him father," Frances said. "I dare say he would behave as a gentleman should, though I would endeavour to make him see the error of his ways."

Casually and with a playful smile, Frances popped a piece of cheese into her mouth.

"I hope you'd do nothing of the kind, child!" Miles said.

"I'd say 'black Tom' should be more concerned about meeting your daughter, my Lord," Harry quipped, though Frances rolled her eyes.

"It's a shame you didn't arrive earlier, for then you would have seen Ralph," Elizabeth said almost casually, and Frances' head turned as open mouthed she stared.

"Ralph was here?" she eventually voiced.

"Yes, he arrived yesterday unexpectedly but left a couple of hours ago to ride to York. I'm surprised you didn't see him on the road?" Elizabeth responded, taking a sip of canary wine.

"I presume it would depend on which route he took," Frances remarked with a deepening scowl. "We came up through Skelton and saw no one."

"Then perhaps he chose the ferry at Poppleton?" Miles remarked absently. "I suggest you return to York the way you came though, my boy. Don't allow this one to persuade you to ride out toward Long Marston, that's where pockets of rebels have oft been sighted, on Hessay Moor."

"You have my word on it, my Lord," Harry assured.

"Why on earth has Ralph come north again?" Frances enquired.

"Granted a brief furlough, so he told us. Anne hoped he would stay for a day or two, but you know what Ralph is like. Brought messages north from Rupert and others and wanted to see them delivered swiftly," Elizabeth explained.

'What's wrong with that man?' Frances thought but said. "Did he not think to take Anne with him, there'd be room for them both at Fitzherbert House?"

With a nervous smile, Elizabeth glanced at her husband before answering.

"I did suggest it, but Ralph said there would be little point, he'd have too much to do in York before leaving for Oxford again," Elizabeth responded.

Frances stared in disbelief, shaking her head slowly.

"What utter nonsense. Mark me on it, he'll receive short shrift from me should he venture to Ingram House," she said, devouring a piece of preserved plum with gusto.

"He did say that he would be eager to see you," Elizabeth said, though Harry leapt in voicing, "I doubt that will be a pleasant experience for him, Countess."

Miles stifled a chuckle, liking the attitude of this young Buckinghamshire Lord, though his daughter was not about to let it pass.

"I don't expect you to voice an opinion on the matter, Harry Broughton. I have known Ralph Bynghame far too long to remain silent about this affront to his wife."

Harry lifted both hands, palms outward. "Oh, believe me, Frances…. I've little desire to get involved," he chortled, exchanging a grin with his host.

CHAPTER FIFTY-THREE

April 1643

Ingram House felt decidedly claustrophobic, the number of souls crammed into the medium sized room, exacerbated by excessive heat from the blaze in the large grate.

Picking her way through the crush, nodding at first one then another, Frances ultimately located her quarry. He stood close to one of the windows, back toward her and in the manner learned from Mary Richmond, she said, "Od's fish, if it ain't Lord Bynghame."

Slowly, he turned about with an almost bemused expression, allowing his gaze to gradually traverse over her before removing his hat and sweeping it to one side when he bowed. Frances looked breath-taking, in a gown of emerald-green, the sleeves pinned together at various intervals with gold and ruby studs, and low décolletage edged with diaphanous material, again decorated with the same ruby studs that almost highlighted the milkiness of her skin.

"Fran my dear, I began to think you avoided me?" Ralph said, forcing a nonchalant smile to his lips. "I went to Haveringham only to be told you were in York, but then when I arrived here, I learned you had ridden out to Haveringham, escorted by this rogue." He turned to Harry at her side. "Well now, Broughton, made a conquest of this lady, have you?" he asked, hoping he hadn't. Broughton was a handsome man with a character any woman might find appealing, and Ralph knew he was being pressed to find a suitable wife.

"If only Bynghame, she's perfectly enchanting," Harry grinned. Both men laughed together, slapping one another on the back exuberantly in a brief, but manly embrace.

"Tis good to see you Hal, you've been missed by the regiment," Ralph beamed, holding his friend by the upper arms.

"I wish I could say I've missed them…." Harry responded, lifting Frances' hand to his lips. "How's Rupert?"

"Oh, you know him, eager for the fight as always and oft criticised for being over-zealous and argumentative," Ralph responded with a grin.

"And disregards it all, I dare say?" Harry laughed.

Ralph perceived Frances exchanging a smile and nod with the Duchess of Richmond across the room.

'So, she's made a new acquaintance, I see,' he thought to himself.

"How long are you here, Ralph?" Harry asked.

"Another three days only alas. Rupert gave me a weeks' furlough but stressed his need for me back in Oxford, as soon as may be."

Frances shot Ralph a look of censure. *'Three days?'*

Ralph noticed her questioning expression but chose to ignore it.

"Are you responsible for restoring the brilliance to Frances' enchanting eyes then Hal?" Ralph enquired.

"Well, I can't really take the whole credit…."

'Then who?' Ralph wondered, glancing at the laughing Duchess beside the Queen. Mary Richmond had a reputation of being one of the brightest stars in the royal court but also for a penchant to flirtatious behaviour. Perhaps she had played a part in Frances' improved spirits. Whoever was responsible, it certainly was a relief to see her so greatly altered and revived.

"You both talk such nonsense," Frances said flicking open her fan. "I feel much improved due to the excitement and diversion the Queen's presence has brought to York. There's been such a lot to enjoy here."

'And a number of handsome faces?' Ralph thought but said, "Ah, that

must be it then."

"Tell me Bynghame, I'm itching to hear what sport I've missed in the south?" Harry asked.

Watching the two Lords, Frances decided to supress the desire to rebuke Ralph, at least until the talk of war had run its natural course. These men were both hardened soldiers after all, both having virtually cut their teeth in the Low Countries whilst still young.

"Rupert led us on a sortie to Bristol last month after Royalist informants wrote of a plot to open the city gates should the Prince deign to approach."

"And?" Harry asked wide eyed.

Ralph shook his head and pursed his lips.

"The information proved false and Bristol's Governor, Nathaniel Fiennes, remained defiantly immoveable. Rupert was in the foulest mood on the return journey to Oxford. You know how he can be if things don't go his way?"

"Our informants in Bristol haven't been unmasked though?" Harry asked and Ralph shook his head.

"We don't believe so. I'm certain the rebels would have taken great delight in making us aware if they had."

"I dare say Rupert will be after Bristol again before too long. I can only hope I'm back with the regiment by then," Harry said.

"Well, we do need to gain a major seaport in the west now and since Birmingham fell…"

Harry's brow creased deeply, and his jaw dropped.

"Are you saying we've captured Birmingham?" he asked, eyes lighting up.

"Not easily, but yes, a few weeks back." Ralph noticed the confused look on Frances' face and wishing to include her, added, "There's a number of sword mills in Birmingham Fran and being staunchly for Parliament, it had to be taken."

"Much resistance?" Harry enquired.

"They tried their best. They'd barricaded the gates but quickly torched 'em in an attempt to keep us at bay. It didn't prevent Rupert though, he pressed on with determination, as always, until finally we were able to break through." Ralph began to rifle inside his doublet, drawing out a folded paper. "Here's what had been put about since, damn 'em."

Harry opened the paper out with Frances peering over his arm to read it herself. A distorted caricature of Prince Rupert was emblazoned in the foreground, on horseback in full armour, one hand brandishing a pistol, a pole axe held in the other. On the ground beside his horse was the cruellest depiction of Boye Frances had ever seen, more like a lion in appearance. The background showed rudimentary images of a town in flames.

'Prince Rupert's burning love to England, discovered in Birmingham's flames,' Frances read aloud.

"The town was fired then?" Harry enquired and Ralph hesitated, pursing his lips.

"A small area can be blamed on the Royalists, but......you know what it's like Hal, some troops grew over-zealous and a little crazed, taking advantage of the townsfolk, looting, damaging property, killing anyone opposing them A priest was butchered, and a number of women were...." Ralph stopped abruptly, as if suddenly remembering Frances' presence. "Forgive me Fran, but I cannot deny some of the events we witnessed.... In the main the culprits were believed to be mercenaries, come over from Europe. They're an ill-disciplined lot at the best of times, reluctant to obey even the most direct of orders. When he was informed, Rupert was furious and dealt with a number of 'em directly, as you can imagine."

Harry nodded his head thoughtfully.

"Makes sense, after all Rupert would know any blame would reflect badly on him personally, as this proves," Harry responded, looking back at the pamphlet. The list of allegations, laid at the Palatine's door went on and on. Direct cruelty, atrocities against the townsfolk, theft, wanton destruction, killings, defiling of innocent women and the ultimate burning of the town, all said to have been done with the Princes' full knowledge and approval!

"I don't believe it, I just don't. Prince Rupert would never have ordered such things to be done," Frances exclaimed, and Ralph reached for her hand.

"That's the point Fran, he didn't, but so many desire to dishonour him at every turn and don't care how it's done. I was there myself and though there was some plundering, most of the wealthiest families had already fled to Coventry, taking their property with them. The rebels set fire to some of the sword mills as they fled and in turn houses close by caught fire too. Rupert actually deployed men to extinguish the flames, I was present when he gave that direct order."

Frances couldn't escape the appearance of what looked to be a mixture of anger and sorrow in Ralph's eyes, nor his breathing which had become erratic.

"Digby's not helped Rupert's cause one bit," he continued. "He was heard saying that were he to have his way, he'd go straight back to Birmingham and destroy the whole town completely, as punishment for harbouring rebels in the first place."

"Pah, ignorant imbecile," Harry snarled.

Frances's attention grew. Digby was a name she had heard John speak of in the most derogatory terms and now both Ralph and Harry seemed to be expressing the same contempt for the son of the Earl of Bristol. Inwardly she hoped never to have the misfortune to encounter that particular gentleman. Loudly, she sighed and said, "Do you realise just how tedious all this talk of war is, both of you?" She threw a smile at each in turn. "I realise you want to hear what you've missed Harry, but I've heard quite enough for one evening…. now be a dear, and allow me some time alone with Lord Bynghame?"

Ralph guffawed loudly.

"I know this lady of old my friend, tis best to do as she says. Listen, I'm lodged at the Olde Starre, come back with me later and we'll continue this over a tankard or two, I've more to speak of Litchfield for example."

"Litchfield? Wasn't Lord Brook shot through the eye by a boy marksman?" Harry said excitedly.

"Oh, enough," Frances said, patience wearing thin, and Ralph dropped a hand on Harry's shoulder.

"We'll talk later, Hal," he said. "If I'm to have any peace, I feel compelled to hear what this lovely lady has to say to me, though I have the strangest notion I won't like it."

"Very well, though it grieves me to leave you, Frances, I'll be over yonder, with Goring," Harry said and walked away.

Frances' smile faded when she turned back to look directly at Ralph.

"Ah, I see I've assumed rightly that I'm to have a tongue lashing. Very well, proceed then Madam, what have I done this time?" he asked.

"I want to know why you are here when Anne is still at Haveringham?" she enquired slowly and precisely.

"What?"

"Mother told me that Anne was distressed at having only a fleeting visit from her husband."

"I explained the need to reach York swiftly," he said fiddling with the sword slung at his hip.

"But you just told Harry you'd be here for a further three days."

"What of it?"

"Then shouldn't you return to your wife and give her the solace of your company for a day or two, I'm sure she'd welcome it, Ralph."

"Once again you question my motives, Madam?"

Ignoring his indignant tone, Frances said boldly, "Not at all, though I'd love to know why your anger is directed toward me?" Her chin lifted as stoically she stared directly into his eyes. Eventually, he reached for her hand, brushing his thumb across the back.

"Mayhap because you constantly seem to interfere in matters that are none of your concern," he ventured firmly. "Anne knows that I have to stay in York until I receive replies to the messages I brought north. Once I have them, I shall be leaving at once for Oxford. In the meantime, at least I have chance to spend time with you?"

Frances snatched her hand away.

"With me?" She stared in disbelief. "For shame Ralph Bynghame, I am not your wife…. she is the one weeping into her pillow not six miles from here, due to her husband's neglect. Heavens, if John had been so close and hadn't shown the slightest inclination to visit me, then I…. I… I…."

Her breathing had grown laboured and swallowing hard, she fought back angry tears. Why did this man have the capacity to make her so annoyed at times. He was friendly enough to be sure, but he had the propensity to treat Anne so badly and Frances always felt obliged to defend her.

"Fran…. how many times do I have to explain that my marriage is naught akin to yours," he said impatiently.

"I know, you've told me often enough," she snapped back but then paused for a moment considering the tips of her shoes peeping from under her green skirts. "Ralph, she adores you…. can you not feel inclined to show her any affection?"

Pressing his lips together, Ralph looked down at his sword, tracing a finger repeatedly over the beadwork decorating the pommel.

"Listen Fran, you don't know the half of it. She and I have spoken at length about this very subject. I do care for her, of course I do. She is my wife and I intend to do my duty by her. I saw her yesterday and again this very morning before I came to York." Frances opened her mouth to speak, but Ralph pressed a forefinger to her lips. "Enough, tis not fitting for a woman to question aught I do…. least of all you!"

Frances hung her head. He was right, no woman should ever question the motives of a man and yet Ralph was like a brother, so Frances felt she could speak freely to him, obviously not on this particular matter.

"Ralph, forgive me," she said softly, grimacing until he lifted her chin.

"You care Fran, and whilst that's an admirable trait, you cannot change something that is unchangeable, no matter how much you would wish to," he said.

"Then in a way, I'm saddened for you both," she whispered.

"Don't be. Anne and I both know the match was arranged for us and that love would not be involved. But we shall both be obedient to what our families require of us and one day, God willing, we shall have children together."

He knew she would be inclined to respond to that and almost reading her thoughts, gave her no chance. "No more, Madam," he snarled, raising his hand.

Frances turned to look through the window, conscious of being under scrutiny from curious eyes. What would be made of this; first rumours about Montrose and now heated words with Lord Bynghame. Silence fell between them until she felt his hand lightly touch her shoulder.

"You look better than you did last autumn," he murmured.

"Those were such cheerless days," she admitted.

"Aye, but it gladdens my heart to see you so greatly recovered."

"You mean you do have a heart after all?" she quipped.

'If you only knew....'

As if he had been struck across the face, Ralph forced a smile to his lips and said, "Of course I do, and to appease you, dear Fran, I shall ride to Haveringham tomorrow to pay my wife another visit...."

CHAPTER FIFTY-FOUR

May 1643 - York

"Captured? But Goring was supposed to be escorting us south to Oxford," Alys gasped after Harry Broughton told of an unexpected occurrence resulting from a recent sortie to Wakefield.

"Well, he'll not be doing so now," Harry admitted.

"But Wakefield was supposed to be a safe royalist garrison, wasn't it?" Frances asked.

Harry gave a shrug and pursed his lips.

"That's what we all thought, but the rebels elicited a night attack. The garrison was alerted of course, barricades manned, musketeers deployed, and for a while we stood firm, but Fairfax proved determined, his aim doubtless being to take prisoners to trade for those we secured from him at Seacroft Moor…"

When a deep scowl scarred Harry's features, one of Goring's own officers, Captain Reeve Vickerman, took up the tale.

"It took two hours for the rebels to breach the defences, Fairfax himself leading a cavalry charge through the gap in the barricade, directly in front of us," he explained. "Goring had to be roused from his sickbed, but was straight to horse, yelling for us to counterattack."

"He was unwell, Captain?" Frances asked.

"Abed with a fever of some sort, Viscountess," Vickerman said with a glance at Harry.

"That or another incidence of inebriation," Harry quipped, though his attempt at humour this time appeared half-hearted. Harry had come to have great admiration for Goring, a man often maligned for dissolute habits, though without doubt commanding respect as a gifted and able soldier by the majority of his men. When Goring had declared intent to head for Wakefield to counter any rebel interest in the town, Harry had requested permission to go too.

"Numerous captives were taken, Goring among 'em; Vickerman and I were lucky to escape ourselves," Harry explained.

"They will consider Goring a worthy prize, and transport him to London," Vickerman added.

"Not The Tower?" Frances said, a hand to her throat.

"Where else," Harry voiced.

The thought of Goring being incarcerated in the one place so many feared, made Frances shudder. Though the General had been inclined to overindulge at times, often seen asleep in quiet corners or carousing in the streets of York with at least one woman beneath his arms, nonetheless Goring appeared the epitome of a military specialist whenever leaving the city ahead of his troops. Before long he would be resident in that dank, dark fortress that few escaped alive, not something many wished to consider for long.

When the days began to lengthen, increasingly the talk turned to the time when the Queen would depart for Oxford. Frances often sat beside a window in Ingram House, staring out at nothing in particular, bothered by troubled thoughts and this day was no exception. Since Ralph's departure for Oxford and then the unhappy news from Wakefield, Frances had begun to wonder just where her life would lead once the Queen had gone. Everything the courtiers spoke of now sounded exhilarating and the more she heard of the upcoming arrangements, the more depressed Frances grew. Then one day Mary Richmond made an almost frivolous suggestion that had refused to leave Frances' mind ever since. Looking up, Frances noticed the Queen making her way across to the window where she was seated. Instantly, she stood and dipped a curtsey.

"Ah some new arrivals battling this inclement weather," Henrietta announced almost casually. "They are sure to be soaked, *nest pas, Viscomtesse?*"

Incredibly, Frances felt as though she had been offered a rare opportunity, one she was not about to let pass.

"Indeed Majesty, the rain seems relentless," she said, then taking a deep breath, bravely added, "Your Majesty, might I be permitted to speak privately with you?"

Even though she knew such a direct request went against every form of propriety and that if she had heard, her mother would have been completely horrified, Frances waited, poised for the Queen's response. When the royal head turned, Henrietta appeared completely at peace, a gracious smile Frances' only reward.

"Bien sûr. Vous êtes troublés, Viscomtesse?" she asked in her native tongue.

"Not troubled exactly, Your Majesty…. tis more I have pondered something for some considerable time and should welcome your opinion on it?"

Henrietta wandered closer, sitting on a chair, and indicating Frances should take the one beside her.

"We shall not be disturbed *'ere;* pray you, speak freely," Henrietta said, kindness in her eyes.

Hesitating momentarily and biting her lip, Frances took another deep breath.

"I would speak of silver and plate, Your Majesty," she said simply.

A deep frown scarred Henrietta's feature.

"Que voulez-vous dire…. silver and plate?" she enquired.

"Well, Your Majesty, I know that those loyal to the King are requested to relinquish such treasures…. for the cause," she said, watching the Queen's expression steadily. Thankfully, a broad smile spread to Henrietta's lips, revealing front teeth that protruded slightly.

'Oui, c'est vrai… there is great need for such items if we are to equip our troops sufficiently to defeat these *'roundheads'* once for all. Despite that need, I do not understand how this might concern you?"

"Only that such items are concealed at my home, including an amount of silver given to Lord Fitzherbert and myself, upon our marriage. My father thought to eventually bring those items here to York to the Mint, but my own view is that it might be of greater use were it to be transported south to Oxford."

Frances paused, staring into dark eyes that seemed totally engrossed with no indication of animosity or annoyance.

'Mon dieu. You have given this much thought, haven't you?" the Queen ultimately said and lowering her gaze, Frances felt heat infusing her cheeks.

"I confess I have thought of little else recently, Your Majesty," she finally admitted honestly.

"*Oui, fois étrange, madame*, but… why do I suspect there is something you are not saying?"

Frances' stiffened and her mouth went dry.

"Her Grace, the Duchess of Richmond recently made a proposal that has refused to leave my thoughts ever since," she admitted, and Henrietta's brows lifted.

"What kind of proposal?"

"A suggestion that I consider accompanying the party to Oxford. If so, then as she implied, any silver would be under the direct protection of the vast number of military men guarding your good self," Frances stated.

The Queen's dark eyes narrowed to the point where Frances feared she might have overstepped the mark.

"You seem to have thought of many facets, save one, *peut-être?*"

"I cannot imagine what Your Majesty means?" Frances answered.

"Why that the journey will be arduous with many discomforts and hardships. Tents are not always the most salubrious of accommodation and also, we may not always be granted fair weather?" Henrietta indicated the rain still hammering against the windows. "There is in addition, the fact that the *'roundheads'* will do their utmost to intercept us at every turn. Perhaps the biggest dilemma for you though, will be that you will have to leave your family and home and I can give no assurance of when you might be able to return."

Frances had pondered these aspects long and hard over the past days. It would be of some concern to be separated from her parents and to leave Haveringham Manor would not be easy, but then had she not been destined to leave Yorkshire for Kent only months ago? Now she felt that if the Queen of England could endure the hardships and dangers of a journey that would end in Oxford, then could she do any less? Despite threats from Parliament to impeach her and if captured, divest her of her head, Henrietta Maria remained strong and determined; this alone filled Frances with all the more resolve.

"Your Majesty is willing to endure trials and threats from our enemy with unshakable courage… May I not be permitted to do the same?"

Henrietta's expression softened and very gradually the smile spread to her eyes.

"Well spoken, my dear," she said. "There is perhaps another issue you may not have considered and that is your widowhood and resultant personal wealth, *n'est pas*? That alone may provoke interest in you that you may well wish to avoid. Are you prepared for such an eventuality?"

"I have given much thought to all eventualities, Your Majesty and believe it will be worth the risk…. if I am to serve my King as boldly as your good self," Frances stated firmly.

"And if the rebels should unexpectedly strike at us?"

"I shall stand beside you Madam; with the bravery and tenacity you will doubtless show to them."

The Queen settled back on her chair, studying the young woman opposite for some time, interlinking her small hands, nodding to herself as if reviewing everything carefully.

"Very well, I give my consent," she eventually said.

A series of tiny bubbles burst forth within Frances's stomach, waves of excitement mingling with a trace of trepidation.

"There may yet be a slight impediment, Your Majesty," Frances admitted, and the Queen's eyes slowly widened. "I fear my father might declare some reluctance in allowing me to do this," Frances explained.

"When I give my permission, there can be none," she voiced stoutly. "Lord Benningford will never object when I express the need to have you as one of my own ladies?"

"Your Majesty?"

"Leave your father to me."

Frances momentarily chewed her lip.

"Should I send word that Your Majesty requires to see him?"

A royal hand unexpectedly gave that of Frances' an almost affectionate squeeze. "Do so, *Viscomtesse.*"

CHAPTER FIFTY-FIVE

May 1643 – Ingram House, York

Miles continually fed the brim of his rain-soaked hat back and forth through his fingers in an attempt to prevent droplets from spilling onto the polished oak flooring.

"You wished to see me, Your Majesty?" he enquired.

Receiving what sounded to be a direct summons, Miles had assumed it to be urgent enough to have his horse saddled for the short ride to York, a decision he now regretted.

"Hardly the state in which to approach one's Queen, my Lord?" Henrietta remarked taking note of the damp appearance of the man before her. Miles comprehended, realising how dishevelled he must appear, every bit of his outerwear completely soaked through, even to the shirt that felt decidedly damp against his skin. Rain had been falling steadily for days turning the roads into little more than impassable quagmires. Now as he stood before Henrietta Maria, water dripping steadily from the hem of his cloak, Miles wished he had used a carriage.

"I crave Your Majesty's pardon for my somewhat unusual state but as your summons sounded urgent, I chose to travel on horseback," he explained.

"As I see," the Queen answered. "In that case, I shall come straight to the point, my Lord. I wish to speak of your daughter."

Miles stiffened, throwing a hasty glance at Frances standing quietly to one side with lowered head and down cast eyes. *'Unwilling to look at me daughter?'*

"What has she done, Your Majesty?" Miles enquired tentatively.

"Tis not what she had done, more what she intends to do, Lord Benningford," Henrietta said with a tinkling little laugh.

"I'm afraid I don't quite understand, Your Majesty," Miles finally admitted.

"Then I shall make it clear. Your daughter is desirous of undertaking a mission for her King," the Queen said slowly and precisely.

Miles suddenly felt compromised, dumfounded, and more than a little annoyed.

"In all honesty, Majesty I cannot see how my daughter might...."

"You do not consider there is aught....'les femmes' can do for our great cause, Milord?" Henrietta interrupted.

Miles offered a hesitant smile and said, "Gracious lady.... I beg your pardon and await your pleasure."

Offering a further bow and a flourish of his hat, Miles noticed the trail wet plumes had left on the floorboards.

"The Viscountess told me of the silver and plate you have concealed within your manor house, Lord Benningford," Henrietta declared with an authoritative voice.

In the process of pulling off his gloves, Miles paused, turning his head only slightly to encompass his daughter with a look of absolute dismay.

"Forgive me Your Majesty, but my daughter has little to do with whether there is.... or is not such items within my home," he said.

"Be not alarmed Milord, the conversation was undertaken in total privacy and your daughter was at pains to mention her own wedding gifts as forming part of the possible cache. I am now hoping fervently to persuade you to surrender such items willingly, in order that they may be transported with my party, directly to Oxford."

For once Miles was almost lost for words. His daughter never ceased to amaze him and yet her willingness to hand over gifts that had been received as marriage tokens proved how serious she just might be. The Queen was not yet done with surprises for Miles.

"In addition, my Lord, the Viscountess has expressed the desire to accompany those treasures to Oxford herself," she said.

In the almost deafening silence that ensued, Miles tried his best to assimilate what had just been declared. In essence, none of the last few minutes felt real somehow though deep within he felt that the notion might be of Frances' instigation, but not necessarily. He could hardly argue with the Queen of England but felt aggravated at having been placed in such a position where it felt as if everything were already arranged.

"I confess to being somewhat astounded Your Majesty," he began. "I never believed my daughter capable of subterfuge?" He shot a further swift glance at Frances.

'I'll be speaking most firmly with you Madam, have no fear about that' he thought.

"Might I request a moment or two to consider these proposals, Majesty?" he asked at last.

"No need, Lord Benningford. I am already aware that you were considering conveying an amount of silver to the Mint here in York. I merely suggest changing the ultimate destination to Oxford. It will be guarded by several thousand Horse and Foote; can there be a better means to ensure its safety…. as well as that of your daughter?"

Miles sighed, shaking his greying head, and pursing his lips.

"At this very moment, Majesty, I cannot think of a single objection," he eventually admitted.

Henrietta's smile grew magnanimous and satisfied.

"Then allow me to allay any concerns regarding the welfare of your daughter, for I shall insist she be lodged close to me, in Oxford, with my other ladies. Have no fear, my eyes shall continually be upon her, I give you my word, Lord Benningford."

Miles suddenly felt as if a brace of wily females had brow beaten him into submission, ensnaring him hook, line and sinker. In a way it was faintly amusing, but women could be such cunning creatures making men unaware of just what they might do next.

"It seems I'm left with little alternative but to agree, Your Majesty," he finally said.

"Excellent, then tis settled," Henrietta said rising to her feet and holding out her hand to be kissed. "As to the exact details, they can be left to you and your daughter." She began to walk away but then turned back. "Oh yes and I know there must be others in the locality who might be…. shall we say…. persuaded to part with their silver?"

"Well now, this is a fine to do, daughter. I've been soaked through and for what…. a forgone conclusion," Miles snarled, giving his cloak a shake before laying it across the back of a chair by the fire where it began to steam. "I am heartily disappointed Frances, for this feels like sheer madness in my view."

"I don't see it that way, father," Frances answered, unused to what appeared to be a trace of contempt on his face.

"No that much is patently obvious," he snapped.

"I'm only going to Oxford, father."

"In time of war, when God alone knows what might happen to you on the way and when you're there, what then?"

Frances heaved a sigh.

"Father, please…."

Miles stared down the room for some time at a portrait on the wall until with a sigh, he reached for her hand.

"I can hardly gainsay the Queen of England, now, can I?" he admitted, in much softer tones that made Frances feel tearful. "Know this dearest daughter, tis obvious that you and our monarch's wife conspired to achieve something you alone desired," he suggested firmly.

"Not quite like that father," she said. "I have to admit though that ever since General Goring spoke of our silver all those months ago at Haveringham, I have thought on it constantly."

Miles shook his head and sighed.

"So, you've been giving it thought, have you? Now you've come up with the idea of going to Oxford too?"

"I have father, yes. The party is to be vast, and I honestly cannot see an easier way to ensure the silver is delivered directly to Oxford, in what must be relative safety...."

"Relative safety? Damn it girl, don't you think the rebels will try to intercept the convoy? I'll warrant they've plans afoot already to do just that once the Queen leaves here. They'll be after her, mark me on that and yet you want me to agree to you putting yourself at risk?"

"But there'll be thousands of troops guarding us. The rebels would never dare to attack such large numbers and we've already learned that Prince Rupert is intent on clearing a route through the midlands... everything is in place, father."

Grasping her elbow, Miles led her to the window, where outside the rain was still pouring relentlessly.

"We can only pray the young Palatine does just that," he said with more than a little exasperation. "He's certainly working hard, took Litchfield from that hard-nosed John Gell last month."

"Yes, Ralph told us he'd breached the defences with explosives and last we heard, he was heading south to counter Lord Essex' movements; he's certainly continually active," she said, and Miles' brows lifted stoically.

"I dare say you'll hear far more than I do, these days, being here," he admitted.

"Messengers do arrive occasionally with communications," she admitted as Miles considered the rain-soaked vista outside.

"This damned weather grows worse by the hour," he said. "I'm in for a second soaking on the way back. That'll make your mother fuss about, she considered me foolhardy coming here at all in this weather. She certainly won't be eager to let you travel all the way to Oxford, you know."

"Ah but I'm sure you can talk her round, father. If you tell her how the Queen is desirous of me becoming one of her ladies, that should work admirably, you know how mother is?"

Miles searched the face framed by perfectly formed ringlets. Her eyes were sparkling in a way that he couldn't ignore. She'd faced such joy and tragedy in so short a time and yet now the Queen had arrived, her spirits certainly seemed much improved, and he felt glad of that change in her. Her throat was encircled by pearls that shimmered in the candlelight and the deep blue satin gown set off her complexion flawlessly. He laughed and took hold of her hands.

"You know, I really do not know where you get this cunning from, my girl," he said, tracing a finger down her cheek. "Where has my gawky, excitable little girl gone eh?"

"Gone forever father, changed irrefutably by marriage, war and widowhood," she answered with a reflective smile.

"Ain't that the truth, my dearest," he said sadly with a sigh. "Very well, in both matters, I give you my blessing, but before you crow too loudly, I need you to make me a promise."

"What kind of promise?" she asked suspiciously.

"To be on your guard constantly. Not everyone you meet in

Oxford will be of reputable character even if their manner appears the best. Some men hide their true character behind beguiling words in the attempt to dupe innocent, vulnerable women with a fortune to offer. Never forget that you are widowed and a Viscountess. Despite all her fine declarations, the Queen will not be able to watch you continually, and I won't be there to protect you!"

CHAPTER FIFTY-SIX

May 1643 - Haveringham Manor

Frances stopped just inside the large, oak front door, placing a finger to her lips to show Harry, a little way behind, that they should remain silent as muffled manly voices drifted out from the Great Hall. Carefully removing her gloves, she set them down on a table next to an ornate blue and white vase bursting with fragrant spring flowers before removing her cloak and laying it across a chair.

A note had arrived in York from the Earl of Benningford, stating that he had convened a meeting of local gentry and should be obliged if she too would attend, even sending a carriage to convey his daughter the relatively short distance to Haveringham. Harry Broughton had insisted on escorting her, once more organising a number of armed cavalrymen to accompany them.

"Surely you must have stable hands who could be spared to undertake the task Miles?" One voice could be heard saying.

"That's not possible," Miles said. "All I have left here to undertake the running of the whole estate are mere boys and old men and I can't spare any of 'em."

From the tone of his voice, Frances could tell Miles was frustrated, but nevertheless, she wasn't inclined to enter the Great Hall just yet.

"The men have gone round to your kitchens…. I may as well join them," Harry whispered.

"No, no, I'd quite appreciate having you beside me… if you don't mind?" she whispered back, hopefully. Harry complied at once, despite the attractions a tankard of ale and possibly a morsel of food might have. In reality, the young soldier felt more than a little inclined to hear exactly how these men might respond to the proposals he was already aware of.

Edging s little nearer to the archway, Frances listened.

"How about your man with one arm, Miles? I'd vouchsafe he and my gamekeeper could accomplish the task?"

Frances recognised the voice of Sir William Hunt and though there were mutterings and murmurings, she couldn't quite hear exactly what was being said until her father snapped, "Walter? Why he can scarce hold a weapon now and as for your gamekeeper, he's older than my own and Jake is three and sixty at the very least!"

Frances stifled a giggle.

"Father's growing tetchy," she whispered to Harry who had moved to stand beside her.

"What's wrong with the Mint in York? Why the sudden suggestion to have items sent south?" another asked.

"Naught, though it would be of greater benefit to the King were it taken direct to Oxford," Miles explained coolly.

"I confess to being reluctant to part with any of my treasures, Miles, no matter the urgency of the King's need."

"George Radcliffe," Frances whispered to Harry.

"Selfish rogue," Harry hissed back.

"George.... are you not aware that the King's men could pay you a visit at any time to simply take your property without prior consultation?" Frances recognised the voice of Sir Arthur Redbourne, a man she knew very well indeed, due to his close friendship with her father. "T'were best to part with it willingly, wouldn't you say? Unless you're declaring some form of inclination to run with both the hare and the hounds, like some?"

"That is a direct insult, Redbourne," Radcliffe snapped. "I'm no Matthew Boynton with wavering loyalty and Burton Agnes Hall standing in such a prominent position whereby either side might find it of value?"

"Tis of little military concern being a manor house, much like this," Miles said, gesturing with one hand. "The issue is more that I need to know that you still stand firmly for the King?"

"You know I do Miles; I'll not support rebellion against our monarch. All I need to know is if we are to have any assurance of our treasures being returned," Radcliffe continued.

"What?" Harry gasped and Frances snapped, "hush!"

"Return it? Don't you realise it'll all be melted down...." Redbourne snarled angrily.

"Arthur!" Miles' tone held more than a measure of vexation.

"Your pardon Miles, but it makes my blood boil to hear such selfishness. If we were all of that mind, our aims would be totally unworkable and His Majesty's cause eventually lost," Arthur snarled.

"Are we then to be recompensed in some way?"

This was Thomas Barratt, a well-balanced, stout-hearted Yorkshireman, always known for being a true supporter of the Royalist cause.

"At last, a rational question," Miles declared. "In answer, yes Tom the hope is that eventually, everyone will be fully compensated."

"That's all very well, but when?" another asked.

Out in the corridor, Harry and Frances exchanged a swift look of disbelief.

"God alone knows when and how this conflict will end and until it does, no one can answer that," Redbourne said with scarcely disguised impatience.

"And if the rebels intercept our goods during transit, what then?" Henry Fletcher, a man with a small estate some fifteen miles east of Haveringham, enquired and even from the hallway, Frances could sense the depth of her father' frustration.

"What are you proposing Henry, that I invite His Majesty here to collect it in person?" Miles asked, somewhat sarcastically.

"Of course not, but if our valuables are to be taken to Oxford, then all we ask for is some form of assurance of its protection," Fletcher explained.

"I believe that's our cue, Harry," Frances said and headed straight in under one of the archways. Chairs were hastily vacated at her appearance and bows ensued.

"I bid you good day, gentlemen," she declared brightly, dipping a quick curtsey to her father before kissing him on the cheek. "If you have no objection father, might Lord Broughton join us?"

"Of course, you are most welcome, Lord Broughton, pray be seated," Miles answered, indicating a vacant chair lower down the table, drawing out one beside himself for Frances.

"Your pardon gentlemen for interrupting your meeting in this manner but I am hopeful of offering the perfect solution to the concerns expressed regarding your treasures being transported to Oxford," she announced, encompassing each with a pleasing smile.

"If you are able to present a suitable solution, then I am sure we would all be eager to hear it, Viscountess," Tom Barratt said.

"Then allow me to explain. For some time now, I have been resident in York attending Her Majesty, the Queen. Arrangements are well underway for her onward journey to Oxford, and I intend to be part of the entourage myself. Tis also my choice to surrender my own silver, along with that offered by my father and hopefully…. your offerings too, should you be willing to part with them."

She paused, eyeing every man once more, waiting for their reaction as Harry, arms folded across his chest, nodded his head appreciatively.

"I presume Her Majesty's party is to be adequately guarded?" Radcliffe eventually dared to ask.

Frances tried her best not to allow anyone see the intensity of her vexation. Could these men be serious in asking just how the Queen of England might be guarded on a long journey that was sure to present possible issues with an enemy that was all too real.

"If you consider thousands of horse and foote adequate protection, Mr Radcliffe, then yes," she said, ignoring all the murmurs around the table. "However, should the need be for greater assurance still, I can inform you all that His Highness Prince Rupert is even now endeavouring to secure a safe route through the midlands. The hope is to rendezvous with the Prince and his army, at Stratford on Avon. Now gentlemen, can there be a safer means of transporting such a precious cargo?"

Miles watched his daughter with increasing pride. Was this really the same girl who only a few months ago had attended a quite different meeting, sitting shyly beside her new husband, afraid of saying anything other than a timidly delivered request on his behalf. Now she appeared not only completely at ease, but perfectly confident in what she had to declare to the group of local gentry.

"Her Majesty has given approval to this notion my friends, so all that is required now is your accord," Miles declared firmly.

"Shall we receive acknowledgment for what is handed over?" Radcliffe enquired.

Taking this as his cue, Lambert came to stand beside his master.

"If I might be permitted to answer, my Lord Earl?" he enquired.

"Go ahead, Lambert," Miles answered.

"Every item sent here will be catalogued most carefully and a receipt issued to every donator," Lambert explained.

"Might I now assume that this weighty issue is settled, thanks to the solution provided by my daughter, with the full knowledge of Her Majesty?" Miles asked and Thomas Fletcher rose to his feet, setting a plumed hat firmly on his head.

"I can declare that you'll have my offerings within the week, Miles." Then to Frances, he said, "Congratulations Viscountess on what can only be described as a brave and most courageous venture, on your part."

Fletcher's acquiescence seemed to open the flood gates, one after another voicing similar pledges, until only George Radcliffe remained, sombre and contemplative.

"I appear to be out manoeuvred," he admitted. "Very well, my treasures will be sent here in two days." He offered a hand to Miles and then turned to Frances. "May God protect you on your journey, Viscountess. Tis well done, yes well done indeed," he admitted and with a bow, sauntered off down the room.

CHAPTER FIFTY-SEVEN

June 1643 – Haveringham Manor

With mixed emotions, Frances watched her trunk being loaded onto the back of a wagon in Haveringham's courtyard, alongside innumerable crates containing silver and plate destined for the Royal Mint in Oxford.

Close by and despite lowering his voice, she clearly heard her father addressing Harry Broughton.

"I am trusting you to behave as befits a gentleman…. with absolute honour toward my precious daughter," he said.

'Oh father, must you, really?' Frances thought.

Harry as always, showed no sign of being scandalised or even annoyed by what the older man had just said. If anything, he smiled even more.

"On my honour, Lord Benningford," he eventually said. "Frances will come to no harm whatsoever, not whilst I'm about."

"And when you reach Oxford, what then?"

"Father…." Frances said, joining the two men.

"Your father is merely concerned for your welfare Frances and quite frankly, I'd be concerned if he wasn't," Harry said and then to Miles himself, "Whenever I am in Oxford, my Lord, I shall endeavour to keep to my promise, though I'm sure you will comprehend that my duties with Prince Rupert might mean my absence from time to time?"

Harry never would voice the worst-case scenario that every soldier faced, the undeniable risk of never returning from battle at all, resigning the impression to the back of his mind, unwilling to contemplate it further.

"Of course," Miles said. Reaching for his daughter's hand covered now with the finest leather, he momentarily recalled how tiny hers had once been and how easy it had been to encircle it completely with his own. That had been the way to calm her fears and worries in those days. Looking in her eyes, he addressed Harry directly, "I ask your pardon if I pressed you a little harshly my boy. I can be a little over-protective of Frances but… for the time being, I commit her to your charge."

With that, he placed Frances' hand onto Harry's, the strange comparison to a marriage ceremony not missed on Elizabeth who widened her eyes with a satisfied smile.

"Will you send word of her safe arrival in Oxford, Lord Broughton?" she asked brightly.

"As soon as I am able, Countess," Harry replied, looking down at Frances' hand still resting lightly in his.

"You must pass on greetings from the Benningfords to your father, when next you write to him," Elizabeth added and with a scowl, Frances withdrew her hand, realising at once, just what her mother referred to.

"I shall be over yonder, bidding the servants farewell," Frances said heading toward a row of faces displaying a variety of expressions and emotions. Martha in particular was trying not to show how upset she was, and Frances drew her into an informal embrace.

"Don't take on so," she urged.

"I just wish I could come with you, Mistress Frances," Martha bleated but then her eyes widened. "Don't forget to fold your gowns the way I showed you… and the way to style your own hair." She stopped abruptly, sobbing. "Oh Milady, I shall miss thee so much.…"

Martha wiped the tears from her cheek but not before one had spilled onto her pristine collar.

"Just think Martha, when I return, you'll be able to reprimand me for not looking after myself properly," Frances quipped.

Her thoughts did not match her words, in truth Frances really had no idea when she would be able to return, if at all. Unwilling to consider that further, she moved on to Moll Gilbert, the faithful, loyal housekeeper who had known Frances since birth. With unshed tears glistening in both eyes, Moll repeatedly fingered a kerchief. Reaching out, she straightened Frances' cloak and briefly touched her face.

"Watch out for those handsome gallants who come bearing gifts, quoting poetry and such like; they're as much to be wary of as these rebels, you know," she said, and Frances kissed the older woman's cheek.

"I shall, Moll," she promised.

"I had Martha pack your warmer petticoats and your two thickest cloaks, the nights may be a tad on the chilly side, and you'll be glad of the extra warmth, I dare say."

Moll's voice cracked, the kerchief promptly pressed to her lips and Frances moved swiftly on, each servant bowing or curtseying in turn until finally, she reached Lambert at the very end.

"God be with you, Lady Frances," he said but then hesitated. "I should deem it a great honour should you agree to me keeping you in my prayers?"

Frances smiled.

"I should be delighted to have you do so Lambert, we may need all the help the Almighty can afford us," she said and leaning closer added in a whisper, "look after father for me?"

"As always, my Lady." Affectionately patting her hand, his eyes flicked to the waiting wagon and men. "It appears as if they're ready for you."

When Frances glanced round, Harry was already in the saddle, retaining Phoenix' reins.

Retracing her steps, she wandered across to where her parents waited, embracing first Anne Bynghame and then her mother who appeared close to tears.

"I shall often write mother…. though whether you will receive…?" Frances said; her own voice unexpectedly husky with emotion. With his usual adroitness, Miles comprehended this female propensity for emotion and stepped in.

"Now, now, don't you give in to that. Lift your head girl for you ride out from here on a brave mission as the Viscountess Haveringham, heir to the ancient Benningford estate but more importantly… as my daughter." With that, he hoisted Frances onto the chestnut mare's back and reaching up, whispered, "I love thee…."

Stoically, Frances squeezed his hand, their joint expressions silently declaring feelings of equal depth and intensity. Frances knew this parting would be as difficult for him as it was for her, and gathering the reins, she waited as Harry boomed out instructions.

"Coates, you, and Jackson go ahead and report back anything of concern. I want the return to York to be as uneventful as the journey here." Then turning to Frances, he asked, "Ready?"

She nodded and Harry moved his mount forward. Just for a moment, Frances hesitated, overwhelmed by uncertainty and apprehension, but taking a deep breath, she urged Phoenix onward.

'*You can do this,*' she told herself, falling in beside Harry. The wagon of silver was immediately in front, guarded by a small troop of cavalry supplied by the Queen herself to ensure its safe conveyance to York. As they neared the gatehouse, Frances pivoted in the saddle to take a long look at the house and the group of people standing outside. The house stood proud and erect as it always had, the family standard fluttering in the breeze as if offering a farewell of its own. The building had witnessed so much in just two short years. Firstly, Robin's return from the Low Countries and her initial meeting with John Fitzherbert, then the unexpected visit of the Palatine brothers on the eve of her marriage, the wedding celebrations themselves followed swiftly by civil war with all its resultant sorrows. The war had wrought suspicion, brutality, and robbed Frances of the husband she had loved but known so briefly, after which the Queen of England had arrived along with many others, including the Earl of Montrose. Now Frances was leaving it herself and for an indefinite length of time.

'God keep this house, and all within it, safe,' she silently prayed, turning back to concentrate on riding beside Harry Broughton under the gatehouse, and onward to an unknown future.

THE END

Read more about Frances in Oxford

and beyond in:

This Realm of Hatred

"Conflict of Conscience"

by

Christina Wells

HISTORICAL NOTE

I am perfectly aware that anyone reading this novel might well find fault, disagree with some aspects of the story, or even misunderstand the reasons behind using certain facets. However, this being an entire work of fiction, as a novelist, I have resorted to using portions of 'poetic licence' regarding certain personalities and events as do many writers. I have tried my utmost, where possible, to position real personalities in places where they were actually recorded as being, with the exception of Prince Rupert and his ride north to oversee the training of troops at Haveringham. I doubt very much whether he would have chosen to ride so far merely to oversee training, but with his so called, 'flying army' who knows? Certainly, Rupert gained a reputation for turning up unexpectedly in various places, despite distance! Parliamentary pamphlets of the day did accuse him of many incredible feats, as well as numerous, unproven, atrocities, so I believe any reader might forgive anomalies for the sake of this work of fiction.

My heroine's rank is such that it would have been possible for her path to cross some of the major players in the civil war, and as I have written, it would not be improbable for her to have undertaken some of the exploits she was involved in.

Records still exist proving that 17th Century women did undertake incredible acts of bravery in this time of civil unrest. Grand ladies often protected their homes, ran estates on behalf of absent husbands, dealt with financial matters and even became involved in acts of spying (for either side). Some evidence exists of women dressing as men to be involved in the fighting or merely to stay close to husbands or lovers!

One aspect to mention, is that it is debatable whether the Benningford family could travel from the north to London in the Autumn of 1641. I have, for the purposes of this work of fiction, used it as a definite possibility. Once it was realised how dangerous situations were growing with. increasing amounts of unrest, many fled the capital, therefore I made sure that the Benningford's returned to Yorkshire swiftly.

All the military engagements I have mentioned really occurred, though I have often tried to make the accounts more interesting, either by introducing facets by conversation, or letters, rather than merely relating what happened in text

Prince Rupert, his brother Maurice, and several others did land at Tynemouth in the northeast of England, and would have ridden south through areas of Yorkshire, therefore it would have been entirely feasible for them to divert briefly to Haveringham Manor had it existed of course!

It is unclear whether Mary, Duchess of Richmond did venture to Holland with the Queen, though for the purposes of this novel, I have her doing so. Apologies to anyone knowing differently.

Haveringham Manor itself is completely fictious, though in describing it, I had in mind a wonderful Tudor building not far from the east coast of Yorkshire.

Fictitious Characters:

Frances, Viscountess Haveringham

Robin, Viscount Haveringham

The Earl and Countess of Benningford

The Earl and Countess of Melton

John Fitzherbert

Ralph Bynghame

Anne Bynghame

Alys Holcroft

Harry Broughton

The Benningford servants

Lambert, the Steward

Martha, Frances' personal maid

Haveringham Villagers.

Ladies of the Queen's entourage, (with the exception of Mary, Duchess of Richmond)

Most fictitious characters have been woven into events, places and situations involving actual personalities of the English civil war.

Factual Characters

King Charles I

Henrietta Maria

Prince Rupert of the Rhine

Prince Maurice

Mary, Duchess of Richmond

James Graham, the Earl of Montrose

Mortaigne (little is known of this man, or his first name, though he was constantly beside Prince Rupert – for the purpose of my novel he is named Jacques!)

Richard Crane Commander of Prince Rupert's Lifeguard

George Goring

William Cavendish – Earl of Newcastle

Henry Jermyn

ABOUT THE AUTHOR

Christina Wells is Yorkshire born and bred, living in Leeds, West Yorkshire. She has always had an avid interest in history, particularly the Tudor and Stuart eras of 16th and 17th Century. During a visit to York with friends in the early 1970's, her interest in the English Civil War was initially ignited. Seated upstairs in the bowed window of a well-known coffee shop, her attention was drawn to a group of historically dressed, long haired 'Cavaliers' strolling unexpectedly along Stonegate. Two in particular, stopped in their tracks, looked up at the window and swept off their plumed hats bowing low. Christina was hooked!

A movie of the early 1970's was to prove significant to her. That film was "Cromwell," staring the late Richard Harris in the title role, and the late Alec Guinness as King Charles I. Only after many years of study of the English Civil War, did Christina realise the amount of 'blatant historical errors' that film contains, though it still remains a favourite.

During the 1980's her interest had to be virtually put on hold whilst raising her family, but a TV series entitled "By the Sword Divided" was not only to reignite it but proved significant in triggering the rudimentary skeleton of a novel. Following extensive reading and during one of the frequent visits to the battleground of Marston Moor, between Tockwith and Long Marston near York, she first encountered members of The Sealed Knot Society, an English Civil War re-enactment group. In 2010 she was persuaded to join, thus affording opportunity to actually experience a taste of 17th Century life herself. Invariably dressed as a "Lady of Quality," Christina invariably found herself involved in cameo roles at grand houses, most of which were unavoidably 'lost' to the enemy! In a time when women were considered of lesser standing to men, other than to bear offspring to continue family lines, it is well documented that heroic acts were performed regularly by females, particular in regard to family dwellings. This novel is the story of one fictitious lady and the adventures, tragedies, and brave escapades she finds herself caught up in.

Printed in Great Britain
by Amazon

25483559R00215